T0384320

The
WILDERNESS
of GIRLS

The

WILDERNESS
of
GIRLS

MADELINE CLAIRE FRANKLIN

ZANDO YOUNG READERS
NEW YORK

The
WILDERNESS
of GIRLS

MADELINE CLAIRE FRANKLIN

zando young readers

NEW YORK

**zando
YOUNG
readers**

Zando Young Readers is an imprint of Zando.
zandoprojects.com

First Edition: June 2024

Text design by Pauline Neuwirth, Neuwirth & Associates, Inc.
Trees by Oh Rian from Noun Project
Cover design by Jessica Handelman and Sarah Schneider
Cover illustration by Tim O'Brien

Library of Congress Control Number: 2023948987

978-1-63893-100-3 (Hardcover)
978-1-63893-101-0 (ebook)

10 9 8 7 6 5 4 3 2 1
Manufactured in the United States of America

This book is dedicated to a twelve-year-old girl who has just spent her life savings on her very first personal computer in the hopes of writing her novels a little bit faster. She is probably pacing her bedroom floor in a cardboard crown and novelty sunglasses, trying to figure out the best way to start the next chapter.

Stay weird, kid. And stay wild.

A LETTER FROM THE AUTHOR

I wrote this novel for many reasons: the native compulsion of a storyteller, the raw rage of my awakening feminism, my love of and confusion about natural magic and how it fits into my worldview. What I didn't realize until I struggled to write this story for several years was that I was writing this novel to express some very deep wounds. And unfortunately, if I wanted to tell this story, I had to do the healing work. (Likewise, if I wanted to heal, I had to write this story.) None of the specific events of this novel actually happened to me, but fiction is often a harmonic of our lived reality, passed through several filters, sharpened and balanced, the noise cut away to create a satisfying narrative melody.

Given what I know about the all-too-common wounds that were explored to write this book, I feel it would be irresponsible as a storyteller not to inform you, Reader, that these pages contain moments that may bring up strong, uncomfortable feelings. While I hope this book heals or strengthens something in every reader who comes to it, please be aware of the following content warnings and take care of your personal well-being.

This book portrays, describes, or discusses in detail: complex PTSD, suicide and suicidal ideation, disordered eating, body shaming, family and domestic violence, emotional abuse, cannibalism, and sexual assault.

In the Beginning, We Were Wild

Excerpted from *Savage Castle:*
A Memoir of the Wild Girls of Happy Valley

ONCE UPON A TIME, deep in the wilderness, in a land beyond maps and borders and human-claimed things, there was a beautiful castle.

This castle was not like other castles in tales you may have heard; it was wild and alive, hewn from the earth itself, grown and shaped over hundreds of years, just for us. Our castle was the hollowed body of an ancient tree, wrapped and latticed in an exoskeleton of vines and magic. It was a giant of a tree. A mountain of a tree.

And it was our home.

The castle protected us: four untamed princesses and, sometimes, a wise old man named Mother. Mother was more than just his name; he was our prophet, our protector, our teacher. He gave us the gift of magic, the truth of naming, the treasure of stories. He gave us the mooring of a past, and the promise of a future. Mother was our heart, the castle our bones. Together, they held us upright through every storm.

In the wilderness, we lived in perfect rhythm and harmony, like the wilderness itself. When we were hungry, we hunted with our wolf-kin, the forgiving earth beneath our hardened feet, the hot slick of the kill on our jaws. After long days of foraging and play, we slept peacefully in the shelter of our castle, with only the stars to light our dreams. We woke with the sun as it broke over the mountain, flooding our forest with the streaming gold promise of a new day. We gorged ourselves on bear fat and tree nuts in the dying season, and crawled through the frozen months in a haze of hunger and dreaming, snowbound days and dogpiled nights. Come the return of green and light, we plucked fish from the streams with our bare hands and ate them raw, errant scales painting rainbows around our mouths.

We were a part of the wilderness and all it contains. We were a part of the magic in the unfurling of new leaves, the power that cleaved the world when lightning cracked the sky. We were a part of the spiral dance of life and death; the wonder of light dancing on the water and leaves on the wind; the mystery of seedlings and cool black earth; the beauty of decay, the violence of life. We were a part of the magic of it all.

Until, one day, the spells were broken.

One day, the castle fell.

One day, we left the only home we had ever known, and our beloved wilderness betrayed us.

ONCE UPON A TIME, THERE was the wilderness. There was violent beauty and devastating calm. There were clouds in migration, the punishing sunshine, the gemstone sky.

Once upon a time, there were four young girls and a man named Mother, the wolves we called family, a tree we called a castle, and the forest we called home.

Once upon a time, *we were* the wilderness.

And then, we were caged.

1

THE NIGHT HER FATHER IS ARRESTED, Eden is sitting on the long side of the dinner table, facing the wall that separates the dining room from the kitchen. Her back is to the broad picture window that looks out onto the manicured backyard that abuts the edge of the forest.

This is her seat. When Eden was a child, her stepmother, Vera, couldn't stand how Eden would stare and stare into the trees during dinner, so she made Eden face the wall instead. The wall in question is blank; no pictures of friends or family; no commemorative plates or interesting artwork—certainly none of Eden's artwork from childhood.

Of course, Eden is not a child anymore. She knows how to survive, now. She learned long ago not to remark upon, or even think about, the bare white walls. She learned long ago not to look over her shoulder for a glimpse of the wilderness.

Eden's father and stepmother are sitting to her left and right, respectively, each at a head of the table. A glass of water and a glass of red wine sits at each place setting. Vera always says alcohol is an appetite suppressant in moderation, and it seems to be true for her. She sips her third glass of wine tonight, her salad sitting mostly untouched as she glares back and forth between the window, Eden, and Father.

Eden is acutely aware of the tension at the table. Father has been on his phone for the entirety of the meal, arguing with one business partner or another. His tone is aggressive and sharp, even though he is not yelling. There is a grilled cut of red meat on his plate that smells divine, but he has barely cut into it. The soft pink of it is so alluring to Eden's senses, it is almost vulgar.

Eden wishes there was something she could do to distract Vera from Father's rude behavior; she wishes there was something she could do that would get Father to put his phone away and pay attention to his unhappy wife. But to please either parent would mean potentially angering the other, so instead Eden focuses on her salad of bitter greens and grilled white chicken meat. She discovers their cook, Mariya, has hidden a little pool of herbed olive oil beneath the salad, which Eden carefully dips pieces of chicken into before sticking them to the greens to cover the shine. Vera would be furious if she suspected Eden was going off her "diet."

Black coffee and half a grapefruit for breakfast, two hard-boiled eggs midmorning. Lean meat and vegetables for lunch and dinner. Protein shake after a workout, but only if the workout is more than sixty minutes. Raw broccoli for snacks—the fiber will fill you up faster. No fats after seven o'clock. And red wine at dinner. It helps with digestion.

That is how Vera lives her life, so it's how Eden lives, too.

She was only six years old when Vera first started criticizing her body, restricting her food, bringing Eden with her to the gym. She is now sixteen years old and cannot eat even so much as an apple without recalling its caloric density. Vera has made sure of that.

If it wasn't for Mariya hiding liquid calories beneath her "approved" foods, or her stepbrother, Kevin, sneaking her treats at night when he stayed with them, Eden thinks she might have wasted away by now. She is always tired, always hungry. She fantasizes about food constantly, and not even anything special: furtive spoonfuls of peanut butter, a classmate's ham and cheese sandwich, butter on her steamed vegetables, a fucking slice of fresh-baked bread.

Staring at her salad, Eden takes a silent deep breath and lets her anger go. Anger doesn't help. It only makes her suffer more. The only way to keep going—to have any hope of escaping this house someday—is to feel nothing at all.

Eden takes a sip of her wine. She likes how it warms her, how it makes her brain soft, open, fuzzy. Eden thinks she understands her stepmother better when she's had a glass of wine or two. Like she's tuned in to a different radio station and can finally hear what Vera is really saying.

"This chicken is dry," Vera mutters, prodding it with her fork. *I'm unsatisfied.*

"Mariya had better not be using frozen chicken breasts. I've told her over and over again that it ruins the texture." *Why don't I have any control over my life?*

"For what we pay her, she should be able to make chicken that isn't dry." *I have everything I want and none of it makes me happy.*

Vera puts her fork down and takes a long drink from her wineglass. She glares hard at Father when she's done. *I blame you.*

She glances at Eden, briefly, before turning back to her wine. *And you.*

When the doorbell rings, Father rolls his eyes heavily, still talking on his cell phone and ignoring his family. Eden tenses, wondering who could possibly be at the door, wondering how infuriated Vera will be at the interruption. She would answer the door herself, but Vera hates it when Eden does the housekeeper's job for her.

Nearly a minute passes before the noise at the front of the house makes its way to the dining room, before the sound of several pairs of footsteps moving purposefully across bare marble floors registers as aggressive—as an invasion.

Two suited men appear in the archway behind Vera, flanked by four police officers, hands on their guns, ready to draw. She twists to see them, confusion and anger on her brow, but the men flow around her, past Eden, so swiftly that Father doesn't even have time to put down his phone as shock flashes in his eyes.

"Lawrence Chase," one of the suited men says loudly as the officers take hold of Father's arms. "We have a warrant for your arrest."

Father's phone clatters to the floor as the officers haul him to his feet and pin his arms to his back. He doesn't struggle, but he doesn't make it easy for them, either. Father's body and limbs are stiff, every muscle clenched as if he believes that if he can just keep his body under his own power, they can take no rights away from him.

But to Eden's astonishment, that's exactly what they do. She thrills as they read him his Miranda rights and accuse him of crimes she isn't surprised to hear he's committed: embezzlement, money laundering, drug trafficking. Her stepmother, furious at first, soon begins sobbing loudly, picks up her phone to call her lawyer, and hurries from the room without a backward glance.

As Father is maneuvered out of the dining room and toward the door, he looks ahead like a soldier, blank and cool. Never once does he look in his daughter's direction.

One of the suited men—a detective, maybe?—puts a hand on the back of Eden's chair, causing her to jump. He leans down a little to say, "Sorry to interrupt dinner, sweetheart. Daddy's been a bit of a naughty boy."

Eden looks up at him with what she thinks is an expressionless face, but whatever the detective sees in her eyes makes him whip back to his full height and snatch his hand away from her chair. Whatever self-satisfaction he had been wearing on his face slips away as he nods coolly to Eden and follows his men out through the archway.

Mariya is standing in the kitchen doorway, twisting a kitchen towel between her hands, her dark eyes tracking the detective as he leaves. When the front door slams shut and quiet settles over the house, she says to Eden, "He will be fine. The system is made for men like him. Here." She comes around the table and picks up Father's plate, then sets the steak down in front of Eden. "No sense in letting good food go to waste."

Eden senses the goodness in the gesture, the affection, the maybe-even-love, but what she wants is for Mariya to put her hand on her shoulder, or to wrap her in a hug. Not because she is sad about Father being arrested, but because she is *starving* for human touch—to feel just a tiny bit connected to someone in this world.

But Eden has known for quite some time now that the hunger for human touch is the most dangerous appetite of all.

She cuts into the steak with her fork and her father's knife, like a girl whose father has not just been arrested, who is not starving for human connection, who is not aching for the love that comes easily to those who belong. She is only starving for food, Eden tells herself. Her body only needs food, water, and shelter to survive. That's it.

That is it.

That is all you need to survive.

2

NOT LONG AFTER THE POLICE drive away with Eden's father in handcuffs, Vera clambers down the main stairs with two huge suitcases. Weeping, she shouts from the foyer, "I am done with this place!" and shoves her way through the large front door.

Eden imagines Vera tossed her hair dramatically and donned her largest pair of Gucci sunglasses before climbing into her Uber. But her disgust at Vera's behavior doesn't spare her from the sting of abandonment; if she ever thought, even for an instant, Vera might have *any* maternal feelings for her, that thought is now completely dashed.

Child Protective Services knocks on the door before Vera's Uber has even pulled away from the curb. When Eden answers, the agent, a nondescript white man in his early thirties, who seems nervous to be there, tells her to pack a bag.

"Enough for a long trip. You'll be away for a while."

Eden hasn't been on many trips. She spent a long weekend with her stepbrother, Kevin, in Harlem last summer before he left for his year abroad—but that's not very helpful to think about right now. This isn't a weekend away in the city.

This is a turning point. A threshold.

As she heads to her room, Eden realizes—not for the first time in her life—that she is truly alone. Only this time the knowledge does not sink her like a boulder strapped to her chest. This time, her chest constricts with nervous wonder as she considers the possibilities unfolding before her: Father in jail; Vera gone; Eden legally removed from their house.

She can start over, maybe.

She can forget everything that's ever happened to her.

Maybe.

Eden grabs a backpack but there's not much she wants to bring with her into this potential *after*. Some toiletries. A picture of her mother. She glances at her overstuffed bookshelf, drooping from the weight of tattered pages, stories she has escaped into over the long, lonely years, but decides to leave the books behind. Instead, she throws in her schoolwork, clean T-shirts, bras, and underwear; several pairs of soft well-worn jeans; her phone charger; and her late mother's old Syracuse University hoodie.

"That's all?" the agent asks when Eden comes downstairs with only her backpack.

"Yeah," Eden says, bracing for him to scold her or tell her she's packed wrong.

The agent only shrugs. "Suit yourself. Let's get you downtown and processed."

WHILE EDEN IS SITTING IN the hard plastic chair by the CPS agent's desk, she tries not to think about the fact that her father is in the same building somewhere, outraged someone has had the audacity to catch him committing crimes, or about how her stepmother abandoned her to go God knows where. (Actually, Eden knows exactly where: Vera will fly to a tropical resort where she will sit by a pool or on a beach all day getting elegantly blitzed on fancy cocktails.) Would Vera even bother to call Kevin? Eden thinks, like a reflex, that she should be the one to tell him what's happened. But her stepbrother is gone/not an option/studying in Germany for his last year of grad school. Father's arrest won't touch him, assuming his tuition is already paid.

He's far away. Too far away to rescue her this time.

"Good news, kid," the agent says. "We tracked down your uncle. He's ready to take you in—unless there's a reason you don't want to stay with him. Just know that foster homes can be . . . well, let's just say they're a bit of a crapshoot."

"My . . . uncle?" Eden is drawing a blank.

"James Abrams. He is"—he squints at his notes—"your late mother's younger brother."

She straightens. "Uncle Jimmy? Yeah. Yes. I'm fine staying with him."

"All right then!" The agent grins and shoots two finger guns at Eden before picking up the phone.

It turns out Uncle Jimmy is not only coming to pick Eden up, but dropping everything to come and get her, right *now*. The agent says she's lucky. Half the time a new guardian can't be bothered and kids have to spend the night in the holding cell until CPS can drop them off the next morning.

Eden doesn't feel particularly lucky right now, but she knows better than to say so. She doesn't know much about Uncle Jimmy other than that he is her mother's much younger brother. Eden wasn't able to visit him after her mother died when Eden was four, and she hardly remembers life before then. She had seen her uncle at her mother's funeral reception (he'd been a teenager then, and Eden had been too shy to say much to him at all), then again, a few years later, when he came to the house for his first and only visit, when Father wasn't home. Jimmy had been in college then, at SU (just like Eden's mother), and Eden had been about ten years old and shyer than ever. It was a pleasant enough visit, considering he was (and is) a virtual stranger to her, but she'd felt his earnestness then. After all, what college student makes the time and effort to visit a ten-year-old niece he's hardly ever spoken to?

Two hours into her visit to the police station, Eden's phone chimes. She stirs from a half sleep on a chair in the waiting area and pulls out her phone from her backpack.

Message from: NO

Suddenly, she's wide-awake. Warmth drains from her face as she holds the phone tightly in her hands, debating for a long moment whether she should read the text or not. In the end, Eden swipes the notification away before she even reads the message preview.

She can't think about that right now.

Thankfully, her uncle arrives at the Saratoga Springs Police Department minutes later, just before midnight, snow dusting his shoulders as he looks around the waiting area for his niece. He is just as tall as she remembers, easily six feet or more, with the same dark eyes and ethnically ambiguous complexion they both share with Eden's mother: a honeyed beige in the winter that turns a deep olive in the summer. From what Eden understands, they get their coloring from her grandmother, whose entire family tree was Jewish.

When he spots her, Uncle Jimmy gives Eden a hearty bear hug, even though they haven't seen each other in years. Despite herself, their estrangement, and the fact that she is fine, she is fine, she is fine (*if anything, this is going to be for the best, right?*), Eden nearly bursts into tears when he wraps his arms around her. She isn't sure what she's feeling, but it tries to overwhelm her, flooding her chest and eyes with pinched wet heat. But before the first sob can break from her lips, Eden reels the impulse in, clenching her teeth, barely breathing until the pressure in her throat abates. She doesn't need to cry about any of this, she tells herself. Especially not in front of a stranger.

"Okay," Uncle Jimmy says after signing the requisite forms and hearing the CPS agent's spiel on his legal responsibilities as her guardian. He and Eden are now standing in the vestibule, preparing to step out into the wintry night air. "You got everything you need in that backpack? I don't generally keep necessities for teenage girls in my home, so we can either stop somewhere and grab you a few essentials, or we can wait until tomorrow. We won't get back until pretty late either way, but that's fine. We're both playing hooky tomorrow. So what do you think?" His voice is forcefully cheerful, his slight Central New York accent not as strong as Vera's New York City accent, but obviously related. Eden wonders if she has an accent, too, and just never noticed it.

"Whatever you want to do is fine," Eden says quietly. "I think I've got what I need."

From the corner of her eye, Eden sees her uncle studying her. She doesn't turn to meet his eyes. She looks instead at the gray concrete steps visible through the clear glass doors of the police station, big lacy snowflakes blowing across them like whorls of the most fragile confetti.

Uncle Jimmy strokes the dark stubble on his jaw. "How about some food? You hungry?"

Eden shrugs. She is always hungry, but she is used to that.

"I heard the cops interrupted your dinner. Pretty rude of them, if you ask me."

"It's okay," Eden says, stomach rumbling at the thought of the steak she didn't get the chance to finish. Eden hopes Mariya ate the rest, at least. And she hopes she raided the pantry and the wine cellar for all the good stuff before she left.

"Well, I'm hungry. Late-night road trips have a way of working up a person's appetite, eh? I could go for a meal at a good old-fashioned greasy spoon. How does that sound?"

Eden isn't sure what that means. Her pinched brow must say as much.

Uncle Jimmy chuckles. "A greasy spoon—that's what they call those old diners with the twenty-four-hour breakfast menus and burnt coffee. There's a spot between here and Happy Valley that does a hell of a cheeseburger. Do you eat meat? They've got vegetarian food too, I'm sure. Or cheese fries, pancakes . . ." He stops, and when he speaks again his voice is softer, as if he's made himself sad talking about diner food. "Whatever you want, Edie. It's on me."

Eden's skin feels raw. She hasn't heard anyone say her name with any true kindness in such a long time, it almost feels dangerous. "Yeah, that sounds good," she says, because it seems like that's what he wants her to say.

"All right then," Uncle Jimmy says, pleased to have a direction to head in.

Or maybe pleased that Eden agreed with him—she isn't sure. She can't read him just yet.

He opens the police station door and gestures for Eden to go first. As they walk across the parking lot, lazy snowflakes landing weightlessly upon their hair and shoulders, Uncle Jimmy says, "I think I'll get myself a chocolate milkshake and some fries. You ever try dipping the fries into the milkshake? It sounds weird, but it's a classic combination. You like chocolate-covered pretzels? I think it works the same way, flavor-profile-wise."

Eden hasn't had a milkshake in years. Or French fries, for that matter. Or pretzels.

"I've been learning a lot about *flavor profiles* lately," Uncle Jimmy goes on nervously as they approach his truck. It's big and hunter green, with a white Happy Valley Wildlife Preserve logo on the side: a deer's head with two mountains rising between the antlers, a pine tree, and a soaring bird beneath a crescent moon. He unlocks the truck with a *beep* and a flash of headlights, then opens the passenger-side door for Eden before walking around to the driver's side. "I've got a friend who is a chef, really into flavor pairings and the like . . ."

In the car, Uncle Jimmy continues talking about his chef friend. Eventually, Eden understands this friend is someone he is trying to impress romantically. At first, this makes her cringe, but as he proves himself to be just as earnest as she remembers him, some of the tension slips away and Eden begins to *really* see him, without the veil of dread over her eyes. He appears to be a genuinely good guy—the opposite of the men Eden has known.

"What's this chef friend's name?" Eden asks eventually.

Uncle Jimmy pauses. "Oh." He chuckles again. "Their name is Star."

"Star," Eden repeats.

What a stupid name, she thinks, but that's not her own voice she hears in her head. It's Vera's.

Eden considers the name, tries it on herself. She decides she likes it. Maybe she should steal it.

"That's a unique name," she says.

"Oh, Star is quite unique," Uncle Jimmy confirms with a grin. "They chose that name for themself when they moved to Happy Valley. To start a new life, you know?"

Eden doesn't answer. She stares out the windshield at the black ribbon of highway lit only by the truck's halogen headlights, but she sees none of it. She is too busy trying to swallow her heart as it attempts to climb up her throat.

Is that an option? To become a different person as soon as you leave behind everyone you know? Is she allowed to just *stop being* Eden Chase and forget all the pain that girl carries with her?

INSIDE THE DINER, EDEN SHIVERS as she looks at the menu. She knows Uncle Jimmy wants her to eat something, and she wants him to like her and not think she's a freak with crazy hang-ups about food. She also knows Vera is far away and there is literally no reason Eden can't order anything her taste buds and stomach desire. But there's still the nattering of Vera's voice in her head, warning her about saturated fats and sodium and bloating and acne and cellulite and always, always, warning her against "getting fat."

I don't care about "getting fat," she thinks.

Yes, you absolutely do, she also thinks.

Well, right now I care more about telling Vera to fuck off.

The waitress comes over, a soft-looking woman in her forties or fifties, curvy and short. Eden thinks she looks pretty as the harsh fluorescents bounce off her hair and do nothing to hide the powdery finish of her makeup sitting on the fine peach fuzz of her round cheeks, or the tiny flakes of black mascara speckling the slight bags under her eyes.

Vera would never, Eden thinks, which makes her automatically warm to the waitress.

"Good evening, ma'am," Uncle Jimmy says. He looks to see if Eden is ready.

She nods but keeps looking at the menu so he'll order first.

"I'll get a cup of coffee and the house burger, medium rare, with cheese, bacon, and no lettuce, please. Oh, and fries for the side please."

"And you, sweetheart?" the waitress asks, turning to Eden as she finishes scratching down Uncle Jimmy's order.

Eden looks up and notices the waitress's name tag says *Doris*. "I'll have the same, but no onions on mine, please. And a Sprite. And a chocolate milkshake, please."

"Thatta girl," Uncle Jimmy says. "Make that two chocolate milkshakes, ma'am. Please and thank you."

"Of course," Doris says. "Coming right up." She dots something on her notepad and smiles at them both before walking back to the counter with their orders.

"Glad you found your appetite," Uncle Jimmy says, picking up a sugar packet from the plastic tray full of sweeteners at the end of the booth and tapping it against the table. Though his tone is playful, there's another note to his voice, like the sheer drop of a cliff. Eden can tell he is about to veer into something more serious. "There's nothing like a good meal to steady you after an ordeal."

There it is. Time to talk about the *why* and *how* of the night. Or at least the *what's to come*.

Doris returns swiftly with Eden's Sprite and pours Uncle Jimmy a cup of coffee. After a whirl of *thank-yous* and *you're welcome, sweethearts*, she is gone again.

"Listen, Edie," Uncle Jimmy begins, peeling open a thimble of cream and pouring it into his coffee. "I know we don't know each other very well, but I want you to know—I *hope* you know—it's not because I haven't tried. You're the only family I've got left. I've *wanted* to be in your life. But I think it must have been too hard for your father. I think I reminded him too much of Angie."

Eden hasn't heard anyone call her mother *Angie* in so long, she almost doesn't know who he's talking about. Her father only ever called her *Angela*. But Eden looks at her uncle with his tanned skin (like Eden's) and dark-brown eyes (like Eden's) and dark-blonde hair (like Eden's mother's), and she supposes she might see a resemblance.

"And it's a bit of a drive to Happy Valley, so it's not like he could just drop by with you for dinner or anything." Uncle Jimmy stirs the sugar into his coffee as he makes excuses for her father that Eden doesn't need him to make. "But I hope you know—"

"Uncle Jimmy," she stops him, her face warming with her own audacity—but if she's going to seize this opportunity to start over, then she's going to do it right. "My father wouldn't have stopped by for dinner even if you lived next door. He wouldn't have invited you over even if you looked completely unrelated to my mother. That's just who my father is."

Uncle Jimmy studies her. She immediately worries she shouldn't have said it, should have played along with the idea of her father being a decent-but-brokenhearted man. Forget honesty, forget being truthful or real—

"Yeah." Uncle Jimmy chuckles nervously, then stops himself. "Okay. Yeah, you're probably right. Well, the point is, I know we don't know each other very well, but I owe it to you and your mother to keep you safe and healthy. To be frank, I have *no* idea what I'm doing." And as he says those words, he really does look utterly lost for a moment. "But I promise you, I will do my best." His brow furrows. "You're not allergic to cats, are you?"

Eden blinks. "Um, not that I know of?"

"Okay. Well, I've got a cat named Purrdita. She looks like a Dalmatian. Have you ever seen *101 Dalmatians*?"

Eden shakes her head.

"Hmm. Maybe we can fix that one of these days." Uncle Jimmy sips his coffee. "You understand this is a big change, right? New home. New town. New school."

Something in Eden yawns and stretches at this acknowledgment, like a seedling unfurling beneath the soil. "Yes."

Uncle Jimmy nods. "Okay then." He lifts his mug toward her. "To new beginnings."

Eden hesitates, tapping her short, chewed nails on the translucent red plastic of her cup. "Uncle Jimmy," she says, casting her eyes down to the creamers Doris set on the table earlier. "Since I'm getting all these new beginnings"—she looks up at him—"I don't want to go by *Eden* anymore. I want to pick a new name, if that's okay."

Eden braces herself for him to question it, to ask why, to argue. She even starts questioning it herself, arguing that *Eden is a perfectly fine name. So what if it has been spat out like curdled milk and whispered like the cinching of a corset around your insides? You should be stronger than this.*

But Uncle Jimmy has a shiny look in his eyes, a watery-eyed kind of restrained happiness that takes Eden a long, *long* moment to recognize as pride.

"Okay. Whatever you want to be called is fine by me." He raises his mug a little higher. "To new names *and* new beginnings."

She smiles genuinely for the first time in God-knows-when. In her mind, she shoves the girl known as *Eden* into the closet of her childhood bedroom, along with all the ugly memories. Then she locks and barricades the door and tries to forget the horrified look on Eden's face before it closed on her.

She raises her red plastic cup to her uncle's off-white ceramic mug.

"To new beginnings," she says.

DRAFTS

FROM: "Eden Chase" <e.r.c.2007@springmail.com>
TO: "Kevin Hartwell" <hartwell.kevin@irving.edu>
DATE: December 12
SUBJECT: Greetings from the end of the world

Kevin,

I'm sure you've heard about Father. Are you surprised? I'm not. Surprised he got caught, maybe. But not that he's a criminal.

I'm living with my uncle now in Happy Valley, about an hour from home. Life is definitely different here. There's nary a sushi bar nor cold-pressed juicery in sight. (Vera would hate it.) It's not exactly *worldly*.

Which reminds me—you know what I was thinking about the other day? The first time we met. I asked what you wanted to be when you grew up. You said you didn't care, as long as you got to travel the world. Now you're living in Germany, probably flying off every other weekend to countries I've never even heard of.

How did you do that? Make your life happen the way you wanted it to?

I need some of that magic. I need to make my life *happen*. Or maybe I just need to have been born someone else's daughter. Or son, realistically.

You know what else I was thinking? As bad as it was, you're probably the only reason I survived in that house as long as I did.

But you're gone now. And I'm free.

For now, anyway.

Is Vera happy wherever she's run off to?

(Who am I kidding? I won't send this.)

I miss you.
Merry Christmas, Happy Hanukkah, & Happy New Year too, I guess.

3

"ICE SHIRT," A GIRL SAYS, passing behind Rhi in the locker room. Rhi hunches her shoulders and doesn't respond or even turn to see who said it. She's not sure if it was meant as an insult or a compliment, and she doesn't really care to find out. She just closes her locker and rolls up the sleeves of the Happy Valley Wildlife Preserve T-shirt her uncle had brought home from work for her when she first moved in with him.

It's February now, and Rhi has been in Happy Valley nearly two months. She has still not made a single friend besides Purrdita.

In gym class, she partners with another solemn outcast for basketball drills, but even they seem chagrined to be in such close proximity to her. Rhi doesn't know what it is about her—maybe some pheromone she gives off that warns other students how much of a weirdo she is. She never fit in at the private schools her father sent her to, and now, coming from said private schools, she doesn't seem to fit in at Happy Valley Public High School, either. She gets the sense they think she's a snob, and maybe that's her own fault.

Despite her best intentions to make a fresh start, Rhi can't seem to keep her head up in the hallway; she can't meet anyone's eyes; she can't smile at a single stranger to see if they might smile back. She's too self-aware, as if watching herself like a character in a movie. But unlike the plot of a movie, she is not taken in by a popular kid who sees something unique in her; she is not adopted by a bored extrovert from any part of the social strata; she is hardly noticed by anyone.

Except the gym teacher, who keeps trying to get Rhi to join one of the many sports teams. She sees "potential" in Rhi, who single-handedly crushed the opposing team during the floor hockey unit her first week at HVPH (affectionately called "HPV High" by its students), and who can run a six-minute mile without even pushing herself. The coach can thank Vera's obsession with cardio for that. But Rhi declines to join the girls' field hockey team, lacrosse team, or volleyball team. She declines track and field, basketball, swimming. She declines it all.

"Why?" the coach finally asks Rhi after gym class, cornering her while the other girls are filing out to the locker room. "Don't you want to meet new people? Find your place in this town?" She leans in, lowering her voice. "I know it's hard transferring schools in the middle of the year. But joining a team—that's how you form lifelong friendships."

"Sorry," Rhi says as she inches toward the locker room doors. "I'm just really busy studying."

But as she changes back into her school clothes, guilt nibbles at the back of her head. She hasn't actually been able to study since she started at HVPH. Every time she opens a book or pulls out a set of flashcards, it's like she's had a sleeping spell cast over her. She has woken up slumped over the desk in Uncle Jimmy's guest room more than once, with a blanket draped over her shoulders that she didn't put there. After school, sometimes Uncle Jimmy lets her help with dinner, but when he can convince her to let him manage things alone, Rhi always ends up asleep in front of the television or napping in the guest room she's been staying in. Thankfully, her grades haven't begun to suffer yet.

When school lets out, Rhi walks to the ranger station like she's been doing every day since the semester started. Crunching over the snow as she cuts through downtown, she can't help but compare her life now to the life she was living just two months ago. Instead of the fine dining and upscale home goods shops of Saratoga Springs, downtown Happy Valley consists mainly of hardware shops and general stores. Instead of the horse racing and spas and other tourist attractions of Saratoga Springs, Happy Valley has only the vast wilderness of the wildlife preserve and the accompanying campgrounds, which are hardly in use in the winter.

And instead of being trapped in her father's cavernous house with its sterile tile and glossy new hardwood floors, Rhi now lives in her uncle's converted two-bedroom cabin, which is quite possibly as old as Happy Valley itself, with wall-to-wall high-pile brown carpet that no amount of vacuuming will rid of all the cat hair that has accumulated over the years from Purrdita. Cat hair, in general, is a new phenomenon to Rhi—it's *on* everything, *in* everything, shedding *from* everything, even when they have *just* finished cleaning. But she doesn't mind it. There is something safe about living with someone who allows that kind of untidiness.

When she gets to the ranger station, Rhi waits in the break room for her uncle to finish his shift. She is fighting to keep her eyes open as she leans over the chapter on family life in her Latin textbook (*avunculus; genitive avunculī; second declension—maternal uncle, mother's brother, mother's sister's husband . . .*), when she overhears Uncle Jimmy talking with his coworker, Jessica, about opening the trails for the spring.

"We need someone up there on foot after the snow melts," Uncle Jimmy says. "Someone to keep the maintenance trails clear for vehicles, notify us of any trees that have fallen, that kind of stuff. But we don't have the staff for it since Harry retired last fall."

"We could hire a part-timer," Jessica suggests. "What about your niece? She doesn't seem to have anything going on right now."

"Hey, she's got *a lot* going on," Uncle Jimmy says, defensive.

Rhi flushes, immediately awake as embarrassment floods her cheeks. Besides her excessive sleeping, most of what she's had "going on" since she came to Happy Valley is sitting in front of the forced-air heat vent in Uncle Jimmy's guest room, wrapped in a blanket, staring out the window as the snow falls, trying to imagine (and not imagine) what her future might look like.

She gets up and walks to the door of the break room, peeking her head out. Her uncle spots her right away and straightens, causing Jessica to turn and look at her, too.

"How much does the job pay, and what are the hours?" Rhi asks.

She starts her safety training that weekend, and, within a month, she's on the job.

THE FOREST WELCOMES RHI the way no other place ever has. She is still overly self-aware and vigilant, especially after hearing about the black bears that came down to Oneida Lake late last winter and tore through several empty cabins looking for food. But once she's on the path, her vigilance loses its edge; her awareness melts more completely into her surroundings. Even though the first part of the trail is entirely uphill—or maybe because of that—Rhi finds herself relaxing into her task in a way that energizes her, makes her feel capable and alive like she hasn't felt since—well, ever.

It's now the end of March, and Rhi has grown comfortable with the woods. Today, she sets off on the trail like she has every Saturday morning since she started. She enjoys this first part of the trail most of all, a subtle path cutting straight through the wilderness to get to the too-wide maintenance trail above. She can almost feel the trees moving with her, bending toward her in curiosity, or opening up for her to pass. She is often reminded of the scrubby tangle of woods behind her father's house, the lone sanctuary of her childhood, but that thought is laced with pain and she turns away from it.

Rhi notices the forest has grown unexpectedly loud since the equinox. Even in the too-early, misty hours of morning, birds sing, squirrels scurry about in search of their hidden food stores, melting snow rushes down the mountain in whispering rivulets and streams. Rhi's boots crunch over leaves and twigs as she hikes up the small mountain, clearing larger branches out of the way.

When she steps onto the maintenance trail, dense with pale morning fog, Rhi expects to see the familiar wide swath of flattened grass stretching out in both directions, the occasional utility pole stabbing up at the sky, the dense wall of hemlocks on the other side of the path.

Instead, the first thing she sees through the fog are two huge silvery wolves.

Rhi freezes. The wolves' teeth are bared, muzzles pinched into snarls, pinning Rhi in place with eyes like raw egg yolks, four bold points amidst the morning haze. Her body wants to turn and run, but Uncle Jimmy taught her better than that. Instead, Rhi takes a careful step backward, fingers wrapped tight around the straps of her backpack.

A movement draws Rhi's focus to something just beyond the wolves.

Her eyes widen.

Crouched behind the wolves, peering through the fog under the shelter of the hemlocks, is a tangle of wild girls.

4

RHI STARES, TOO SHOCKED to accept what her mind is telling her. The gauzy quality of the fog does not help—denser than it has ever been on the trail, and glowing pink-gold with the sunrise, turning the girls and wolves into something out of a dream.

As the fog dissipates, parting as if to reveal a path between Rhi and the girls, it becomes even more clear that these girls are not hikers lost in the woods. These girls are *wild*, snarling and half-naked, clad in damp ragged furs, their bodies covered in dirt. Their hair is caked with mud, twisted away from their faces in crude plaits and knots, studded with twigs and feathers like some kind of camouflage, or crown, or halo.

Rhi counts four of them tangled together: three knobby, half-starved girls, possibly teenagers, huddled around a smaller one. The fourth girl is lying on the ground, half on the carpet of hemlock needles and half in the lap of another girl. She is snarling even harder than the wolves are, her eyes wide and wild in her pale face. But when she tries to push herself up into a sitting position, she hisses and squeezes her eyes shut, her snarl turning into a grimace, her ferocity into pain.

A cord snaps tight inside Rhi's chest, pulling her toward the girls even as her feet stay firmly planted. She wants to help them, but the presence of the wolves—still snarling—stops her. Did the wolves hurt the girl? Will they attack *her*?

Then she notices: one of the girls, the only one with dark skin, is resting her hand on the flank of the nearest wolf, fingers sunk deep into the fur, as familiar as a pet.

Do the wolves . . . *belong* to the girls?

Or do they all belong to each other?

The smallest girl tries to shift her weight again and winces. Through the shifting web of limbs, Rhi sees a bold spot of color: purple and dark red. She swallows, that cord in her chest going taut again. She has to do something.

"*Hey*," Rhi calls, bracing herself as her voice breaks the long silence.

The wolves lower their heads, still snarling, but make no move to attack.

"Are you hurt?" Rhi asks.

No one responds, but the smaller girl's expression says enough.

Slowly, Rhi lowers her hand to the two-way radio clipped to her belt, watching the wolves to make sure she isn't agitating them. She unclips the radio and turns the volume down before she turns it on.

Her mouth is dry when she murmurs into the receiver: "Ranger One, this is Rhi-Rhi. Please acknowledge." After a moment she remembers to add, "Over."

"Roger Rhi-Rhi. Go ahead," Uncle Jimmy's voice crackles from the speaker.

"Uncle Jimmy, there are some girls up here. One of them is injured. Over."

"What kind of injuries are we talking about? Over."

"I don't know exactly. I can't get close enough to see, and it's pretty foggy up here. There are two wolves with them. Over."

There's a brief pause. "Say again?" he says, surprised, forgetting radio etiquette.

"There are two wolves with them. Over."

His reply comes fast this time. "What's your location? Are you safe? Over."

"I'm okay. The wolves don't seem interested in attacking. I think—I think they're protecting the girls?" Rhi flushes after she's said it out loud. "I know it sounds insane, but I'm looking at them right now. Over." She wants to say more, to explain more, but she shouldn't tie up the frequency in case he's trying to respond.

"Hey, I believe you, kiddo," Uncle Jimmy reassures her. "What's your location? I'll get help up there ASAP. Over." After Rhi tells him, Uncle Jimmy says, "We're on our way. You stay safe, okay? Over and out."

Rhi clips the radio back to her belt and breathes deeply. Knowing help is on the way makes her feel a little more in control of the situation—but not by much.

The wolves have stopped snarling, but they remain sharply focused on her, a febrile energy in the bristling of their fur, the twitching of their tails. The girls remain wary, their bodies angled toward one another. Their attention also stays on Rhi.

"Hey," Rhi calls to the girls again. "Help is on the way, okay?"

A brief look passes between the girls before they return all eyes to her. The smallest one flinches again, a grimace pinching her face.

"Do you mind if I take a look at her injury?" Rhi asks, keeping her voice steady. None of the girls answer. She isn't even sure they understand her. But growing up with her father and Vera, Rhi has learned to be exceptionally good at reading people, and her instincts tell her the girls—maybe even the wolves—are waiting for her to do something. Anticipating it, even. Strangely, Rhi feels it too: a bated-breath compulsion to see where this story goes.

Rhi steels herself and takes a careful step into the fog, finally allowing the taut cord in her chest to pull her forward.

The wolves don't move. The girls don't slink away. Encouraged, Rhi dares another step, and another, nerves thrilling as she moves closer. Closer. Closer, until she can see the breeze ruffling the wolves' fur, the mud spattered on their sides.

Rhi can see the smaller girl a little better now. She can see more of her injury, too: her right leg is covered in blood from mid-calf down, and there is something wrapped around it, some kind of shackle or snare or—

No. Rhi has seen one of these at the ranger station: it's a spring trap, one of those serrated, jawlike bear traps she'd only ever seen in cartoons before moving to Happy Valley. But they're real, and illegal. Poachers set traps like these deep in the mountains sometimes, far away from the campsites and trails, in hopes of catching foxes or black bear cubs.

And this poor girl stepped in one.

"Oh my God," Rhi says, her calf suddenly aching in sympathy.

The wolf on the left cocks its head, a growl at the back of its throat.

"P—please," Rhi says softly, unsure if she's talking to the wolves or the girls, her eyes flickering back and forth between them until she's almost dizzy. "I just want to help. You can trust me."

She can sense their hesitation. Cautiously, she sinks down onto her knees, demonstrating her submission. "My name is Rhi," she says. "What are your names?"

The girls' eyes go wide and they shrink down like petals closing on a bloom, huddling together. An odd repetitive sound builds between them, like cicadas striking up a chorus in the trees. It hums across the maintenance path, swirls around Rhi's head, barely touching her ears before the hairs on the back of her neck stand on end.

"*Reereereereereereereereereeree . . .*"

They are saying her name, she realizes. They whisper it over and over again like a mantra, giving Rhi an unsettled feeling, making her strangely possessive of the monosyllable that has come to belong to her. She almost wishes she could take the name back from the girls, can almost feel them tugging at it, examining it like a costume Rhi never knew she was wearing. But when the girls stop whispering and look at her in confusion, Rhi's curiosity outpaces her discomfort.

What *was* that?

Before Rhi can figure it out, one of the girls moves.

Slowly, the girl peels away from the tangle of lanky dirt-streaked limbs, her pale eyes like ghosts against the cool ebony of her face. The others touch her as she goes: familiar caresses, palms against her bare back, the muscled lengths of her legs.

Rhi is filled with a creeping, uncanny dread. There is something unsettling about the way the girl moves through the fog: spiderlike, crouched with her knees near her head, arms reaching across mud and pine needles and moss, fingers long and rigid. Her elbows rise over her ears as she sinks her chest to the ground, her head low, long mud-capped twists of hair scraping over the forest floor. But her eyes are lifted.

She's staring straight at Rhi.

As she crawls past the wolves, she sniffs the air with quick, sharp inhalations, as if trying to catch a scent. Feeling equal parts scared and ridiculous, Rhi lifts her hand and offers it to the girl, just as she would to an unfamiliar dog.

The girl creeps a bit closer, graceful and wrong at the same time. She lifts her head and sniffs again, inches from Rhi's outstretched hand. Rhi can see the dirt under her nails, smell the rank wet fur of the pelts hanging about her waist. What can the girl tell from the scent of Rhi's palm, she wonders?

Whatever she smells, the girl's features relax and she sits back a few inches as both wolves move in to press against her, shoulder to shoulder. Then the girl sits up straight, shifting all her weight onto her heels as the wolves close rank ahead of her.

Without warning, the wolf on the right pushes its muzzle into the palm of Rhi's still-outstretched hand, sending a thrill of fear through her. It sniffs heartily and flicks its tongue at her skin while the other wolf circles around to her other side, shoves its nose into her fist, forcing her palm open. Before she knows it, Rhi is surrounded: a wolf at each hand and the wild girl before her. Watching. Staring.

Rhi stares back. The girl's eyes are suddenly intensely real—too real—as if Rhi is looking into her *own* eyes. She is pinned by her gaze, the acute clarity of it holding her in place, stealing the speed from her pulse, the fear from her body. Rhi is no longer aware of anything except the wild young woman before her, her crown of knots and feathers, her ghost-gray eyes.

Satisfied with whatever she has discovered, the girl lifts her chin in acknowledgment and crawls back to her companions. The wolves follow.

Rhi is shaking—exhilarated, but shaking. They're welcoming her. They trust her. *Right?* She moves toward them again with caution, desperately hoping she is not misinterpreting their actions.

Rhi kneels by the injured girl's dirt-blackened foot, looking her in the eye as she does so. The girl's expression is twisted and feral, all snarling lips and wrinkled nose, with a deep furrow between her pale eyebrows. Now that Rhi is closer, she notices the girl's eyes are heterochromatic, one blue and one brown. There is an air of eerie madness about her, like someone possessed—or maybe it's just the juxtaposition of what Rhi has been told a young girl *should* be, versus what this one is.

Rhi leans down to examine the bear trap, making sure to move slowly and keep her hands visible. Up close, Rhi can see the serrated steel teeth are sunk deep into the flesh, the wounds crusted with blood. There is only a narrow gap between the jaws of the trap. Rhi wouldn't be surprised if the girl's bone is shattered. Her calf, badly swollen, has turned a foreboding shade of purple. Rhi knows only a little bit about first aid from the safety training she did for this job, but she knows for certain that prolonged loss of circulation is a sure way to lose a limb.

"This trap has to come off," Rhi says, trying to sound confident, looking up at the girl's pale face streaked with dirt and tears. "I know how to release it. Will you let me?"

The girl scrutinizes her for an interminably long moment, weighing factors Rhi can't begin to guess at. Finally, she gives Rhi a stiff nod. With a deep breath, the injured girl presses her back into the girl behind her, who holds her steady and does not yield. The other girl is also white beneath the mud dried on her skin. Her thick black hair is knotted atop her head, held in place by small animal bones curving around her skull. Her eyes, so dark they are nearly black, shimmer as she nods at Rhi to continue.

Rhi examines the trap, hoping it's the same as the ones she's seen at the ranger station. This one is older and covered in rust, not like the smooth stainless-steel traps poachers use to prevent damage to their goods. This one has either been long forgotten, or is meant to cause serious damage. Regardless, the basic principle of the spring trap is the same: two levers on either side and a pin to set the trigger plate. Pressing the levers will compress the springs, releasing the jaws and the girl.

Rhi searches for the levers—and lets out a breath when she finds them.

She stands and looks at the others, clenching the shiver from her hands. The adrenaline that was coursing through her before feels like it has tripled now with the fate of this girl's leg in her hands. She's decided to trust Rhi with her pain, and Rhi is determined not to break that trust.

"It might hurt when the trap moves," Rhi warns, beads of sweat trickling down her back as she speaks, despite the cool morning. "But I'll get it open, I promise."

The girls stare at Rhi and say nothing.

She takes that as permission to proceed.

With extreme care, Rhi bends down and folds out the levers on either side of the jaw, trying to maintain an even distribution of pressure to avoid needlessly jostling the wounded leg. She straightens, takes a deep breath, exhales. Before she can lose her nerve, she sets her weight into her heels and puts one hiking boot on a lever, then the other, and leans her weight forward onto the balls of her feet, compressing the spring beneath the trap.

But the jaws don't budge.

The teeth are sunk too far into the girl's swollen flesh.

Rhi looks to the other girls for help, but they don't understand the mechanics of the trap. They look back and forth between Rhi and the trap, their eyes wide and expectant, impatient for the release she promised.

Rhi takes another shaky breath and sinks all her weight into her feet as she squats down, desperately careful to maintain even pressure on both levers. When she is sure of her balance, she reaches for the metal jaws with both hands, willing herself not to tremble. As gently as possible, she starts to pry the metal teeth from the girl's leg.

The girl gasps.

"I'm sorry," Rhi says through gritted teeth. "I'm sorry, I'm sorry, I'm sorry . . ." She pinches the metal and pulls—evenly, slowly, firmly—until the jaws finally give. The serrated teeth slide from the wounds and a new gush of dark blood rushes to fill the space, trickling down the girl's calf. But the jaws are open, lying flat between Rhi's feet, and the girl is free.

One of the other girls slips a hand under the knee, lifting her leg away from the jaws. When the girl's leg is clear, Rhi warns them to stay back. She lets herself fall back on her butt and the trap snaps shut.

She looks up to find everyone's expression grim, except for the injured girl whose face is scrunched up in fearful pain. The wolves move in, crowding Rhi out, forcing her to shuffle backward. As the wolves start to lick the wound, the injured girl bites her lip so hard she draws blood. She stares achingly up at the sky as a dark cloud passes over the sun, dampening the already hazy light. She moans as her sisters smooth her white-blonde hair back from her forehead, press their palms over her chest, under her neck and back. When she grimaces and moans louder, they lean into her, lean their foreheads against her, against one another, a soft, unearthly humming passing between them like a prayer. At the sound's epicenter, the girls are linked, skin pressed against skin pressed against skin. Even the wolves are leaning against the girls, flank to flank.

As Rhi watches them, some burgeoning, unpleasant emotion tries to claw up from the pit of her stomach, but it's pointless—absurd. She crams it down and climbs to her feet, forcing herself to think of practical things instead: *Uncle Jimmy and the others will be here soon. He'll help. He'll make sure she doesn't lose her leg. They'll be okay*—

Enveloped by her sisters, the injured girl finally parts her lips and lets out a loud, agonized sob. As if in answer, light flashes from the darkened sky, making Rhi look up. The clouds light up blue and white as lightning flickers and skewers through them. Thunder follows fast on its heels, cracking the sky open wide to unleash a torrent of rain.

Rhi gasps as it hits her skin, cold and fast, raising goose bumps on her arms and sending shivers up and down her spine.

It doesn't surprise Rhi when the first girl howls, or the second, or the third. She sinks back, farther away from the huddle of girls and wolves, watching with unexpected reverence as every last one of them lifts their face and their voice to the sky, howling at the clouds. They are elusive, mournful cries, slipping straight past the storm and into the heavens.

Impossibly, Rhi understands what they are saying, even as they say nothing at all. She understands their pain, their grief, their loss, even though she knows nothing about them. Her throat aches to join them.

She swallows instead.

When their howls trail off, the rain slows to a sprinkle, then a spitting mist, as if a faucet has been turned off somewhere overhead.

In place of the girls' voices, Rhi hears a distant crunching of debris and the low whine of engines propelling vehicles up the mountain. One of the wolves looks over its shoulder at Rhi. It slinks over to her, nuzzling her hand again. The wolf looks up at her with huge yellow eyes, then at the girls, back and forth and back.

They're in your world now, the wolf seems to be saying. *Take care of them*.

"I will," Rhi whispers, trying to make the animal understand. "I'll make sure they're okay. I promise."

The four-wheelers round the curve of the maintenance trail, high beams cutting through the fog—still some fifty yards away, but approaching fast. The wolves, hackles raising, turn to see the girls one last time. They paw the ground before bolting into the cover of the forest, mist, trees, and shadows swallowing them whole.

For a moment, as Rhi watches the rangers park their vehicles and climb down from the cabs, she wonders if the wolves were ever really there at all.

A Name for All Things

Excerpted from *Savage Castle:*
A Memoir of the Wild Girls of Happy Valley

IT WAS A WINTER NIGHT when Mother taught us about naming.

"A name is not a simple thing," he told us, circling the fire with a long stick in hand. We were seated around the firepit dug into the center of the castle floor, burning low to keep the hollow tree as warm as possible without scorching us. We did not feel the cold like Mother did—we had adapted to the elements long ago, the fine hairs on our bodies growing thicker and thinner, our blood rushing warmer and cooler, as the seasons demanded. But Mother was old, even when we were very young. He was a sage back home, after all, and a prophet— and no young person had ever seen enough of life to be both a sage and a prophet.

"When words are true, they hold great power," Mother told us, moving carefully in the space between us and the fire, pausing at each of us to scratch the dirt floor with the tip of the stick. "But when a name is true, it holds the greatest power of all."

Oblivienne looked up at him, firelight dancing in the pitch of her eyes. "How do you know if a name is true?"

"The same way we know anything, child," he said. "You *feel* it. Take this fire, for example. Doesn't the word *fire* feel right to you? Fire. Feu. Vuur. Vatra. Eldur. In almost any language of this world, they have captured the essence and the feeling of fire."

In the glow of the flames, Sunder's mismatched eyes widened as she sat up, whispering, "Fire."

Epiphanie, sable skin gilded by the flames as she leaned forward, whispered it back. "Fire."

And when the two of them, and Verity, too, whispered it together, the fire flickered and roared. It rose an inch, then two, stretching high to banish the shadows overhead.

Mother chuckled. "Yes, yes, good. You see? A name is a powerful thing. And that is why I have concealed each of yours."

Four pairs of questioning eyes turned to Mother, searching for the gleam of secrets always present in his gaze. None of us remembered being called by names other than the ones we knew, but there was much we did not remember about our earliest years: the time before the wilderness, the castle, four girls and a gentle old prophet, huddled together in the mountains of a foreign world. There was very little we remembered about our first home besides darkness, fear, and ruin, and nothing that we missed.

"Whomsoever holds the knowledge of your name, also holds power over you," Mother went on. "I have hidden your old names from the world, and from your memories. I've done this to keep you safe, yes. But I have also done this to ensure that the four of you will always be free of masters and kings."

Mother stepped over to Sunder and scratched a symbol into the dirt, using both hands to steady the stick as he moved. He lowered his voice to a whisper. "No one will believe the names I have given you are your real names. But the secret is, these names are truer than any name you wore before." Mother sidestepped over to Epiphanie, smoothing the dirt in front of her with a naked foot browned by years in the sun. "These names are the sounds your sisters call out when they are in need. They are the invocations of your wild selves—adventurers, explorers, survivors in a new land."

"But what does that mean?" Verity asked as she traced the shapes in the dirt before her with the ragged nail on her pinky finger. Her shapes were different from Sunder's on her left, from Oblivienne's on her right.

"These may not be the names that your parents gave you," Mother said. "But they are the names written on your destiny." He finished with Epiphanie's drawing, stepped outside of the circle, and gazed at us with pride.

Oblivienne scratched at her arm, copying the shapes in the dirt before her and watching red lines rise on her forearm. "What are these symbols, then?"

"These are your sigils, that you may invoke your power even in silence. Even in secret." Mother leaned on his stick and began to walk, circling at our backs. In the shadows, we could not see how much he depended on the walking stick, how stiffly his legs moved. We could not see how old he truly was.

"You have your names," he told us. "And now, you have your sigils. Learn them. Remember them. Use them wisely. To invoke one's name is no trifle, whether by sound or sight."

Each of us looked up, away from the scratches in the dirt or on our own skin. We watched Mother move to the open doorway, close his eyes, and feel the cold on his face, leaning heavily on his stick. The low pinkish night sky made a surreal background of the forest outside, turning him into a jagged silhouette as the fire cast his robes in sharp shadows, flickering like the flames themselves.

"Does this mean you are not called Mother back home?" Epiphanie asked.

Mother chuckled, gazing out into the falling snow through the archway between the castle's roots. "No," he admitted, inhaling the cool, fresh air of the pink night outside. "But it is a truer name than any I wore before coming to this new world."

He reached out and laid a hand against the smooth dry wood of the castle walls, perhaps feeling the last of his magic seep out of him and into the tree, strengthening its rotting skeleton against another winter.

We knew he would have to leave us again soon. He would have to wander to replenish his magic. And this time, like the last time, we were afraid he would not make it back.

5

OBLIVIENNE CLINGS TO HER SISTERS as they pour out of the vehicle, staring up at the enormous building rising from the ground not thirty paces ahead of them. Wrapped in crinkling silver blankets, given to them by the people who removed them from the forest, they follow the girl who calls herself *Rhi*, the one the wolf-kin said could be trusted. They follow her, reach for her, hold on to her as if she is their only torch in a moonless night. But it is full daylight—a cool and bright spring day—and the girls have never felt so lost.

The ground is unnaturally flat beneath Oblivienne's bare feet, hard as stone and rougher than sand. She curls her toes against it as she watches the boxy vehicle that arrived ahead of them, lights flashing and swirling on top. Someday soon she will learn this vehicle is called an *ambulance*, but today all she knows is that Sunder is inside it, injured and vulnerable. The rear doors fling open and a man and a woman hop out, reaching in and pulling to slide Sunder, strapped to a narrow bed, out of the tiny room inside. Wheels unfold from the bed and extend to the ground as the people on either side work some kind of magic. Oblivienne wonders if they are some kind of healers, like Mother. Sunder is growling on the bed, gritting her teeth as they push and pull her toward the building in a half-jog, eyes aimed at her feet and the wide sheet of glass blocking their way.

Oblivienne thinks nothing of it as the glass splits and slides open, then closes once they have gone through, without any human assistance. She has seen greater wonders with Mother in the wilderness.

Even so, to see Sunder vanish inside this mountain of pale brick and mortar makes Oblivienne's stomach clench. She and her sisters press closer to Rhi as she leads them toward the doors.

"It's okay," Rhi assures them. "They're going to fix her leg. This is a place where they help people."

The calm in her voice reminds Oblivienne of the way Mother could restrain a storm with nothing but his firm determination—a lone frail human holding back the whole howling force of nature. But even Mother could not hold a storm back indefinitely—nor would he want to. Nature, like humans, can only be manipulated. Eventually, all true things run their course. Still, Oblivienne is grateful, as she knows her sisters are, that Rhi has made herself an island of peace in this storm.

Rhi and the man she calls "Uncle Jimmy" lead them to the glass doors of the building. On the glass, just before it slides open, Oblivienne reads the words as Mother taught them to:

ONEIDA SISTERS OF MERCY HOSPITAL
EMERGENCY ROOM

The words make little sense to Oblivienne, but once inside, she forgets them anyway. The floor is smooth and startlingly cold underfoot—waxy, almost, with a thin layer of filmy grit. The air smells sharp and foreign, full of strange odors Oblivienne has never encountered. A hum of noise and activity fills the space: people talking, alien sounds of ringing and buzzing, nearly overwhelming Oblivienne's senses. They approach a sign hanging from the ceiling that reads CHECK IN HERE, and Oblivienne is grateful when the voices falter and fade—but then there are eyes on her skin, crawling like beetles. She and her sisters huddle even closer together before they turn to look.

To their right is a room *full* of people—more people than came to the forest to help Sunder—more people than Oblivienne or her sisters have *ever* seen in one place. They are sitting on benches and in chairs, staring unabashedly at the cluster of girls. Oblivienne and her sisters stare back.

"What in God's name happened to these girls?" someone asks loudly behind her, tone both irritated and concerned.

Oblivienne turns and sees a woman dressed all in bold rosy pink, the same clothes that several other people are wearing in this building, hurrying around like ants at work. The woman bends to pick up the silver blanket Verity has let fall to the floor and returns it to Verity's shoulders—a good head higher than the woman herself—but Verity glares at her and shrugs it off again, puffing out her bare chest in confrontation. The woman sighs and takes Verity by the arms, turning her away from the roomful of clawing eyes.

What happened *to us?* Oblivienne thinks, looking at her sisters. *We lost Mother's protection. We left the castle. The wilderness betrayed us.* But that is not something she can explain to these strangers.

"Someone had better make certain the police are on their way," the woman mutters to another woman in pink. She looks at Rhi. "Are you the one who found them?"

"Yes, ma'am," Rhi says.

"Do they speak, or do they just snarl like the other one my EMTs brought in?"

Rhi looks annoyed. "They understand everything you're saying."

The nurse turns her attention to Oblivienne. "What is your name?"

Oblivienne's face closes off, goes slack. She knows better than to give their power away so easily.

The woman sighs. "Suit yourselves." She scribbles something down on a board with paper clipped to it, pausing momentarily to spin Verity back toward her sisters when she tries to turn around again. The woman looks up at Rhi. "What's your name? Aren't you Ranger Abrams's niece?"

"Rhi. Yes."

Oblivienne and her sisters startle. This is the second time she has given her name away. Does she not know the power of a name?

"Well, you've done your best for these girls. We can take it from here." She takes Rhi by the elbow and tries to send her away.

Epiphanie grabs hold of Rhi's hand. "Rhi," she says with urgency, her pale eyes wide.

"Rhi," Verity whispers, staring at the girl.

"Rhi." Oblivienne adds her voice to the chorus, murmuring the sound over and over again, invoking the name like Mother taught them. Their voices blend and overlap until the sound forms a bubble around Rhi, around Oblivienne's sisters, around the suddenly wide-eyed woman. The power of the sound envelopes them, buzzes across their skin—but somehow does not penetrate the girl before them.

Something is not right.

But is it the name, or is it their magic?

Rhi looks at them in surprise, her eyes suddenly bright with an emotion Oblivienne cannot name, but recognizes; it is the feeling of being on the outside and then drawn in—something Oblivienne knows well. For as much as she is a member of this pack, she has often felt that the thread that ties her to her sisters is more tenuous than the rest. She has often felt inexplicably alone, even when undeniably connected.

That is simply your nature, Mother told her once, a long time ago. *Some of us are born with borders that are less permeable than others. It can be both a strength and a weakness.*

Oblivienne blinks the memory away as Rhi shakes her head, as if to clear it of a similar distraction.

"Let me stay with them a bit longer," Rhi says to the woman, straightening. "I think I can help."

Oblivienne feels a rush of emotion, a swelling in her chest that makes her cling tighter to the girl. *Help. Yes. We need help. Sunder needs help. We need to heal her leg and find our way home . . .*

The woman tightens her mouth into a thin line, eyeing their pack.

She cocks an eyebrow at Rhi. "Ranger Abrams," she says, sliding her gaze over to the man in the tan uniform at the counter, writing on a small stack of papers. "Do you hear what she's saying?"

Ranger Abrams—*Uncle Jimmy*, Oblivienne realizes, and thinks perhaps they *do* use false names in this world?—glances over at the woman, the cold rectangles of light on the ceiling illuminating the silver hiding in his dark-blonde hair.

"Rhi's a smart kid. She can sign whatever forms you need." He looks at Rhi and a small, proud smile turns up the corners of his mouth.

Mother used to smile at us that way, Oblivienne thinks, and the thought passes between her sisters as a twist of grief blooms in their chests. They press even closer together, tightening the circle around Rhi.

The woman shrugs and swivels around on her white shoes. "Come on then," she says mildly, but her shoulders pinch as she leads them down the hall, uncomfortable with having the girls at her back where she cannot see them.

They pass through a maze of hallways and doors, and after a brief inspection of the girls' bodies for signs of injury, Rhi confers with one of several pink-clad women accompanying their pack before turning back to the girls.

She squares her shoulders, calm and confident despite the chaos. "The nurses are going to get you cleaned up now, okay? You can trust them."

Oblivienne wonders how they plan to do that without a body of water anywhere near this place.

OBLIVIENNE STARES, AWED BY THE water shooting from short metal branches sticking out of the walls, the incredible amount of steam filling the room. Stripped of their tattered wet furs, she and her sisters are maneuvered into the slippery square room and, after great hesitation, they touch the water and find it impossibly warm. Verity is the first to realize the pleasure of this as she dives beneath the spray, relishing the hot water, barely noticing when the nurse hands her a fragrant waxy brick and a square of white woven cloth, and tells her to wash.

Oblivienne and Epiphanie follow Verity's lead as they move to stand beneath the spraying water, take the pungent bricks from the nurses, and create a thick, floral lather. They washed regularly with soapwort in the wilderness, but the lather from the dried plant roots had never been anything like this.

"Don't forget behind your ears," one of the nurses calls out.

"And your toes."

"And behind your knees."

The girls follow the inane instructions, covering themselves in dense white foam.

"Okay, now rinse off."

Oblivienne bristles. Never in their lives have they taken orders from anyone—not even Mother. Mother had only ever offered gentle suggestions and guidance. But what choice do they have? Sunder is their captive. Until she is returned to them, the girls must make allies of these strangers.

The nurses help them dress in strange clothing after drying off as best they can, pulling hard combs through Oblivienne and Verity's hair to dislodge the feathers and bones still entangled. Oblivienne tugs at the uncomfortable gown, hating the feeling of the collar against her bare throat. They are handed thin robes to wear over the gowns, and horrible papery covers to put on their feet that whisper and crunch with every step, every shift of their weight. Oblivienne looks to Epiphanie with disgust, but Epiphanie indicates with a nod to accept it.

They find Rhi waiting for them in the next room, sitting on a bench. She stands and looks surprised when she sees them. Oblivienne looks at her sisters, too, tries to see them through Rhi's eyes, but all she can see is the garish pale swaths of overwashed fabric, the unflattering coldness of the artificial light, turning her sisters' brilliant colors flat and dull. Panic pricks at the back of Oblivienne's mind: Is this really what Mother intended for them?

"Are you doing okay?" Rhi asks, eyes moving over each of their faces.

Oblivienne and her sisters shift in their uncomfortable new clothing, clasping one another's hands.

"We'll take them out through the back entrance," the nurse says. "I have an ambulance waiting to transfer them to the psych unit. You should get out of here after we load them up, though."

"Psych?" Rhi repeats, her concern making the girls more vigilant.

"Where else do you think they're gonna go, hun? They're half-feral, nonverbal, and look like they'd sooner bite us than let us help them if you weren't around. They need to be *fully* evaluated. Lord knows what they must have been through to make them like this." Her mouth twists sympathetically as she fusses with a tangle in Verity's long blonde hair. "Someone is responsible for the state they're in."

"Come on," one of the nurses says. "Girls, we're taking you somewhere where we can feed you and take care of you. Your friend will join you soon, after we've fixed up her leg. Do you understand?"

Oblivienne's brow furrows, and she knows her sisters' brows are wrinkling just the same. They understand the meaning of the words, but not the heart of them.

"You can go with the nurses," Rhi assures them. "You'll see your sister again soon."

But Oblivienne's heart only beats faster, swept up by an internal storm she senses she will not be able to hold at bay much longer.

The nurses gather their clipboards and push the girls back into the corridor, guiding them once again through the twists and turns of the building until they end up at two large gray doors beneath a glowing green sign that says EXIT. Two of the nurses slip through the doors ahead of the rest, and Oblivienne can hear people on the other side—many people, from the sound of it. When the other nurses open the doors wide, a swell of bodies surges forward toward them.

Strange men and women crowd all around Oblivienne and her sisters, even as the nurses push them away. There are so many people, so many eyes and voices and new and different faces, it feels like *hundreds* of people—but Oblivienne knows that cannot be right.

She is blinded by a powerful flicker of light, like lightning striking nearby. The first burst of flashes makes her flinch and shrink back, covering her face with her forearm. As the voices begin to shout, her eyes narrow and the hair on her body stands on end. Electricity hums between the girls, wild and frenetic, like the air before a thunderstorm.

Their bodies know before they do: these people are not safe.

When someone shoves a blunt black wand just a little too close to their faces, the storm breaks.

Verity rips the robe from around her shoulders and flings it at the crowd. It falls over a handful of people and they fumble backward, into other bodies. Taking advantage of the confusion, Epiphanie darts into the crowd roaring like a mountain lion, headbutting the nearest woman waving a black wand, knocking her into the people behind her. Epiphanie and Verity whale their fists against the gaping black mouths of the boxy objects pointed at them. They knock one from a man's shoulder and it hits the ground with a *crack*, pieces of it flying off in all directions, trampled underfoot.

Oblivienne is the last one to join the fray, diving at the attackers' knees to take them down. She thrashes with her ropy but powerful arms at anything that does not get out of her way, feels the satisfying collapse of joints all around her as bodies tumble to the unnaturally flat ground.

"Are you getting all this?" someone shouts gleefully from the outer edge of the crowd. "This is incredible!"

Oblivienne does not understand the joy in the person's voice. She does not understand the objects being thrust in her direction. She does not understand why huge men in unnaturally white clothes are pulling her off the people attacking her and her sisters. She does not understand why there is a prick in her arm, or why a sudden uninvited weariness washes over her.

What she does understand is the thing she has been trying to ignore since the day they left the castle; since Sunder stepped in that awful metal trap; since the moment the wolf-kin gave their approval of the girl named Rhi now leaning over Oblivienne with a stricken expression, holding her hand.

As she sinks into the gray prison of an unnatural sleep, Oblivienne finally understands: she and her sisters are never going home again.

PRIVATE: The Girls

Can't include these notes in the official file. I'm too angry. The ER nurses botched this situation badly and now VIOLENT is scrawled on the girls' official records. Can anyone blame them for reacting that way? After what they've been through?

Preliminary examinations have not found evidence of sexual activity or abuse, so that is something. But the girls refuse to speak to us. They are wary, frightened. I need to find a way to gain their trust.

Until then, here's what I've gathered just from my observations:

- Many attempts to hoard food & water. Typically, an indication of food scarcity, but aside from the injury, the girls are surprisingly healthy, if underweight. Was someone taking care of them out there?

- Long bouts of what seems like group chanting. Possibly a method of self-soothing?

- Very interested in the arts & crafts supplies—though it seems they've never seen markers or crayons before. They appear to be mesmerized by the colors.

- Normal-to-above average dexterity & fine motor skills

- Why are they writing the word "sunder" over and over again?

LATER: Nurse Leticia says, since the youngest (we think?) was returned to her companions yesterday, the girls have added three more words to the mix, but they're spelling two of them wrong. I'm relieved that they have some reading and writing abilities, which will make rehab that much easier. Though—can they write anything beyond these four words?

So many questions. Who taught them to write? How long have they been out in the wilderness?

Who is missing these poor girls?

6

THE MEDIA IS IN LOVE with the "Wild Girls of Happy Valley." Even though all they have to go on is speculation (or maybe *because* that's all they have), the news stations and their audiences are captivated by the story. Rhi spends hours switching between news channels with Purrdita nestled in her lap, shedding her black-and-white fur on Rhi's black pajama bottoms.

"Four allegedly feral girls were discovered at the Happy Valley Wildlife Preserve early this morning by a junior at the local high school. We've reached out to her for more information, but there has been no comment at this time . . ."

Or at any other time, Rhi thinks, silencing another call on her cell phone from an unfamiliar number.

"Word on the street is that four teenage girls have been brought to Oneida Sisters of Mercy Hospital today after a local high school student found them in the wilderness, surrounded by coyotes . . ."

Not coyotes. Wolves.

Right?

Rhi isn't so sure, now. Recalling the events of that morning both fascinates and embarrasses her; she knows what she witnessed—what she *experienced.* But how could it possibly be real?

"Allegedly, the girls have been living in the mountains on their own for quite some time. No word on what's become of the coyotes. More as the story develops . . ."

"One of the girls was rushed to the emergency room with a severe leg injury. Instead of letting doctors treat her, witnesses say she displayed animal-like behavior, snapping and biting at the nurses . . ."

"Witnesses say that the feral girls attacked a group of reporters at the hospital, causing over ten thousand dollars in damages and more than a few black eyes. Let's take a look . . ."

The footage is the same on every channel: brief interviews with overeager witnesses, then shaky video of three girls in hospital gowns wrestling grown men and women to the ground, flashes of white eyes and teeth bared in ferocious growls, spittle and limbs flying.

In some of the footage, you can spot Rhi in the background, watching the chaos with an almost preternatural calm on her face.

"You're lucky you didn't get hurt in that brawl," Uncle Jimmy says as he walks into the living room and slumps down in his tattered green armchair. He's changed into his pajamas for the night as well: Warhol-inspired *Star Wars* pajama bottoms and an old black undershirt with holes in it.

"They were just defending themselves," Rhi says, petting Purrdita a little more aggressively than she means to.

Rhi's phone vibrates again on the seat cushion next to her. She reaches to ignore the call but stops when she sees it's not a call from an unknown number—it's a text message from someone in her contacts.

> **Message from: NO**
> Did I just see you on the news???

Rhi clears her notifications and puts the phone face down on the coffee table, ignoring the sensation of her heart trying to crawl out of her mouth.

ALL WEEKEND LONG, Rhi watches as the reporters and journalists keep circling back to the same questions:

"Who are these girls?"

"Where are their families?"

"Were the Wild Girls of Happy Valley kidnapped?"

"Have they escaped from a religious cult?"

"Are they victims of human trafficking?"

Without much else to go on, the reporters have all landed on the same conclusions, too:

"These girls were probably torn from their families at a young age and have been missing for years."

"They must be reunited with their parents," the voices repeat, as if scripted.

"Whoever kidnapped them must be brought to justice."

By Monday, Rhi is exhausted from all the late-night scrolling through think pieces and Associated Press regurgitation. Thankfully, Uncle Jimmy lets her skip school—"Just this once"—to avoid the questions that will be waiting for her and catch up on sleep.

Rhi sleeps all day but wakes up in time to see Sheriff Elroy's tele-vised press conference in the town hall. According to Uncle Jimmy, there's never been a need for a press conference in Happy Valley be-fore, but the sheriff does his best to look official and composed behind the lectern.

Rhi and Uncle Jimmy watch from home. Star is coming over later with Chinese takeout and board games; they and Uncle Jimmy both want to distract Rhi from the wild girls, even if only for a single evening.

But Rhi can't imagine focusing on anything else. She feels at once protective of the girls and voracious for any information about them, anything that might help her comprehend the connection she felt with them in the forest—that pure, wordless understanding, like a doorway thrown open in her heart. It was as if Rhi had been sleepwalking her entire life, up until the moment her path crossed with theirs. Only *now* is she awake, and she does not want to fall asleep again.

On her uncle's flatscreen, Sheriff Elroy gives his official report, sweat dotting his forehead as he leans a little too hard into the microphone. After he covers everything they know and are able to share (which is very little), a reporter jumps up.

"Thomas Kyle, Fox News. Can you tell us if these girls are a threat to your town?"

The sheriff laughs. "Of course not. They're just little girls."

Rhi rolls her eyes at both the question and the answer.

"Clearly Sheriff Elroy has never had an older sister," Uncle Jimmy jokes, scratching Purrdita between the ears.

"These are feral children, is that correct?" Thomas Kyle continues. "After their display of violence the other day, what measures are being taken to make sure no one else gets hurt? What's being done to keep the hospital staff and the other patients safe?"

Rhi watches as a familiar-looking middle-aged Latina woman stands up from a chair behind the sheriff and moves toward the lectern. The woman is wearing a sensible skirt and blouse in shades of blue; her dark hair is pulled back into a loose bun, and she is wearing dark-framed glasses. She whispers to the sheriff and he nods, stepping down with obvious relief on his face.

"Hey, that's Mari!" Uncle Jimmy says. "You remember her, right?"

When the camera cuts to a closer shot of the woman at the lectern, Rhi recognizes her as the psychologist she met with during her first few weeks in Happy Valley, when CPS made Rhi go in for her own psychiatric evaluation a few days after her father's arrest.

"My name is Dr. Mariposa Ibanez," the woman says clearly, loudly, pronouncing her name with the correct Spanish accent, though the rest of her accent is firmly rooted in Upstate New York. "I am head of the psychiatric clinic at Oneida Sisters of Mercy, and I am personally overseeing the evaluation and treatment of the young women rescued from the woods on Saturday. I would like to make it clear, right now, that we will *not* be answering any questions about their care, at *any* time. I can assure you that the other patients at the hospital are as safe as they have ever been. I can also assure you that whatever violence previously displayed and captured on film was a fear-based reaction motivated by self-defense.

"We have taken DNA samples and fingerprints, and we are working with the FBI to identify them," Dr. Ibanez continues. "However, if anyone has any information about them, we ask that you contact the police department immediately. These girls need their families now more than ever. That is our priority at this time, and we hope the press will assist us in seeking this information." She gives the crowd of reporters a long, meaningful look. "That is all. Thank you for your time."

The crowd erupts with questions as Dr. Ibanez steps away from the lectern.

After a moment, the feed cuts back to the local news station, the anchors looking momentarily lost before the male anchor comments: "Keeping it short and sweet, I guess."

"Mari's never been one to soak up the spotlight," Uncle Jimmy says, turning off the news as it switches to sports coverage. Before Rhi's evaluation with Dr. Ibanez, he had told her that he had gone through the Happy Valley public school system with Mari, and although she's a few years older than him, they've run in the same circles for nearly his entire life.

"Speaking of Mari . . ." Rhi bites her lip, thinking. "Uncle Jimmy . . . do you think you can do me a favor?"

7

THE NEXT DAY AT SCHOOL, Rhi tries to keep her head down, but her regular shroud of anonymity has been yanked away. Every classmate who ever looked away when it was time to partner up for a group activity, or shouted an abrasive "what?" when Rhi answered a question in class too quietly, or simply pretended she was not there in the hallway, is suddenly hovering around her before and after every class.

"Weren't you so scared?"

"Do they speak, or can they only growl?"

"Was that girl's leg like totally mangled?"

"Did you see them beat the crap out of those reporters?"

"Are they dangerous?"

"No," Rhi answers, sometimes, trying to remain neutral, inoffensive. "They were just scared."

When the kids become bored with her insufficient answers, they speculate instead, just like the reporters.

"Do you think they're in a cult?"

"Do you think someone kidnapped them?"

"Do you think they were sex trafficking victims?"

"Do you think they're just faking this for attention?"

Rhi shakes her head at their questions, but they're not really asking her anymore. It becomes progressively harder for her to maintain a neutral expression as the day goes on. Then, after lunch period, someone finally makes her suffering worthwhile.

"Did you see someone at the hospital leaked the girls' names?"

Rhi looks up at the boy who says it, then at the smartphone he is surreptitiously sliding across her desk so all the students can see before their teacher notices. There are four grainy, washed-out pictures—four girls, hollow-cheeked and haunted, as if shocked to be presented with a camera lens so soon after smashing all those cameras the other day. Rhi quickly scans the names beneath each photo.

Verity. The tall stoic blonde.

Sunder. The smallest one, whose leg was injured.

Oblivienne. The dark-haired girl who'd held Sunder's head in her lap while she wept.

Epiphanie. The ghost-eyed girl who stared into Rhi's soul until the world dropped away.

Ignoring her classmates, Rhi pulls up the news article on her own phone and stares down at the four photos, chanting their names in her head until the teacher says her name in a warning tone, and she's forced to put her phone away. But even as she watches her teacher give her lesson at the whiteboard, Rhi's mind remains with the wild girls.

Immediately after school, Rhi takes the city's only bus to the psychiatric hospital. She continues to study the girls' pictures on her phone on the way there, not for fear of forgetting their names, which are now seared into her brain, but to ground herself, to calm her nervous, doubting mind until she can see them again. She needs to see the girls with her own eyes to make sure they're okay, but more than that—to make sure finding them wasn't a dream.

THE FRONT DESK PAGES DR. IBANEZ when Rhi arrives and explains why she's there. After a few minutes, Dr. Ibanez appears, a woman-shaped patch of color in the drained sepia hallway. She is wearing a lavender blazer and matching slacks, her blouse a paisley of greens and yellows beneath. She smiles and offers her hand, the coral flash of her nails drawing Rhi's eyes.

"Hello again, Rhi. Good to see you." They shake hands briefly before the doctor gestures for Rhi to follow. "Right this way."

The halls of the psychiatric hospital are quiet, just a few patients ambling through the white corridors, aides at their sides. Muted voices seep from beyond closed doors: muffled conversations, the jabbering of daytime television, the occasional moan of weeping.

Rhi clears her throat, uneasy in the murmuring hush of the corridor. "So . . . how are they?" she asks.

"Not here." Dr. Ibanez raises a finger to her lips. "The cameras are gone, but these walls have ears. *Someone* here leaked the girls' names and photos to the press." She side-eyes an empty nurse's station before leading Rhi into an office that reminds Rhi of her guidance counselor's office, only without the cringey motivational posters: overstuffed, sagging particleboard bookshelves; dented metal file cabinets, half open and half closed; mismatched upholstered chairs for visitors; a torn white vinyl swivel chair on the doctor's side of the desk, patched with rainbow duct tape at the corner.

The desk itself is minimalist blonde wood, remarkably cleared of clutter. All that sits on the desk is a nameplate reading MARIPOSA IBANEZ, PSY.D., M.D., a wireless phone charger, a purple-and-green stoneware coffee mug, a closed laptop, and on top of that a clipboard with official-looking forms.

"I was very glad to hear from Jimmy yesterday that you wanted to see the girls," Dr. Ibanez says, gesturing to the mismatched visitors' chairs as she sits down at her desk. "The truth is I'm having a hell of a time getting them to talk to me. They seem to *trust* me, in a way, but they won't answer any of my questions . . ." She takes a breath, looks Rhi in the eye. "But before we get into all of that, how are *you*?"

Rhi lowers herself into the deep, green velvet chair. It's been three months since she's sat across from Dr. Ibanez like this. When she had first arrived in Happy Valley, Child Welfare had asked Dr. Ibanez to evaluate Rhi to determine if she needed "elevated care," or if next of kin was good enough. Rhi doesn't know what Dr. Ibanez's report said, but she's been living with her uncle ever since with no indication that will change. At least until her father gets out of jail.

"Um, I'm fine," Rhi says, playing with a loose thread on the knee of her jeans. "A little weirded out by everything, I guess."

"That's perfectly understandable," Dr. Ibanez says. "You experienced something very intense in those woods."

You don't know the half of it, Rhi thinks.

"Yeah," she says. "But I think it's more the attention that's difficult to deal with, you know? The reporters calling. My classmates asking me all these questions I can't answer. To be fair, I guess I've got the same questions as everyone else. Only, I feel . . ." She trails off, embarrassed she started to say anything at all. Talking to Dr. Ibanez is strangely easy, but also slippery. She wonders if therapists are trained to put you in some kind of hypnotic state.

"Go on." Dr. Ibanez eases forward in her chair. "I work at a psych ward, remember. There's not much you can say that will shock me."

Rhi hesitates. "This isn't, like, a *session*, right?"

Dr. Ibanez chuckles. "No. But if you're going to talk to the girls, I do need to make certain you're prepared for what you're going to see behind these doors. So, yeah: I am doing a *little bit* of an evaluation. But just a little one." She smiles at Rhi. "Go on. What were you going to say?"

Rhi shrugs. "It's stupid."

"Nothing a person feels is stupid."

Rhi thinks that's exactly what a psychologist is supposed to say, but goes on anyway. "I just . . . I feel like I have more of a *right* to know, if that makes sense?" Her cheeks warm. "I *know* I don't. But I found them, you know? I'm kind of a part of their story now."

Dr. Ibanez nods. "Do you feel like your actions should be rewarded?"

"What? No." Rhi crosses her arms over her stomach. "No, it's not like *that*. It's just . . . when people go through a crazy experience together, sometimes you feel like you have some kind of connection."

"Do you feel like you have a connection to the girls?"

Rhi chews on the inside of her cheek, wondering how much is safe to tell Dr. Ibanez—then thinking: *If I'm hiding something from a psychologist, isn't that kind of a red flag?*

"Sort of," Rhi says. She uncrosses her arms, starts to pick at her cuticles. "Like you said, it was intense out there. And the way they trusted me, in the woods and in the emergency room . . . it felt like I just *knew* how to help them almost every step of the way. And they knew that, too. Somehow. So yeah, that felt like a connection."

Dr. Ibanez makes a thoughtful noise. "Some people are much better than others at picking up on nonverbal cues. And when someone is very good at it, like you are, Rhi, it can almost feel like a superpower at times—like you're reading their mind instead of their body language or facial expressions. It's not uncommon when you've grown up in an unstable environment."

Rhi looks up at her, flushing at the implication. "So you think that's all it was?"

"Oh, no—not *all*. Human connection is very hard to define, and only scientifically understood as chemical processes in the body, which hardly does it justice, I think. If you felt a connection to the girls, I can only take your word for it. And hope they felt it, too, and will be more open with you than they have been with me so we can get them the help they need." Dr. Ibanez smiles sadly, absently twisting the gold watchband on her wrist. "But the truth is, Rhi: regardless of your connection with someone, you are not entitled to their story. And there is no one who has any right to *your* story, either. That's what makes helping these girls so challenging—they have to *want* our help."

"Oh, I didn't mean—I don't think I'm *entitled* . . ." Rhi stammers, cheeks burning.

Dr. Ibanez waves her embarrassment away with a disarming smile. "Of course you didn't. Just some words of wisdom from an *elder*." She rolls her eyes at herself, then settles a warm gaze on Rhi. "I believe you and I have the same goal, Rhi. We want to see these girls happy, healthy, and reunited with their families. And hopefully, able to heal from whatever they've been through. We both want what's best for these girls, right?"

Rhi nods.

Dr. Ibanez hands Rhi the clipboard with its thin stack of papers. "Before you go in, I'll need you to sign this waiver, a HIPAA compliance form, and a general confidentiality statement. I'll fax these over to your uncle to have him cosign, too."

Rhi takes the clipboard and a proffered pen, and eagerly hunts for the blank signature lines at the bottom of each page.

WHILE AN AIDE GOES TO fetch the girls, Rhi waits in the "family room" on a misshapen armchair upholstered in the same dingy blue-and-white microfiber as the adjacent love seat. Dr. Ibanez has not joined Rhi for her visit—they both want the girls to feel free to speak their minds, and Dr. Ibanez's presence has not proven conducive to that. Dr. Ibanez has promised Rhi she will not be observing their visit—both because Rhi feels better not having to conceal that, and because observing patients' private conversations without their consent is a morally gray area, even if the patients are not legally capable of giving consent.

While she sits, she has time to worry, to convince herself the girls never actually trusted her, that she has misread the entire situation. Or even if they did trust her at any point, they won't trust her now, because she left them.

But before Rhi can work herself into a frenzy of disappointment, the door opens and the girls enter, pushing the youngest—Sunder—ahead of them in a wheelchair. When Rhi stands to greet them, they rush over without the slightest hesitation, immediately extinguishing Rhi's anxieties in a puff of wonder. They surround her, murmuring her name, pulling her into a tangled embrace, laying palms against her face, touching her hair, lifting her hand to touch their faces. One of them clutches Rhi's hand and squeezes it tightly.

For a moment, Rhi's entire body feels like a live wire, rigid from too much unexpected contact. But the relief radiating from the girls reaches her like a sunbeam, warming her frozen muscles.

Finished with their greetings, the tall blonde one—Verity—helps Sunder out of her wheelchair, lowering her to the ground by the love seat. Sunder stretches her broken leg out in front of her, clad in a huge black removable cast. The rest of them crowd around on the love seat, still stuck together as if they cannot stay upright without one another.

"Rhi," Sunder whispers from the floor.

"Rhi," the others echo, voices dry and hushed.

"Hello again," Rhi says, suddenly very shy. In their pale-blue hospital-issued pajamas, with the animal ferocity missing from their eyes, the girls don't look half as surreal as they did when she first discovered them, crouched among wolves and howling at the sky. Rhi doesn't know why it bothers her, but she can barely see the resemblance between these girls and the girls she found in the wildlife preserve. They are all freshly washed and scrubbed, hair detangled, combed, in some cases freshly cut: Verity's long and loose, Oblivienne's in a blunt Cleopatra bob, Epiphanie's in tight braids, Sunder's pixie-short. Their faces and forearms are maps of scrapes and scars, some new, some old, visible now that all the mud has been washed away. Their skin looks waxy under the fluorescent lights; their eyes, tired and bird bright, follow Rhi.

For a moment, Rhi pities these poor girls. She doesn't *mean* to pity them. She knows they probably don't want her pity, anyway. But pity is more than just the reaction of someone who cares—it is also the reaction of someone who is powerless.

Rhi knows that, too.

She half smiles at the girls and swallows her pity. "You all look well," she says, even though it's not exactly true. She lowers herself to sit on the stiff mold-green carpet, facing the girls. "How is your leg?" She gestures to the cast on Sunder's leg.

"It will heal," she says, stroking the rough texture of the cast with a calloused finger. "Though I could be healed faster in the forest."

Rhi is surprised. The girl's voice is clear and youthful, but unexpectedly *regal*.

"Why is that, Sunder?" Rhi asks.

Sunder looks startled. She casts her contrasting eyes up to her sister on the couch—to Epiphanie who, along with the wolves, deemed Rhi to be trustworthy before, in the wilderness. Epiphanie is strikingly beautiful, even under the unflattering fluorescent lights. Rhi notices her posture is exceptionally straight, without appearing stiff. She looks at her sisters in turn, first Sunder, then Oblivienne, then Verity, who, only now, cleaned up and hair brushed, looks oddly familiar to Rhi. A conversation is passing between them, she realizes.

"Who gave you our names?" Epiphanie asks, deadly serious.

"Someone released your names . . . to the press." She knows as soon as she says it that this will mean nothing to them. "Someone told me. Is that okay?"

"They are not our original names," Sunder says with a warning look. "But they are the only names we have ever known. They were given to us."

"Oh." Rhi's mind races at this revelation. "They are very beautiful names. Can I ask who gave them to you?"

The girls look at one another, another unspoken conversation passing between them. Rhi decides to back off and take Dr. Ibanez's advice: they don't owe her their story.

"You don't have to tell me if you don't want to," Rhi says, and means it, even if the thought of them not trusting her stings. "So, have they been taking good care of you here?"

Sunder turns back to Rhi, her eyes bright. "There is *so much food*," she says, more in shock than appreciation.

"And it is just . . . *here*," Oblivienne adds. "There is no hunting, no gathering."

"Some of it makes my stomach hurt," Verity says. "But they have medicine for that."

"They have medicine for *everything*," Sunder says, trying to scratch under her cast.

"So . . . this is all new to you?" Rhi asks carefully. "You don't have any memories of a life like this? Before the forest, maybe?"

"No. Nothing like this," Sunder says.

"Here, there is water—clean water, everywhere," Epiphanie says, a brilliant smile spreading on her lips. "Almost every room we walk into has a—what was it? A sink. Or a water fountain."

"And the *showers*," Verity reminds them. "*Hot water.*"

They all nod, expressions reverent.

Rhi smiles, relieved to see the girls loosening up. "Believe it or not, that's what it's like in most places. Running hot and cold water, access to food. You haven't even mentioned electricity."

Oblivienne makes a face at the bright panels overhead. "The light has confused our bodies. We no longer know when the sun is rising or setting. We wake and sleep at an arbitrary hour dependent on the feeding schedule. I do not like this part of your world."

Rhi notes the clarity of their words, the intelligence in their speech. How could these be the same girls she found crouched and snarling in the woods? The wild gleam has not gone entirely from their eyes, but now Rhi sees that they are cunning, too. They are decidedly *not* feral or violent, as the media would have the world believe. These girls are something else entirely.

"Rhi," Epiphanie says, staring boldly at Rhi. "Have you come to help us? Are you bringing us back to the wilderness?"

Verity, honey blonde and green eyed—who looks so familiar to Rhi, and yet not—adds in a low voice: "We miss being free."

Rhi's heart sinks. "I promise you, I *am* here to help. But I don't have the power to decide where you go." She frowns. "I'm . . . I'm sorry. This was the only way to help Sunder. She could have died out there—"

"This is the only world you have known," Oblivienne says. Her voice is soft, forgiving. "You do not have to apologize. This is how you have learned to do things."

Rhi bites her lip. "I want to be honest with you," she says. "The people in charge here, the ones who *do* have the power, they aren't planning on letting you go back."

"They have explained," Epiphanie says.

"We knew the risk of leaving the castle," Verity adds. "Mother warned us."

Sunder looks sharply at Verity.

"So . . . you lived with your mother?" Rhi asks, leaning forward slightly. "In a castle?"

"Not *our* mother," Sunder says, turning back to Rhi. "*Mother*."

The girls all seem to sit a bit taller, a bit straighter.

"And who is . . . Mother?" Rhi asks. She pictures a forest crone, long white hair braided down to her knees, a necklace of small animal skulls thumping against her chest as she walks, leaning against a crooked wooden staff. Had Mother been cruel? Wise? Fearsome? Insane?

"You would not understand," Oblivienne says, crossing her arms over her chest.

"She might," Sunder says, eyeing Rhi with curiosity.

"She is not from Leutheria," Verity says, though she states it as a fact, not a judgment.

Leutheria? Rhi repeats the word in her head. She can't recall having ever heard of a place by that name before.

"But she is the fifth," Epiphanie says. "We must trust her, or else everything Mother taught us was for nothing."

The girls look at Rhi, many shades of wary and hopeful.

"We were *told* to trust her," Epiphanie reminds her sisters. Her voice is clear, melodious, commanding attention. "After all, Mother said this kingdom is vast. They might know something of our world."

Kingdom? Rhi thinks. *I am the fifth? The fifth what? The fifth . . . girl?*

"Mother told you to trust me?" she asks, trying to keep the eagerness from her voice.

The girls scrutinize her, peering at her through eyes that seem to know so much more than Rhi could ever understand. Sunder starts whispering a word over and over until her voice sounds like the wind rushing through the trees. It takes Rhi a moment to realize she's saying her name.

Sunder stops whispering and squints at her. "*Rhi* is not your true name, is it."

"It's short for Rhiannon."

"Rhiannon." She looks up at Epiphanie, who shakes her head. "No, that is not your true name, either."

Rhi's stomach clenches. "What do you mean?"

"It is a false name," Oblivienne says. "It is a name you took to protect yourself."

Rhi leans back, rubs her damp palms on her knees. "How—how do you know that?"

"It feels like something with shallow roots," Sunder says. "Like a sapling you can pluck from the dirt."

Rhi nods slowly, astounded by the impossible accuracy of their words. "*Rhi* is what I go by now," is all she can think to reply.

"If you tell us your true name," Verity says, "we will tell you about Mother."

"Verity!" Sunder hisses, twisting to strike her sister's knee, but she's not quite able to reach because of the cast.

"No," Epiphanie says, her voice a balm to Sunder's agitation. The smaller girl settles back on the ground, rubbing her leg under the cast. "Verity is right. We were told to trust her. We should not ignore that—so long as she remains trustworthy."

Rhi swallows her discomfort. She can't let the past interfere with what she's trying to do here and now, which is *help these girls.*

"My legal name is *Eden*," she says. The syllables feel clumsy in her mouth; immediately, she can hear the memory of it barked from her father's lips, slurred from her stepmother's mouth, whispered from the dark. The only voice she can't remember saying it is the one she wishes she could: her mother's.

Epiphanie lifts her chin and raises her eyebrows, as if understanding something that she could not grasp before.

"Eden," Sunder says, but the way she caresses the name in her mouth is like a prayer—almost an invocation.

Each of the girls tastes the syllables for themselves, repeating the name in overlapping whispers and murmurs. Rhi's heart swells and collapses at the sound of her birth name, frightened by the ghosts that have been given new life. But it's more than that—in the twisting of her stomach, she can feel the name being sanctified, the impurities burned away, carrying the name to the brink of reincarnation. As if they're casting some kind of spell.

When the girls go silent all at once, *Eden* is no longer just a name that Rhi abandoned. She's not sure what *Eden* is now, but her memories have stopped flashing the gut-punching sound of it spoken in other people's voices.

Instead, when the name echoes through her mind once more, she feels a kind of pity for it—the same pity she felt for the girls minutes earlier.

"That is not your true name either," Verity says.

Rhi, startled, is about to protest, but Oblivienne continues her sister's thought.

"But it has power over you," she says. Her dark eyes are soft when she says this, and Rhi has the uncanny feeling that the girls have heard every thought that passed through her mind over the last sixty seconds.

"It is our secret," Epiphanie says, inclining her head toward Rhi. "That name will not leave this room."

Rhi looks at each of the girls before her, astounded. How did they know about *Eden*? What happened when they were chanting that took away the nerve-stomping power of her former name? Do the girls *know* what they did?

What does Rhi think they *did*, anyway?

Something. She's not sure what, but they've done *something* to her, and she's not sure if it started in the woods, or right here in this room.

"Thank you," she says, trying to collect herself. "And thank you for trusting me. Will you . . . will you tell me about Mother and the castle, now? Will you tell me about . . . Leutheria?"

The girls look between one another, from girl to girl, then back to Rhi.

Finally, Epiphanie nods. "We will tell you."

Our Savage Castle

Excerpted from *Savage Castle:*
A Memoir of the Wild Girls of Happy Valley

WE HAD ALWAYS LIVED IN the castle. Mother brought us there when we were young: first Epiphanie, then Verity, then Oblivienne. Sunder was the last to arrive. We remember that day quite clearly, when Mother returned to the castle, a squirming bundle of white gold in his arms, her tiny hands stretched out and up, grasping at the blue, blue sky.

The castle was always a part of our lives. Never in all our years have we seen a tree as mighty as the one we called our home. It had the footprint of a small house, the height of a mountain, and inside where the bugs and rot had hollowed out the trunk, there were shelves and walls and stairs and ladders, climbing high along the walls to each of our individual platforms, where we made ourselves cozy nests to sleep on the nights when we desired to be alone, or when we wanted to rest during the day without being disturbed. There were places for us to store nuts and roots and smoke-dried meats during the winter, and shelves for our amphorae of fermented berries and honey. There was a high, dry spot for storing furs in warm weather, and where we hung herbs to dry, making the furs smell of sweet wood sorrel, vetiver, and wild sage.

And somehow, despite the age of the thing, despite the decades if not centuries of storms and worms and insects and rot, the castle stood tall and broad, impervious to the ravaging of nature and her weapons of decay.

Between two massive roots there was an opening in the smooth outer layer of the trunk, the width of two arm spans and the height of a bear. In the summer we hung a sheet of woven grass over it to keep the heat away. In the winter, we sealed the opening with tanned hides to keep the cold out and the heat from our bodies and our fire in. On temperate evenings we might sleep outside the castle, under the stars, sun-chapped skin bathing in moonlight. We were rarely bothered by mosquitoes or horseflies or other biting things. They moved around us as if we were stones, as if they could not even sense the flesh and blood of us.

When we were ill, we sheltered in the castle, on beds of pine needles and furs, the scent of hot broth and body sweat swirling in the air. Our sisters would bring us water and food, and stories to pass the time. Mother would come too, sometimes, and use his magic to cast off the sickness from our bodies. But Mother was not always there.

One summer, when we were still very young, Sunder was gravely ill. She was vomiting for days on end, soiling herself, unable to eat or keep water down for nearly a week. She was gaunt and gray by the time Mother returned. When he did, he made a poultice from a handful of bear fat and wild herbs, and we smoothed the mixture over Sunder's abdomen. It smelled sour and minty and felt like a fresh owl pellet in our hands, but it soothed her quickly. Within minutes, she was able to lie comfortably for the first time in days. Within the hour, she was able to eat and keep things down for good. It took another two days of resting, eating, and hydrating, but she recovered completely.

"Will you teach me to make that poultice, Mother?" Epiphanie asked on the second day, when she brought a bladder of fresh water back to the castle. "So I can make it in case you are not here?" Epiphanie twisted her braids back with nimble hands and a well-placed stick before pouring some water into a bowl and drinking from it.

"Yes, what plants did you use to cure her?" Oblivienne asked from where she sat beside our sleeping sister, her dark eyes shining. Verity had gone out into the forest in search of more wild strawberries and blackberries, and the sour green apples that grew farther away.

Mother smiled and looked up from where he was seated, cross-legged on the other side of Sunder's sickbed. "Oh, this and that. But it was not so much the specific plants I used as it was the *intention* I put into the poultice, and the life force of the plants themselves. Any good green thing could have done the trick with the right person mixing them and giving them purpose."

"Will you show us how to do that?" Epiphanie asked as she handed a fresh bowl of water to him.

"Of course, my child," Mother said. "But first, we need a desire. A powerful desire—not just any flight of fancy. My love for Sunder made my desire to heal her very, very strong. And when I charge the castle to protect you, my love for all of you girls is what makes that intention so powerful." Mother looked at Oblivienne and Epiphanie in turn. "What powerful desires do you have, my children?"

Both girls looked down at their hands, as if their answers were written there.

"I want to see Leutheria again," Oblivienne said, clenching her hands into fists. "I want to see the place where I was born." She looked up at Mother through a curtain of mud-twisted black hair, her jaw set.

"The time will come, Oblivienne," Mother said softly. "When the heavens meet the Earth and your fifth sister has arrived, the way home will be revealed. You will return to Leutheria and save your kingdoms."

"I want the time to come *now*," Oblivienne said with deep longing. "I am tired of waiting."

Epiphanie put a hand on her sister's shoulder. "We cannot rush the heavens any more than we can rush the seasons. We cannot rush destiny."

"And you, Epiphanie?" Mother asked. "What do you desire?"

Epiphanie looked at Sunder, pale skin glowing in her healing slumber, asleep on her bed of furs, and then at Oblivienne, frowning as she gazed out the castle door and up at the blue, blue sky.

"I desire, with all my heart," Epiphanie said, brushing the hair away from Sunder's face, "for my sisters to be safe . . . and happy."

8

RHI TRIES TO STOP HERSELF from gaping at the girls.

"It sounds like Mother taught you a lot," she says, wild with imagination, with worry, with questions. She asks the one that tugs the hardest on her mind. "Will you tell me . . . what is Leutheria? Or where?"

The girls look at one another, then dive back into their story.

The Five Kingdoms

Excerpted from *Savage Castle:*
A Memoir of the Wild Girls of Happy Valley

WE DON'T REMEMBER THE FIRST time Mother told us our story, but we know it by heart.

"Once upon a time in a world called Leutheria, there were five princesses, in five kingdoms, that together formed a perfect star across the land."

Mother always began the tale this way, in his labored, scratchy voice. He would be sitting by the fire at night, or under the shade of the castle by day, or leading us to the top of the mountain when the moon came full and lit a clear path between the trees.

Our brightest memory of Mother telling our tale is of a sweltering summer night when we had decided to sleep outside, lying between the two broad roots of our castle that framed the gaping entrance. The night air was hot and sticky; Mother wore his pale-blue robes that reflected the moon as he gazed at the sky; we girls were stretched out naked on a bed of cool green fronds gathered from the forest, listless, hoping the icy glare of the stars might cool us. None of us suspected this was the last time we would hear Mother tell our tale. If we had known, we might have asked more questions.

"Once upon a time, in a world called Leutheria, there were five princesses," Mother began that night as he always did. He shrugged his robes a little closer despite the heat, leaning against the castle's root, turning his gaze to the forest. "Five princesses in five kingdoms, that together formed a perfect star across the land. For thousands of years, these kingdoms lived in peace and prosperity. And how could they not? Paradise was their home, and their people were descended from the heavens."

"Were you alive back then?" Verity asked, staring up at the heavens, imagining a parade of celestial beings dancing down to the mountains of the planet below, shimmering with starlight.

"At times, yes," Mother said. "Each one of us has come and gone many times over the centuries. But it is not often we remember from lifetime to lifetime who we have been and what we have done."

"But you do?" Oblivienne asked.

"Of course he does," Sunder said. "He would not be a prophet, otherwise."

"I wish *I* remembered," Verity said. "I would be so smart by now. Think of all the things you would not have to learn over and over again. How many times do you think we have learned how to count, or how to skin a rabbit? We could be figuring out how to open the sky by now, if we did not have to keep repeating our lessons."

"Why would you want to open the sky?" Epiphanie asked.

"To go home," Sunder answered for her sister, reaching an arm toward the sky.

"Homecoming cannot be forced, my girls. You know that." Mother returned his gaze to the sky, at the stars framed by the castle's barren branches. "When the heavens meet the Earth and your fifth sister has arrived, the way home will appear. You will know it when the time comes—and it will come only once in this lifetime."

"But how do you know?" Verity asked.

Mother sighed, but it was not in exasperation. "All that I have foreseen has come to pass. Some things that I delighted in, but much that

I did not." He nodded, more to himself than to the girls who were mostly not watching, who were more enthralled by the stars and the night than by the old man whose voice insisted on filling it. "I foresaw the darkness that consumed Leutheria. I foresaw the savagery and disease that brought her to ruins. The darkness of mankind is a force as destructive as any storm, and it cannot be underestimated. Even in this world, we are not entirely safe from its reach."

"Then how are we ever going to save Leutheria?" Oblivienne asked, scarcely concealing the hopelessness in her voice.

Epiphanie reached across the furs to take her sister's hand, clasping her fingers gently between her own. "We will find a way."

"The way will be shown to you," Mother corrected her, gently. "Just as it was shown to me. I knew Leutheria was falling and I foresaw that the only way to save it was to bring the four of you here, to this world beyond the veil, before you, too, were lost to the decay." His gaze turned down from the sky to the girls, to the wildflowers wilting in their hair, to the crude symbols and decorations they had painted on their skin with water and ash. "You are royal blood, each of you a princess of the remaining kingdoms. It is not only destiny, but birthright, that has chosen you for the task of saving your world."

"But what about the fifth princess?" Sunder asked, turning her mismatched eyes to Mother. "Our fifth sister. When will we finally meet her? You have been speaking about her for as long as I can remember, but when will she arrive?"

Mother smiled, mysterious as ever. "When the time is right, and no sooner. When the time to save Leutheria is nigh, and no later."

"But how will she know this is her path if no one has told her?" Oblivienne asked. "How will she know to find us?"

"My children, this is not a matter of setting out on a journey and reaching a destination," Mother chuckled. "This is *life*. This is *destiny*. You girls are already on a path that will lead you home to Leutheria, and so is she. No force in the universe can alter that path except for your own will. You four are fortunate enough to know where your path leads, but foreknowledge is not a part of her path. *I* am not a part of her path. But *your* paths are entwined." Mother closed his eyes, as if to peer into his own mind to find the words he was looking for.

"How will we recognize her?" Verity asks.

"She is like you—a daughter of wolves. You will know her as your kin from the first time you see her, at the border between the two worlds. And she will recognize herself in you."

The girls fell silent, trying to imagine their fifth sister as they often did: Would she be fierce and brave? Would she be contemplative and wise? Would she be reckless and frightening? How would the world beyond the forest shape her differently? Who was guiding her, if not Mother?

"Mother," Oblivienne whispered. "Even if—when—she finds us, what you have described, the shadow that has fallen over our kingdoms . . . it is too big of a burden for just five girls."

"Not *just* girls," Mother insisted. "There is no such thing as that."

"Then what are we?" Verity asked.

"You are warriors. Healers. Wonderers. You are the wild wolf and the towering black bear, lean of pride and strong of purpose. When I brought you here you were pure—untainted and untamed—and so you have remained. You are unmarred by greed or selfish loathing. Harmony comes naturally to you. Magic flows easily to you. Your wonder has never ceased, your wildness remains intact. That is what keeps you openhearted, and that is what makes you *strong*."

His voice trembled, but it was more than just conviction that caused Mother to shake. He gripped his robes more tightly to hide how he pressed his knuckles into the pain in his lungs, how his chest shook with each labored inhale.

"And what about you, Mother?" Epiphanie's voice carried through the dark.

"I am no hero." Mother chuckled with quiet resignation. He didn't want the girls to know the vision he had seen for himself, but soon there would be no avoiding it. "When the path to Leutheria is revealed, I will remain here."

"No!" Sunder cried, sitting up, shedding a blanket of moonlight in favor of shadows. "Leutheria needs all of us!"

"My girl," Mother soothed. "I have served Leutheria for many years, and I will serve her for many more. But never again in this life. Surely you all must have noticed, I am an old man."

"So?" Sunder begged. "You can use magic. You can heal yourself. You have healed us a hundred times before!"

"Healing cuts and bruises is very different from healing the thousands of lacerations left by the passage of time." Mother reached out to Sunder, who took his bony, papery hand—swiftly, firmly. "You will be okay, my girl. You will survive, and you will fulfill your destiny."

"All of us?" Oblivienne asked softly from the pile of furs on the ground, still lying on her back. Her damp dark eyes were full of shadows and starlight, shedding glistening streamers that trickled down over her temples, into the black mess of her hair.

"Yes," Mother lied.

9

WHEN THEY FINISH SPEAKING, RHI feels as disoriented as a child waking from a nap. She blinks, her mind grasping at the vivid images, like trying to capture the vestiges of a dream. Only it is no dream—it is the real lives of these four young women. Four young girls.

But the story they've been living is too full of fantasy to hold up under scrutiny. They may believe these things, may have been told these things, but what they spoke of—alternate worlds and magic and knowing the future—these things are impossible. Unbelievable.

And yet . . .

And yet.

Who is the fifth princess they've so long awaited? Was that what they meant when they said "she is the fifth" earlier today? Is that why the wolves gave her their approval? Why Mother told them to trust her without ever having met her?

Is *Rhi* the fifth princess?

Rhi cannot even begin to imagine how she could possibly share any of this with Dr. Ibanez, but she finds herself daring to dip her mind into impossible waters more often than usual when it comes to these girls—these wild but regal girls who chant and howl and invoke a power Rhi does not understand, but cannot deny. What if there really is some kind of natural magic at their fingertips—or perhaps their lips, called by the sound of their voices raised as one?

Hadn't she felt it, that day in the forest, when Epiphanie looked her in the eyes and the world fell away?

Hadn't she nearly thought, when the rain and thunder came so suddenly, just as grief overtook Sunder and the girls howled at the sky?

Hadn't she almost believed, mere minutes ago, when the girls knew unaccountably that she had a secret name?

The ticking of the clock high on the wall pulls Rhi's attention back to the present. She swallows, looks at each girl in their hospital-issued baby-blue pajamas, on the worn blue love seat, on the stiff green carpet.

She knows that, in all likelihood, if the media and the police are to be believed, these girls are merely the brainwashed victims of a mentally ill old man who stole them away from their families.

And yet . . . if Rhi had to choose which version of their story she wishes were true, it would certainly be the girls'.

"So," Rhi says after several beats, pausing to clear her throat. "You've lived in the forest for as long as you can remember? With Mother. Inside a tree."

"A *castle*," Sunder corrects her.

"Castle." Rhi nods, fighting to keep the concern off her face. An old man and four young girls living alone in the wilderness . . .

"He *protected* us," Oblivienne says, catching Rhi's eye.

Rhi leans back, stunned. Did Oblivienne read her mind, or was her horrible notion that obvious?

"They *both* protected us," Oblivienne continues with a frown. "We never should have left."

"We did not have a choice," Verity counters.

"We agreed the signs said it was time to go," Epiphanie reminds them, touching Oblivienne's shoulder. "This is just another part of the path we are meant to travel."

"To get home," Rhi confirms. "To Leutheria. To *save* Leutheria."

The girls nod.

"That's quite a weight to carry."

"It is our destiny," Sunder says, fixing her eyes on Rhi.

Rhi isn't sure if Sunder is trying to communicate something to her or intimidate her, but there is a message in the girl's two-toned eyes that she is not quite grasping—or perhaps she does not want to grasp.

"Do any of you remember anything from your life *before* the forest? Anything about your families before Mother?"

They shake their heads, not quite in unison, like stalks of wildflowers waving in a breeze.

"We know our families did not survive the darkness that came for Leutheria," Oblivienne says. "We would not have survived either, if it were not for Mother. He rescued us."

"So then . . . Mother," Rhi says. "Where is he right now?"

Epiphanie puts a hand on Sunder's shoulder, takes Verity's hand as Verity takes Oblivienne's hand in hers. They breathe as one for a moment, heads bowed, eyes cast off to a place where Rhi cannot follow.

Finally, Sunder looks up at Rhi and says, "Mother is with us. Always."

"WE MADE *INCREDIBLE* PROGRESS TODAY, and that's entirely thanks to you," Dr. Ibanez says as she walks Rhi back through the byzantine halls of the hospital. "I can't thank you enough."

"I'm just glad I can help," Rhi says, fighting the blush burning her cheeks.

At the end of their visit, when the girls did not seem inclined to elaborate on their answer to Rhi's question about Mother's whereabouts, Rhi asked the girls if she could share what they'd told her with Dr. Ibanez. It didn't feel right to report back to the doctor without their permission. Fortunately, they agreed that if Rhi trusted the doctor, they would trust her, too. Dr. Ibanez recorded Rhi's recounting of the conversation on her phone, keeping her face neutral to mildly interested even when Rhi told her about Mother and the magic—even when she told her about Leutheria.

"Ah, that makes sense," Dr. Ibanez had said at one point—her only interjection. "They've been making drawings of five people around a circle—the moon, I think. I thought the fifth figure might be someone who lived with them out there, but maybe it's this supposed fifth princess?" Despite her carefully neutral face, her eyes had shone with curiosity—maybe even excitement.

"Would you be willing to visit with them again soon?" Dr. Ibanez asks now as they approach the main exit. "Maybe another time this week?" She clears her throat and sticks her hands in the little pockets of her blazer.

Is she . . . nervous? Rhi wonders.

"They really do seem to have a connection with you," Dr. Ibanez explains. "And I want them to feel safe while they're here."

"Yeah." Rhi nods. "Of course, whatever I can do to help." Rhi understands Dr. Ibanez's nervousness now: she is asking for Rhi's help, which probably isn't exactly standard protocol for a state-run mental health facility.

Before they reach the automatic sliding doors, Dr. Ibanez turns and holds her manicured hand out to Rhi. "Thank you again, Rhi. And, you know, if you need anyone to talk to about all of this, how it's affecting *you* . . . my door is open."

Rhi shakes her hand firmly. "Yeah. No problem. Thank you."

"Oh, and tell Jimmy I said hi."

She smiles a little. "I will."

Outside the hospital, the parking lot seems unnaturally dark beyond the immediate glow of the floodlights by the entrance, distant pools of lamplight illuminating cars and empty parking spaces. As Rhi scans the lot for her uncle's truck, her phone buzzes in her pocket. Thinking it might be him, she pulls it out to check the screen.

> **Message from: NO**
> Edie, please talk to me.

Rhi swipes the screen to delete the message, but not before her heart reaches into her throat to choke her. Her hand is on her neck before she realizes it, pressing against the delicate skin over her tendons, pushing away the memory of another hand, another night, another life entirely.

Almost as quickly as the memories rear up inside Rhi, the double honk of a car horn pulls her back to the sidewalk, to the hospital, to Happy Valley and the life she's living now. She looks to the source of the sound and sees Uncle Jimmy's forest-green pickup parked on the other side of a median, amber parking lights flicking on in the murky dark.

Rhi hurries over and opens the passenger-side door, slips inside, and heaves the door shut. She forces a smile, partly for her uncle, partly to convince herself.

"Hiya, stranger," Uncle Jimmy says, handing her a paper coffee cup Rhi recognizes from the ranger station. "How'd it go in there?"

Rhi takes the warm cup between her hands and instantly she smells the salty-sweet flavor of instant hot chocolate, mixed with a spoonful of instant coffee, just how she likes it—and how Vera would *never* have allowed her to have it.

"Thanks," she says. Rhi sips the "general store mocha," as she has dubbed it—named after the odd assortment of inexpensive-but-overpriced, often-expired but technically nonperishable goods found on the shelves of the general store near the campgrounds by the wildlife preserve. The beverage has had time to cool on its trip from the ranger station, and its syrupy sweetness is just the thing to jolt her awake for the ride home. "It went really well, actually."

"I can't imagine what those poor girls have been through. You're doing a good thing, Rhi, letting those girls know they're not alone. Getting them to talk. It could be the key to figuring out who they are. When I think about the families that are missing them, *grieving* them . . ." Uncle Jimmy shakes his head.

"I know." Rhi hesitates. "But I also think they miss being out there, you know? All that freedom is just . . . gone now."

Uncle Jimmy eyes her as he pulls out of the parking spot. "You're not feeling guilty, are you? For calling me up there and getting those girls to safety?"

"No. Maybe. I don't know."

"You saved that kid's life, Rhi-Rhi. Maybe all of their lives."

"Yeah." Rhi can't explain it to her uncle, not without seeming borderline delusional. But she can't help it. The more she thinks about their story and the strange things she's seen—the things she's *felt*—the more she's inclined to believe *all* of it.

Still. Whether or not any of it is true, what else could she have done?

"Speaking of *life*," Uncle Jimmy says, pulling onto the main road, "guess who just had a baby? Sheriff Elroy's daughter, Samantha. I dated her for a month in middle school—can you believe that?" He chuckles. "I guess I'm getting old. Suddenly I've got a kid in high school and all my friends are having babies."

Rhi makes a sound halfway between a laugh and a scoff. "I don't think I count as you having a *kid*."

"Sure you do, kiddo."

"You're only twelve years older than me!"

"As long as you drink those nasty general store mochas, I get to call you *my kid*. Got it?"

Rhi's lips pull back into the still-unfamiliar shape of a grin. "Got it."

10

OVER THE NEXT WEEK, RHI returns to the hospital after school to visit with the girls as much as she can. For every question she asks about their life in the wilderness, they ask a million more about her: about her life, and her family, and the world outside the hospital walls.

This time, when Rhi shows up, the girls are waiting to ask Rhi for a favor.

"We need your help healing Sunder's leg," Epiphanie explains. She is seated on the floor beside Sunder, whose leg is stretched out in front of her in the black cast. Oblivienne is sitting behind Sunder, and Verity is kneeling at her foot.

Epiphanie gestures for Rhi to sit across from her and complete the circle.

"I . . . don't think I can help with that," Rhi says, taking her assigned seat.

"You can," Sunder says, waving her foot a little impatiently.

"The magic will be more powerful now that we are five," Oblivienne says, placing a hand on Sunder's head. Sunder leans into it, closing her eyes. A contended expression settles on her face.

"Magic," Rhi repeats, a little breathless.

"For healing," Verity explains, putting both hands on the foot of Sunder's boot.

"It is not difficult," Epiphanie assures her, taking Sunder's hand. "The most important thing is our desire for Sunder's leg to be healed. Focus on that, and the rest will follow."

"Oh," Rhi says as Sunder slips her other hand into Rhi's. Her hand is warm and dry, and her grip is surprisingly firm for its size, grounding Rhi even as her excitement sends her mind racing. She is riveted to the girls as they close their eyes and take long, slow breaths.

Rhi thinks about what happened in the woods, when they seemed to summon a storm cloud with their keening; or what happened in this very room, when their incantation cleansed her discarded birth name. Would there be singing now? Would there be an incantation?

Rhi waits with bated breath for instructions, directions, a guided visualization, maybe, like she has seen modern witches and astrologers do on their Instagram Lives around the new and full moons—until it dawns on her that Epiphanie's words *were* the instructions.

She quickly closes her eyes and focuses her intention on Sunder as embarrassment momentarily heats her face, but then something else, something much more important washes over Rhi. She feels the warmth in Sunder's palm rush into her, turning cool as it hits her core, vaguely shimmering as it wraps around her from the inside out.

This must be what magic feels like, Rhi understands, aware of the flow of it now, passing between them all like a static charge, or a mist, or the illusory touch of moonlight. She revels in it for a wild moment before remembering the purpose of the magic, then turns her mind toward her desire to see Sunder whole and healed. Rhi has not attempted much visualization in her life (she has tried some of those guided meditations with disastrous results; her psyche does not lend itself to exploration), so despite her best efforts to focus, her mind wanders to adjacent desires: to see all of these girls happy and healthy; to see them free and wild; to see their destinies fulfilled, whatever that might look like. Every time she realizes her mind has wandered, she pulls it back, a tiny little tail of self-flagellation trailing behind. But the magic, or perhaps the feeling of the other girls' energies winding around her, dissolves any negative feelings before they can take root.

Rhi senses that the ritual is finished from the slowing of the momentum in her own mind. She feels the withdrawal of the magic, feels her hands wrapped around Sunder's, feels her butt half-numb on the hard carpeted floor. She opens her eyes, blinking to clear away glimmers in the corners of her eyes, and sees the other girls opening their eyes, too. Sunder is half-asleep, her head in Oblivienne's lap just like the day Rhi found them, only at peace instead of in pain.

Rhi glances at the clock on the wall and is shocked to see how much time has passed. It felt like only a few minutes, but the clock indicates they've been working this magic for nearly an hour. (*Magic. Was that really magic? What else could it have possibly been?*)

"Were we successful?" she asks, her voice soft so as not to shatter the quiet.

"It is a serious wound—healing will take some time," Epiphanie says with a tired smile, smoothing a few strands of hair from Sunder's face as she blinks her way back to wakefulness. "But magic will mend the wound faster."

That makes sense to Rhi, even if she is a little disappointed there would be no instant miracle, no black-and-white evidence to declare, "Magic is real!" But even her disappointment disappears in the afterglow of their ritual, or spell, or whatever it might be called. The powerful flow of energy is gone, but is fresh and real in her memory, and has left shimmering fingerprints on her heart.

After, in Dr. Ibanez's office for her "debriefing" as the doctor calls it (with a somewhat nervous laugh), Rhi finds herself obscuring the details of the ritual. She gives only the facts and none of the feelings, none of the sensations that still electrify Rhi's mind when she recalls the magic.

"It was basically a meditation," Rhi says. "But they seem very confident in its power. Which . . . you know . . . some people feel that way about prayer, too." She shrugs, feigning a nonchalance that she desperately wants to laugh at.

Dr. Ibanez taps a purple Bic pen against her bottom lip as she looks past Rhi, mind clearly churning away as she takes in what Rhi tells her. "You know, cult leaders often utilize breath work and a bastardized kind of meditation to put victims into an altered state of consciousness. The first few breaths feel good, but after a while it messes with the brain—too much oxygen, or not enough. People report feelings of euphoria, out-of-body experiences, intense connection to the divine, which of course they think is because of their divinely chosen leader or whatever." She stops tapping the pen and holds Rhi's gaze. "Did they do any weird breathing?"

Rhi shakes her head, her mood dimming slightly. "Not that I noticed."

Dr. Ibanez makes a thoughtful noise.

Later, before she releases Rhi back out into the world, Dr. Ibanez pauses. "Rhi, I hope I'm not asking too much of you, having you spending all this time with the girls."

"No," Rhi assures her. "I want to help them."

"Yes," Dr. Ibanez says. "But you do have quite a bit going on already. And sometimes when things feel overwhelming, it can be easier to focus on someone else's life."

Rhi's face burns. "Is that what you think I'm doing?" she asks quietly. "That I'm using these girls as some sort of escape?"

"No, I don't think so. But I can see how it could be tempting. Frankly, Rhi, you've handled everything with a level of calm that even trained therapists would have a hard time maintaining. Quite similar to the girls, in fact."

"I don't understand. Is that a bad thing?"

Dr. Ibanez glances at the pockmarked ceiling tiles while she gathers her thoughts. "When a person has lived in a perilous situation for a long time—such as the girls, surrounded by wild animals and unpredictable weather, and who knows what other dangerous things—the body and mind adapt to maximize potential for survival in part by de-emphasizing the importance of emotional well-being. In action, this can look like staying quite calm and clearheaded in the face of danger—like, say, a wolf encounter. In regular life, well. We see this kind of *calm under pressure* frequently in the children of alcoholics, or—"

"I'm not—" Rhi blurts. She flushes. "My parents aren't alcoholics."

"Okay." Dr. Ibanez nods. "I will take your word for it."

On Saturday, after her morning shift on the trails is interrupted by a handful of intrepid local journalists who had hiked out early to intercept her, Rhi showers and changes at the ranger station, then has Uncle Jimmy drop her off at the hospital. The girls have finally been cleared to join the other residents, so today, Dr. Ibanez meets Rhi at the front desk and walks her back to the common area.

While waiting to be checked in, Rhi peeks through the window of the nurses' station into the room. She sees several patients she does not recognize before Sunder swings into view on her crutches, hobbling across the room. Her leg is free of the boot now but clad in a heavy plaster cast, already covered in furious scribbles and angular symbols, scrawled on the plaster as well as her skin. Rhi is a little disappointed to see the cast—it means the healing spell didn't work. At least, not yet.

"I'd like to join you for your visit today," Dr. Ibanez says, signing something on a clipboard. "The girls won't elaborate more about their time in the wilderness beyond what they've already told you, and I'm getting pressure from the police department." She sighs, dotting the paper and handing it back to the nurse.

"So no one has found *anything* more about who they are?" Rhi asks, watching through the window as Sunder maneuvers up to an arts and crafts table. She sticks her hand deep into a bin and pulls out a fistful of markers before dropping to the floor between two aluminum-frame chairs, letting her crutches clatter down beside her. Nearby, another patient angrily covers his ears before walking away. Sunder wrenches the cap off a marker and starts to draw on her cast.

"Not . . . exactly," Dr. Ibanez says. "That's part of why I need to dig a little harder for information from the girls. I've been told the FBI is sending an agent out here today, but we'll see. They're notoriously slow with cases where there's no clear evidence of a federal crime being committed. But the police would like to try to find the place where the girls were living, see if there are any clues there about this Mother character. The agent will want to ask the girls questions, too. I was thinking they might be more inclined to talk if you're there."

"Whatever I can do to help," Rhi says.

Dr. Ibanez touches her arm, drawing Rhi's attention back to her. "I just want to warn you, Rhi, this place is a lot to handle. Some of the folks behind that door are very unwell. Not dangerous, but . . . it can be distressing. Even the family members of patients can have a hard time visiting." She looks Rhi in the eyes, her own deep brown eyes clear and kind. "If it gets to be too much for you at any point and you need to walk away, let me know. No one would fault you."

Rhi raises her eyebrows and says, "But *I* would." To leave now would not only be a betrayal of the girls, but a betrayal of herself—especially her younger self, hiding in her bedroom from her stepmother's critical eyes, her father's cold indifference, wishing that she had even one ally in this world besides her stepbrother off at boarding school nine months of the year.

"Well, you hold yourself to a very high standard," Dr. Ibanez says warmly. "But remember, if you need someone to talk to—about this, or anything else . . ."

Rhi nods. "I'll remember. Thank you."

"The other patients should be heading to group therapy shortly. Let's go say hello, hmm?"

The nurse buzzes them in through the main door. When the lock clicks undone, the door pops open an inch, as if startled by its own sound.

Inside the common room, Rhi searches for the other girls and immediately spots Verity on the floor studying a magazine, looking in awe and confusion at the glossy men and women, the inscrutable advertisements, the curious text. Nearby, Epiphanie is sitting on a couch with a bespectacled older woman, holding a ball of yarn as the older woman knits with blunt plastic knitting needles. The woman is telling Epiphanie about her late husband; Epiphanie listens intently.

"Oh, Sunder," Dr. Ibanez says with a grimace, drawing Rhi's attention to the girl.

Sunder is still sitting on the ground with a fistful of uncapped markers. She's managed to break several open and rip out the squishy, pigment-soaked tubes inside, turning them into the most uncooperative finger paints Rhi has ever seen. Her cast is now smeared in color so dark it is nearly black, but more than that, Sunder has painted her arms, her neck, the sharp cut of her cheekbones and nose, with streaks of red and orange, like the pattern on the fur of a wild cat. She's still looking at Rhi and Dr. Ibanez when she squeezes a dark tube between her fingers and smears the black ink over both eyes, painting herself like a raccoon.

Rhi bursts out laughing at the sight of Sunder, so serious and ridiculous, all at once.

"She does like to innovate." Dr. Ibanez sighs. "I'll alert the aide."

Alone now, Rhi heads over to Sunder, still holding back laughter. "I like it," she says secretively to Sunder, bending down to help pick up the discarded marker shells.

"Nothing is good here," Sunder says suddenly and sharply. "Nothing is sacred. Nothing has purpose."

Rhi's smile fades. "What do you mean by 'purpose'?" She offers the girl a hand to help her up.

Sunder looks up at Rhi but remains seated on the floor, ignoring the offered hand. "We have been trapped here for days. Why does Dr. Ibanez keep trying to separate us?"

"Dr. Ibanez is a good person," Rhi says, cocking her head. "She's trying to help you."

"Then why does she keep us here when we want to go home?" Sunder demands.

"Because we cannot go home," Oblivienne says from across the room.

Rhi looks up. Oblivienne is standing in the corner, pressed against the window: clear plexiglass fastened over metal mesh, dulled by years of other hands and faces pressing against it. "That home is *gone*."

"But our wolf-kin are still out there," Sunder insists. "We can make a new home—"

"We just have to wait, Sunder." Oblivienne looks over her shoulder at her sister. "Until we can return to . . . our *true* home." She gives the nurses' station a wary glance before turning back to the window.

"Come on." Rhi offers her hand again. Sunder takes it, sighing deeply as she lets Rhi pull her to her feet.

Rhi picks up Sunder's crutches and hands them to her. "Is that why you were out in the woods when I found you?" she asks delicately. "Did something happen to your castle?"

Sunder's face tightens. She lifts her chin and swings away on her crutches, toward the window at the nurses' station. She plants herself there, staring intently through the glass. One of the nurses looks up from her computer monitor and jumps in surprise. Sunder hardly seems to notice.

"She likes to watch the halls for new faces," Dr. Ibanez says quietly, returning to Rhi's side. "But I also think she likes to make the nurses uncomfortable."

Rhi looks between Sunder and Oblivienne, both pressed against windows, yearning for the freedom of what lies beyond the common room walls.

"What's going to happen to them if we can't figure out who they are?" Rhi asks.

"The same thing that will happen if we *can* figure out who they are," Dr. Ibanez whispers back. "Rehabilitation. Reintegration, hopefully. School. Friends. Jobs. Eventually—ideally—they will live normal lives."

Rhi nods. She needs to believe what the doctor tells her, even if the idea of "normal lives" still, unaccountably, breaks her heart. If Rhi has ever been sure of anything, it's that these girls are not meant for normal lives. But then, what kind of lives *are* they meant for?

Epiphanie places the yarn on the couch beside the old woman and walks over to Rhi. Her braids have been tied into low pigtails. Under the fluorescent lights, her ghost-gray eyes are paler than ever.

"Do you know how to knit?" she asks.

"I do, actually," Rhi says, as if that surprises her, too.

Epiphanie's eyes light up. "Can you teach me?"

"Yeah, of course. Next time I come in, I'll bring some yarn."

Epiphanie grins—actually grins, full-on, her face and eyes brightening with excitement.

"Dr. Ibanez?" a nurse says, sliding the window open between her station and the common room. Sunder is right there, staring intensely at her. The nurse pretends she doesn't notice, but her gaze keeps sliding back to Sunder's mismatched eyes, to her war paint, to her white-blonde hair now streaked with red and black from her ink-stained fingers.

"Yes?" Dr. Ibanez looks up.

"There's an Agent Tyler asking for you at the front desk." The nurse side-eyes Sunder.

Dr. Ibanez looks surprised. "Oh, that was fast. Thank you, I'll be right there. Rhi?" She turns back to her.

"I'll be fine," Rhi insists. And she will be. She can sense it, like she can sense when a neighborhood cat can be approached or when it should be left alone. Sometimes these girls might give her the cold shoulder, might twitch their tails or narrow their eyes at her, but none of them want her to leave them alone.

When Dr. Ibanez has left and the nurse's window is closed, Epiphanie throws her arms around Rhi and pulls her against her chest, like a mother holding a child, almost stoic, almost soothing. Verity comes next, touching Rhi's head, stroking her long wavy hair, pressing her forehead against hers, as if they've always belonged to each other. As if it's always been like this.

Rhi's surprise is quickly overcome by the intimacy of their touch, the vulnerability, the inclusion. Her barriers are stripped away by the comforting press of their bodies. She feels like parched soil soaking up a flood. Rhi embraces the girls back. Melds into them. Tries to become one of them.

But she's not like them. She's not wild or fierce. She doesn't know what it is to have a pack. Rhi is not a princess. Rhi does not have a destiny. She's just a girl trying to do the right thing, a background player to the real heroes, the real story.

But maybe Mother was right. Maybe there is no such thing as *just a girl*. Not if the girl doesn't want to be.

And maybe Rhi feels such affinity for these girls because they speak to that secret part of herself, begging to be wild—to be fierce—to be free.

Or maybe—just maybe—she really is the fifth princess, after all.

The daughter of wolves, Mother had told the girls. Rhi could certainly call her father and stepmother *dangerous animals*, but *wolfish* wasn't quite right . . .

A loud bang jolts Rhi out of her thoughts.

Sunder smacks the nurse's window with both palms, rattling the glass in its metal tracks, causing several of the patients in the room to shout expletives at her.

The other girls pull back—they are still huddled close to Rhi but are watching Sunder with keen interest. Their sister is scowling so hard that her lips pull back from her teeth. Her eyes are wild and extra bright against the painted black mask from the markers.

"Sunder?" Rhi asks in alarm, stepping toward her.

Epiphanie tugs Rhi back, shakes her head.

Sunder growls. She slams her palms against the window again, and this time Rhi can see the nurse move on the other side, standing up, shouting at Sunder to *get away from that window, young lady*, but Sunder doesn't hear her, doesn't care that the poor woman is furious and frightened, just bangs on the window again and again, her growl transforming into a snarl, then a furious wordless roar.

"Sunder!" Rhi gasps, but the girls hold still, clinging to Rhi, faces tight with alarm. She realizes they understand something about this moment that she cannot—not until later, when all the facts are laid out before her. They know there is no way to stop Sunder's rampage now.

Sunder stumbles backward on her crutches, throws one to the floor and takes up the other like a club. Limping, barely balancing on her good leg, she swings the crutch with the strength of a creature much larger than she is, slamming it into the window with a *whoosh* and a splintering crunch.

The sound hits Rhi like a thunderbolt, making her jump, and then jump again when the secure door buzzes loudly and pops open.

Dr. Ibanez slips in, hands up, palms forward, two orderlies dressed in white behind her.

"Sunder, put it down. Put the crutch down. Listen to me. Sunder, don't!"

Sunder thwacks the crutch against the glass again, her shout as huge as a lion's roar, her face contorted with ink and creases of fury. Jagged lightning bolts appear in the safety glass as the window fractures. The nurse on the other side has fled.

"What's wrong?" Rhi cries out, to Sunder, to Dr. Ibanez—to anyone who might have an answer.

"She saw something she shouldn't have seen just yet," the doctor answers in a low, calm voice, much calmer than her body language suggests.

Sunder, panting, red-faced and growling, hobbles backward, into one of the chairs around the table where her broken markers are still lying in a heap. The other patients have taken up defensive positions, covering their heads where they sit or pushing into the corner farthest from the raging girl, watching with burning curiosity even as some of them groan and shield their ears.

Ignoring the distress she is causing, Sunder pitches her last crutch at the orderlies advancing on her and grabs hold of a chair. The cheap chrome finish on the metal frame glints as she drags it over to the window.

"Sunder," Dr. Ibanez tries, one last time. "Put. The chair. Down."

Sunder limps faster, crying out from the pain when her weight falls on her injured leg, crying out from the agony of whatever it is she has seen. Her whimpers become a battle cry as she lifts the chair over her head and hurls it at the nurses' station window.

The chair embeds itself in the window and the surrounding plaster. Safety glass crumbles into a million little blue-green cubes, spilling from the window tracks, scattering across the floor. A patient at the back of the room screams.

The orderlies grab Sunder by her arms and legs, bringing her to the floor in a swift, practiced takedown. They pin her arms to her sides and press her face into the carpet as her battle cry becomes a wail.

Even with her leg in a bear trap, Sunder did not cry. But this—whatever she has seen—has her keening on the floor as if her soul has been wrenched from her body.

Rhi finally notices the other girls have tightened their grip on her, on each other. Oblivienne, even, has come to stand with them, hooking her arm through Epiphanie's, clinging to Rhi's elbow. When a nurse rushes through the door brandishing a syringe, the door gets jammed open on the chunks of glass, giving them a wide view of the corridor beyond.

Through the doorway, Rhi and the girls see a tall middle-aged woman and an equally tall teenage girl, both with honey-blonde hair and piercing green eyes that cut across the distance like traffic lights. Rhi wouldn't have noticed the color if not for the fact that their eyes are so wide with shock, and the fact that their eyes, and their faces, and everything about them, is terribly familiar.

The same way Verity's face has always been terribly familiar.

The woman—the mother—rushes forward, dragging her daughter up to the door, but not through it. She can't bring herself to cross the threshold into this world, as if they might catch whatever the patients have. But she stares hard at the girls and her face turns white as a sheet when she finds the face she's looking for.

"Mathilda?" the mother calls through the door.

Every last one of them—including Rhi—stares back.

"Mrs. Erikson, please, this is not the right time," Dr. Ibanez says, hurrying over to the door.

But it's already too late.

Verity breaks free from the cluster of girls and locks eyes with the teenage girl just beyond the door.

Rhi recognizes her. She goes to Rhi's high school. She has passed her in the halls a hundred times or more.

"Mathilda!" the mother shouts. "Oh, please, Dr. Ibanez, please, just let me see my baby—"

"It's not a good idea—"

"Who *are* you?" Verity demands, coming up behind the doctor as she tries to bar their way.

"Verity, please, go back to the others." Dr. Ibanez is barely restraining the frantic plea in her voice, turning now to place a hand on Verity's shoulder, to gently urge her away.

Verity presses into the doctor's hand combatively, but her eyes don't leave the girl on the other side of the door, who is nearly the same height as her mother, who is easily the same unusual height as Verity. In another life—where Verity lived in comfort, with secure access to food, without constant exposure to the elements—looking at this girl might have been like looking in a mirror.

"*Who are you?*" Verity asks again in a low, steady voice.

The girl in the hallway swallows, glances up at her mother, then back at Verity. She sticks her hand over the threshold, offering it to the tallest of the Wild Girls of Happy Valley.

"Hi, Mat—V—Verity," she stammers. "My name is Grace. I'm . . . I'm your twin sister."

CLICKMONSTER NEWS

Trending Articles

The First Legit Family Has Come Forward to Claim a Wild Girl

Meet the Wild Girl's Long-Lost Twin Sister, Grace:
An Instagram Deep Dive

Whatever Happened to Baby Mathilda? What We Know About
the Original Case of the Missing Infant, Mathilda Godefroy

Where Are the Other Families of the Wild Girls?
Our Experts Guess Why They Have Yet to Come Forward
(And Discuss the Frauds Who Have)

This Survivalist Doesn't Believe the Wild Girls Were Living in
the Wilderness Preserve Without Help, and Here's Why

This Girl Gang Calling Themselves "The Wilder Girls"
is Being Threatened with Expulsion for Refusing
to Wear Bras to School

Rhiannon Chase Does Not Exist: One Social Media Sleuth's
Quest to Find Out ANYTHING About the Girl Who Rescued the
Wild Girls

DRAFTS

FROM: "Eden Chase" <e.r.c.2007@springmail.com>
TO: "Kevin Hartwell" <hartwell.kevin@irving.edu>
DATE: April 3
SUBJECT: Reunions

Verity has a family. Here. In Happy Valley.

I can't imagine what it must have been like for her mother to see her again. Or for her twin sister. After so long apart . . .

Do you remember that first Christmas, after our parents got married? I was so happy you were finally home from boarding school, that it wouldn't just be me and them, at least for a little while. But then we had that snowball fight, and you tackled me and shoved ice down my shirt, and I accidentally kicked you in the nuts . . . you were *so mad*. Even after I begged forgiveness, you refused to acknowledge my existence for DAYS.

You have no idea how painful that was for me. How much I depended on you. How much I needed even the *idea* of your kindness, just to survive.

Or maybe you did understand. Maybe you did it on purpose. To make me need you a thousand times more than you could ever need me.

I don't remember how we reconciled, but I remember the night before you went back to boarding school we were cuddling on the couch watching scary movies after our parents went to bed.

You always wanted to watch horror movies. I never argued.

I hate horror movies now.

I don't know if I ever liked them.

What do you think of that?

11

Sunder tries to curl into a ball on her bed in the corner, but the clunky cast on her leg prevents her from doing so. She presses her forehead against the cool white wall, squeezing her eyes shut. She slept for hours after the men in white tackled her and put the needle in her arm; then she could not sleep for two days. She could not *speak* for two days, either.

How can she speak about anything when her world has been torn apart?

"Sunder," Epiphanie says, sitting on the foot of her bed. "Please talk to us."

They are all there. Even with her eyes closed, Sunder knows the feeling of a small space full of her sisters. She can feel Verity sitting on the floor beside the bed, Oblivienne next to her, perched on the chair by the tiny desk. She can even sense Rhi's energy now, hovering by the closed door.

"We need to discuss this," Epiphanie says. "As sisters. Before that man comes back to ask us questions again."

She means Agent Tyler, the one who brought Soft-Verity to the hospital and blew up their lives. He has been taking each of them into a small room, one by one, questioning them about their time with

Mother, trying to get them to reveal a place, a timeline, an identity. He tried to get Sunder to say awful things about Mother—that he touched them in wrong ways, that he stole them away from loving families. But none of that is true. Mother was good. Mother was kind. Mother *saved* them.

"I have a twin sister," Verity says. "In *this world*. That means . . . that means I cannot really be from Leutheria."

Sunder presses her forehead harder against the wall, her head humming with *no no no no no*.

"They told me . . ." Verity continues, unhappy. "They told me that I was taken from my mother when I was barely two years old. That someone stole me in the middle of the night. What if . . . what if that was Mother?"

"But Mother said he *saved* us," Epiphanie insists. "From a great darkness consuming our kingdoms. He would not lie about that."

"The man," Oblivienne says, too quietly, "Agent Tyler. He wants us to take him to the castle so they can collect information. They want to try to figure out who Mother is—who *we* were . . . before he brought us there."

The unspoken thought between them is: *Should we help them?*

No no no no no, Sunder thinks.

How can this be happening? Because, no matter what else is true or untrue, Sunder knows the magic Mother taught them to use is real. Even though magic is scarce in this new place, she remembers the feel of it in her fingertips and her bones, the way it flowed through them in the wilderness. She remembers how she flew from treetop to treetop; how they sailed through the flames of their bonfire without being burned; how they summoned prey for hunting when they were hungry; how they could call forth a storm with their hearts. That was all *real*.

And if the magic is real, then Leutheria must be, too.

"It couldn't hurt," Rhi says. "To return to the castle. Right?"

"Mother never wanted anything to do with this world," Epiphanie says. "Why should we help these people?"

"Because Mother may have been lying to us," Oblivienne whispers.

Understanding squeezes Sunder's heart. A hot rage ignites in her belly and rises into her mouth. "You betrayed us," she says, rolling over to scowl at her sister. "You have already agreed to help Agent Tyler."

Oblivienne looks devastated for a split second before she lifts her chin. "I want to know who Mother really was. If he was not the seer and prophet he claimed to be, why did he take us? Why did we spend our childhoods in the wilderness struggling to survive?"

"It was not a struggle," Sunder argues. "We were happy out there."

"We were *children*," Oblivienne snaps.

"And Mother *loved us*," Epiphanie says.

They are all silent at that. Of one thing they can all be absolutely certain: Mother *did* love them. He showed them a million times in a million different ways, by how he spoke to them, how he cared for them, how he believed in them.

"What does it matter?" Oblivienne asks, voice weak. "Our lives before are over. We can never go back to the way things were, and we no longer know what the future holds for us."

"But we *do* know!" Sunder insists. "Mother *told us* we would return to Leutheria, and Mother never lied." She shoves her doubts away, out of her heart and out of her mind.

"Then explain how Verity has a twin sister in *this* world," Oblivienne says sharply.

Verity winces.

Sunder looks to Rhi for help, as if she might know the answer, but Rhi looks about as stricken as Sunder feels.

"Verity," Rhi says, and Sunder can feel her spirit reaching for Verity—for all of them. "Girls . . . I'm . . . I'm so sorry."

It takes a moment for Sunder to understand, but when she does, she reaches for Rhi with her heart, pulling Rhi into the tangle of their spirits, the web of their lives, the power of their sisterhood: Rhi thinks their grief is her fault. That since she is the one who brought them into this world, she is the one responsible for the aftermath.

But Sunder knows she is wrong. She puts her hand out to her new sister. Rhi steps forward and takes it, letting herself be drawn down to the bed between Sunder and Epiphanie.

"You had no choice, Sister," Sunder whispers. "We have always been meant to find you. It was always going to be this way." Mother was right about Rhi. Surely he must have been right about the rest of it.

Oblivienne turns away, drawing her knees up to her chest, staring at something no one else can see.

Let her doubt, Sunder thinks, clutching Rhi's hand even tighter, as if her mere presence can anchor the girls to the path Mother foretold. *Let Oblivienne doubt. Fate will give her no choice but to believe, in the end.*

When the Heavens Meet the Earth

Excerpted from *Savage Castle:*
A Memoir of the Wild Girls of Happy Valley

MOTHER HAD TOLD US COUNTLESS TIMES, *When the heavens meet the Earth and your fifth sister has arrived, the way home will be revealed,* but he had never been able to tell us more than that. Finally, one night, many moons before we left the castle, Mother sat us down on the flat rocks beside the creek and pointed to the reflection of the full moon, fat and shimmering on the black water. The distorted shape of it shimmied and fluttered, dancing to the quick rhythm of the current.

"Look there, my children." Mother's fingers spread out, as if to grab the reflection and lift it from the water. "Do you see how she visits us in this world? Do you see how she comes down to be among us?"

We nodded and studied the opalescent bloom upon the water. We had watched the Moon on her visits before, seen her hover and glide between firefly stars, all the way across the river until she disappeared from the sky and the sun had burned away all evidence of her visitation. We were fond of the Moon in all her many phases, and fonder still of her visitations.

"You have seen the lunar eclipse many times, have you not? Some partial, some full." Mother placed his staff in the divot of a rock close to the water and leaned on it. "But always you have watched her change up in the heavens, from brilliant to blood red, like summer to fall. You have never seen her vanish here, on Earth. But you will, one day."

At this, Sunder sat up straight, looking between Mother and the reflection of the Moon.

"Girls, you must listen to me carefully and retain all that I tell you, for I may not be around to tell you again before the day arrives. I have had a final vision concerning your journey to Leutheria. One day, soon after your fifth sister arrives, you will see the Moon in all her fullness, and she will begin to disappear before your very eyes. And when that happens, you must take yourselves to the nearest body of water and watch for the Moon's image here on Earth. For when her spectral body is eclipsed, you will see a black nothingness and a shimmering red halo, dancing on the water. That, my dear girls, is the doorway to the world beyond."

"Through the water?" Epiphanie asked.

"Through the portal," Mother replied.

"But what if we cannot reach it?" Verity wondered. "What if it is too far out in the water, or the water pulls us away?"

"The portal will be accessible," Mother assured us with a painful smile. "The Moon knows you, my princesses, and is eager to guide you home. She wants to shine on Leutheria once more, free from the bondage of greed and vice. She wants to bring you home so that you may save your people from the shadow that has fallen over your kingdoms." He looked at us each in turn, arm trembling as he gripped his staff.

"But what if we are not ready?" Verity whispered.

"You will be ready," Mother assured us. "You have been preparing for your destiny all your lives. There is nothing you will meet in

Leutheria that you cannot conquer, that you cannot overcome, so long as you stick together. So long as you remain sisters."

Sunder clasped Epiphanie's hand, who clasped Verity's, who clasped Oblivienne's.

"But our fifth sister," Oblivienne whispered, one hand empty.

Mother smiled. "She will be there. She is coming. This I promise you."

We gripped one another tightly, looking out onto the water where the Moon was hovering. She seemed to whisper to us, *I will guide you home, my daughters. I will guide you to your destiny.*

And Mother, listening, nodded his agreement to the stars.

12

"Should I bring anything else with me?" Verity asks Rhi, looking at the brand-new backpack Blood Mother brought to the hospital for her so that she could pack her belongings.

Verity has already dumped in all the food she has hoarded over the weeks, the spare set of *pajamas* the hospital gave her, a few items she made at the crafts table with her sisters. She has nothing from her life before. She can hardly believe that life is over.

This past week, Verity has spent more time away from her sisters than ever before, either in meetings with police officers or Dr. Ibanez, or visitation hours with Blood Mother and sometimes Blood Sister Grace. While she has been occupied, her sisters have been away meeting with a *behavioral therapist* to help prepare them for life at the *group home*. Even now as Verity is packing, her sisters have already packed up what little they want to bring with them and are being given some kind of lecture to prepare them for their transition today.

Verity and her sisters are all leaving the hospital, venturing out into this strange new world of rules and walls . . . but they are not leaving together. And though she *knows* it is not her fault, Verity cannot help but *feel* like it is.

"You don't have to bring anything from here unless you want to," Rhi says. She looks around the small hospital room where Verity has been sleeping these past few weeks, but Verity knows there is not much to see: a bed, a desk, a chair, a stack of drawers called a *dresser*. "Your family will have everything you need. And I'm sure they'll be happy to get other things you want, too."

"Can they get my knife back?"

Rhi half frowns. Verity can tell Rhi wants to say the thing that will give Verity the most comfort in this moment—she is good at that when she needs to be. But instead, Rhi chooses honesty, and Verity is grateful.

"No. The police took it for evidence, which means it's probably gone for good." She sits down on the bed, picking nervously at her thumbnail, and tries to smile. "Generally speaking, folks get nervous around people carrying knives."

Verity blinks at this. "What if they need to cut something?"

"Well . . . that doesn't come up as much as you'd think. The more important concern is, what if someone gets mad at you and they *do* have a knife?"

She blinks twice this time, thrown by the implication. All her life Verity has had her knife by her side, until she came here. Never once has she been tempted to use it in anger—not against a person, at least. And anger is no stranger to her. She has fought with her sisters, and with their wolf-kin, and she has been angry at herself from time to time. (She is not angry with herself now—it is something else. Something heavier, and shifting, like the slow melt of heavy snow.) But anger is just another emotion. No more important than all the other hundreds of feelings she experiences throughout the day. Certainly not more powerful.

"Is that something we must be aware of? Out there?" she asks Rhi as she zips up the backpack. She tests the weight, notes the tight stitching on the straps, the almost waxy texture of the new-leaf-green fabric that she was told repels water. Had she owned such a pack in the wilderness, it would have made things much easier. "Should we be on guard against violence?"

She can tell Rhi is choosing whether to be honest, again, and it makes her wonder how often Rhi has had to lie in order to survive. (Is that something Verity has to look forward to as well?)

She is relieved when Rhi chooses honesty again.

"On the whole, violence is not an *everyday* problem for most people." The corner of her mouth quirks a little. "But gun violence is a problem in this country. And police brutality. And violence against women is a whole *other* thing. But day-to-day, it's not something you have to worry about. Just . . . if anyone touches you or makes you feel uncomfortable, and for sure if anyone hurts you, tell someone. Me, or Dr. Ibanez, or . . . do you know about nine-one-one?"

Verity has seen the numbers before, but she cannot recall exactly where. On signs, mostly, and small machines around the hospital. She shakes her head.

Rhi takes out the slim rectangle from her pocket—a *cell phone*, Verity has learned it is called, and she has been told it can speak to nearly anyone in the world who also has access to a phone. (Verity does not think people are lying when they tell them this, but she certainly finds it difficult to believe.) Rhi comes to stand beside Verity and shows her the glass face of it. It is cluttered with colorful sigils and icons Verity cannot even begin to decipher. Rhi points to the bottom, where there is a small green square with a white shape in it that resembles a clunky, stretched-out *C*.

"That's the *phone* icon. You tap it," Rhi says, tapping the square gently with her index finger. The face changes to a list of words—names, Verity realizes. "Then tap on *keypad*." She taps again, and the face changes again, this time to numbers. "If you need to call anyone, you tap out their number and then hit the phone icon again. This one." She points to another stretched-out *C*.

"How will I know what anyone's *number* is?" Verity worries.

"Here." She takes a piece of paper from Verity's desk and writes some numbers on it, along with her name, then hands it to Verity. "That's *my* phone number. Hopefully your mom will get you a phone, in which case numbers can be saved. But that's why nine-one-one is special—it's easy to remember in case of emergencies. Even if your mom doesn't get you a phone, they'll probably have a landline, which is even easier. Just hit the numbers—no tapping around or hitting *call*." She winces, perhaps realizing she's ventured into territory that's still muddy for Verity. "But if anything dangerous or scary happens, you just find a way to call nine-one-one, okay?"

Verity nods. "Thank you," she says, hoisting her backpack onto her shoulder. "For looking out for us."

"Of course," Rhi says, sliding her phone back into her pocket. "Is there anything else I can do?"

Verity smirks. "Can you get Blood Mother to keep all my sisters?"

Rhi's smile looks sad. "I really wish I could." The smile weakens further. "Are you going to be okay? Away from them?"

"I am certain I will survive," Verity says. She knows Rhi will understand. It has been apparent since they met her: Rhi knows all about doing what it takes to survive. "I may even, someday, appreciate my new family. They are kin, after all."

"Just . . . don't let them try to replace your sisters," Rhi says, a crease of worry between her eyebrows.

Verity smiles, even though her heart is heavy and her eyes are suddenly stinging with tears. "They could not do that if they tried."

13

THE GIRLS HAD ASKED RHI to be present today as Sunder, Epiphanie, and Oblivienne head off to the Happy Valley Group Home. They know Verity will not be coming with them, but they don't fight it. The fight has gone out of them, it seems—even Sunder.

Rhi offered to go with Verity to her new home, to be a familiar presence in a foreign place, if only for a few hours, but Verity declined. Rhi can tell she wants to do this alone, feels it is a burden she *must* bear alone, but doesn't say that out loud—she doesn't need to. Rhi can read between the lines of the few words she does speak, the language of her body, her expressions. And if Rhi can see it, surely her sisters can as well: the discovery of Verity's family in this world has made her feel like a villain—like it is something she must atone for.

Rhi watches from a few feet away as the girls stand together on the sidewalk of the psychiatric hospital in a square, standing close, but not touching. Epiphanie is the first to speak.

"This is our first true parting," she says aloud. Her regal voice almost breaks from the truth of those words.

"I do not want to go," Verity admits, reaching for the girls nearest to her—Sunder on one side, Oblivienne on the other.

Her touch triggers the square to collapse as all the girls press in on one another, tightening until they are linked arm to arm, chin to shoulder, chest to back. Sunder drops her crutches on the sidewalk with a clatter and throws her arms around her sister, whispering Verity's name, as if she could keep her, if only she could find the right spell to utter. No more words pass between them, only crushing embraces and desperate kisses, dry lips planted on foreheads, cheeks, the bridges of noses.

Several feet away, Rhi notices Grace Erikson lean close to her mother to whisper, "Is this the right thing to do?"

"Of course it is, sweetheart," Mrs. Erikson insists. "Mat—" She stops and corrects herself. "*Verity* needs her family right now."

Grace purses her lips and turns back to the girls, swiping at her eyes and muttering, "That's my *point*." She glances at Rhi and gives her a curt nod of acknowledgment.

Rhi turns to Dr. Ibanez, concern scrunching her brow.

"It's for the best," Dr. Ibanez says quietly before Rhi can say anything. "To let them break apart a little. To encourage them to become individuals instead of a pack."

"Some of us would be lucky to have a pack like theirs," Rhi says.

"You're not wrong. But you of all people can see that the girls feed each other's delusions. We've made progress since Mrs. Erikson showed up; they're starting to doubt Mother's stories. If we want them to live normal lives, they're going to have to grieve those identities and claim who they are in *this* world, and this world alone."

Rhi feels a little sick, picturing the girls ten years in the future dressed in business casual, sitting in a cubicle tapping diligently on a keyboard; or waitressing at a diner, waiting on old men whose eyes never quite make it all the way up to theirs when placing an order; or falling in love with someone and forever making compromises to keep that person close, until they become a shell of who they used to be.

Finally, Verity extracts herself from her sisters and wipes the tears from her cheeks with her sleeves. She turns, stone-faced, to Grace, her mother, and the tall balding blonde man—her stepfather—behind them, waiting by a green Volvo hatchback. She does not look away or avert her eyes. Her gaze is unknowable. Unsettling.

Mrs. Erikson runs to meet her halfway and throws her arms around Verity. "Oh, my girl, my girl, my little girl," she whispers, eyes squeezed shut as she embraces her lost daughter. Verity stands stock-still and does not hug her back, but it doesn't seem to matter. Mrs. Erikson has probably never been so happy in all her life.

Rhi thinks of her own mother and wishes she could tell Verity to return the embrace. Up until this moment, the discovery of Verity's family had felt like a blow—to the fantasy the wild girls had shared with Rhi, and to the girls' very understanding of the world. But as she watches Mrs. Erikson's tears fall freely onto Verity's hair as she rocks her daughter in the tightest embrace, Rhi feels a swell of grief for the woman—for Grace, too—for all the years where they thought they had lost Verity forever.

While Mrs. Erikson walks her daughter to the waiting car, Epiphanie, Oblivienne, and Sunder are ushered onto the small bus idling at the curb. Rhi gives them comforting looks and mutters reassuring things as they pass her, climbing aboard the vehicle that will take them to yet another building, even farther away from the wilderness they once called home.

In her pocket, Rhi's phone chirps. She pulls it out and looks at the screen.

> **Message from: NO**
> Sentencing is tomorrow. Will you be there?

Another text appears in the preview window while she's reading.

> Edie, please call me. I need to know you're okay.

Rhi clears the notifications and casually slips the phone back into her pocket, even as she struggles to keep her mind from the undertow of memories threatening to pull her out to sea.

You're still my best girl, right, Edie?

Rhi swallows her nausea and forces a smile, waving to the girls as the bus rolls away.

14

A T SCHOOL THE FOLLOWING MONDAY, the students have resumed ignoring Rhi. They are talking about Grace instead, asking one another, "Did you even know she had a sister?" and "Did you read that ClickMonster article about the kidnapping?" and "I had no idea Grace's mother was a recovering addict, did you?"

Rhi does not want to eavesdrop, but it helps distract her from stewing in her own disappointment—and embarrassment. She hadn't realized until it was ripped away from her how much she had begun to believe in the girls' story—Mother's story, really. She feels silly that she'd even entertained the idea that she might be the fifth princess—a *daughter of wolves*, whatever that meant.

But the girls are still real, even if their foretold destiny is not, and so is the connection Rhi feels to them. Rhi is now even more determined to help the girls adjust to their new lives. Verity's mother has asked for a few weeks without visitors or doctors or officers or anyone else intruding on their lives, but Rhi has managed to visit the other three girls at the group home by riding Uncle Jimmy's bike there after school. To Rhi, the girls seem like a three-legged chair, unsteady without Verity to hold them in balance. But they are adapting to the group home, to the other children there, to the staff that always seems alternately frustrated or amused by everything they do.

ON THURSDAY, RHI, EPIPHANIE, OBLIVIENNE, and Sunder are sitting in a circle on one of the hanging bridges of the deserted playground at the Happy Valley Group Home when Oblivienne announces that Dr. Ibanez has cleared her to guide Agent Tyler's search party through the forest, to the castle.

"I know this does not make you happy, Sisters," Oblivienne says, taking Sunder's hand in hers. "But I hope you understand why I must."

"We understand," Epiphanie says, taking Oblivienne's other hand, looking her in the eye so intently Rhi almost feels like she should turn away.

"Do what you want," Sunder says, leaning back against the nylon rope railings to look up at the moon visible in the daylit sky. "It will not change Mother's vision."

It does not surprise Rhi to hear that Sunder still believes in Mother's stories, but it does hurt a little. She can only imagine what the other girls are feeling.

"Rhi," Oblivienne says, somewhat shyly. "Would you come with me?"

"Yes," Rhi says, without hesitation. "Of course." As a park ranger, her uncle is also a part of the search party (or "expedition," as Uncle Jimmy has been calling it with a mischievous grin), and the moment she'd heard it was finally being put together, Rhi had let herself fantasize about what they might find.

Now she is going to see it with her own eyes.

ON SATURDAY, OBLIVIENNE LEADS AGENT TYLER's search party as far as she can into the forest, toward the castle, before dusk begins to fall and the rangers stop to make camp, a tidy circle of pop-up tents and portable stovetops. There is a debate among the rangers as to whether they should build a fire—they have enough gear that it's not a necessity to keep them warm, and it would carry the general risks of all campfires, but eventually the others in attendance (police officers, forensics team, Agent Tyler, Dr. Ibanez) say "come *on*" enough that the decision is made.

Rhi and Oblivienne watch as Uncle Jimmy gathers kindling for the fire. Per a murmured request from Dr. Ibanez at the start of the hike, Rhi has been keeping an eye on Oblivienne. Dr. Ibanez is slightly worried she might decide to make a run for it, but with a pang of regret, Rhi knows Oblivienne has no desire to run now. To Rhi, despite her secondhand jeans, thrifted hiking boots, and marigold-colored jacket, Oblivienne looks for all the world like a zoo animal in an enclosure, a parody of freedom. And just like those broken-spirited animals, she has resigned herself to captivity.

One of the park rangers lights a match to start the campfire and Oblivienne's dark eyes consume the fiery miracle with hunger. When the ranger goes to fetch more wood, Oblivienne picks up the box of matches and whispers, "At the castle, we used magic to light our fires."

Goose bumps prick at Rhi's skin, all up and down her body, but she tries to ignore them.

"But magic did not always work. If it had been raining, or if we could not focus well enough. And toward the end, after Mother . . ." Oblivienne's eyes are distant with memories, but she shakes her head to clear them, replacing the matchbox on the log where the ranger had left it. "Anyway. Having those would have been nice." She hugs herself and watches the fire burn.

Rhi feels split in two, between the Rhi who desperately wants to believe that the girls conjured fire with magic, and the Rhi who knows that can't be true. Alarmingly, she's not sure which one she is.

As dark begins to settle in, someone hands out little tin trays stamped with MRE on the cardboard sleeves ("meals ready to eat," apparently), and the party finds various places to sit and eat. Oblivienne, squatting on her heels by the fire, looks out into the forest as the night drapes itself around their camp, half of her government-issued dinner left untouched at her feet.

Uncle Jimmy comes by, holding something up like a prize: a gleaming green apple. "Look what I was able to rustle up. Oblivienne, would you be interested in some food that doesn't come out of a tin?"

He tosses her the apple and Oblivienne catches it in one hand, studying it intently before biting into it.

Rhi smiles at her uncle. She is grateful he is the person who took her in after her father's arrest, not just because he is kind, but because he is genuinely *good*. Yet still, Rhi finds it hard to completely relax near him. She is always trying to predict what he wants from her, what he needs her to be. What if she disappoints him one day and he decides he hates her? What if she upsets him and he kicks her out—or worse?

Everyone else Rhi has ever trusted has let her down. She doesn't want to make the same mistakes again.

AFTER DINNER, RHI AND OBLIVIENNE turn in early and head back to their tent.

Scooting into her sleeping bag, Rhi confesses: "I'm glad you asked me to come with you." She lays her head on her pillow and turns to face the other girl. "I hope my being here is . . . helpful."

Oblivienne sits on her sleeping bag and examines her feet, red and irritated from the hiking boots.

"I do not like traveling without my sisters," Oblivienne admits, twisting her leg with nearly inhuman flexibility to position her foot in front of her face, poking at a blister on her pinky toe. The bottoms of her feet are calloused and stained dark from a lifetime of wandering barefoot through the forest. Her toes are curled even at rest, as if seeking something to grip, but her toenails have been freshly cleaned and clipped, probably by one of the aides at the group home.

"You are not them," Oblivienne continues without malice, unfolding her legs and inching backward to get into her sleeping bag. "But in some ways, you are more like me than they ever were."

"What do you mean?" Rhi asks, tucking a hand under her pillow.

Oblivienne lies down on her side and faces the wall of their tent, her back to Rhi. "You want to be a part of the pack, but you will never be able to lose yourself long enough to become part of something else."

Rhi stares at the other girl's form as a weight blooms in her chest and presses the air from her lungs. She rolls onto her back and looks up at the tent ceiling doused in shadows.

Neither of them speak again until morning.

IN THE MIDDLE OF THE AFTERNOON the next day, Oblivienne pauses at the head of a well-worn path. She closes her eyes and takes three deep breaths before leading the party forward. They cross over a border that Rhi feels as much as she sees: long white stones laid into the dirt, projecting some kind of energy into the air that makes her hair stand on end when she steps into the small clearing.

Oblivienne stops, looks sidelong at Rhi, and nods.

"This is it," Rhi tells the others, taking it all in as goose bumps rise on her skin.

It looks like any other abandoned, illegal campsite at first: the dry, bare ground beaten down by foot traffic; a firepit filled with ash. But the firepit is fenced in with curving animal bones, and there is a massive, long-dead, uprooted tree on the eastern side of the site, and a half-collapsed stone wall on the northern side, made of shale and river clay.

The first thing Rhi notices are the markings. They aren't obvious at all—rather, they seem to emerge, gradually, out of the texture of the place, and come into focus as her eyes are drawn across the scene from tree to rock to bone. Everything is carved, painted, or branded with a symbol, pictograph, or handprint. As her eyes become practiced at picking out the shapes, Rhi is overwhelmed by the extent of what *is* covered in markings versus what is not. Even the bare ground has been marked, inlaid with more rough white stones that glare in the high sun to form a bright many-armed spiral around the firepit.

When Rhi's gaze finds the stones in the ground, it is like a veil is yanked from her eyes. The entire scene transforms into something glistening and enchanted; wild spring buttercups and flowering ivy pour out of the woods to form a green ring around the sacred space; the fallen tree on the opposite side of the camp appears magnificently large all of a sudden, and its hollow trunk, collapsing in on itself, reminds Rhi of the ruins of ancient temples, or of castles toppled by war. The huge tentacles of near-petrified roots reach toward the sky, casting thin shadows over where it once loomed. There is no dirt clinging to the underside, no living things crawling where the roots should have been—just smooth naked wood.

Oblivienne makes a soft sound at Rhi's side.

"It looks so helpless," she murmurs, an edge of distress in her voice. She turns away, as if she cannot bear to look.

But Rhi continues forward, drawn to the tree. At one time, it must have stood taller than any building Rhi has ever seen, and easily as wide as a house. Now it lies toppled, the gaping opening to its cavernous insides only partly turned up and out to the world, a half entrance that both beckons and demurs. Rhi puts a hand on the tree and feels a strange thrum within its smooth gray trunk, like the distant marching of a million tiny feet—as if she can feel the insects inside, or fungi digging roots and spores deeper and deeper into the remains of the tree, speeding along its inevitable decay.

Rhi ducks and sidesteps into the mouth of the castle. Inside, she can stand at full height with more than enough space above her head. There is plenty of debris inside, leaves and brambles that have blown in or been brought in by animals, bird feathers and fur and still more bones. But even with the entropy of nature taking its toll, evidence of long human habitation remains, as obvious to Rhi as phosphorescent lichen glowing in the dark.

The air still smells of burning wood and the clean carbon of ash. There are woven grass baskets, toppled and spilling their contents: piles of tanned hide and furs, skeins of leathery strings made from jerky-like substances, dried flowers and butterfly wings, hand-carved wooden animals, stone knives, red clay beads and jewelry made from the same, weather-beaten glass bottles, and *so many* bones, especially skulls, of all species and sizes. There are carvings on the walls, scratched and scrawling in a panorama of natural observations, attempts at telling stories through stick figures and celestial bodies and smears of color.

She follows the artwork up, onto the now-ceiling, the once-wall, and finally, there, at the top, is a depiction of a figure in some kind of robe, bathed in light indicated by streaks of white and shimmering pyrite, radiating outward. There are stars painted all around him—or maybe sparks?—and five figures around him, dancing in his radiance.

"He was everything to us."

Rhi jumps, spins around, hand to her throat. "You scared me."

Oblivienne doesn't respond to that. She stands just inside the castle, her hands on the wall, gazing up at the drawing. "He was our parent. Our teacher. Our best friend." She smiles, just a little. "He gave our existence meaning. He gave us *magic*."

"Because . . . of your destiny?" Rhi asks.

"No. Because he loved us."

Rhi's heart aches at this, for the things these girls have lost; for the things *she* lost, long ago: a home, and someone who loved her without any conditions at all.

Oblivienne steps deeper into the castle, toeing at the spilled chaos, the downy feathers of old birds' nests rustling around their feet. "He left us sometimes for moons at a time, but when he returned it was always like seeing the first buds on the trees in spring. All that possibility, and power, and life, just pouring out of him, into us. It was . . . completion."

"So, you never fought with him?" Rhi asks.

Oblivienne shakes her head.

"You never questioned him, or resented him?" Rhi feels a tightness rise in her, thinking of her own family. She pushes it away.

Oblivienne shakes her head again, squatting to rummage through an overturned basket. "It was not perfect, if that is what you are asking. I asked questions, and he would not always give me satisfactory answers."

From the contents of the basket, Oblivienne pulls out a nearly destroyed book, easily the size of a dictionary, missing the cover, the whole thing swollen and crisp with water damage. There are two more books in similarly terrible condition that Rhi can now see peeking out from under a stack of furs. One appears to be a copy of *The Odyssey*; the other looks like a hardback edition of *Grimms' Fairy Tales*.

"I know I was not the only one who suspected he was hiding something," Oblivienne says. "But we did not talk about it. If he was keeping something from us for some reason, we believed that it was a *good* reason."

Rhi tilts her head. "And now?"

Oblivienne's eyes glisten. "Now, I do not know what I believe." She gazes at the book in her hands for a long while before asking, "What do *you* believe?"

Rhi's eyebrows shoot up. "Me? I—I can't even say. I wasn't there, you know? I didn't live it."

"No, but that is what gives you clearer sight than the rest of us. Your mind is not clouded. You do not *need* to believe that your entire life until now was not merely . . . the whims of a mentally ill old man." Her voice breaks on the last word.

Rhi's insides twist. Her mind *is* just as clouded as Oblivienne's, in a way. Despite all logic, she is desperate to believe in the magic of these girls, in their vital sense of belonging and purpose. She needs to believe that there really is a world out there that needs to be rescued by four magical princesses waiting for their lost fifth sister.

Grace would be their fifth, if anyone, Rhi thinks, scolding herself. *But is she the "daughter of wolves" that Mother described?*

Rhi bites the inside of her cheek to bring herself back to reality. "I don't *know* if Mother was lying to you or not, Oblivienne. But if he loved you . . . if you loved him . . . does it matter?"

Oblivienne ponders this reply before tossing the ruined book aside. She lets out a deep sigh. "We should go. They will have found the bones by now."

"Bones?" Rhi asks, but Oblivienne is already ducking through the opening, heading outside.

WHEN RHI EMERGES FROM THE castle a few paces behind Oblivienne, she sees the forensics team has spread out over the camp, their investigative tools set up like plein air painters at a park: still cameras, LED and UV lights, biohazard bags, evidence bags, and a hundred other tools that Rhi can't begin to name. Uncle Jimmy is talking to someone over the radio, sending back coordinates from his GPS. They'll be looking for somewhere nearby to land a helicopter, to expedite removal of evidence and replace personnel as the investigation persists. Rhi and Oblivienne will probably be on the first helicopter out.

Right now, Oblivienne is watching Agent Tyler squat, prodding at one of the long white stones at the very edge of the clearing where they first entered the site. The unevenly sized stones appear to make a full loop around the place, vanishing under the carpet of wild buttercups, then reappearing on the other side. When the stone under Agent Tyler's nitrile-gloved fingers pops free from the dirt, Oblivienne jumps, clutching Rhi's arm.

"What is it?" Rhi whispers.

Oblivienne looks grave as she shakes her head, the thick waves of her dark bob falling into her eyes.

Agent Tyler lays the stone back in place, pulls a brush from his utility vest pocket and sweeps away some of the dirt. "Dr. Ibanez, can you take a look at this please?"

"I see it." Dr. Ibanez's expression is wary as she walks over to Agent Tyler. "That's human. Tibia."

Agent Tyler snaps a picture of the bone before lifting it, peering over the marred surface where mud and rain have stained the indentations the color of earth. He cocks an eyebrow. "Do those look like teeth marks to you?"

Dr. Ibanez crouches across from Agent Tyler, pulling thick-framed glasses out from the pocket of her fleece jacket. "Yes," she confirms. "And those are human, too."

To the Bone

Excerpted from *Savage Castle:*
A Memoir of the Wild Girls of Happy Valley

MOTHER HAD WARNED US HE would not live forever, but we were still not prepared when the time came.

It happened when we were gone, out with our wolf-kin harvesting mushrooms and berries and other things we'd watched the black bears enjoy, that we enjoyed, too. Mother, after securing the perimeter of magic around our well-loved bit of land, sat in the crook of the root on the left-hand side of the castle's doorway, wrapped in his rich red robes. Perhaps he thought of Leutheria when he lifted his face to the sun and fell asleep.

He did not wake up again.

When we returned to our castle, we knew by something more than sight that Mother was no longer there, even as we looked upon. In the wilderness, we were intimate with Death; she was a sacred and necessary partner in the dance of survival. We ushered her in daily with blunt stones, sharp spears, bare teeth and hands. We knew very well what it was for life to be vibrant and full one moment and gone the next. But we had never before dwelled on what it would mean for one of our own to depart.

We stood in a semicircle and stared for a long while. It was clear Mother's life had not been *taken*—there was no sign of injury or struggle. He had merely left his body behind, as if he had shaken it off like one of his robes before bathing.

We knew Mother had died, but the *meaning* of that—the understanding of our loss—was slow to trickle down from our heads, into our hearts. When it finally happened, it was like a vital organ was ripped out of us. One by one, we fell to our knees and pressed our palms to the hot, baked dirt, spines arching, soaking up the stability of the earth to make up for what had been stolen.

Mother was gone.

Mother, so regal and powerful in life, was now frail and inconsequential in death.

We could not bear to see him like that, slumped unceremoniously against the roots of the castle. Acting as one, we hauled ourselves over to Mother and gripped his arms and legs. We carried him out onto the spiral arms of cool white stone we had embedded in the earth, many years ago. Carefully, we laid him out, flat and straight, with his back to the earth and his face to the sky. And then we circled him, crawling on hands and knees, half-crouched, half-broken as we moved. Even our wolf-kin circled, vigilant, waiting.

"Mother?" Epiphanie was the first to say his name, hiccupping at the end as the first of many realizations struck home: *Mother is not there.* She started to reach for him, but faltered, fingers falling short of their goal.

Verity whispered his name, "*Mother. Mother,*" as if testing to see if she could call him back.

Oblivienne shook her head and paced around the body on fingers and toes, but could not bring herself to say his name, could not bring herself to part her lips, for fear of what might escape.

Finally, Sunder, who sat rocking on her heels, hugging her knees to her chest and biting the meat of her arm, rolled forward onto her knees and flung her head back, crying out in miserable wordless sorrow. Her arms hung limp as all her strength was sent to her voice, roaring at the trees and the mountains and the sky, who dared continue on as they always had instead of collapsing to the ground in mourning. When her throat was raw, she folded forward, grinding her knuckles into the earth, pounding the dirt over and over again as she sobbed, "*Mother! Mother! Mother!*"

Sister and Brother wolf barked and howled, settling onto their haunches as they pressed against Sunder's sides. Epiphanie crawled over to Sunder. She embraced the younger girl from behind and held her close, rocking her.

Verity and Oblivienne continued to pace on hands and knees, whispering, grasping at Mother's lifeless body, at his blood-red robes, at his calloused palms, until our limbs ached and our hearts ached more.

When we were numb with loss, we sat vigil, watching, thinking, waiting, until the sun began to sink, draping our home in the cloak of gloaming. Sister and Brother wolf lay on the ground between us, eyes wide and sorrowful, staring at the body at the center of our circle.

Verity struck up a fire in the bone-fenced pit of ash and char. When the fire was blazing, it painted everything in flickering red and gold. Shadows washed up and down Mother's chest, as if it was still rising and falling with breath; shadows crawled over his face, as if he was stirring from sleep. For a moment, we could almost believe Mother had returned to us.

But we knew he was gone, no matter how the flames seemed to animate his corpse. And the hole that knowledge made within us felt like an echoing chasm that we could never hope to fill. All of Mother's wisdom, all of Mother's magic, all of Mother's comfort and love and reassurance—all of *Mother* was gone, except for the shell he used to inhabit.

What happens when such a prominent fixture of your life is ripped away? How do you fill the unbearable emptiness left behind?

Epiphanie was the first to think it, but thoughts are contagious in the wild. Like burrs carried from flank to flank, the thought passed from girl to girl as we looked around the fire at one another's slowly lifting faces, and finally at Mother, draped in red. Mother, who taught us everything we knew. Mother, who had been a source of wisdom and wonder for as long as we could remember. Mother, who was made of stories, and magic, and the love that used to fill the aching in our bellies.

Without a word, Epiphanie drew her flint blade from its sheath looped around the belt of her deer-hide skirt. She stood, tears streaking her face with gold as she passed the blade through the flames, cleansing it.

Verity crawled over to Mother's body and began tugging at the cord around his waist. His robes were always clean, always bold and rich in color, but tonight they had transformed into something less. The fabric was suddenly threadbare, suddenly dull and faded like the color in Mother's cheeks, suddenly paper-thin like the weight of his ancient skin. We untied the cord—once golden-threaded, now nothing more than sun-bleached rope. We undressed him, drawing his arms from the sleeves and laying him back down on the bed of time-worn cloth. We cast our eyes up and down the frail, sun-darkened limbs, hairless and withered, speckles of black painted along his hands and arms. His chest was narrow, concave, bones sharp and rigid beneath his skin. His ribs made deep shadows, like fingers reaching up from the ground to wrap around his torso.

All of Mother was ancient and withered. But there was some meat left on the shoulders, the legs.

We spread out, surrounded Mother, grabbing arms and legs, lifting them, washing them with our spit and the cloth of Mother's robes. A low hum built between us, reverberating off the bones around the fire, the bones inside our bodies, the bones inside Mother. It vibrated through our chests, our hands, sent shivers through the packed earth beneath us. The wolves stood, ears pricked, eyes narrowed on the ritual at hand.

As the pitch rose, so did the magic rise from the earth. The sigils carved upon rocks and trees lit up warm and coppery in the dark, radiating power into the night. The spiral arms of stone reaching out from the firepit turned opaline and radiant, shining their starlight back to the heavens. And when Epiphanie approached Mother with her stone blade in hand, the spiral arms began to sway, as if dancing beneath us.

Oblivienne lifted Mother's arm over her shoulder. Epiphanie put her foot against Mother's ribs, gripped his bicep with her left hand,

and plunged the blade into the soft tissue under his arm where it met his shoulder. She moved forcefully, shoving the blade up, then down, cracking the joint apart while Oblivienne pulled. The cartilage gave way as she sawed. Mother's arm came apart from his body, much lighter in Oblivienne's hands than she had expected it to be.

While Epiphanie circled around to the other side, Oblivienne pulled her own blade from her belt and cut into the skin of the arm she now held in her lap. She made a long incision, then gently peeled the skin away, tossing it to our wolf-kin.

Our humming had lit up the forest by then, calling creatures to the perimeter of our space, their eyes flashing in the dark. The glow of our sigils and stones began to outshine the fire itself, turning the whole world pale and silvery like the moon. We cut and cut, honoring Mother as the deep scarlet of his lifeless blood stained the white glow of magic all around us.

We continued to hum, louder, higher, until our throats reached the pitch of mourning: a high, open-mouthed note, like a hymn or a battle cry. Each of us took our own blade and cut long strips of meat from Mother's shoulders and thighs. We raised the flesh high over our heads as our song reached a fever pitch, howling at the stars as we ran out of breath.

And then the song was over.

Night swooped down and stole the light from the world, leaving nothing but fire and shadow, and four young women chewing on the raw, red, mortal remains of the man we had known as Mother.

"Mother," we muttered, between mouthfuls.

"Mother," we whispered when we cut more from the limb.

"Mother," we breathed when we had swallowed the very last bites.

And when the bones were bare and we were sick from our feast, we lay down by the fire, bloodstained and weary, willing the weight in our bellies to fill the holes in our chests.

Mother was gone.

Mother was truly gone.

But at least, now, he would be a part of us forever.

THE HAPPY VALLEY HERALD

FBI Takes a Step Back from "Wild Girls" Investigation

(CONTINUED FROM PAGE 1) despite strong reservations from the community.

"Our goal is to reunite the other three girls with their families if possible," said Paul Rupstein, director of the Happy Valley Group Home for Boys and Girls. "If the FBI can't help, then it's better they let these poor girls move on."

We spotted Agent Robert Tyler of the FBI leaving the Happy Valley Police Department with his case files today and asked him why the FBI is pausing its investigation.

"At this point, there's nothing more for the FBI to do," Agent Tyler said. When pressed about the late-night activity at the coroner's office over the weekend, he added, "We did discover human remains at an undisclosed location. The remains broadly match the description of the suspect that the girls gave us, someone they refer to only as 'Mother.' But it's going to take some time to collect a clean DNA sample, and there are no dental record matches, so the suspect—and the rest of the girls—remain unidentified. Either way, the suspect is deceased. For all intents and purposes, that means this case is closed while we focus our attentions on more urgent cases."

But even if the official criminal case is going inactive, the speculations surrounding the Wild Girls of Happy Valley and the mysterious "Mother" are alive and well . . .

15

GRACE IS DREADING GOING BACK to school today. It's been just over two weeks since the FBI contacted their family and blew up their lives, but there isn't enough time in the world to adjust to something like this.

Her mother fusses over Grace's clothes before school, wants to make sure she looks youthful and carefree in case anyone decides to snap a picture or interview her, or in any way potentially put Grace's image out there for the world to consume—an image that ultimately represents the Erikson family, her mother reminds her. Grace understands some of this comes from her mother's own shame over a past that has been dragged out for all the world to judge. But Grace, too, is bracing for judgment, and is too angry with her mother to be very compassionate or understanding, now.

Her mother asks if Grace is wearing makeup. When Grace replies, "No, you don't like me wearing makeup to school," she puts a few dabs of something red on Grace's cheeks and lips, blends it with her thumb until it looks almost natural.

"Cameras always make a person look washed out," she says. "I don't want you looking sickly, like no one is taking care of you."

Mathilda—*Verity*, Grace reminds herself—is across the hall in the office/guest room (which is now her bedroom, Grace supposes), listening to their conversation. Grace can't see her, but she can feel her eyes on them, feel her ears swallowing their words.

"Smile, Gracie," Mom says with her own chalk-white grin. "You have a sister again. People are going to want to hear all about the excitement of having her back."

Grace frowns. She can't hide her disappointment as well as she can hide everything else.

Her whole life she has thought about the day Mathilda would be returned to her. Her whole life she has clutched the sparse memories she has of her twin sister—the comfort of her body next to Grace's, her hand in Grace's hand, her mind linked to Grace's mind. Grace had fantasized about the strong, powerful, protective sister who would come home to her one day—maybe then Mom might be happy, and their stepfather less of a prick.

But here she is, not *Mathilda*, but *Verity*: a freak in need of more care and education and rehabilitation than Grace can wrap her head around.

She thought she was from a parallel world?

She thought she was a princess?

She thought some random dude in the woods was using magic to protect her?

Grace flushes, hot with annoyance.

Later, at the breakfast table, Verity approaches so silently that Grace jumps when she pulls out a chair. She stares at Grace; Grace stares back.

It's like looking into a mirror in a parallel universe.

They are identical twins, but telling them apart is as easy as if they were total strangers—which they also are. Grace sees how her own life, however cursed it has felt at times, has been full of veritable *luxuries* that have shaped her into a glossy, Instagram-ready young woman. Verity is gaunt, skin prematurely aged by the elements, hair bleached and brittle from the sun, lips full but frequently dry and cracked (even though Grace has given her like a hundred different flavors of lip balm to try). She has scars all over her face and body that make pale slashes across her tanned skin, the map of a life Grace can scarcely imagine. She looks like an end-of-season contestant on *Survivor*, and Grace looks like an American Girl doll. It's no wonder none of Grace's friends recognized her from Verity's picture on the news.

But Grace also sees strength in her sister that she has never even come close to knowing, and it makes her furious.

She pours a bowl of Special K and adds unsweetened soy milk, just until the flakes begin to rise. Her mother slides a mess of eggs and bacon onto a plate for Verity.

"Gross," Grace mutters.

"Grace," Mom warns her.

"What? I don't eat dead animals."

"Verity, just ignore her, sweetheart."

Verity looks between them, the premature wrinkle between her eyebrows from endless squinting in the sun deepening as she tries to decode what she is meant to do.

Ugh.

The anger rushes fast, then scatters. Grace takes pity on her. She, too, knows what it's like to perform.

"It's fine, Verity," she assures her. "Go ahead. It's not gross."

Verity picks up a piece of bacon and nibbles on it, sullenly.

IT'S BEEN NEARLY A MONTH since the girls were discovered, but the students at "HPV High" School don't have much to entertain them, and nothing fascinates them more than the "Wild Girls of Happy Valley."

"She's doing great," Grace says when her friends ask about her sister.

"We're getting along great."

"It's so great to have her home."

"Verity is just . . . great."

Everyone wants more than her evasive answers, though, no matter how happy Grace tries to sound.

"Is she like, totally savage?" Aidan, Grace's ex, asks, sitting on her desk in homeroom.

"She's actually really quiet."

"Does she climb trees like a monkey?" someone else asks.

"No." She cocks an eyebrow.

"Does she walk around the house naked?"

Grace rolls her eyes. She doesn't mention that Verity did in fact leave the bathroom door open while she was showering, and then also left her bedroom door open when she was getting dressed, until Grace told her doors were meant for closing, *especially* when you are naked, and especially when you have a shitty stepfather loitering around the house. Verity's lack of concern was reassuring, at least—she was probably telling the truth that this Mother character did not molest them. He was just regular crazy instead of pervy crazy.

Grace is grateful, at least, that no one has brought up her mother's past. The articles about the formerly cold case of Mathilda Godefroy's kidnapping love to point out that "the mother had been high on fentanyl the night her daughter was abducted." As if the opioid crisis hadn't touched nearly every family in this country in some form or another.

In the cafeteria, Grace spots Rhiannon Chase huddled alone in a corner. She can't help but wonder *why* Verity and her "sisters" have taken her in. It's not like she has any similarities to them at all. Rhi comes from a wealthy family in Saratoga Springs—everyone knows her father is in jail for the kind of crimes only rich people get convicted of. Not to mention, she has the personality of a hedgehog with none of the cuteness. Maybe no one bothers her about the "wild girls" anymore because trying to talk to her is like trying to squeeze blood from a horse chestnut; prickly, unpleasant, and hopeless. Instead, Rhi just goes to class and gets good grades and makes an art of disappearing completely even though she's attached to the craziest news story of the decade.

"When can we meet your sister?" Victoria asks as she takes her seat at the table, raising two perfectly drawn eyebrows.

"Can we talk about something else?" Grace finally snaps. "I'm kinda over it, to be honest."

Brett groans dramatically and flops over onto the table. "But everything else is so goddamn boring!"

Grace remembers when she felt the same way. She wishes life could be so boring again.

16

V ERITY UNDERSTANDS TABLE MANNERS, NOW.

There was a time when she ate charred red meat off the bone, or scraped fish scales with her flint knife and ate the raw pink flesh the way one might bury their face in a slice of watermelon. She used to play-fight Sunder for the last cracked bone to suck the marrow dry. She used to fall asleep with berry-stained lips and bear fat on her chin.

But now Verity places a napkin on her lap and ignores the part of her that wants to grab the roasted chicken at the center of the table and tear it apart with her bare hands. She ignores, even, the hunger gnawing in her belly. Ever since coming to live in this house, for the first time in her life, Verity does not have much of an appetite.

After Verity declines everything, Blood Mother serves her anyway. She slices the chicken into thin, dignified pieces. She spoons a perfect globe of mashed potatoes onto the plate, and then a neat pile of bright green peas and crimped orange carrot slices.

"Go on," Blood Mother encourages. "Eat up."

Verity picks up her fork and pokes at the food. She has watched them all do this, from time to time, to give the impression of engaging with their food when, really, they were eating none of it. Blood Mother is the most masterful at this deception. Verity has seen her go entire days without eating. And yet when Grace attempts the same trick, Blood Mother scolds her.

"Eat your dinner, sweetheart," she says now to Grace.

Verity raises and lowers her fork from plate to mouth a few times, but she fears if she puts food in her mouth right now, it will not go down. And she knows how much vomit disturbs Stepfather. She was violently ill the first few days while her blood family got used to her dietary restrictions. He seems to hold it against her, still.

But it has been three weeks since she came to live here. And Verity understands table manners, now.

"How was school, Grace?" Blood Mother asks.

Grace shrugs. "Mrs. Anderson asked me to ask you to bring Verity in, to talk about her going to school."

"Absolutely not," Blood Mother says. "They'll throw her in with the remedial kids. I don't want that label on her for the rest of her life."

Grace scowls. "As opposed to the label of *feral child*?"

"Or one of the 'Wild Girls of Happy Valley,'" Stepfather snorts, looking sidelong at Verity.

Verity mixes up her mashed potatoes with her peas and carrots like an obedient, *civilized* daughter. It is not yet time to be her true self. She has not yet decided if that time will ever come here. Part of her knows this place—these people—are her life now, but another part of her, the greater part of her, cannot yet imagine a future that does not lead her to Leutheria, with her sisters at her side. The faces around this table tell her that future is impossible, but the faith she has nurtured all her life cannot be washed away by a single storm.

"Verity is *not* feral," Blood Mother says, gazing fondly at her. "She's been through a traumatic, harrowing experience. She needs love and support and security, not labels."

Everyone has so many ideas about what she needs but not one of them has asked Verity. If they did, she would tell them: *I need my sisters.* But she knows they would only reply, *Your sister is right here. Is it not wonderful to be reunited?* And Verity would feel, once more, like she has let everybody down—her real sisters, and her Blood Sister. In the forest, Verity would have confessed these feelings by now and unburdened herself to her sisters. But in the forest, shame like this was scarcely even imaginable.

"She needs to be socialized," Stepfather says. "Verity, would you like to spend some time with other kids your age?"

Verity shrugs, in the way she has seen Grace respond when she does not really want to respond.

"Grace, maybe you should have some of your friends over to meet her."

Grace looks up at Stepfather, eyes wide. "Are you kidding me?"

"Christopher, no," Blood Mother says. "That's far too much stimulation right now."

"I'm sure the kids at school have been pestering you to meet her, anyway," Stepfather says to Grace, ignoring Blood Mother.

"Exactly," Grace says, quietly but fiercely. "And I've been trying to get them to drop the whole subject. Not *only* to protect Verity, but because, frankly, I'm sick of being known as the *twin sister* of a 'Wild Girl of Happy Valley.'"

"What were you known as before?" Stepfather wonders. "The girl who gets caught smoking pot in the school bathroom?"

Verity does not understand how one could smoke a pot, but Grace turns pink, and Verity understands that her sister has been embarrassed by Stepfather's words.

"Christopher." Blood Mother glowers.

Dinner is often like this. This is why Verity cannot eat, usually.

LATER, WHEN THE FAMILY HAS gone to bed and Blood Mother has performed her nightly ritual (of stopping at Verity's room to tell her she loves her and is so glad she is home, then gazing at her with tearful eyes, hungry for something Verity cannot give her), Verity sneaks downstairs.

She opens the refrigerator and pulls out the leftovers. Stomach growling, she stuffs handfuls of chicken into her mouth, chewing and swallowing frantically until her own hunger is sated. Then she cleans up every last speck of evidence. She has gotten used to the idea of *tidying*. It is not so awful to be *tidy*, but she misses the dirt between her toes.

When everything is spotless, Verity goes to the sliding glass door in the family room that looks out onto the wooden deck and the big backyard. She slips behind the sheer curtain and presses her fingertips to the cool glass. There is a padlock on the door—on every door of the house, in fact ("a temporary precaution". Blood Mother says)—but Verity does not try to escape. Even if she did, where would she go?

The yard is a dark impression upon an even darker night. The moon is hidden behind the clouds, but Verity's night vision is exceptional. She can still see the deer nosing around the flower garden at the edge of the woods, where the trees meet cut grass. She can see the twitch of its ear as it listens to the distant sounds of traffic. Verity watches the deer eat every last tulip and daffodil before it springs off, swallowed whole by the forest.

Verity's hearing is quite exceptional as well. While she is watching the deer, she is also listening to the slippery sounds of Blood Sister Grace as she creeps down the stairs and into the living room.

"What are you doing?" Grace asks, her voice just above a secret.

Verity parts the curtain to speak to Grace, but does not fully emerge from behind it. "Looking," she says.

"At what?" Grace asks.

Verity thinks about the question. *Looking* is an activity that encompasses many things. Besides, Verity was looking with her heart as much as her eyes, and how could she even begin to describe that with words to someone like Grace?

Apparently, she takes longer than is acceptable to answer, because Grace gets impatient and moves on. "Can I ask you something?" She steps down into the family room and plops onto the oversized ottoman. "Do you remember me?" she asks, raising her voice just enough to shake it free of her whisper. "At all?"

What Verity remembers is not Blood Sister Grace. She remembers fear; her fat little hand melded into someone else's fat little hand; kneeling on something unsteady in a dark cramped space; a cage full of knees and elbows and bated breath; and then, an emptiness. A longing. She is not certain whether that is a true memory, or merely a nightmare she has carried with her for as long as she can remember.

"In a way," Verity says. She slumps down to sit on the carpeted floor, pressing her toes together, one after the other, in an eerily dexterous motion that makes Grace look away.

"In *what* way?" Grace asks.

Verity lifts her eyes to her. "Like staring at the sun. Like an afterglow."

Grace's brow wrinkles. "What the hell does that mean?"

Verity's brow wrinkles, too. Her sisters would have understood. She knew how to talk to them. To Mother. She knew which words fit into the waiting places in their minds. She thinks Rhi understands that language, too. But Grace does not seem able to hear it in the first place.

"I do not remember you," Verity says.

Grace's eye twitches.

"But I think I remember feeling the absence of you."

Blood Sister Grace looks down at her hands. "For how long?" Her voice is a whisper again.

Verity searches her mind, but the memory is not there. "I do not know."

Grace chews on the inside of her cheek for a moment. "I remember when you were taken. I was the only one who saw him take you."

"You saw Mother?" Verity asks, her heart thumping harder in her chest.

"He *kidnapped* you, Verity. Don't you *get* that?" Grace looks into her sister's eyes. "Don't you *understand*?"

Verity rolls onto her feet in a smooth, agile motion, her hands clenched into fists at her sides. Slowly, she releases her fingers, lets them dangle limp and buzzing. "It is late," she says in a stiff voice. "We should be asleep."

Grace looks wounded. If Verity had seen that expression on her sisters' faces, she would have felt it like a bone spear to the heart. But she feels nothing now but a niggling sensation in her insides, a squirming, nauseating thing that she cannot bear to look at. Not yet.

Maybe not ever.

"It was one of Mom's friends," Grace says sharply. "I guess you don't remember, but Mom used to be into some really bad shit. She's been sober since you were taken. But I recognized him." She looks at the ceiling, avoiding Verity's gaze. "There was a party one night, and one of her friends came in and took you." Grace frowns. "It could have just as easily been me, but your crib was closer to the door."

"What did he look like?" Verity asks, a sour feeling winding through her stomach. "The man who took me?"

Grace shrugs. "Short, pale, brown hair. He'd been at the apartment lots of times."

"Short?" Verity asks. "Shorter than us?"

"Yeah. He was way shorter than Mom, at least."

Verity exhales loudly. "That was not Mother," she says, relieved. "Mother was taller than me."

"*Okay* . . . then he must have given you to someone else. The point is, *I* remember the night you were taken. And *you* don't remember a thing."

"Does that anger you?"

"Yeah!" Grace says, raising her voice. "All these years I've worried about you, mourned you, imagined the worst. And you didn't even remember us. You *miss* the person who took you."

"That was not Mother—"

"But he *still took you away*," Grace says bitterly. "And you'd still rather be with him than with us."

Verity shakes her head imperceptibly. She has been playacting Blood Daughter and Blood Sister long enough that she no longer knows *what* she wants from this world, or this life. Once upon a time, her purpose had been clear. Her desires had been clear. But now . . .

"I just want to be with my sisters," Verity says, quietly.

"But that doesn't include *me*, does it?" Grace says, her eyes shining with tears.

Verity does not know how to answer.

Dr. Mariposa Ibanez's iCloud > Notes

PRIVATE: The Girls

Sunder walked into today's session loudly clomping her cast on the floor and complaining that she doesn't need it anymore. It's only been two months since they set her fracture, and the doctors said it would take 4-6 months to heal, MINIMUM. But sure enough, when they examined her, they said (with about as much shock as I felt) the cast can come off early. They cut it off right then and there.

I've seen a lot of unexpected things in this hospital, but this is . . . something else. Or maybe it's nothing. Maybe she's just young and heals quickly. Maybe the ER doctors misdiagnosed the injury to begin with. But I can't help but think about when the girls were in the psych ward with me, how every evening they would kneel around Sunder, performing some sort of healing ritual or "meditation," as Rhi explained to me.

I'm not sure what to do with these observations. My colleagues would laugh me into oblivion at best, and take away my license at worst.

But I can't help but think of the faith healings my grandmother used to go to, or the Qigong "miracle" videos my mother sends me from time to time. I'm a woman of science, but that doesn't mean I think we have nothing left to discover. What is the saying? "Any sufficiently advanced science will look like magic"? Something like that. Maybe magic is a science we have yet to break ground on.

I suspect these girls could teach us more than we realize.

17

OBLIVIENNE IS THE FIRST TO be placed into foster care.
Muriel Lynch is a semiretired psychiatric nurse, and the girls'
caseworker, Shelly Vance, thinks Mrs. Lynch and her husband, who
owns a small travel agency downtown, will be good caretakers for a
girl who has a tendency to isolate herself, frequently has insomnia, and
sometimes refuses to leave her bed for days.

Oblivienne has no feelings about Mrs. Lynch or her disinterested
husband, Mr. Lynch. It is the other foster children who have her
attention.

There are two small boys who both harass and ignore Oblivienne
from the moment she walks in the door. They howl at her in a poor
imitation of wolves, making each other laugh. Besides the boys, she
shares a bedroom with an older girl named Allison, who keeps everything locked away in boxes and drawers, even locking the door on her
wardrobe so that Oblivienne cannot be tempted to "borrow"
anything.

"It's not personal," Allison explains. "I've just been burned by
roommates before. And foster parents." She tosses her mass of curly
brown hair as she dabs something shiny to her lips. Allison is

seventeen, tall in a way that reminds Oblivienne of cattails, wears glasses with thick blue frames, and frequently asks questions about Oblivienne's life *before*.

"What was it like living out there?" Allison had asked the first night, sitting cross-legged on her bed, watching Oblivienne unpack her few belongings. "Weren't you ever scared?"

"Rarely. Mother . . ." Oblivienne hesitates. Mother may have lied about some things, but he always took care of them. Didn't he? "Mother kept us safe. He made sure our home was secure against predators and—"

"Hold up. You've gotta explain something to me. Why do you guys call him *Mother* if he was a dude? Shouldn't you call him *Father*? I mean, I'm not the gender police or anything, but . . . it's just kind of weird."

Oblivienne does not understand why that is weird. "We did not call him *our* mother," she says, hoping to offer clarity. "His *name* was Mother. At least . . . that is the only name he ever gave us. It is the name he gave himself when he came to this world." The words—*came to this world*—which once seemed so normal to her, now feel clumsy on her lips, heavy with the doubt that has infested Oblivienne's mind like so much rot.

"Riiight," Allison says. She leans back, arms behind her on the bed, nodding. "I guess that makes as much sense as anything else. So, are you trying to find your real mother and father now?"

"Agent Tyler said there were no DNA matches in their database"—more words Oblivienne had not understood until recently—"so it would be up to my family to come forward now. If they are still alive."

Allison laughs. "Oh, you've *had* family come forward," she says, raising curled fingers in the air when she says *family*. "A case like this brings all the nutjobs out. People are *obsessed*. Look." She taps a little rhythm against the screen of her phone before showing Oblivienne.

r/WildGirlsofHappyValley

valley_of_wolves · 24 days ago

Read First: Posting Rules & Everything We Know So Far

Odd_cRavings · 1 day ago

Theory: Mother was a child trafficker who had a psychotic break when the guilt got to him

valley_of_wolves · 1 day ago

CNY ties to the "burned-over district," a prime spot for cult activity

midnightsnax · 1 day ago

(IMG) Oblivienne looks just like my neighbor's daughter who ran away 3 yrs ago

aurtisticmystic · 2 days ago

(IMG) Possible match for Epiphanie?

SpecialMandelaFX · 2 days ago

(IMG) Ran the composite sketch of "Mother" through AI and it turned him into elderly Taika Waititi

SeriousGoose · 2 days ago

Theory: the girls are just runaways and the bones are some poor homeless dude

Odd_cRavings · 2 days ago

What do we know about the park rangers at the wildlife preserve?

aurtisticmystic · 3 days ago

(IMG) Little girl in this missing poster looks just like Oblivienne, but I think she's half Japanese?

Oblivienne looks at Allison with surprise. "What is this?"

Allison laughs. "Do you mean Reddit, or the internet?"

"Who is . . . writing those words?"

"They're posts," Allison says. "People have a lot of theories about how you guys ended up out there. They're fascinated by you and your sisters. You're our generation's JonBenet Ramsey, only this time the girls might be the murderers."

Oblivienne narrows her eyes.

"Do you really not know how insane your story is?" Allison sighs and pushes herself upright. She holds up her hand and starts counting on her fingers. "For one, y'all lived in the woods for the last . . . who knows how many years, and no one ever found you until that Rhiannon girl. Two, you were raised by a man who, according to this article I read, told you that he was a prophet, which just screams 'cult.' Three, aside from Verity, they still haven't found any DNA matches on any of you in any forensic databases, aside from some like seventh-cousin-three-times-removed-level shared DNA, which means almost nothing. Which means three of you were never even reported missing when you were kidnapped. What are the odds? Like, did he have something on your parents? Did they *give* you to him?"

Kidnapped. That word again. Is that what Mother did to them?

Oblivienne does not like the way she feels when Allison asks her so many questions, but it does get her mind working. She has questions of her own—questions she needs to ask herself and her sisters. Questions she is desperate to find the answers to.

Oblivienne is overwhelmed and confused, but she glimpses a hopeful light to follow, like the first star in the sky at dusk. She knows a little bit about the internet from the children at the group home, but she does not know how to get to it or use it.

"*Where* are people asking these questions?" she asks sharply—urgently. "What is *Reddit*? Can you show me?"

Allison's smile fades a little at Oblivienne's brittle intensity. Oblivienne leans forward, almost over the other girl, and despite being much smaller, she knows she is starting to make Allison nervous.

"Yeah, yeah, okay," Allison says, scooting away and climbing off the bed. "Let's borrow Mom's laptop. I'll show you how to . . . *use the internet*, I guess."

Oblivienne enters the bedroom a few days later in search of Allison. Allison is lying on her stomach in bed, gazing into her phone, which is emitting a tinny electric song. She does not acknowledge Oblivienne, but Oblivienne knows she is just distracted. Phones seem to make people very distracted.

Oblivienne takes a seat, cross-legged, on her own bed. "Do you know about . . . *podcasts*?"

Allison snorts without looking at Oblivienne, sliding her thumb along the screen of her phone. "You're really getting deep into Reddit, huh? They *love* podcasts on there." She bobs her feet in the air to the beat of the song, pristine and pink, not a scar in sight.

Oblivienne shrugs and looks down at her own feet, still stained brown from a lifetime of being barefoot, but cleaner and softer now than she has ever seen them. She flexes her toes one by one.

"Ugh, I hate it when you do that," Allison says.

When Oblivienne looks up, Allison is watching her, phone temporarily forgotten. "There's something so . . . *off* about it." She makes a disgusted face, then laughs when she sees the hurt on Oblivienne's face. "Hey, don't take it personally. So you're a bit of a freak. So what? Embrace it."

Oblivienne tucks her feet under her bottom. She suddenly feels itchy in the black cotton T-shirt she is wearing, like the collar is too tight around her throat.

Allison sighs dramatically and drops her phone. "So why do you want to know about podcasts? You want to listen to one? My friends back in Camden have a great podcast about horror movies. Ooh, we could watch the movies first and I could use them as, like, teaching tools or whatever. I'll have you civilized in no time."

Oblivienne twitches at the word *civilized*. "I—no. Well, yes. There is a podcast I would like to listen to. It is about what happened to my sisters and me."

Allison nods. "Ah, okay. There are like a million podcasts about that."

"I have been asked to be *on* it."

"For real?" Allison asks. But then the excitement on her face melts into worry. "Have you been *posting* on Reddit? Oblivienne, Mom said you should only *look* on the internet for now, and while she's a little uptight about these things, I think she's probably right in this case. There are still so many people who are obsessed—and I mean that in the literal, scary way—with the story of the Wild Girls, there could be stalkers out there, or people who would like to be stalkers if they could find out where you live. Like, you have no idea how many questions I still get about you from other kids at school. It's actually really annoying."

"I *know* about names—I would not give mine away," Oblivienne says firmly, summoning the confidence that she used to feel in the wilderness. "I have hidden under a *username*. I told the Reddit people I was a foster child in the same house as one of the . . . *Wild Girls.*" She does not like to use that title, but she has begun to grow numb to it after hours and hours of reading through articles and posts that consolidate the complexity of her family into two words.

Allison raises an eyebrow. She twists and swings her legs over the bed, climbing to her feet. "You'd better show me what you've posted. And *then* we can talk about the podcast. Do you *want* to be interviewed? Haven't y'all been *avoiding* the press?"

Oblivienne is not sure how to answer that. Just like with Agent Tyler, she wants to help the people who are still seeking answers. But Agent Tyler—the FBI—all the officers who had interviewed the girls at the start have not reached out in weeks, leaving Oblivienne adrift in a sea of questions. She needs the help of someone who has infinitely more understanding of how this world works if she wants to find answers, and that might mean letting herself be interviewed. But Oblivienne also knows that her story is not wholly her own. If she shares it with the world, she is doing so for all her sisters, too. It is not a choice to make lightly.

"I want to find out who Mother was," Oblivienne says, her voice much smaller than it had been moments ago. "And who we were before the wilderness. Who we could have been if none of it had ever happened."

Allison's face goes soft. "Yeah. I bet you do," she says. She pats Oblivienne's arm. "Come on. Show me the posts you made as a very normal foster child who happens to live with a Wild Girl of Happy Valley. I'm sure they're very convincing."

18

Sunder is the second girl to be fostered out, much to the surprise of the entire staff at the group home. Sunder has the most violent tendencies, the most stubborn nature of all her sisters. But these things only helped her find a placement, for as soon as she was listed as an "elevated needs" foster case, the choice of foster parents was narrowed for her.

The caseworker, Shelly, escorts Sunder to the front porch of a massive brick house located at the end of a long driveway, far from the main road, surrounded by fields and pastures. She has not yet noticed that Sunder took her shoes off in the car.

"So, are you nervous to meet your foster family?" Shelly asks before ringing the doorbell.

Sunder is very nervous to meet more strangers, but she is also very calm, because she knows it does not matter—that someday soon, though she is not exactly sure when, the portal to Leutheria will open, and she will be with her sisters again.

But there is no time for her to answer, even if she had intended to, before an older pale-skinned woman with two long gray braids opens the door wide with an exclamatory "Hello!"

"Oh!" Shelly jumps. "Hello, Mrs. Quaker."

"Oh, my, you must be our girl. Sunder, is that right? Am I pronouncing it correctly?" She clutches both hands to her ample chest, over a white-dusted apron stitched together from squares of old blue fabric.

Sunder nods.

"Well then, welcome! Welcome, both of you. Please, come in."

Inside, the farmhouse is all dark timeworn wood, thickly waxed or polished to a dull shine. The rooms are clean but cluttered, with lots of small tables and armchairs, cabinets and shelves, framed photographs, artwork, and harvest festival posters from years past. On the shelves, there are all kinds of things: old metal toys, potted plants, dried flowers, hand-carved soap figurines, lopsided homemade clay bowls, crystal vases. And there are *books*—so many books. An entire wall of books in one room, with even more books piled onto other shelf-like spaces, everywhere Sunder looks.

As Sunder walks into the carpeted room, an old white man in overalls stands up from the sofa. He has sun-darkened skin and closely cropped gray hair.

"Sunder, this is Jack, or Mr. Quaker, whichever you prefer," Mrs. Quaker says.

Mr. Quaker offers a leathery hand and says with a smile, "Welcome to our home. We're so happy to have you."

Sunder knows this greeting ritual. She puts her hand in his and shakes it.

"And this is Dallas," Mrs. Quaker says, gesturing to the young man standing behind the couch with tanned skin and curly black hair. "He's been with us going on two years now."

"Pleased to meet you," Dallas says as he shakes her hand, his serious brown eyes the same rich color as the glossy woodwork around him.

"And this," Mrs. Quaker says, "is our precious Giovanna."

A girl, maybe about ten or twelve, scampers over to Sunder. She stops a few feet in front of her and smiles.

Sunder is struck by Giovanna's bone-pale skin and beautiful auburn hair, done up in a circlet of braids. There is something about the placement of her eyes, the flatness of her profile, the shortened neck, that mark her from the rest. Sunder does not fear this difference, though. It only leaves her curious.

Sunder starts to reach to shake her hand, but is confused when Giovanna looks at the floor, pinches the sides of her dress, and holds the skirt up a few inches, while crossing her ankles and bending her knees.

"Pleased to make your acquaintance, Sunder," Giovanna says. Sunder notices her voice is unique, the words coming softly and slowly.

Sunder nods at Giovanna, then looks around at everyone in the room, smiling politely as she has learned to do. Rhi has taught her about the importance of manners: how even though it is a waste of words, it is a form of reassurance among strangers. *Like offering your belly to a baby mountain lion so it will let you stroke its fur when it comes near?* Sunder had asked. *Exactly like that*, Rhi had replied.

"Hello," Sunder says. "It is nice to meet you all."

Dallas's eyes widen. "She speaks perfect English!"

"Dallas, please," Mrs. Quaker says.

"What? I heard she was feral, not—"

Giovanna shoves him hard. "Stop talking, Dallas. You're embarrassing yourself."

Dallas chuckles and smiles at Giovanna, then more sheepishly, he smiles at Sunder. "My apologies."

Sunder's face tightens with annoyance. She has heard this kind of exclamation before, from the children at the group home. At first, she believed their shock was genuine, but gradually Sunder realized they were mocking her sisters and her. She glares at Dallas until he raises his hands in submission.

"Seriously," he says. "It was an honest mistake. Won't happen again, I promise."

Sunder looks him in the eyes, both aware of and unconcerned with the thick tension in the room, and decides she believes him. She relaxes and turns to find a seat on the shaggy brown rug. Sunder takes a handful of cookies set out on the low table and bites one tentatively. Giovanna goes to sit near her, choosing a yellow armchair.

"So, Mr. and Mrs. Quaker," the caseworker says when the room begins to breathe again, "you've read her file?"

"Yes," Mr. Quaker says. "And we've gone over some of the more delicate points with Dallas and Giovanna."

"Then you know Sunder has had the most difficulty adjusting in the group home, but as you've just seen, she's quieted down. There are no concerns of pathological tendencies, just behavioral. She lived a life without inhibition before, which—"

"Yes, we read the file," Mrs. Quaker repeats. "We have no doubt Sunder can be happy here. We think the order and routine of life on our farm can help her adjust to her new life while keeping her close to the natural world. Isn't that right, dear?"

Mr. Quaker nods, looking kindly at Sunder as she shoves a fourth cookie into her mouth.

"I bet Sunder will love the ponies," Giovanna says excitedly. "Can I show them to her?"

Mrs. Quaker chuckles. "In good time, my dear," she says.

Sunder is not sure what ponies are, but the way Giovanna lights up makes her curious to see if she does, in fact, love them.

"Maybe your friends can come see the ponies, too," Giovanna says. "You must miss them a lot."

"Not friends," Sunders says, swallowing the last of the cookie. "Sisters."

"Well," Mrs. Quaker says. "We know how close you are with your sisters, so we'll make sure you can keep in touch. Dallas here knows how to use all the modern technology the kids use to communicate."

"I'd be happy to show you how to use video chat," Dallas says, clearly eager to make amends for his earlier words. "So you can see and talk to your sisters whenever you want."

"That would be good," Sunder says solemnly. "I must remind my sisters to watch the moon. We are waiting for an eclipse."

"Well," Mr. Quaker says with a chuckle. "You might not have to wait too long. I believe there's a lunar eclipse coming up this summer that will be visible right here in Happy Valley. My old almanac can tell you about things like that. I'll show it to you later if you'd like."

Sunder stares at Mr. Quaker, riveted. *This summer?*

"Sunder, how old are you?" Giovanna asks.

When Sunder does not reply, eager to ask Mr. Quaker more questions, Shelly answers for her. "The doctors think she may be anywhere from twelve to sixteen years of age."

Annoyed, Sunder corrects the caseworker. "I spent thirteen winters in the wilderness."

"I'm *twelve* years old," Giovanna offers with pride.

Sunder remembers then that people in this world sometimes ask questions as an offering of friendship and peace, and that they like to have questions asked of them; curiosity means appreciation, which Sunder can understand, even if she would rather ask to see Mr. Quaker's almanac now. There will be time for that later, she supposes.

"Have you . . . lived here . . . long?" Sunder tries on a question.

"Since I was seven. The Quakers legally adopted me last year."

Mrs. Quaker nods. "Giovanna is our daughter in every way but blood. Like your sisters are your sisters in every way but blood. The bond you have with the other girls is extraordinary, Sunder. *And* it's something to be cherished."

Sunder feels the heart of Mrs. Quaker's words and is surprised. No one but Rhi has done anything but try to pull her sisters apart since they left the wilderness.

Living with this pack may not be the worst thing after all, she decides.

At least until the portal to Leutheria opens.

19

SHORTLY AFTER SUNDER LEAVES THE group home, Epiphanie is finally placed in foster care. Shelly, their caseworker, said it was important that Epiphanie be placed with a Black foster family, if possible, so Epiphanie can spend time with people who understand what it is like to be Black in America (the kingdom they are in, apparently) and who would be more attuned to supporting Epiphanie's transition into society.

Dr. Ibanez had explained that Epiphanie shares an *ethnicity* with other Black people that her sisters do not. Of course, Epiphanie knows that her skin is significantly darker than her sisters', but what surprises her is the discovery that here, she has a different culture and different needs from her sisters, simply because of the color of her skin.

"Being Mexican American, I know a little of what that's like," Dr. Ibanez had said. "I'm a different shade of brown than you are, a different culture and ethnicity, with a different history in this country. But I've had to work twice as hard as my white colleagues to get where I am today. Our experiences have been different, and will be different, but because of the color of our skin, we do share something your sisters will probably never have to deal with." She smiled thoughtfully. "But it's not just the difficult things. There is so much to celebrate about being Black and brown. I love my culture and my community, and my hope is that your foster family can help you embrace your identity, too. I'm sure you have a lot of questions, and you'll have more as time goes on. But know that I'm here to help you process."

"I am . . . confused, more than anything," Epiphanie had told her. Confused, conflicted, overwhelmed—that was true about a lot of things these days.

In the wilderness, the rich black-brown of her skin had always been obvious to them all, but no more noteworthy than Oblivienne's sleek black hair, or Verity's height, or Sunder's mismatched eye color—something unique and beautiful to each of them. The way that Shelly and Dr. Ibanez speak about Epiphanie makes her feel suddenly *apart* from her sisters, and this, more than the physical distance, feels like a true separation.

What should this new culture mean to Epiphanie if she is fated for Leutheria? Except Epiphanie does not even know if she still believes in Leutheria, even if she wants to, more than ever.

As it turns out, Shelly had not been able to find a Black foster family in Happy Valley, or even in the townships beyond. "This is a very white part of the state," she had explained, a note of apology in her voice.

And so Epiphanie, more fearful and confused than she would have been if they had never mentioned anything to her about her race at all, had been placed with Maggie, a kind but frazzled white woman who also cares for six other foster children full time. Epiphanie is not the only Black foster child in the home, so Shelly is happy with that.

That first day, the house is filled with the sound of wailing. Epiphanie follows the cries to the small nursery, where she finds Maggie trying to rock a very small, very unhappy baby to sleep.

"He will be okay," Maggie insists when she sees Epiphanie's concern. "The doctors think he's just depressed. He's only six months old. Can you imagine being this small and being depressed?" She looks exhausted even when she smiles. "His name is Romeo. Say hi, Romeo!" She tries waving the boy's tiny hand, but he scrunches up his already wrinkly pinkish-brown face and threatens a toothless scream.

The boy is tinier and more fragile than any human Epiphanie has ever seen, even more so than when Oblivienne had come to the castle. Oblivienne had been old enough to crawl then, but so nervous and thin-limbed, she had looked more like a baby bird, hunched there on hands and knees, clinging to Mother's robes.

"May I help in any way?" Epiphanie asks.

"Oh, you sweet girl," Maggie says as something crashes in the living room, making the baby wail louder.

Epiphanie goes to see what the noise was, and finds the three next youngest children looking shocked, standing beside a short, toppled bookcase. As she helps the children replace the bookcase and the books, she thinks to herself: *Alita is Black like me. Simon is Black like me. Olivia is white like my sisters.* She glances at the two older boys in the kitchen and thinks, *Caleb is Black like me. Bradley is white like my sisters.* She is annoyed suddenly, because both are old enough to be taking care of these younger children.

Caleb looks at her, catching on to her irritation. He laughs, a short unhumorous laugh. "Hey, it's not our job to babysit them. It's not *your* job, either." He gives her a meaningful look that she knows she does not fully understand.

Epiphanie has always been a natural leader with a keen eye for what is needed, so after two weeks, she's dug her way into a necessary, if not comfortable, position in the household. It is easy for her to take on responsibility when she is not completing the workbooks assigned by their behavioral therapist, or the workbooks assigned by their tutor, or talking to her sisters on the phone and on video chat.

Now, Epiphanie is waiting for Rhi to pick her up and take her to Sunder's foster family home, where the sisters will be reunited for the first time since the hospital. All the doctors and therapists and people in charge have finally decided the girls have "settled in" enough to be able to visit one another. Epiphanie overheard Maggie discussing this visit with Dr. Ibanez on the phone, and they agree that Rhi is "a good influence on them." The cloying pressure of so many opinions on who they can and cannot see makes Epiphanie so mad sometimes, she feels like she could howl. But there is always so much for her to do in this new home, so many younger ones to steer away from accidents and harm, Epiphanie hardly has time to properly feel anything.

When Maggie lets Rhi in the front door and turns to call for Epiphanie, tiny Romeo bundled in her arms, Epiphanie is already in the entryway, having left the younger children occupied with the television, Bradley scoffing at her request to mind them. She goes awkwardly through the motions of preparing to leave the house: sticking her arms into a jacket, fumbling her feet into sandals. Her hair is in fresh box braids that Maggie sent Alita and Epiphanie to a salon to get done, because "white women don't know how to do Black women's hair." Epiphanie enjoyed the experience. The woman at the salon was gentle, and if she closed her eyes, she could almost pretend it was her sisters braiding her hair like they did in the forest.

Maggie tries to insist that Epiphanie put on sneakers instead, but Epiphanie's shoulders slump when she looks at the clunky shoes her foster mother purchased for her, sitting on the shoe rack, still bound together by a little plastic loop.

Rhi notices and says to Maggie, "It's going to be warm out this afternoon. The sandals might be the better choice."

Maggie presses her lips together but gives in. "Have a good day, sweetheart," she says, leaning in to side hug Epiphanie goodbye.

Epiphanie smiles gratefully and leans into the hug. She does not resist Maggie's kindly contact like she used to. She waves a finger in goodbye to Romeo, who laughs at her before she turns to leave with Rhi.

They walk up to an unfamiliar, small, beat-up blue truck in the driveway.

"Uncle Jimmy bought it off a friend of his so I could drive myself around this summer while he's at work," Rhi explains. "It's nothing special, but it's nice to have my own transportation. Hop in."

Epiphanie climbs into the truck and buckles in. She has gotten used to riding in motor vehicles by now, something that seemed unfathomable a mere moon ago.

"How have you been, Epiphanie?" Rhi asks once they get on the road. "Maggie says you've been adapting well?"

Epiphanie looks at the sleeves of her jacket and the plastic thongs of her sandals and is alarmed to realize that she *is* adapting, if only to avoid conflict. She does not eat with her hands anymore. She wears clothes that cover her body in places she never felt the need to cover before. She engages in polite conversation as a means of ritualistic calming, like trying to soothe bear cubs by tossing them scraps of meat.

"I am tired," Epiphanie says finally. She finds it exhausting to constantly think about *how* she interacts with the world: where she is looking, what her face is doing, whether she is allowed to move or is expected to remain still. She finds it exhausting to be so aware of herself.

In the wilderness, she just *was*. Her sisters just *were*. They lived their lives with minimal effort, only instinct and understanding. They built fires when they were cold and swam in the creek when they were warm. They ate when they were hungry and drank when they were thirsty, slept when they were tired and woke when they were finished dreaming. They spoke when they had something that needed to be said, which was not often. They played when they were feeling playful, and listened to the rhythms of their bodies, of the earth, of the sky, and let the rhythms sway them into movement, into action, into rest.

It seems to Epiphanie that the way of this world is to disconnect from all that is easy and natural. Cover your body so it cannot feel the sun's rays or the shadows of clouds or the sparkle of starlight. Cover your feet so they cannot touch the sacred earth or feel the running of the deer in the woods or the worms in the dirt. Strip the oils from your body so all record of your day is lost, so that you are unnaturally clean and unprotected, then protect yourself with things that come from a plastic tube or bottle. Eat by the clock, sleep by the clock, wake by the clock.

"That's not surprising," Rhi says gently. "I can't imagine how stifling it must be, even now that you're in a home where you have more freedom."

Epiphanie is grateful for Rhi's guidance, who understands how this world works, but also how it is broken.

"Freedom is not something we had a word for, before," Epiphanie says as Rhi turns the truck down a long, winding driveway and begins driving up to the brick house, past the livestock grazing in the fields and tossing their tails. "It was just how we lived. We may no longer be caged or medicated now, but we are not free. I fear we may never truly be free again."

Rhi stays silent as she parks her truck beside another truck—this one huge and red—and turns off the engine. She stares ahead at nothing, a dark cloud descending upon her.

"I don't think I've ever been free," she whispers.

"I do not believe you have ever been free, either," Epiphanie agrees sadly.

Rhi looks up at her, eyes glistening. "Do you miss Mother?"

"All the time."

"Even though he"—she hesitates—"may have lied to you?"

Epiphanie cocks her head. "I do not believe he lied. I believe he meant every word, even if they no longer seem true. I believe he was motivated by real love for us." She is not sure how to explain how her mind has reshaped itself around the idea of Leutheria. Where before her reality had been neatly defined by Mother's stories and her own lack of experience, reality now seems softer, hazier, like the gray blindness of dusk.

"How can you be so certain he loved you?" Rhi asks, looking away.

"By the way he made us feel," Epiphanie answers. "Safe. And powerful."

Rhi wipes something from her eyes and Epiphanie realizes, not for the first time, that Rhi is nursing a wound so deep it will kill her if she does not pull back the bandage and look at it properly.

She wants to ask Rhi about it, but then Sunder is at Epiphanie's door, screaming and yanking it open and hauling Epiphanie out of the truck so that Sunder can embrace her with all her might. Verity is there too, and since Sunder will not let go, Verity wraps her arms around them both and kisses her sister on the cheek with a laugh and a smile.

Behind them, an older woman steps out through the front door of the house, onto the porch, wiping her hands on her apron, smiling as she watches the girls. Oblivienne stands next to her, eyes shifting away from them like a cornered animal. She looks almost . . . guilty.

Over Sunder's head, Epiphanie studies Oblivienne, burrowing into her heart.

What has her sister done?

20

MRS. QUAKER FEEDS THE FIVE of them a lunch of roasted chicken and braised vegetables in the dining room, but the girls do not speak much while they eat. They are too focused on recalling what they have learned about table manners and cutlery to think of anything to say. And in Oblivienne's case, she is distracted. She knows what she has to tell them will be difficult to hear.

It is only later, in the stables, among the sweet stench of animals and hay and manure, when Sunder is showing her sisters how to brush the horses and begins to talk about how much she wishes they could take the horses with them to Leutheria when the portal opens, that Oblivienne knows she must speak.

"I have decided to be on a podcast," she says.

They all look at her with trepidation. Her sisters know what a podcast is—she has explained, during stilted video calls, what she had learned on the internet about *true crime podcasts*, specifically the ones following the case of the "Wild Girls of Happy Valley."

"Why?" Epiphanie asks.

"I spoke to a man who is trying to figure out where we came from and why Mother took us," Oblivienne says. "I would also like to know those things."

"Oblivienne," Rhi says, concerned. "Literally anyone can make a podcast. Are you sure you want to trust a complete stranger with presenting your story to the world?"

"He is not a complete stranger." Oblivienne brushes the golden horse in front of her slowly. "We have been speaking for several weeks. On Reddit."

Rhi looks alarmed, but before she can say more, Sunder cuts in, more shocked than angry. "So you have completely abandoned Mother?"

Oblivienne purses her lips. She has stopped brushing the horse and it is nuzzling her arm, trying to get her to start again.

"I am not abandoning Mother. I just want to know who he was. Before he was Mother."

"What does it matter?" Sunder asks, raising her voice.

The golden horse snorts loudly and prances in place, suddenly nervous.

"Because if it turns out he really was just a man from *this* world, then . . . well. We will know for sure. That Mother lied. And Leutheria is a lie. And the magic he taught us was just a trick . . . and our whole lives—"

"How can you speak like this?" Sunder snaps, throwing her brush on the barn floor. "And how can you *listen*?" She glares at Oblivienne, at Verity and Epiphanie, then bolts away from them, through the barn doors, into the streaming afternoon sunlight.

She passes a young man on her way out: tan skinned and dark featured, clad in jeans and a black cotton shirt with the sleeves cut off. He watches Sunder with a creased brow as she goes.

"Should I be concerned about that?" the boy wonders, looking at Rhi.

The girls are silent. Oblivienne regrets causing her sister pain, but she refuses to hide the truth from her, either. The horses stamp and fling their heads back, snorting with anticipation.

"Calm down, ladies," the boy murmurs, putting both hands out, palms down. When Oblivienne gives him a perturbed look, he says, "Oh, I was talking to the horses, not you girls. Sorry. Name's Dallas. I'm Sunder's foster brother."

Rhi takes the lead, wipes her hands on her jeans. "Right. Sorry, Dallas. This is Verity, Oblivienne, and Epiphanie." She gestures to each of them in turn.

"Ah, the other princesses," Dallas says, grinning.

"Perhaps," Verity says.

"And perhaps not," Oblivienne finishes.

Dallas approaches the chestnut mare Rhi has been brushing, pulling a carrot from his pocket.

"I do not know if it is wise to trust these podcast people," Epiphanie says quietly, leaning close to Oblivienne.

"Who else can we go to?" Oblivienne asks, pushing away the urgency that wants to flood her voice. "Agent Tyler has given up. Dr. Ibanez keeps telling us we may never know who Mother really was."

"You're right," Rhi says warily. "But you still need to be careful, Oblivienne. People on the internet can be . . . untrustworthy. And weird. Most of them just want the tawdry details. Elizabeth Smart was rescued over twenty years ago and people are *still* asking her about it."

"Who is Elizabeth Smart?" Verity asks.

"Mother did not do that to us," Oblivienne says quickly, loudly, clutching the bristles of the horse brush to her chest. She has read about Elizabeth Smart and her kidnappers and all about the "tawdry details" of that case. "Mother never—*never* . . ."

Epiphanie puts her hand on Oblivienne's back and Rhi steps toward her, taking her gently by the arms.

"I know, Oblivienne," Rhi assures her. "But the podcast people . . . they will want more than just stories about making friends with wolves."

"Don't know why," Dallas says, pulling out a second carrot from his back pocket and feeding it to the golden mare. "I think your story is fascinating enough on its own without any embellishment."

Rhi cocks an eyebrow at him. "But no one is entitled to it," she says firmly, then looks at Oblivienne. "And it's not just your story, Oblivienne."

Oblivienne looks at Epiphanie and Verity. "Will you be angry with me if I tell our story, Sisters?"

Verity looks to Epiphanie for guidance, just as they have all, always done.

"You must follow your heart, Sister," Epiphanie says, taking Oblivienne's hand. "But you may not like where it leads you."

21

R HI AND THE OTHERS HAVE been looking for Sunder for almost twenty minutes when Dallas thinks to try Giovanna's bedroom. When they enter, Giovanna is lying on the carpeted floor, looking at the ceiling, talking loudly about the book of fairies she has been reading.

"More girls!" she exclaims as she sits up. "Dallas, you and Dad are way outnumbered now."

"I'll just have to find a way to bear it." Dallas sighs with a grin. "Is Sunder here?"

"No," Giovanna says, glancing under her bed.

"Then who're you talking to?" Dallas asks.

"Fairies." Giovanna giggles.

"Sunder," Rhi says gently, kneeling at the foot of the bed. "We'll have to leave soon. Don't you want to spend more time with your sisters?"

After a moment, they hear a loud sigh. Sunder rolls out from under the bed, almost into Giovanna's lap, dragging a huge hardback almanac with her. She pushes herself up on her elbows and looks at her sisters with red-rimmed mismatched eyes.

"Are you still planning to betray Mother?" she asks Oblivienne.

"I am not going to betray him," Oblivienne says, kneeling beside Rhi, before Sunder. She puts a hand on Sunder's cheek, runs her fingers through her little sister's tousled, choppy blonde hair.

"You used to dream about Leutheria just as much as I did," Sunder says, not bothering to brush away the tears starting to trickle from her eyes. "More than that, even. Do you no longer believe at all?"

Rhi finds herself holding her breath, waiting for Oblivienne to answer.

"It is more complicated now, Sister. You know that. Verity's Blood Sister, her Blood Mother—"

"There is an explanation," Sunder insists. "There must be. Maybe there is a version of each of us in both worlds. Maybe it is all a *mistake*. We do not need to *know* how it all works, we only need to have faith in Mother and the things he taught us."

Rhi looks at the others, sees the wrinkle between Verity's eyebrows, the conflict on Epiphanie's face, the pain on Oblivienne's. She is not certain where the girls stand on their destiny these days, but it is clearly not a subject any of them take lightly.

"But *I* need to know," Oblivienne says, so softly it is almost a whisper. She brushes the tears from Sunder's cheeks with her thumb. "I need to know who Mother was before he was ours."

Sunder speaks in a voice so weak it is almost nonexistent. "We already know everything we need to know about him."

Rhi catches herself sharing in Sunder's heartbreak, wishing Oblivienne would stop her search. Not just because she questions the motivations of the podcasters, but because she wants to keep believing in Mother.

Because if he really was a prophet, then I might be the fifth princess. I might have a destiny in another world.

Rhi shakes off the thought before it can take hold because she's already learned: hope can be just as dangerous as anger. She and Oblivienne help Giovanna and Sunder to their feet. As the girls are leaving the bedroom, Rhi points at the large book Sunder is still hugging to her chest.

"Some light reading?" she teases, trying to make Sunder smile.

"This is an almanac," Sunder whispers. "It tells me the phases of the moon and when and where she aligns with the sun and the Earth. I am going to figure out when the portal will appear."

With her heart in her throat, Rhi watches Sunder lay the almanac lovingly on the bed before she runs downstairs, outside, so the sisters can spend the rest of their time together with their bare feet on the earth.

Our Lone Wolf Girl

Excerpted from *Savage Castle:*
A Memoir of the Wild Girls of Happy Valley

WE WERE ALWAYS ONE—A SINGLE pack that moved and thought and felt as one. But we had our separate lives as well.

Mother used to say, "Just as the pack cannot exist without the wolf, the whole cannot be served without the whole individual." We did not quite understand what that meant until many years later, when it was far too late. But he encouraged us to have interior lives distinct from one another, as much as he encouraged us to bond as a pack.

And for the most part, we were successful. Each of us was quite comfortable alone, with nothing but our own thoughts. We often spent hours by ourselves getting lost in the wilderness, fumbling our way home, with nothing but the conjured light of fireflies to guide us. Sunder went alone to visit the wolves, and would sometimes return with injured baby animals that she nursed back to health with warm blankets and incantations; Epiphanie spent hours in meditation or making sculptures out of the clay we gathered from the riverbed, sometimes practical, most often not; Verity spent days floating in the water, composing long stories in her head that she would tell the rest of us by the firepit at night.

Oblivienne spent a great deal of time on her own, but never told us where she went. When we asked, she would say "walking," or "exploring," but she never elaborated beyond that. Sometimes she would return with unusual objects she had found on her wanderings, like glass bottles the color of changing leaves, or gleaming metal circles bigger than her head, that looked like little silver suns (we later learned that these were called *hubcaps*).

One day, several moons after Mother's death, when the freezing time had come again, Oblivienne went out in the snow and did not return before nightfall. It was not uncommon for this to happen, but in the cold, we worried about her. When dawn came, we set out with our wolf-kin to follow her tracks through the snow. After several miles through the forest, we found her higher up the mountain than any of us had any need to go.

She was seated in the middle of five hand-sculpted castles—castles just like *our* castle—each one taller than Oblivienne herself when she was standing. They were made from stones, clay, and mud, but also the vertebrae of large animals and round pieces of the colorful bottles Oblivienne sometimes brought back to the castle. They even shone with the sugared purple and white crystals we sometimes found inside river rocks. Each castle wore a haze of a different color, tinted from the culmination of its various parts: black, green, purple, blue, red. And on top of each castle was a small pile of coins, which we sometimes found at the bottom of the creeks that ran off from the river.

At the center of the ring of castles, Oblivienne had created a mosaic out of pebbles and polished bones, depicting the moon and the sun and thousands of stars in the sky. And between the moon and the sun, there was a big empty circle.

Oblivienne was digging deep down into the circle when we found her.

She knew right away why we were here, even without our words. "I am fine, Sisters. The cold will not harm me."

She patted down her fur-lined vest and long pants, made from the bear carcass we had found by the river last summer—a pelt Mother had cast a spell on to keep us all warm and safe until spring.

We came to embrace her, nonetheless.

"What is this place, Oblivienne?" Epiphanie asked. "Did you create all this?"

She nodded, smiled with pride, and flushed pink. "These are the five kingdoms," she gestured to the castles as the wolf-kin nosed around the structures. "And here are the heavens, meeting the Earth. And here." She tossed a pebble down the hole between the sun and the moon. "This is the portal that will take us back to Leutheria."

We did not need to ask her why she built that place, for the presence of it was pure magic. We did not have the words for it then, but we knew in some way what it was: a shrine. A holy place. Its presence alone justified its existence.

"It is beautiful," Sunder said, her hand hovering over the side of the blue castle, uncertain if her touch would pollute it.

"I started building it years ago," Oblivienne told us. "But finding the right materials took a long time . . . until recently." She bites her lip, looks at each of us before she confesses. "Ever since Mother died, I have been finding treasures everywhere. Shiny metals, and colorful bottles, and perfectly cleaned bones, and so many coins, practically flooding the banks of the river when I come looking for them." She grins, her dark eyes wide and shining. "Mother has been providing for me, even in death. I wanted to tell you—I wanted to *show* you—but I needed to keep this place to myself. Just a little bit longer."

"Have we ruined it for you, Sister?" Epiphanie asked.

Oblivienne took Epiphanie's hand and squeezed. "No. You have helped me finish it. Mother's spirit has guided you here today to tell me it is done."

We looked around in awe, each one of us drawn to a different castle, a different corner of the mosaic, a different piece of the magic of that place.

"What happens now?" Verity wondered.

"I think," Oblivienne said, a little breathless. "It must not be long now."

"Until the heavens meet the Earth?" Sunder asked.

Oblivienne nodded. "Until we are home."

22

WHEN RHI AND UNCLE JIMMY come home after grocery shopping that Sunday, there is a message on the answering machine. Uncle Jimmy presses play on the ancient device and it beeps hideously before an even more horrible sound comes out of the speaker.

"Eden, this is your father."

Rhi freezes in the entryway, one shoe off. Uncle Jimmy's face goes rigid.

"I don't know what's going on with you up there in Happy Valley since you won't visit me, but I keep seeing your face on the news." Her father's voice pauses, and Rhi imagines him frowning, vein bulging on his forehead.

Visit him? What is he talking about? There is no world where Lawrence Chase wants his daughter to visit him in jail (and despite everything she's been through, that fact still skewers through Rhi's insides).

"You're not responding to my lawyer's phone calls or any of our emails or texts, so I thought I'd call you myself. We were granted an appeal, but I need you to take the witness stand this time. It's the least you can do, considering you didn't even show up for my sentencing."

Another pause, this time filled with a sigh. "Look, I know I haven't been the best—I know I didn't handle your mother's death well, and I . . ."

Rhi feels her face scrunch up with rage and forces herself to look away. She's gotten more comfortable with Uncle Jimmy over the last few months, but she doesn't want him to see her like this.

". . . could have done better." Another sigh. Then, more angrily, "You're not the only one who lost someone, you know? Maybe I wasn't always the best father, but I worked long and hard to provide for you, and I think the least you can do to show your appreciation is sit in a chair and explain why your own father doesn't belong behind bars."

Rhi's breaths come fast, shallow, as if her lungs already know how fast she would run to get away from the sound of his voice.

Her father's voice is still speaking, but Rhi doesn't hear the rest as she kicks off her other shoe and strides directly to the guest bedroom. She closes the door and sinks to her knees beside the bed, buries her face in the teal comforter Uncle Jimmy bought her when she first moved in, and tries not to scream.

After a moment, there's a knock at the door and a worried "Rhi?" from the other side. "Can I come in?"

Uncle Jimmy. Rhi recalls the tense look on his face when the message started to play. She stands and smooths the comforter out before she sits on the bed, arms crossed over her chest. "Yeah," she says, heart hammering.

"You okay?" he asks as he opens the door, stepping inside. Purrdita darts in from behind his legs, makes a curious little trilling sound as she rubs her face on the foot of the bed.

Rhi takes a deep breath, tries to breathe through the rage boiling inside her. Anger has never helped her get anywhere—it has only ever caused her pain. Besides, she's not mad at Uncle Jimmy. She doesn't want to take this out on him. She nods, silent, unable to trust her mouth just yet.

"I'm sorry," Uncle Jimmy says. "The lawyer called almost every day when you first came here, but you were in no state to be participating in that trial. You had your own stuff to process, and you were starting a new school, and I could just tell . . . I mean I thought . . . it seemed to me . . ." He stops, his face tight.

It makes Rhi's heart pound even faster.

"It's okay," she says gently, because the anger has transmuted from fisted rage to fluttering panic, and all she can see now is that her uncle is upset. She knows she needs to make him feel better somehow. She softens herself: puts her hands in her lap and widens her eyes, loosens her spine, looks *up* at him instead of just at him. She makes herself small, docile, grateful. She *is* grateful. She needs him to know that, especially with all the chaos she's brought into his life. "Really. It's okay."

"No," Uncle Jimmy says, shaking his head. "I'm not gonna justify it. It was wrong to hide things from you. Because now you've found out, and you won't trust me. And you're right, I haven't earned your trust."

Oh. Rhi blinks. His concern for her feelings shouldn't shock her, and yet it does.

"Uncle Jimmy," Rhi says, letting herself breathe. "I'm not upset with *you.*"

His face widens from contrition to surprise. "You're not?"

Rhi wants to scowl when she imagines her father trying to reach her in those early days, but she neutralizes her face and her voice, speaking almost in a monotone. "No, I'm upset at my father. Did he ever even ask you about how I was handling his arrest? If I had a roof over my head? If I was still going to school?"

Uncle Jimmy comes and sits by Rhi on the bed, rubbing his palms on his jeans. Purrdita starts weaving around their ankles, purring loudly.

"I'll be straight with you, Rhi-Rhi: I don't like Lawrence. I don't think he's a good man, let alone a good father to you."

Rhi scoffs before she can stop herself.

"But that doesn't change the fact that he's your father," Uncle Jimmy continues. "And it fucking sucks to have a father like that."

Rhi startles and looks at him. She's never heard him curse before.

"It's okay to be mad, you know," he says. He jerks his arm in a way that Rhi knows means his instinct is to put his arm around her, but he's stopping himself. She's glad. She doesn't want to be touched right now—

—except she absolutely *does* want to be held, squeezed tightly in someone's loving arms, cradled like a child, have her hair stroked and her mind soothed by the grounding certainty of a body against her own. She wonders if Purrdita senses that as the cat aggressively rubs against Rhi's shin, standing on hind legs to press her face nearly up to Rhi's knee. Rhi desperately scrounges in her brain for memories of her mother's embrace, but when her mother was alive, they were too frequent, not rare enough to hold on to and preserve—until one day, they were gone forever.

"What did my mother ever see in him?" Rhi whispers, bending to pet Purrdita.

Uncle Jimmy sighs. "I don't think he was always this bad. At least, he was good at pretending he wasn't." He twists his mouth to the side, trying to remember. "When I met him, before they got married, I was only maybe ten, eleven years old. They came to visit your grandmother and me here in the valley. He charmed the hell out of your grandmother. Even took me to an arcade for the day; paid for *unlimited* tokens. I liked him, then." He scoffs. "What ten-year-old boy wouldn't?"

Rhi remembers being ten years old. She remembers Kevin coming home from boarding school for spring break and taking her out for ice cream, taking her shopping with his mother's credit card, taking her to Adirondack Animal Land and buying her endless bags of feed for the petting zoo. It was one of *so few* memories where she was actually happy—where she actually felt safe.

"He does that with a lot of people," Rhi says, pushing the memory away. "Anyone he wants to impress, he throws money at them and plasters on a smile for as long as it takes to get them on his side. It doesn't take very long for him to win people over. Folks love to feel loved by wealthy, handsome men."

"Handsome? Hmm." Uncle Jimmy grunts in disagreement. "Not my type. But I can't blame Angie for falling for him. We all did, in our way. It wasn't until he had your mother locked down that he showed his true colors."

Rhi straightens, leaving Purrdita pawing at her leg. "What do you mean?"

Uncle Jimmy hesitates.

"Please. Tell me."

He makes a face, but continues anyway. "Well, part of why they got married so fast was because your mother was pregnant. Then about four months into their marriage, Angie was calling every week, worrying she'd made a mistake. Our mother told her to forget Lawrence and come home, but . . . she was scared. *And* she was proud. She'd made her choices and she'd made a vow, and she was determined to keep that vow."

Not in the end, Rhi thinks, suppressing the image that floats to the surface of her mind: her mother waking her in the middle of the night, a finger to her lips as they snuck out of the house with trash bags hastily stuffed full of their belongings.

"After you were born, they had your grandmother and me out to meet you *once*," Uncle Jimmy says. "They never came to visit us, never invited us out again. Angie stopped calling. We kept calling her, but she stuck to pleasantries, talking about you mostly, or asking us about ourselves. She sent us a lot of videos of you. Her way of keeping us from asking questions, I guess."

Rhi lets her eyes linger on the worn carpet and finally understands something about the cavernous emptiness inside herself that she has carried with her for her entire life: even when her mother was alive, Rhi had never lived in a happy home. Angie Abrams had never been a whole person while she was with Lawrence Chase. She had never been free.

All these years since her mother's death, Rhi has been aching for the memory of a home that never really was.

It's fine. I'm fine, Rhi thinks to herself, crushing down the tremors from the tears she does not want to shed. She takes a deep breath, lets it out slowly. "So . . . I take it you don't think I should testify."

Uncle Jimmy makes an abrupt choking sound, stopping himself

from shouting. "That's up to you," he says in a tight, measured voice. "But I don't think you owe your father a *damn thing.*"

"No," Rhi agrees, but doubt lingers on her tongue. She has never disobeyed her father in her entire life. Can she really start now? "But what if . . . like he said . . . maybe he regrets . . ." *Being a bad father? A bad human being? Himself?* "I mean, he apologized, kind of. Maybe he . . ." *Sees the error of his ways? Actually cares about me? Genuinely wants to make up for the thousands of ways he's let me down?*

"Rhi-Rhi," Uncle Jimmy says gently. "I'm pretty sure he was just saying those things so you'd have the doubts you're having right now. *I* don't believe he's sorry for anything, besides not covering his tracks well enough to keep himself out of jail. If he is . . . well. Let him be sorry enough to prove it to you."

"But what if I testified and it was enough to get him out of jail?"

Uncle Jimmy tilts his head, not understanding.

"Don't you think, even if he's not really sorry now, if *I* was the reason he won his appeal, maybe he'd finally see that I'm . . ." Rhi trails off as she hears the words coming out of her mouth.

If I just do the right things, say the right words, become the right person, maybe I can make them love me.

She's thought something like this a million times or more, whether about her father or Vera or Kevin. But the deep sadness in her uncle's eyes right now, bordering on horror, is enough for her to realize how wrong she is—how wrong she's *been*, all these years.

Rhi's cheeks flush with hot shame and she looks away, lips pressed tightly together.

"Sweet pea," Uncle Jimmy says, his voice hoarse. He puts his arm gingerly around her shoulders and pulls her into a sideways hug, kissing her roughly on the top of her head. It is a very avuncular embrace: earnest and awkward, and unearned by its recipient.

It is almost more than Rhi can stand.

"You don't need to prove your worth to *anyone*," Uncle Jimmy says quietly, his cheek still pressed to her head. "Least of all *him*. If he can't see what an amazing person you are, that's his loss."

"But . . ." she starts. "I still have to live with him, eventually."

"Not right now you don't. Not for two years. And then you'll be eighteen and you can live wherever you want. And there will always be a place for you in my home."

Rhi glances around the guest room, at the bare walls, the piles of her belongings on desks and dressers and chairs, nothing put away, nothing hanging in the closet, nothing to indicate she's claimed ownership of the room at all. Because she hasn't. Because in her mind, she's only a guest here.

And it dawns on her that this is exactly how she felt living in her father's house, with one exception: instead of dreading the day she might have to leave, Rhi had always feared she would never escape.

Purrdita leaps onto Rhi's lap and immediately begins headbutting her chest, purring loud enough to fill the silence. Rhi strokes her head, making the cat squint her eyes in ecstasy.

She is half-numb, fighting against the fear gnawing at her insides and the yearning threatening to wreck the precarious safety of her expectations. Every emotion is a war inside of Rhi, a struggle between what she instinctively feels and her thoughts about that feeling. She wonders if the girls have ever felt this way but cannot imagine they possibly could have. The girls had never been taught to fear their desires, or pass judgment on their own emotions. They learned to survive harsh winters and coyote attacks, but they had never needed to learn how to protect themselves emotionally, like Rhi had.

Could Rhi ever feel that safe? Could she ever feel that free?

For a moment at least, with her uncle's gentle hand on her shoulder and the buzzing weight of a purring cat in her lap, Rhi doesn't feel like the concept of *safety* is quite so impossibly out of reach.

PODCAST TRANSCRIPT

Valley of the Wolves: The Mysterious Case of the Wild Girls of Happy Valley
Episode 7: The Silence is Broken

Brian Cornwell [narrating]:

[lo-fi music fades in, 20 seconds]

I'm Brian Cornwell. It is June seventeenth, and this is VALLEY OF THE WOLVES. On today's special episode, Oblivienne, the veritable middle child of the wild girls, has agreed to speak with me via video chat.

[rustling and clicking noises]

Brian: Are you okay there? All set up?

[muffled speaking]

Brian: What was that? I think you need to—yeah, there you go. Better?

Oblivienne: Yes?

Brian [narrating]: Oblivienne is the second youngest of the Wild Girls of Happy Valley. She is small, white, scrawny for her approximate fifteen years, with bobbed dark-brown hair and eyes so dark they are almost black. But despite what one might expect, those eyes are not deadened from trauma. Instead, they are alive with questions.

Brian: So, it must be strange for you, living in a house, with people you don't know.

Oblivienne: No more strange than everything else about this world.

[Brian chuckles]

Brian: It's a lot of change though, I'd imagine. And with the discovery of Verity's family here, in this world, that kind of puts a damper on what Mother told you, doesn't it?

Oblivienne: I do not know what a damper is.

Brian: It's just a saying. It means the story doesn't exactly hold water anymore.

Oblivienne: What water?

[Brian laughs]

Brian: No, sorry. "Doesn't hold water" means there are holes in the story, like a bucket that can't hold water anymore.

Oblivienne: Oh. Yes. And no. What we experienced in the forest was real, even if our doctors tell us it was not.

Brian: And what sort of things did you experience that make you still believe in Mother's story?

Oblivienne: . . . magic.

Brian: Magic? What kind of magic? Like, witchcraft?

Oblivienne: Well . . . natural magic. Magic was EVERYWHERE in the forest. It led us to food when we were hungry, to water when we were thirsty. It carried us to safety when we fell from tree branches or rocks, and protected us when the storms tried to blow the castle away.

Brian: Wow. And do you still have this magic?

Brian [narrating]: This is the first time in the interview that Oblivienne looks away.

Oblivienne: Sometimes. Magic requires belief, above all else. And it is hard to believe in something when most of the world is telling you it does not exist.

[lo-fi music fades in]

Brian [narrating]: Something in her eyes tells me she still wants to believe, that she WOULD believe. If only there wasn't so much evidence stacked against it.

According to the FBI, the human remains found at the girls' former campsite belonged to a male, approximately six feet tall, aged between sixty and seventy years. The remains themselves were less than a year old when they were discovered. They place the date of death somewhere between August and September of last year. But a source tells us that the forensics team has had trouble getting a clean DNA sample from the bones, finding the samples too contaminated from their time in the ground. And even if a viable sample is obtained and analyzed, unless Mother's DNA is already in the federal database as a criminal or a victim, he may very well remain unidentified.

The only hope they have in identifying the man who called himself Mother is through the police sketch Oblivienne has helped create. The sketch shows an ethnically ambiguous older man with suntanned, weather-worn skin, a moderately sized crooked nose that appears to have been broken at some time, a wide mouth, deep-set eyes, and hollow cheekbones. His forehead is broad, hairline receded, with a long gray braid of hair that hangs over his shoulder, almost down to his elbow. There is a red tattoo on his neck, or possibly a birthmark, that happens to look like the sun and the moon colliding.

The artist's rendering of Mother has been posted to news outlets and websites for several weeks now, but there haven't been any real leads. A Nova Scotia man claimed to have gone to a summer camp in the Adirondacks forty years ago with a boy who had a similar birthmark, but he cannot remember the boy's name, and the camp is now defunct. A retired nurse who volunteers at the City Mission in Buffalo, New York, claims she once treated a man for heat stroke who looked just like the police sketch, but no one else is able to corroborate. A Happy Valley local reported seeing him in the stacks of the town library just before New Year's—long after Mother died.

[music fades out]

These sightings, if they are in fact true sightings, imply that Mother wasn't always with the girls at the enormous tree they called their castle. Oblivienne confirms this.

Oblivienne: He came and went as he needed in order to keep his spiritual powers intact. Toward the end, he stayed with us more than away. But I wondered sometimes . . . if he was going to be with other people.

Brian: Did any of the other girls share that thought?

Oblivienne: I think Epiphanie wondered. He never used to leave when we were very little—so why did he need to when we were older?

Brian: But you and your sisters never spoke about the subject? Never discussed theories with each other?

Oblivienne: No. It felt wrong to think Mother could be keeping a secret.

Brian [narrating]: Oblivienne's eyes have begun to shine with tears, but she doesn't wipe them away. She continues:

Oblivienne: It STILL feels like I am betraying myself, Mother, my sisters . . . even just speaking to you about this.

Brian: Well, what would have happened if you had brought this up while Mother was still alive? What do you think he might have said?

Brian [narrating]: Oblivienne gazes into the distance for so long, I am sure the screen must be frozen. But the glisten in her eyes tells me otherwise. She is trying to conjure up the ghost of the man who raised her, to hear him once more after all these months. When she speaks again, her eyes are hooded, almost as if she has indeed managed to enter into a trance and summon Mother from beyond the veil.

Oblivienne: He would have praised me for my curiosity. He would have been proud of me for questioning him. Mother always told us to follow our instincts, trust our guts, never trust authority for authority's sake alone. I failed him by not speaking my questions out loud.

[lo-fi music fades in]

Brian [narrating]: If Oblivienne's assumption is correct, that is definitely not the reaction of a cult leader. Indeed, nothing about Mother seems to fit the standard profile of a kidnapper. He may have been delusional, but his delusions were consistent and, for the most part, centered around people OTHER than himself. In fact, Mother seems to have empowered the Wild Girls of Happy Valley, teaching them survival skills, self-reliance, and encouraging a positive self-image.

But I wonder often about the other families who lost their daughters. Are they still out there, searching?

If you think one of the girls could be your missing daughter or sibling, we here at VALLEY OF THE WOLVES would recommend ordering a genetic testing kit through ChromoFile to have your DNA analyzed and added to the public databases, where much of the independent investigation in this case is taking place. Check out the show notes for a coupon code.

Brian: So you really don't have any memories of your family? No memories at all before the wilderness?

Brian [narrating]: Oblivienne closes her eyes for a long moment, during which she looks livid with frustration, and then just as quickly, resigned.

Oblivienne: There is nothing before the wilderness.

TIKTOK LIVE TRANSCRIPT

An off-screen dialogue between @0dd_cRavings and @BrainDocBrian, voiced over a prerecorded Subway Surfers speedrun.

June 18, 20— 11:36 p.m.

@0dd_cRavings [11:36 p.m.]: Right, but, like, this is not the behavior of a cult leader. This is not the behavior of cult MEMBERS, even.

@BrainDocBrian: Uh except the girl is clearly obsessed with the man who kidnapped her—who RAISED her, sorry. Wait, what? Dude, you've got so many people in your comments defending this guy.

@0dd_cRavings [snickering]: Freedom of speech, bro, what can I say? We're here to give them facts, not tell them what to think.

@BrainDocBrian: Right, because WE'RE not CULT LEADERS.

[laughter]

@BrainDocBrian: But, um, anyways, like I was saying: Oblivienne? Clearly obsessed with Mother. Conflicted? Yes. But dude still has a hold on her from beyond the grave. Who's to say she wasn't describing him based on how he described himself? Like when a narcissist gaslights you into thinking they're so great and you're the absolute moron, when really they're the shitstain and you're the victim.

@0dd_cRavings: I don't know though, 'cause don't cult members and like children of narcissists—don't they lose their sense of self or whatever? If we believe what she said in the interview, the dude basically told the girls they were all, like, Xena warrior princesses. EMPOWERING your victims—

@BrainDocBrian [fake shouting]: Empowering victims? In THIS economy?

[laughter]

@0dd_cRavings: No but, in a way? Exactly that.

@BrainDocBrian: Right but, like, how empowered can they be if they're still clinging to his stories? The girl sounds like she's going to lose her shit if she finds out about Santa Claus.

@0dd_cRavings: [giggles] Okay. Okay. Fair point. So, Brain Doc Brian, give us your professional take, given all that we know. For serious now.

@BrainDocBrian: Honestly? The guy was straight-up delulu.

[laughter]

@BrainDocBrian: No, but seriously. No joke. Mother sounds like he was suffering from, like, a very severe and prolonged psychotic break. I don't know if maybe those times he left the girls he was coming back to reality or going even farther away, but I'd be willing to guess psychosis had more to do with it than quote, unquote "spiritual powers."

@0dd_cRavings: IDK man, my tía reads tarot at the botánica on Wednesdays and she's said some pretty uncanny shit. Don't mock spiritual powers is all I'm saying.

@BrainDocBrian: I would never mock your tía, OC.

@0dd_cRavings: I appreciate that, bro.

23

SCHOOL IS OUT FOR THE SUMMER, so Rhi has nothing better to do than to wait for the podcast episode to drop. She listens to it with Uncle Jimmy the minute the notification appears on her phone—"A new episode of *Valley of the Wolves* is available to download!"—and then again after dinner with Purrdita on her lap in Uncle Jimmy's guest room; and then listens to it again every day for the rest of that week. She also skims the articles and other think pieces that have arisen in the aftermath of the interview; the public's renewed interest in the "Wild Girls of Happy Valley" is ravenous, and news outlets and clickbait content writers are happy to oblige with whatever new take they can come up with.

By that weekend, when she gets together with the girls to listen to the interview at Oblivienne's foster home, Rhi has the beats of the interview practically memorized. She watches Sunder's face for signs of outrage or distress, but she seems to have accepted the fact that this interview was going to happen—has happened, now.

Epiphanie looks at the phone, touches the flat screen gently, still amazed by the technology. "You did not sound happy," is all she says.

Oblivienne doesn't reply.

"It's a difficult thing to discuss with a stranger, I'm sure," Mrs. Lynch says, putting a hand on Oblivienne's shoulder. "But it felt good to get it out there, didn't it, Oblivienne? Maybe get that police sketch of Mother in front of a few more faces?"

"Yes," Oblivienne says without feeling.

"People have asked Grace and me for interviews, too," Verity says softly.

Rhi sits up. She hasn't heard about this.

"Blood Mother does not like the idea, but Stepfather believes I owe it to them. Some of the people are offering to pay us a lot of money."

"You don't owe them anything," Rhi says fervently. "You don't have to do any interviews if you don't want to."

"Grace wants to," Verity adds. "She wants the money. And something about 'followers.' She says as long as she is always going to be known as the sister of a Wild Girl, she can at least use the fame to become an *influencer*. Whatever that means."

Rhi raises an eyebrow, but before she can respond, Mrs. Lynch speaks up.

"I happen to know the *Jenny Ro Show* is offering a very large amount of money for an interview with all of you, including Grace. And including *you*, Rhi. What do you think of that? Maybe some cash to help you out with college?"

"*No*," Rhi says, a note of alarm in her voice, a nebulous anger simmering in her gut.

"Oh, well, very well then. But girls, you'll think on it, won't you? You may not have much experience with money but trust me when I tell you how useful it will be to have some of your own stashed away for the day you all become independent women." She smiles sweetly. "Oblivienne, why don't you take your friends outside now? It's such a beautiful summer day."

"Okay," Oblivienne says, rising to her feet. The others rise, one by one, and follow her out the back door to the large backyard studded with swing sets and jungle gyms and faded, colorful plastic slides too small for the girls to use.

Rhi waits until the others leave before turning to Mrs. Lynch, her protective anger flaring. She can't let this woman manipulate the girls like this—the way she's been manipulated her whole life.

"How much are they going to pay *you* if you get us all on the show?"

Mrs. Lynch looks shocked. "Miss Chase, you're being very rude right now, I hope you know. Oblivienne has been reaching out to get interviews on her own. I'm just trying to support whatever she wants to do. Don't you think the girls deserve to take control of their own narrative?"

Rhi shakes her head, her sharp fury turned wordless—useless. When Mrs. Lynch puts it that way it sounds like a good thing, but Rhi knows the media has no one's best interest at heart besides their own.

"Oblivienne is a sweet girl," Mrs. Lynch says. "But she is fierce as hell. No one is making her do *anything* she doesn't already want to do."

Rhi must admit, Mrs. Lynch is right about that.

Rhi joins the girls around the swing set, hands shoved into her pockets, fury transformed into breathtaking embarrassment. She is thinking about how she won't be able to look Mrs. Lynch in the eye again any time soon, when Sunder says from atop the swing set, "We have decided to do the interview that will give us a lot of money."

Rhi's heart sinks. "If that's what you all want, I'll support you."

"You do not want us to do it," Verity says. She's sitting on the swing next to Oblivienne, dragging her feet through the sand beneath.

"You know Jenny Ro doesn't do investigative work like the podcast people, right?" Rhi tells them.

"I . . ." Oblivienne starts. "I know, but lots of people watch her show. If I can get her to show Mother's picture on television, more people will see it. More people will have the chance to recognize him."

"Oblivienne," Epiphanie says, cautiously, from where she's seated in the grass. "This interview is supposed to help us with our *future*, not our past. Let Mother's memory rest."

"I cannot," Oblivienne says, standing abruptly and flinging the swing away from her. "Do you not care that Mother *lied* to us?"

"*He did not lie!*" Sunder snaps. "Why do you insist the person who loved us most in the world is now a villain?"

Oblivienne looks pointedly at Verity, at the undeniable proof that at least one of them is from this world, then back to Sunder. Oblivienne stalks off without saying anything else.

"That does not mean—Oblivienne—wait!" Epiphanie calls after.

Rhi starts after her, but Verity catches her arm.

"She just needs to clear her head," she assures her. "The truth is, Oblivienne was closer to Mother than any of us. When she sometimes felt she did not belong to us, she *always* belonged to Mother. I think she cannot hold an image of Mother in her mind that is anything but day or night. There is no room for . . . complexity."

Rhi studies the girls closely. "And what kind of complexities have *you* made room for?"

The girls look at one another, then away. It dawns on her that the girls have been avoiding discussing the subject since the hospital, except for the times Oblivienne has brought it up.

"I think we just want to move on with our lives," Verity says, flicking a piece of grass from her jeans.

"But the portal is still coming," Sunder says, leaning forward on top of the swing set, eyes sparkling. "And soon. I have narrowed the eclipse down to a handful of dates using the almanac, and I believe it could be as soon as the next full moon."

Verity makes a face Sunder cannot see, but does not reply.

"We still have a destiny," Sunder insists, tightening her grip on the swing set. "Leutheria still needs us."

Rhi looks between Verity and Sunder, between the "proof" that Mother lied, and the nearly blind faith that his stories are true. She doesn't know what she believes, but she knows what she wants to.

"Perhaps you are right, Sunder," Epiphanie says, looking in the direction in which Oblivienne stormed off. "But, in the meantime, I think Oblivienne needs us more."

BEFORE THE GIRLS LEAVE FOR THE DAY, Rhi finds Oblivienne in the kitchen, scribbling in a black-and-white composition journal. Dr. Ibanez gave each of the girls a whole stack of these journals to help them process their experiences, but Oblivienne is the only one Rhi has seen actually using them.

"You want to tell me to let it go," Oblivienne says, still writing.

"No," Rhi says, sitting on the stool next to Oblivienne. "I want to make sure you're okay."

Oblivienne stops writing. She closes the journal and looks up at Rhi. Her expression is tense, as if she is clinging to her anger. Rhi does not have to wonder why she would try so hard to hold on to anger. The alternative is often much more painful.

"If I am right," Oblivienne says. "And if everything Mother told us is a lie, then who is to say . . ." Her voice drops to a whisper. "Who is to say Mother's love for us was not also a lie?"

Rhi feels her insides hollow out at this proposition. The echo of her own pain, buried deep in her past, responds to this line of thinking, tries to penetrate the walls she has built up around it. Rhi is well practiced at pivoting away from that particular agony, but something in Oblivienne's question strikes a nerve.

Rhi swallows an unexpected surge of bile in her throat, the hollowness inside her expanding, thinning those protective walls to tremulous butterfly wings. "I think . . . you can never really know—for *certain*—how another person feels about you. You can only trust what you perceive—the way they spoke to you. The way they cared for you. The way they made you feel about yourself."

And how did he make you feel about yourself? a voice asks from beyond those walls, now too weak to hold back the weight of that emptiness.

Oblivienne looks at Rhi with curiosity, then concern, her own distress momentarily diminished. "Sometimes I look at you and I do not see *Rhi*. I see . . . *Eden*." She whispers the name. "Which is strange, because I have never met her."

Rhi's skin prickles with goose bumps. She feels insubstantial, like a flickering light bulb. She can't keep her eyes steady on Oblivienne's.

Stop, she scolds herself. *I came in here to make sure Oblivienne is okay, not to fall apart myself.*

"Will you tell me why you keep her secreted away?" Oblivienne asks. "Is it to keep your power? Because you know about the power of names?"

Rhi tries to swallow again, but her mouth is so dry, her tongue so thick, it's like shifting sandstones in her throat. "I didn't want to carry Eden's pain into my new life."

Oblivienne studies her and points her finger at Rhi's chest. "But she is still here. And she is still in pain."

Rhi shakes her head. "No. Eden is gone. I'm Rhi now, and none of that matters."

Oblivienne frowns. She turns back to her journal and opens it to a blank page, picking up her pencil once more. "It does not matter, I suppose. The power of names was most likely just another lie Mother told us." She says it with such bitter resignation that Rhi almost doesn't notice the way her chin quivers.

DRAFTS

FROM: "Eden Chase" <e.r.c.2007@springmail.com>
TO: "Kevin Hartwell" <hartwell.kevin@irving.edu>
DATE: July 1, 2023
SUBJECT: why

I don't know why I keep writing these emails. I don't want you to read them. I don't want you in my life at all anymore.

Except I do.

And I don't.

It's very confusing.

Oblivienne asked me/Rhi why I keep myself/Eden hidden away. I don't know what to tell her. I can't lie to her like I lie to myself. I keep telling myself your going-away party last summer never happened, that I didn't leave your apartment at 5 a.m. and go home without saying goodbye. Part of me believes you're still coming home, the same person who made my life bearable all those years when I was too young to stand up for myself. The person who protected me and made me feel—even for a moment— fractionally less alone.

But he never really existed, did he?

The truth is, I was desperate.

The truth is, I still am desperate.

The truth is. The truth is.

The truth is, if I look at the truth, it might kill me.

So I won't look at it. I'm going to be happy here, instead. Maybe I'll go out for track this fall. Maybe I'll go to the homecoming dance, participate in spirit week, all that bullshit. Maybe I'll forget you completely.

I hate you.

I love you.

I wish you never existed.

24

I T HAS BEEN AN EXCITING twenty-four hours for the girls. Yesterday, after packing an overnight bag with Maggie's help, Epiphanie was picked up by a driver in a very long black car called a *limousine*. Together with her sisters, Rhi, Grace, Mrs. Erikson, and Mrs. Lynch, they drove for hours in the long car, through rolling green hills and lush, patchwork farmland. Eventually, they reached the city, where they went to a *hotel*, traveled up nineteen stories in an *elevator*, and entered a *suite* almost as big as Maggie's house. One entire wall of the suite is floor-to-ceiling windows that look out over the Kingdom of Manhattan, spiked with *skyscrapers* and towers made of all kinds of shining things. When the sun set last night, the kingdom lit up like the Milky Way, painting the night with bright signs and flashing lights in colors so impossibly vibrant, Epiphanie is certain she has never seen them before in her entire life.

Now it is morning again and the girls are in the *greenroom* at the *Jenny Ro Show*, sitting on pale pink chairs and couches, nibbling on the tray of food that has been artfully arranged for them on the coffee table at the center. Epiphanie has no idea why they call it the greenroom, since nothing in the room is green except for the stems on the vase of fresh cut flowers sitting on a side table, and the mossy green of

Verity's dress. They are all dressed in strange clothes that do not belong to them, chosen by a *stylist*. In addition to having been dressed by strangers, other people have spent much of the morning putting powders and creams and colors on their faces, rubbing things into their hair and blasting them with hot air. To Epiphanie, they all look like pictures in a magazine—not like real life at all.

Oblivienne, in a black dress with a white collar, her hair shining and straight and held in place with a white plastic headband, looks nervous as she clutches a print of the *composite sketch* she helped Agent Tyler make ages ago. She is sitting on a powdery pink chair, ignoring all the questions Sunder is asking Rhi ("Why did they straighten your hair?" "Because otherwise it's kind of unruly, I guess." "How did they build a castle this big?" "With a lot of really smart engineers and construction workers." "How do the images get from the cameras to the television?" "Um, something to do with information passing through wires, I think."). She seems completely unaware of the awkward looks Verity and Grace are exchanging, looking more identical than ever with their hair styled to match and wearing two different colors of the same dress.

"Oblivienne," Epiphanie says, leaning toward her. "Are you sure you want to do this? You seem distressed."

"I am not distressed," she says sharply, wrinkling the edges of the paper in her hands as she grips it more tightly. "I am impatient."

"We will be called out there soon. The woman who brought us in here said—"

"Not for the interview." Oblivienne shakes her head, frustrated. "Or, maybe for the interview. I do not know." She sets her jaw. "I have not heard anything from the podcast people—no new information about Mother. Allison said showing this on television will reach more people. Millions of people." Her eyes flick to Epiphanie's. "This picture . . . if someone recognizes him . . . it is our last chance to discover the truth about Mother."

"Sister," Verity says, leaning closer to their conversation. This causes everyone to turn and pay attention. "We have discussed this. Plenty of strangers have come forward already, but they only think they may have seen him, or met him. Even if they are right, no one *knew* Mother like we did."

"If we knew him at all," Oblivienne mutters.

"Sister!" Sunder cries, shocked.

Epiphanie is shocked, too. She knows Oblivienne can be dogged in her pursuits—obsessive, almost. And she has been consumed with the idea of connecting Mother to this world for some time now, but she has never heard her speak with such open disdain for the man who raised them.

"Oblivienne," Epiphanie says kindly, carefully. "Have you considered that maybe what is *true* is not quite as . . . specific as what you are thinking?"

"What does that mean?" Oblivienne asks, narrowing her eyes.

"It is just . . ." Epiphanie hesitates. "I worry that if we define *truth* too narrowly, we will be devastated no matter what we do or do not discover about Mother in time."

Oblivienne leans forward, staring into Epiphanie's eyes. "What have you been keeping from us?"

They are all silent now, all watching, waiting, curious—even Rhi and Grace.

Epiphanie has always been the one who took care of the others. That is the only reason she never said anything—she did not want to cause pain or confusion—she is sure that is all.

"I will tell you, Sisters," she says in a tone that lets them know there was never any doubt of that. "I have not been keeping it from you. I have just . . . never found the right time to bring it up." She takes a deep breath and begins. "Once, when Mother came back from his wandering, I found a small plastic box among his belongings. It fell and when it hit the ground, it popped open. You see, I did not know what they were at the time. I had never seen them before we came to the hospital. All I knew was that they were colorful and delicate, and inscribed with tiny letters and numbers—the same inscription on every pill. I thought they must be something Mother had created with his magic while he was away, or found in his travels—"

"Mother was taking pills, and you never told us about it?" Oblivienne asks.

"I do not know that," Epiphanie insists. "I found them, but I did not know what they were then, and I never saw Mother take them—"

"But you have known what pills are for many months now!" Oblivienne shouts.

"Oblivienne," Rhi says gently. "A lot has happened since you came to the hospital. I'm sure it's like Epiphanie said—she just never found the right time to bring it up."

"And having pills does not *mean* anything," Sunder insists, though her face is worried, as if she does not believe her own words. "Mother could have found those in the forest. Or maybe he *did* get them from this world—it does not *mean* anything except he *had* them."

"Of *course* it means something," Oblivienne hisses. "It means Mother had access to all the good things of this world and never shared them with us, even when we were sick or in pain and he was not around to heal us." She shakes her head, tears shimmering in the corners of her eyes. "Mother lied to us about that—he lied about Verity—what *else* did he lie about?"

"Stop—" Sunder starts.

"Did he even care for us at all?"

Sunder jumps to her feet, hands balled into fists at her sides. Her eyes are wide with tears and fury when she speaks. "*Do not say that!*" She starts to crouch, as if preparing to lunge.

"Sunder," Epiphanie says, reaching with her sister in her heart as well as with her hands. She lowers Sunder back to a sitting position, rubbing her back in firm circles to calm her. "Oblivienne, this is what I am talking about. There are many reasons why Mother may have had those pills in his possession. We cannot know for sure what the truth is."

Grace snorts. "Except, I don't know, maybe the truth is exactly what Oblivienne said."

They all turn to her with mixed expressions. Epiphanie is willing the girl to stop speaking with her eyes, but she continues regardless.

"The most obvious answer is *usually* the right answer," Grace says.

"But not *always*," Rhi says.

A knock at the door.

"Five minutes to showtime!" someone calls.

Video Transcript:
The Jenny Ro Show

Air date: June 30, 20—

INTERIOR - DAY - JENNY RO'S TALK SHOW STAGE

[Jenny Ro is sitting in her iconic, throne-like white chair. She's gazing thoughtfully at the girls seated in the interview area on the right: Oblivienne is in a chair next to Jenny; Sunder, Epiphanie, and Verity are squeezed together on a love seat next to Oblivienne; Grace and Rhi are in chairs at the end.]

JENNY RO: And Rhi, what was going through your head when you found them?

RHIANNON CHASE: Um. I guess I was scared when I first saw them. Not of the girls, but of the wolves.

EPIPHANIE [turning to Rhi]: The wolves told us we could trust you, that you would help, not hurt us. They were right.

OBLIVIENNE: Were they?

SUNDER [looking irritated]: Rhi saved my life.

OBLIVIENNE: But at what cost?

[Sunder jumps to her feet on the love seat, staring at Oblivienne with overt rage.

Epiphanie tugs on her wrist to make her sit
down, but Sunder refuses to budge.]

SUNDER [sharply]: Shut. Up.

RHIANNON CHASE [looking nervously between Sunder
and Oblivienne]: I understand, Oblivienne. I've
thought about that day a lot. I'm not sorry I
helped you, but you . . . all of you . . . you were
wild. You were free. And I can't help feeling like
it's my fault the world is going to tame you.

VERITY: No, Rhi. You are one of us. You fight for
us. We do not blame you for the fact that our lives
have changed.

EPIPHANIE: Our lives were always MEANT to change.

OBLIVIENNE: Do not be sorry, Rhi. After Mother
died, it was only a matter of time before we
discovered his lies.

SUNDER [through gritted teeth]: SHUT. UP!

  [The audience gives a collective gasp as
  Sunder lunges into Oblivienne's lap and grabs
  Oblivienne's head with both hands. At the
  same instant, Verity and Epiphanie shoot to
  their feet; Jenny draws her legs up onto her
  chair, gesturing wildly for help; Grace pushes
  backward in her chair and knocks it over,
  sending herself sprawling.]

RHIANNON CHASE [rising slowly from her chair]:
Sunder, it's okay. Listen to me. Just . . .

[inaudible]

[Sunder thrashes, knocking the chair backward
as Oblivienne screams. Jenny looks desperately
at the camera.]

[The network feed cuts to a commercial.]

INT. DAY - MORNING

[Inside a sparkling modern kitchen, two
children are seated at the island with bowls
of mush in front of them. They look bored,
stirring whatever is in their bowls with
disinterest.]

FEMALE ANNOUNCER [in a saccharine voice]: Is it
a chore to get your kids to eat breakfast every
morning?

[A beautiful woman walks in behind her
children, peers over the tops of their heads,
then puts her hands on her hips and shakes
her head.]

CLICKMONSTER
Trending Quizzes And Headlines

It's Strange, But We Know Which Wild Girl of Happy Valley You're Most Like Based on the Way You Would Decorate Your Dream House

---

10 US Wilderness Retreats That Will Give You a Proper Wild Girls Experience

---

5 No-Tools-Required Protective Hairstyles Epiphanie Might Have Worn in the Wilderness

---

10 Times the Wild Girls of Happy Valley Made Us Go "Same."

"I'm Done with Civilization." These Influencers Are Leaving It All Behind to Go Off-Grid in Tree Houses Inspired by the Wild Girls of Happy Valley

---

15 Ingenious Products We Think the Wild Girls of Happy Valley Would Have Liked to Have in the Wilderness

---

Bittersweet Sympathy: An Interview with Grace Erikson—On Her Unfathomable Reunion with Her Long-Lost Twin Sister, Her Dreams for the Future, and Her Hack for Perfect No-Heat Curls, Every Time

25

IMMEDIATELY AFTER THE TAPING, the girls are taken back to the hotel. As soon as they return to the suite, Rhi scrambles to find a way to soothe the situation, but everyone is distracted: Sunder immediately locks herself in the bathroom; Mrs. Lynch fusses loudly over Oblivienne, who has sustained no real injuries; Mrs. Erikson mutters loudly on the phone to Dr. Ibanez with a firm grip on her daughters, not letting them out of her sight. Dr. Ibanez had advised against the interview when first approached, but ultimately told them it was not a decision she had any say in. It was a decision the girls had to make for themselves. Rhi wonders if Dr. Ibanez regrets saying that now.

Rhi glances at Epiphanie, the only other person not caught up in the storm, and they both go to the bathroom door.

"Sunder?" Rhi says, knocking softly. "Are you okay?"

The only sound that answers is the rush of water filling the tub.

"Sister," Epiphanie says. "We are worried about you."

"Worried about *her*?" Mrs. Lynch exclaims. "Look what that animal did to my poor girl!"

From the bedroom doorway, Verity bares her teeth at Mrs. Lynch, but she doesn't seem to notice.

Rhi looks at Oblivienne, sees only tousled hair and tear-stained cheeks, the Peter Pan collar of her dress torn away from her neck. Mrs. Lynch straightens Oblivienne's hair and swabs at the streaky makeup on her face, such superficial tenderness it irritates Rhi. Unexpectedly, that irritation blossoms into anger: anger at Oblivienne for giving up on Mother so easily, so dramatically; for insisting on these interviews despite Rhi's warnings (and Dr. Ibanez's, and the Quakers', and even Uncle Jimmy's—everyone *but* Mrs. Lynch, really); for being so quick to abandon the gifts Mother gave them just because this world, too wrapped up in scandal and rationality, has tested her faith; and finally, anger at Oblivienne for making it that much harder for Rhi to believe it all, too.

"Well maybe Oblivienne should have considered her sisters' feelings before declaring on live TV that everything they thought they knew about themselves was a lie!" Rhi snaps, and immediately regrets it. Shame courses through her as Mrs. Lynch stares at her. Even Mrs. Erikson looks shocked.

"I'm—I'm so sorry, Oblivienne. That wasn't fair—"

"No," Oblivienne says, training her eyes on Epiphanie. "You are right. I deserved my sister's rage. It is a product of her pain—pain that I caused, at least in part."

Rhi opens her mouth to deny this, to soothe the girl's feelings, but she cannot.

Epiphanie wants to say something—Rhi can tell—but she won't say it now, with Mrs. Lynch and the others present.

"Sunder," Epiphanie says, turning to the bathroom door and knocking again. "Please."

To Rhi's surprise, the door clicks open.

The two of them glance back at the others, catch Verity's eye, but she nods for them to go ahead without her as Mrs. Erikson pulls her deeper into the bedroom and closes the door.

Rhi and Epiphanie enter the dimly lit bathroom to find Sunder has filled the large whirlpool tub and is sitting in the water in only her underwear and a tank top.

Rhi looks down. There is no water on the floor, but the tub is clear across the room.

How did the door—?

"Come quickly," Sunder whispers, staring into the water. It is dark—the whole bathroom is dark, tiled in deep sea green, the tub nearly black. Only two square night-lights by the vanity illuminate the room, and their light barely reaches them. Epiphanie pulls her dress off and climbs into the tub, pulling her knees up as she gazes at the water where Sunder is staring.

"You too, Rhi," Sunder says, splashing a little at the place where she wants Rhi to sit.

Self-consciously, Rhi pulls her dress over her head. She knows these girls aren't looking at her body, knows they would never judge her body even if they were looking, but a lifetime of being pinched and poked at and squeezed into a shape she was never meant to be makes her wish she could be invisible—makes her wish she never had to be perceived at all. She climbs into the tub anyway, the warm embrace of the water easing her discomfort.

The three of them form a triangle in the tub, their toes touching at the center, knees poking above the surface. Rhi looks at Sunder. She's about to ask, again, if Sunder is okay, but something makes her pause. Something about her eyes, in the half dark of the bathroom, how they look almost reflective, like fish scales: one brown eye turned shiny copper, one blue eye turned to labradorite. Human eyes should not shine like that, ever, and least of all in the dark.

And suddenly it *is* dark—not half dark, but full, as if the rest of the en suite has dropped away from the world, leaving utter blackness around them. But Rhi can still see Sunder, and Epiphanie, whose ghost-gray eyes are now a holographic rainbow silver. And when Rhi looks down at the bottom of the tub, instead of seeing their toes, she sees the moon.

"What . . ." Rhi starts.

"Just look," Sunder says, inhaling deeply. "And breathe." She exhales, eyes trained on the pale orb floating just beneath the surface of the water. "It is called scrying. Mother taught us. Look into the dark water with a question in your heart, and it will conjure a memory from the future. It is how he knew . . . everything."

The moon rises from the bottom of the tub, growing from a coin to a disc, the details clarifying as it reaches the surface of the water.

"Do you see it?" Sunder whispers, voice barely a breath. "The moon lighting up a pasture of silver grain going to seed. The blocks of stone lying just beyond the field. The ruins of a kingdom."

Rhi does see it. Vaguely at first, like an afterimage, and then as clearly as anything.

"But, how . . ." Rhi stammers.

"Is that . . ." Epiphanie asks.

"Leutheria," Sunder says. "Home."

Rhi stares, unblinking, even as her eyes begin to ache, terrified of breaking the spell. The impossible dark surrounding them closes in on her until there is nothing but the vision on the water. She falls into it, as if flying through the night sky. Beyond the glaring light of the moon, beyond the ruins in the wavering field of grain, she can see a city—dark at first, then silvered, then gilded by firelight, every wall and every building festooned with garlands of fresh flowers—she can smell the flowers, gardenias and peonies and bundles of lavender. The place is prepared for a celebration.

But for who?

It is vacant. No breeze blows through the decorated cobbled streets. No movement comes from windows or doors. No sound echoes through the kingdom.

They are waiting for us.

Sunder's voice seems to come from inside Rhi's head, neither loud nor quiet—no volume at all, just words, unheard one moment and understood the next. Rhi has no sense of how she is here, in this empty city, seeing everything without eyes, without a body—

And then she is blind.

The glaring bathroom lights come on as someone swings the door open. The world re-forms and Rhi is suddenly heavy, slammed back into her body and her head, the vision torn from her like a dream.

"What on earth is going on in here?" Mrs. Lynch asks, exasperated. "Oh, Miss Chase, *really*. You should be a better role model. You're young women, not children—you don't take baths together." She grabs several bath towels from a shelf. "Go on, all of you. Get out of there and dry off. Sunder, you owe your sister an apology, and if you know what's good for you you'll stop pouting in here and go out there and make things right." She turns to leave, shaking her head.

Rhi looks back and forth between Sunder and Epiphanie. "What . . . what did I just see?"

Sunder grins. "Our future."

"Our *possible* future," Epiphanie corrects. "Mother—" She catches herself, questions herself, decides to move forward. "Mother always said we have a choice."

Sunder ignores this and climbs out of the tub, wrapping herself in the huge fluffy white bath towel. Epiphanie and Rhi follow suit, and as they dry off, Rhi looks around her, overhead, at the walls, for some source of light, something that could explain the things she just saw, the things she just experienced—but there is nothing. There is only the square overhead light at the center of the bathroom ceiling and the night-lights over the outlets by the sink.

They find plush hotel robes in a narrow linen closet and wrap themselves in those before exiting the bathroom. In the sitting area, Verity and the Eriksons are on the love seat across from Oblivienne and Mrs. Lynch. Rhi and Epiphanie pause as Sunder marches over to Oblivienne with her head held high. Sunder is practically glowing with confidence and conviction.

Rhi braces herself for another argument, but she senses at the same time Sunder does that the fight has gone out of Oblivienne.

"I am sorry, Sunder," Oblivienne says before anyone else can speak, looking up at Sunder with huge eyes, tears streaming down her face. "The things I said—they were cruel. They are not who I want to be. This is not—it is not the world I wanted for us . . ." She sobs, bowing her head, shoulders shaking.

Mrs. Lynch moves to console her, but Sunder, once in motion, cannot be stopped. She crawls onto Oblivienne's lap and wraps herself around her sister, pressing Oblivienne's head to her heart. Oblivienne is stiff for a long while, before finally melting into her sister, clinging to Sunder's scrawny arms as if they might be able to pull her out of this nightmare.

Sunder's face is serene—regal—even as she sheds her own tears into Oblivienne's hair, even as Oblivienne rocks them both with her sobs. A deep and shameful envy pierces Rhi as she watches them. To have that closeness, that comfort, even in the face of so much pain . . .

Mrs. Lynch stands, visibly uncomfortable, and walks over to Mrs. Erikson. "Honestly, this kind of behavior has got to stop," she says disapprovingly.

"I think it's nice they're still so devoted to each other," Mrs. Erikson counters meekly. "Like sisters."

Verity and Grace glance at each other for a moment before returning their attention to the scene before them: Grace watching with disturbed fascination, Verity with longing.

"It is okay, Oblivienne," Sunder whispers. "I have seen our future in the water, as Mother taught us. Whatever else is true, I know this: the destiny Mother promised us is real. We only have to decide to accept it."

Rhi's breath catches as Sunder's words set fire to something wild inside her. Oblivienne said it before, that magic requires belief—and what is belief except a choice you make in your heart, over and over again?

What if reality, like magic, and like the future itself, is a matter of choice?

Would Rhi choose the future she saw in the bathtub, that vast, empty, alien kingdom, far away from everyone she has ever known?

Or would she choose to stay?

OBLIVIENNE'S JOURNAL

June 28th

∎

Doctor Ibanez said to write down our feelings when they are too much. Today they are ~~crushing~~ drowning me. Head too full. Too fast. My heart is an open wound. Maybe dieing from Mother's betrayl—maybe dieing from this expanding ~~██████~~ vally between me and my sisters.

Mother betrayed us. Feel sick even thinking that. Sisters are the roots of my heart but Mother was the sky. The place of dreaming. His love was the magic that made the castle a home.

If Mother was a liar ~~I do not know how to keep going~~

how can anything good in this world be trustid?

Frustrated. Can not make these things make sense

Grace Erikson ~~ekziste~~ exists

There fore Verity is from this world

There fore we are ~~probly~~ all from this world

But Mother's magic—our magic—it is real. Despyt what this world has told us to believe. Too many memorys to believe other wise.

But ~~magic has abandoned me~~ I can not find magic in any part of this world. Is it because I do not believe? Or because the roots of my heart are rotting?

Ashamed. For doubting Mother. For the pain I have caused my sisters.

But they do not see the pain I am in. Have never seen me when I have needed to be seen. This is my own falt—I hide from them. Ashamed of my pain. Ashamed of always feeling like some thing is wrong with me. Like I do not belong to them.

Scared.

Who are we if not ~~the wild Princesses~~ what Mother ment for us to be?

Who am I if not their sister?

26

"You're not in trouble," Dr. Ibanez says, laughing a little. "You look like you think I'm about to give you detention." She's sitting at her desk, hands clasped in front of her. She looks tired (and Rhi can guess why; Mrs. Erikson called her four more times last night from the hotel, and twice more on the drive back from the city).

"You're not mad about the whole . . . interview thing?" Rhi asks, spine stiff as she sits on the edge of her chair.

"That *was* something of a disaster, wasn't it? But we both knew it would be." Dr. Ibanez sighs. "I'm not mad, and even if I was, how could I possibly blame *you* for what happened?"

Rhi could name a hundred different ways a person could blame her for something that wasn't her fault, but she gets the doctor's point. "Okay. Then . . . no offense, but . . . why did you ask me to come in today?"

"I just wanted to check in. We don't get to have our little talks anymore now that the girls are out of the hospital. And I feel more than a little responsible for your psychological well-being, since I've been encouraging your relationship with the girls so much."

Rhi notes the guilt that twitches the corner of Dr. Ibanez's mouth. She wishes she could wipe it away, explain to the doctor that she has done Rhi a favor, but she also knows some of that guilt is not really about Rhi—it's about her own ethics, as a doctor and a researcher.

"I am *fine*," Rhi says with as much confidence as she can muster. "Really. I've seen siblings fight before. Doesn't faze me."

Dr. Ibanez leans forward, resting her weight on her forearms. "It's true. You remained remarkably calm on the set. I've noticed not much fazes you. Not when Sunder turned violent when the girls saw Grace for the first time. Not even when we found human remains at the encampment."

Rhi starts blushing, bracing for some kind of undeserved praise, but it doesn't come.

"Rhi, do you remember when we talked about children who grow up in dangerous circumstances?" Dr. Ibanez asks.

Rhi's flush reverses as she feels her face go cold. She doesn't want to talk about the reasons she has learned to stay calm, even when all hell breaks loose. It doesn't matter now, anyway.

Dr. Ibanez continues, her voice lower, softer. "It's nothing to be ashamed of, Rhi. It's an incredible thing you're capable of. It's just . . . usually a skill acquired under pretty bad circumstances, at least at your age."

"Always?" Rhi asks, forcing calm into her voice that she is definitely not feeling at the moment.

"No," Dr. Ibanez admits. "But your father is in jail, and your stepmother abandoned you in favor of a tropical time-share. That doesn't paint a picture of a happy family."

Rhi smiles, tries to laugh it off even as her pulse hammers in her throat. "Yeah, well, they won't be getting any parent of the year awards, but I can assure you, my childhood was *very unremarkable*. I'm fine. Really."

Dr. Ibanez keeps her eyes on Rhi's for a beat too long, making Rhi think for an instant that the doctor knows something Rhi hasn't told her. But who could possibly know? Who would possibly tell?

Finally, Dr. Ibanez nods, leaning back in her chair. "Okay. Well then, I am very glad to hear that. But, if you ever need to talk to anyone, about *anything*—" She offers Rhi a heartfelt, lopsided smile. "Well, you know by now."

27

THE QUAKERS HAVE INVITED EVERYONE over to their house for something called a *Fourth of July barbecue*, and Epiphanie is eager to go. It has been several days since their journey to New York City, and Epiphanie wants to make sure her sisters have truly forgiven one another—and more than that, Epiphanie needs a break.

Romeo has a cold again, keeping Maggie up night and day with his crying, so Epiphanie is picking up the slack where she can. That would not be so bad except Bradley has been arguing with her about helping out around the house. Even Caleb has pitched in somewhat, running the dishwasher and doing laundry and even showing the little ones (and Epiphanie) how to fold it. But Bradley refuses to even make a few peanut butter sandwiches when asked.

"They're not *my* kids," he says, putting the finishing touches on a ham sandwich for himself. "And you're not my mother."

Epiphanie looks at him from the floor of the living room where she is kneeling, picking up bundles of freshly washed socks that the other children had recently decided to throw at one another for fun. "This is your home," she points out. "You should help when help is needed."

"Nah, I'm not like you. I don't have that natural maternal instinct."

"Dude," Caleb says, lugging another basket of laundry out from the laundry room. "Just make some stupid sandwiches. It's not that hard."

Bradley glowers. "Fine, but I'm not cutting off the crusts for Simon."

Alarm suddenly shoots through Epiphanie and she jumps to her feet. "Where *is* Simon?"

"Got him," Rhi says as she enters through the front door. Simon runs in ahead of her giggling, hands dusty with colorful chalk dust. "He's fine, he was just drawing in the driveway. Everything okay?"

Epiphanie breathes a sigh of relief. "In a manner of speaking."

"Are you . . . ready to go?"

Epiphanie looks around her at the chaos and wonders if leaving is a good idea. She hears a door close somewhere down the hall and Maggie's hurried footsteps. "Rhi? Is that you?"

"Yes," Rhi says, just as Maggie appears behind Caleb in the living room.

"Oh, good. Here." She hurries to the fridge and pulls out a huge green melon, returning to hand it over to Rhi. "I meant to cut it up and have it displayed all nicely on a platter, but I didn't have time. Still, I don't want to send Epiphanie over for a party empty-handed."

"Maggie," Epiphanie says. "Are you sure you do not need me here?"

"Oh, you sweet, sweet girl. Absolutely not. I appreciate all that you do to help out, but the boys and I can handle this. Right, Bradley?" She says the last part with *meaning*.

"Right, Maggie," he grumbles, slapping peanut butter onto slices of white bread.

"You go enjoy yourself."

"Yeah, Epiphanie," Bradley echoes, too cheerful. "Go *enjoy* yourself."

Maggie urges Epiphanie and Rhi to the front door. "We'll be fine. I'm going to let Caleb and Bradley grill some hot dogs later, and you know how they *love* playing with fire." She rolls her eyes.

"Yes, it is worrisome," Epiphanie remarks.

Maggie raises her eyebrows. "Oh. Well . . . no, don't worry, sweetheart. Just have a good time. Both of you."

"How are things going at home?" Rhi asks once they are in the truck, the watermelon strapped into the back seat like a small child.

"Chaotic," Epiphanie admits, rolling down the window to feel the wind on her face. "But good, mostly."

"Yeah?"

"Yes. It is not like life was at the castle, but that is okay. Mother . . ." She hesitates, not wanting to say anything to disparage Mother, even now. He had given them so much. Was it not a past worth protecting?

"Maggie is very busy," she says at last. "But she is always there for us. And I think that is what really matters."

GRACE DOESN'T WANT TO BE at a stupid barbecue. She doesn't want to be a part of their therapy or their reintegration with society, or *in-tegration* for that matter, but her mother had insisted.

"Hello," a little girl with Down syndrome says to Grace, bending into a curtsy. "My name is Giovanna. Welcome to our farm."

"Thanks," Grace says.

Verity comes up beside Grace, her new green North Face backpack stuffed to the gills and sitting trim and elegant on her back, two reusable water bottles tucked into its netted pockets. Dr. Ibanez has told them they have to make allowances for behaviors like this. *Scarcity thinking*, she calls it. In the wilderness, water only came from so many sources. Verity likes to have her water with her at all times, and hoards unopened water bottles in her bedroom, too. When she gets a glass of water with a meal, she drinks the entire glass, every time. Sometimes she goes to the sink and fills a glass, drinks it down, and repeats until her stomach is protruding, distended with liquid.

Mom and Christopher step past Grace and Verity to greet Dr. Ibanez, Christopher shaking her hand much harder than Grace thinks is necessary. Dr. Ibanez's new girlfriend stands up and offers her hand, and Grace smirks when she sees her fingers wrap tight around Christopher's, giving her stepfather's "proud, firm handshake" a run for its money.

"Do you want to see the ponies?" Giovanna asks Grace and Verity. She points over to the stables where Sunder and Oblivienne are already reaching up to caress the face of a huge black draft horse, standing just outside of a classic red barn. There's a young man holding the bridle, and he's tall—taller than Grace, which immediately makes the evening a whole lot more interesting than she thought it would be.

"Yeah, sure," Grace says as Giovanna leads them over. "I love ponies."

Sunder notices the twins before the boy does. She darts toward Verity and leaps into her arms, nearly knocking her to the ground. They spin and embrace. They clutch each other as if they haven't seen each other almost every other day this week.

"Hi there," the boy says to Grace, stroking the horse's nose with one hand, holding the bridle with the other. "Name's Dallas. You must be Verity's sister, Grace."

"That's me," Grace says, trying to sound casual. "The almost-one-and-only."

His brow creases. "Pardon?"

"Sorry—it's a stupid identical twin joke. Doesn't really work with twins like us who grew up in totally different circumstances and are . . . therefore . . . super easy to tell apart . . ." Grace regrets her fumbling explanation even more than she regrets her joke.

Dallas laughs, charitably. "I get it." He eyes Grace as the other girls go to visit with the horses on the other side of the stable.

"So. What's it like living with the violent one?"

His eyebrows shoot up. "Is that how people think of Sunder? Huh."

"Well, did you see the interview?"

Dallas chuckles. "Yeah. Sunder's intense, but she's a sweetheart once you get to know her."

Straw crunches underfoot and they both turn to see who has arrived.

"Hey, Rhi! Epiphanie!" Dallas says. He meets them halfway and high-fives them both. "How's my favorite rescue ranger?"

"Fine," Rhi replies in her annoyingly soft voice. "How's my favorite farmhand?"

For some reason these nicknames infuriate Grace. Why is Rhi *always* around? Can Grace not have *anything* to herself? To make matters worse, the girls all rush over to Rhi and Epiphanie en masse, even Giovanna, to embrace them both—as if Rhi is just as important to them as their own sisters.

Grace turns and starts heading back toward the open air and the grill and the adults who will have nothing but superficial, innocuous things to talk about. Rhiannon Chase does not belong here, and she can go straight to hell.

"Grace," Verity calls.

And though Grace is not sure if it infuriates her or breaks her heart to do so, she slowly turns back to her sister and rejoins them.

SORE AND FILTHY FROM RIDING, but keyed up and hungry, the girls and Dallas finally sit down to dinner with the rest of the guests just as the sun begins to set. String lights and lanterns on the tables make up for the waning light as they feast on traditional Fourth of July fare: charred hot dogs, hamburgers and veggie burgers, baked beans, potato salad, grilled corn on the cob, red triangles of sliced watermelon, and various other dishes that the girls sample with curiosity.

At the "grown-ups table," Uncle Jimmy and Star are talking animatedly with Dr. Ibanez and her new girlfriend, Chani, who just transferred to the Happy Valley Police Department this past spring. Mr. Erikson is advising Mr. Quaker on when to flip the next batch of hamburgers; Mrs. Quaker and Mrs. Erikson are admiring a sunset-colored rose on a wooden trellis beside the deck, trading secrets on pruning and feeding.

Rhi feels uncommonly at ease watching the people around her. Happy, even.

These days, Rhi has mostly silenced her stepmother's voice to a whisper. She has grown a dress size or two now that she is no longer starving herself, and she feels healthier and more energized than she has in years. She thinks she looks pretty good, too, but mainly tries not to think about how she looks, because that can still be a doorway that invites unwanted voices back into her head.

Rhi fills her plate with whatever looks delicious, then spots Grace picking at her plate with disinterest, and feels a reflexive pang of shame, then a pang of pity. She wonders what else they might have in common.

On the table, Rhi's phone buzzes and a message alert materializes on the dark screen.

> **2 Messages from: NO**
> Happy fourth, Edie. I hope you get to see some fireworks tonight . . .

> I miss you.

Rhi casually swipes the screen to delete the notification, her appetite gone. When she looks up, Grace is watching her.

"Who's that?" Grace asks.

"No one," Rhi says.

Grace studies her with a raised eyebrow, but says nothing.

Across the table, Epiphanie tilts her head at Rhi, as if to ask, *Are you okay?*

Rhi nods. *I'll be fine.* And when she's around the girls, she really thinks she will be.

Beside her, Sunder takes a huge bite out of a half-charred hot dog. "Why is this so good?" she wonders, eyes closed, mouth full.

"Welcome to America." Dallas laughs.

"Aren't hot dogs German?" Grace asks.

"Maybe at some point, but I'm pretty sure Germans wouldn't recognize them in this form." Dallas takes a big bite out of his hot dog, smothered in mustard, ketchup, and relish.

Grace makes a face. "I really don't know how you guys eat that stuff. Hot dogs are like . . . the worst part of the animal."

"It's called *nose-to-tail dining*," Dallas says. "It's actually *less wasteful* than just eating prime cuts."

"Also, they just taste good," Giovanna says, licking ketchup from her index finger.

"I don't get girls sometimes," Dallas says, laughing. "You all have such weird hang-ups about food."

"That's because we're conditioned to believe eating is basically a bad habit we need to break, or else we'll get fat, which we're also conditioned to believe is obviously the worst fate imaginable," Rhi snaps.

Dallas raises his eyebrows. "Really?"

Grace and Rhi exchange a glance before nodding.

"Wow. Then I'm sorry I said that."

"No need to apologize," Rhi says quickly, regretting her honesty, not wanting him to feel bad or get upset with her. "You just made an observation."

"Yeah. But now I realize I was basically mocking how society has traumatized you."

Rhi studies Dallas and decides his remorse is genuine. "Yeah. Okay. In that case, apology accepted." Rhi puts a forkful of starchy, creamy, delicious potato salad into her mouth, thinking: *Fuck you, Vera. Fuck you, patriarchy.*

Sunder's brow wrinkles. "Who is telling you to stop eating?"

"Everyone," Grace and Rhi say at the same time. They look at each other again and share an awkward moment of understanding.

Giovanna looks at them, her plate nearly cleaned. "No one tells me food is bad."

Rhi smiles. "That's because you have amazing parents."

"But Verity and Grace do not?" Sunder asks.

Verity remains silent while Grace snorts.

"Ask me again in ten years," Grace says, biting into a carrot stick.

FIREFLIES ARE JUST BEGINNING TO blink in the shadows beyond the patio by the time they finish eating. As the adults head inside, Sunder builds a fire in the firepit out behind the barn. After a while, Dallas rolls up in a golf cart filled with deerskin drums and ingredients for s'mores.

"Sunder found these in the attic a few weeks ago and has basically turned us into a hippie version of the Partridge Family since," Dallas says, smiling across the fire at his foster sister as he hands the instruments out to the wild girls.

"We had instruments like these at the castle," Oblivienne says softly, examining the craftsmanship of a wide, flat drum in her hands. "Mother taught us how to make them . . ."

"We will get to that," Sunder says. She hands everyone a long stick and a marshmallow, and teaches her sisters how to roast them.

Rhi enjoys the wonder on the girls' faces as they taste the pure sugary joy of the confection, as they examine the texture of the marshmallows, from soft, to crisp, to nearly fluid inside. Sunder beams at being able to bring this thing to her sisters. She glows beside the fire, her shaggy hair lit up like a halo.

Dallas catches Rhi's eye and they share a moment of contentment. Rhi likes that Dallas delights in the girls' delight. She likes that he's gentle and kind, maybe even trustworthy. She likes knowing he's here for Sunder when her sisters and Rhi cannot be, like an older brother.

But Rhi doesn't want to think about older brothers, so she tries to think about something else instead.

Verity sits beside Grace and offers her a s'more, pleased to share this treasure with her Blood Sister. But then Grace takes it and says, "These things are really bad for you, you know. They'll give you zits." She turns and offers it to Rhi.

Rhi bites her lip and looks at Verity.

"Go on, Grace," Dallas says. "Don't let the patriarchy stop you from enjoying the crème de la crème of summer snacks."

Grace's cheeks flush pink. She nibbles a corner of one of the gluten-free crackers until Verity smiles at her. Then she takes a bite— necessarily big, necessarily messy—and self-consciously covers her mouth while she chews.

Bmm.

Bmm.

While they were talking, Sunder has picked up one of the hand-made drums. Between her knees, she is holding a medium-sized drum that is shaped like an hourglass, flat on both ends. Epiphanie, brushing crumbs from her hands, picks up the drum beside her and strikes it twice.

Tmm, tmm, it resonates at a higher pitch. She looks to Verity, who picks up her drum with a smile, and they all lock eyes with Oblivienne, who hesitates. Oblivienne picks up the broad, flat drum, but looks unsure. Finally, she takes a steadying breath and taps it with the tips of her fingers, fumbling slowly into her sisters' song. The wild girls let their hands find the beat with measured strikes, light or hard, cutting the rhythm into thirds and fourths, ricocheting off one another until, miraculously, something beautiful emerges from the chaos.

Dallas and Giovanna hand drums to Rhi and Grace, but only Rhi takes one eagerly. Rhi is still pulled taut inside, torn between the fantasy of full release and fear of the consequences of her own freedom: she is trembling—just slightly—when she closes her eyes, when her mouth bows into a smile, when she pulls her hand back; she is rigid as she brings the meat of her hand down on the hard skin of the drum and thwacks out the first music she's made in what feels like a lifetime.

But as the beats layer on top of one another—bouncing, calling, responding—she quiets her mind and sinks into her bones. She feels the pulse in her flesh and the arrhythmic flicker of the fire over her face, and there, she finds her rhythm—and her release.

Bmmbmmbmm brrack.

Bmmbmmbmm brrack.

Rhi submerges into the pulse of their song, the whole world fading away like it has so many times in the presence of the wild girls. Somewhere in the circle, Dallas beats a simple rhythm with his eyes half-closed; Giovanna slaps happily along with a jangling tambourine. Together—the Wild Girls of Happy Valley, the wallflower, the farmhand, and the child—they weave a tapestry of heartbeats and stomping feet through the pounding of their drums.

Deep in her trance, Rhi feels such an overwhelming sense of connection—an *absence* of separateness and self-consciousness—that she hardly notices that she's on her feet, raising the circular drum over her head as she beats it harder, faster.

"Yeah!" Dallas shouts.

The others are standing too now, drums in hand or tucked between their knees or under their arms. Giovanna dances, twirling with her tambourine, one leg stretched behind her like a ballerina. Sunder starts dancing too, moving the way a leaf whips through a windstorm. Epiphanie calls out in a language no one knows, but each one of them feels, deep in their bones.

Her words become a melody, her voice a low and powerful contralto that makes Rhi's chest yawn open and sets the night ablaze with stars. All at once, they look up at the sky as their hands channel the rhythm of this ephemeral, eternal song. The Milky Way shines overhead, smeared across the velvet sky in swirling, incandescent glory.

Verity begins to sing, too, her voice a notch higher than Epiphanie's, dancing in perfect step with her sister's, always in harmony. The circle of girls and Dallas begins to move clockwise around the fire and around Grace, who is frozen, staring at the sky as if she has never seen the stars before in all her life.

Rhi knows, though she does not know how she knows, that for some of them, they have not felt this alive since the wilderness.

For some of them, they have never felt this alive at all.

All around them fireflies are swarming to their song, illuminating the pasture with pulsating green and blue as they surround them in a ring of light. Perhaps that's why Grace stands up, looks around with wide eyes. When she sees the fireflies, she covers her mouth with both hands.

The drumming and singing are reaching a fever pitch, a climax Rhi feels deep in her fingers and toes and the top of her head. When Sunder falls to her knees, throws her head back, and howls like a wolf, Epiphanie and Verity join her—Rhi joins her—even Giovanna and Dallas join her, knees hitting the soft earth, throats open and howling at the waxing moon.

Only Oblivienne and Grace remain standing, both looking stricken.

"Stop it!"

Rhi turns to the shout.

Oblivienne drops the drum from her hand as if she's just realized she is holding something grotesque. She puts her hands on either side of her head, fingers buried in her black hair, and screams. "*Stop it, stop it, stop it!*"

They do stop. All of them go silent and slack. Her sisters look at her as if they do not know her.

Grace backs away, out of the circle, toward the field of fireflies so dense she does not dare try to move through them.

"Do you not see?" Oblivienne shouts. "We cannot *be* like this anymore!"

"Oblivienne," Rhi tries, still thrumming with connection, sensing Oblivienne's panic as if it were her own. "You're safe here. You're free here."

"No!" Oblivienne shrieks, shaking her head, tearing at her scalp. "If anyone else ever saw this," Oblivienne half growls between clenched teeth. "They would lock us up again. They would cage us again like the animals Mother wanted us to be."

"We *are* animals," Sunder growls back. "And *so are they*!"

"No," Oblivienne says. "No. We are freak shows."

Rhi wonders where Oblivienne learned about *freak shows*.

"Everyone is a freak in their own way," Grace says nervously, surprising the others. "Everyone here is a freak, whether we grew up in the wild or not."

"*You* are not a freak," Oblivienne snaps. "Dallas and Giovanna are not freaks. Mr. and Mrs. Quaker are not freaks."

"Says who?" Dallas asks, putting an arm around Giovanna's shoulders to comfort the frightened girl. "You don't know half the things people say about the Quakers, or Giovanna, or me. We're all different. And some people are afraid of anything that's different from what they expect." Dallas shrugs and tries to offer a smile. "We're all freaks here, but we're doing just fine."

"It is not the same," Oblivienne says, shaking her head vigorously. "It is not the same at all, and you know it. *So many lies* . . . everything we thought we knew . . ." Oblivienne whimpers, before dropping to her knees. "He did this to us. He made us like this. Why? *Why did he do it?*"

It is Sunder who crawls over to Oblivienne, wrapping her arms around her from behind. *We will be okay*, she says with her hands, her arms, her cheek against Oblivienne's hair. *I love you*, she says with the tightness of her embrace, the fierce set of her jaw.

Tears stream from Oblivienne's eyes as she shakes. The sisters look at one another, silent, ashamed, for once in their lives not knowing how to comfort one of their own.

"What should we do?" Dallas whispers to Rhi.

Her throat is still raw from howling when she answers, "I have no idea."

OBLIVIENNE'S JOURNAL
July 4, 20—

■

Can not stop thinking about time Mother brought us peaches. They do not grow in the mountins. Apples, berrys, grapes, sweet roots and tree bark—all we ever knew of sweet things. Mother returned from the forrest that day—4 summers ago? 5?—with round fuzzy hard littl rocks. Pink and yellow and oranje. 4 of them, 1 for each. Mother said he found them while wandering—his spirit gides had shown him to a hidden orchard. But they were not yet ripe. We had to be ~~pashent~~ patient.

Sunder has never been good at patients and she bit in to hers right away. It was hard and tuff like an old dandeline root and tastid like nothing. The rest of us waited a few days like Mother had said to. And when the peaches were just getting soft we took our first bites—Epiphanie shared hers with Sunder—and it was the best thing any of us had ever tastid our entire lives. Still have never eaten any thing as ~~wunderful~~ wonderful as that peach even with every thing this world has given us. The tender flesh. Sweet juice on our chins. Imposibly <u>alive</u> flavor. That used to be a favorite memory.

Now all I can think when I remember that day is <u>where did the peaches come from</u>? Did Mothers spirit gides really show him to a hidden orchard or did he buy them at a super market? Rhi might say the important thing is that Mother cared about us enough to bring us peaches. Epiphanie might say we would have never tastid how good they were if we had not lisened to Mother and waited for the peaches to ripen. Sunder would probably ask why I am trying to re-write our memories. Verity might say regardless of what really happend we can have all the peaches we want now. But I can not help but imagine Mother dressed in JEANS and a T shirt waiting in line at the super market while we are alone in the forrest fully believing every story he ever told us. I hate this image with every drop of my spirit but I can not help but see it. It fills me with so much anger I wish I could bring Mother back from the dead and SHAKE him.

But is it TRUE? It must be. But why does that image feel more real to me than the REAL memorys I cary of magic? Or Mothers love for us? Those are REAL MEMORYS so the magic in them must be real to—and if magic is real that means Mother did NOT lie. Right?

I do not know.

All I know is that I do not want to live in a world where that image of Mother in the super market is real. Even if it is a world full of perfectly ripe peaches.

28

At three in the morning, Oblivienne sits up in bed, the sheets suddenly too cloying, too heavy on her body. She has had enough of her racing thoughts, of the galloping rhythm of her untamable heart. Across the room, Allison sleeps soundly, her dark curls like a spill of night sky on her pillow.

Oblivienne slips out of bed and pads over to the open window. Silently, she lifts the screen. A warm summer breeze meets her as she hoists herself through the opening.

The second-story roof is just on the other side of the sash, inclined but not too steep. Oblivienne maneuvers away from the window to climb up higher. She reaches up to the attic roof and, leveraging her weight between her limbs, hoists herself up once more. She kicks off the side of the exterior wall and flings herself onto the top of the house.

She has done this many times before. The roof is the only place she can be alone, for she knows that even if the other children followed her out here, they would not be able to climb as high as she can. But they do not follow her, because she always goes out here at night, when the rest of the household is sleeping.

Oblivienne scurries, spiderlike, to the peak of the house. The gritty texture of the shingles provides enough grip for her to easily pull herself up the steep incline until she is seated on top of the world.

When she gets there, Oblivienne realizes she is trembling. Not because of the unencumbered breeze whipping her hair around her head, or because she is scared, or because the climb wore her out—it is a trivial matter for her to do these kinds of things, as it would be for her sisters. (*No, not sisters. Companions? They are not my sisters. I cannot keep thinking of them like that.*) Something else is causing her to shiver on this balmy, windy night, something she has been trying not to let herself think these past four months.

She has tried so hard not to let herself think it at all, but it slipped into her mind just recently, during the interview with Jenny Ro. She has not been able to shake it since.

I do not want to live in a world where Mother lied to us.

But the indelible truth is: *Mother lied to us.*

The pain of that fact is like a splinter running under her skin the whole length of her body. She cannot numb it away with distractions. Every movement reminds her of its presence; every clench of muscle, every breath, deep or shallow. Mother has always been at the core of who Oblivienne thought she was: Mother's love. Mother's clarity of purpose. Mother's wisdom. Mother's lessons. Mother's stories.

It was hard enough when Mother died, but at least death is natural—expected. But to lose not only the Mother of the physical world, but the Mother inside Oblivienne as well? To lose the caretaker who shaped them—who shaped *her*—into a strong, capable woman with a definitive, meaningful purpose in this life . . . ?

It is *unbearable.*

Oblivienne has been turning away from this pain for as long as she could, but it refuses to be ignored any longer. She has been glancing at it, sidelong, for weeks now—journaling and meditating and ruminating—listing off all the facts in her head that seem to wrestle with one another, none of them prevailing over the others for more than a moment at a time.

She does not know how to reconcile these two facts:

Mother lied to us.

I do not want to live in a world where Mother lied to us.

Looking up at the scanty stars and the clouds rolling in from beyond the mountains, Oblivienne can still hear Mother's voice in the wind, telling them for the hundredth time, *When the heavens meet the Earth and your fifth sister has arrived, you will return to Leutheria and save your kingdoms.* She recalls the fervor with which they once believed him. What cause did they have to doubt? Here was a kind, nurturing man—the only parent they had ever known—who possessed magic and made the girls believe they had magic in themselves. They had *seen* his magic, had they not? They had witnessed him speaking with beasts, had seen him heal them of wounds and sickness, watched him enchant the castle to protect them. And it *did* protect them. Until Mother died.

They had seen their own magic, too: they had witnessed one another defy gravity leaping from tree branches, and spark fires with nothing but their will, and summon prey for hunting as easily as calling each other home for dinner.

But Verity has a twin sister in *this world*.

So maybe they are *not* from another world. Maybe they *are* from this world of screens and plastics and food so abundant people feel the need to restrict what they allow themselves to eat. And if the "kingdoms" Mother stole the girls from were anything like the household Brian Cornwell described when Verity was stolen, Oblivienne should be glad she was taken away.

But they will never know the truth. The only one who knew that was Mother.

Oblivienne pushes her hair out of her eyes as she looks down at the street below, a smooth black river spotted with amber streetlights. The wind is blowing stronger now, rustling ornamental shrubs and whipping American flags around their poles. She looks at the near-identical houses lining the street in white and pale blue and yellow, filled with families, maybe with children, maybe parents loving their children the way Mother loved them, maybe harming them the way Mother harmed them.

I do not want to live in a world where Mother lied to us.

But the thought comes to her, not unwelcome, and not for the first time: maybe Mother did not lie, and there *is* a way to prove it, so the pain crawling under Oblivienne's skin does not have to continue.

Maybe the magic Mother showed them is real, *has been real*, all along.

They did not imagine when they conjured rain or sunshine, or when they heard one another's thoughts in their minds, or when they held their breath for minutes at a time underwater, without even a moment of discomfort.

And if that is true, Oblivienne could stop hurting.

If the magic is real, she could know who she really is, again.

An exquisite feeling of lightness blooms inside Oblivienne, like a burst of starlight in her chest. For the first time in days, Oblivienne breathes easily. Deeply. She swings her legs over the side of the roof peak and inches down toward the gutter, standing with her toes at the very edge of the roof, looking out over the cars in the driveway so far below. She has considered this before in her journal, but here, now, the opportunity has presented itself for her to prove the truth of things, once and for all.

If the magic is real, Mother was not lying.

If the magic is real, the magic will protect me as it did before.

And if the magic is not real . . .

Oblivienne tilts her face to the sky. She summons the weightlessness of the clouds into her body, and hands made of stardust grip her as she spreads her arms like wings.

I do not want to live in a world where Mother lied to us.

Oblivienne, weightless as a moonbeam, gives herself over to the wind and sky and magic, and lets herself *rise.*

Wolves in the Storm

Excerpted from *Savage Castle:*
A Memoir of the Wild Girls of Happy Valley

SEVEN MOONS CAME AND WENT after Mother died, and in that time the spells he had worked on the castle began to weaken. The place we called home all our lives gradually became nothing more than a shelter—and then nothing more than a rotting, hollow tree. The bunks we had carved into the walls suddenly felt clumsy and small; the places where we stored dry goods and root vegetables grew damp and moldy; the once impenetrable castle now leaked when it rained; insects burrowed through to the interior, chewing away at the walls and biting our ankles when we slept.

Never before had these things been a concern. We had always known some of that protection had come from Mother's magic, the way he charged the castle each time he came home and each time he left, topping off the magic he set in place so long ago when he found the tree and recognized it as our home. But though Mother had taught us other magic, he never taught us that particular spell. Perhaps because he knew his death would be the beginning of the end of our life there. Or, perhaps he simply never made the time.

The nights were miserable enough in those days, knowing Mother was gone forever, never to return. When the castle began to fail us in

all those little, important ways, nights became a small torture—
always damp, always itchy, always skin-crawling, always a dank and
sour smell as fungus took hold and the wood began to rot. When we
built a fire, the smoke no longer evacuated through the high chim-
ney, but instead filled the castle with black smoke and the sound of
our coughing. Snowy nights were a fine balance between keeping
ourselves from freezing to death and breathing.

When the snow began to melt, the end finally came.

A wild, raging storm blew outside that night; we had been bickering all day about unimportant things—Sunder was mad at Verity for
killing the spiders she had summoned to eat the fleas; Oblivienne was
upset with Sunder for losing her best spearhead after killing a rabbit
for our dinner; Verity was sad Epiphanie had not liked the taste of the
rabbit stew she had made for us; Epiphanie was tired of trying to
make peace between us all. The leather curtain was pulled taut over
the door against the rain, and inside the castle had become dusty
with smoke from lard candles.

Suddenly, light flashed high overhead and the whole castle shook
as thunder clapped.

We looked up into the high shadows of our castle. Lightning flashed
again, illuminating a gap in the castle walls above us where the tree
had splintered. Deafening thunder echoed inside as sparks fell from
above and we scattered, covering our heads. We did not have to speak
to know what this meant: the castle was under attack.

Another flash-bang of lightning lit up the inside of the castle, shaking the walls and making the tree groan as the whole thing suddenly
began to tilt, raising the ground beneath our feet with it. The earth
heaved and we toppled away from the entrance, all our scattered belongings tumbling with us.

The curtain snapped partly free and whipped violently in the
wind, revealing an electric blue world outside, swaying in flashes of
storm light. Rain poured inside in fat droplets and sprays, instantly
soaking everything in sight.

Epiphanie gestured wordlessly and we scrambled up the newly
risen floor, leaning now at a forty-five-degree angle. One by one we

slithered over the damp wood and dirt, growing slicker with each passing second, until we were climbing down the massive roots of the tree, landing in a giant puddle below, water up to our waists. Verity, thinking ahead, seized the leather curtain and tore it from its fixtures on her way out.

We scrambled out of the pit and away from the castle as lightning crackled through the sky. Clustered together under the curtain, we watched as lightning struck the castle again and again, sending flaming splinters of ancient wood sizzling into the night.

We watched in horror as our castle fell with a booming groan to the forest floor. The earth shook beneath us as it landed, crushing countless other trees in its path as easily as bird bones. We shivered in the cold, hardly able to comprehend this new loss, and pressed our rain-slick bodies together for comfort.

We stood like that for a long time before our wolf-kin came. They slunk toward us from the shadows, dripping with rainwater, silver fur turned black. When they reached us, they pressed against our cold naked legs with their warm wet flanks, as if to say to us, *Here, we are here, you may lean on us.*

We spent the night with our wolf-kin in their den, too many bodies curled too close, air hot with too much breath. In the morning, the wolves woke us with cold muzzles and urged us out into the day. The sun had come out strong, a shimmering haze over everything as the rain began to evaporate.

With the wolves beside us, we made our way back to the castle in our still-damp furs. When we arrived, we stared at it, wondered at it, with pain and horror—the same way we had once stared at Mother's corpse.

But we were too weary for the heartbreak we afforded Mother. When Mother passed, we'd had a home—a place where we could safely mourn him. Now, it was our very home that we mourned.

But one by one we turned to look at the wolves and wondered the same thing: Did Mother's spirit send our wolf-kin to guide us? Did Mother's spirit mean for us to leave this place, to begin our new journey? Is that why Mother never taught us the magic to protect our castle?

Oblivienne walked across the muddy encampment until she was standing beside the castle. She pressed a hand to the smooth trunk and closed her eyes, saying *thank you* to the tree that had sheltered us our entire lives. Saying goodbye.

The rest of us joined her at the castle's side, pressing palms and foreheads against the trunk, our skin and our hearts flush with grief, and with gratitude, until the time came to do what Mother had intended for us to do.

When we had given all we had left to give, we set off into the wilderness in search of our new home, letting our wolf-kin lead the way.

29

Rhi's phone is vibrating on the nightstand. She almost doesn't hear it over the rain pelting against the windows, the distant roll of thunder somewhere in the valley, but something about the unnatural pitch of the vibration wakes her. The dark room is lit only by the illuminated screen of the phone as it rumbles closer to the edge of the nightstand. Rhi grabs it before it can fall, looks at the caller ID.

| **Epiphanie's House**

Why would Epiphanie be calling at—
Four in the morning?
"Epiphanie?"
"Rhi, please. We need your help. Something is horribly, horribly wrong . . ." Her voice is no longer regal, no longer the firm, steady contralto Rhi has come to trust. It is shaking, as if it might break at any moment.

Rhi turns on the light beside her bed, sits up, blinks away the glare. "What is it? What happened?"

"I think something *terrible* has happened to Oblivienne."

"What . . . what do you mean? Why do you think that?"

There is a long pause, during which Rhi is almost certain she can hear Epiphanie choking back sobs.

"I cannot say it. If I say it, it will be true."

A jolt of panic electrifies Rhi as she jumps up and starts hunting for something warm to throw on.

"Did you call Mrs. Lynch?" she asks, pulling her mother's Syracuse University hoodie on.

"There was no answer."

"Okay. I'm going to drive out there. Is Maggie with you?"

"Yes. She does not believe me."

"Okay. Tell her I'm driving over to the Lynches' house. I'll call when . . . when I have more information."

THE OLD BLUE TRUCK IS noisier than ever in the rainy gray of early morning. The engine growls, the tires rumble over potholes, even the sound of the turn signal is like someone flicking the side of an empty metal can. All of it is blanketed by the insistent tapping of rain on the metal body of the truck, the repetitive swish and squeal of the wind-shield wipers.

Rhi is practically vibrating with anxiety. She feels stupid sneaking out of bed at four in the morning to follow up on someone's frantic hunch; but at the same time, she knows in her gut that Epiphanie is not exaggerating.

So what does that mean?

What is Rhi going to find at the Lynches' house?

Rhi turns at the intersection that will lead her to their house. She prays, silently, to whatever powers might exist in the universe, that this night ends in nothing but chagrin and Mrs. Lynch having one more reason to dislike Rhi. She prays that Epiphanie's anxiety is because of the storm, because of the rift between the girls, the way they've started to hold back from one another and argue, and how none of them seem to know how to process what they've been through. She prays they don't hold her responsible for that rift—that whatever becomes of them isn't ultimately her fault for bringing them into this world—a world that has rarely been kind to Rhi, so how could she have ever thought it would be good to them?

Rhi squints through the rain. Up ahead, there is something lying in the middle of the road.

She slows down as she approaches—she shouldn't be going so fast in a residential neighborhood anyway—and tries to make out what it might be. It's too small for a deer, too big for a raccoon. There are houses on either side of the street; any one of them could have a dog that got out, got hit by a car.

Rhi pulls over and parks when she gets closer to the thing in the middle of the road, her pulse pounding loudly in her ears. She unbuckles her seat belt, pulls the hood of her raincoat over her head, but can't make herself get out of the car.

"It's a dog," Rhi tells herself, as if, like Epiphanie said, speaking it will make it true. She opens the driver's side door and climbs out, the raindrops like a thousand tiny fingers poking at her head and shoulders, wetting her face. She walks toward the form in the middle of the road. In the light from the truck's headlights, Rhi can see something on the asphalt at her feet, wet flecks of dark, shining red fanned out in all directions like the spray of a burst water balloon, all of it rinsing away in the rain.

It is immediately clear that she was not hit by a car.

The sky cracks overhead like a gunshot, lightning flashing, painting everything in stark white.

Rhi fumbles with her phone as she pulls it out of her pocket, dials 911, shoves the phone into her hood, against her ear, out of the rain. Her lips feel numb, her tongue heavy, as she yells over the rain to tell the operator what she's found.

And then she's back in the truck. The door is still open, rain soaking her left side. She can't remember how she got there, what she said to the operator. ("*There is a body in the middle of the road*"? Surely, she never had to say those words in her life.)

Rhi looks out the windshield, through the rain and the windshield wipers and the yellow glow of her headlights, at the too-small body pressed and ruined against the asphalt.

She leans out of the cab of the truck and vomits.

CROWDFUNDME.COM

Official Memorial Fund For Our Sweet Girl, Gone Too Soon

[Press photo of
Oblivienne from
her appearance
on the Jenny Ro
Show.]

Muriel Lynch is organizing this fundraiser.

On July 5, our sweet foster child, Oblivienne—one of the famed "Wild Girls of Happy Valley"—tragically lost her battle with mental illness and ended her life. We've started this CrowdFundMe to raise money to help cover our beloved Oblivienne's funeral expenses and to give her the memorial she deserves. We are devastated to have to ask for help, but we hope that those of you who know Oblivienne's story will feel moved to contribute even in some small way. These funds will cover the cost of her funeral and will also help us pay for the necessary grief counseling for our other foster children. Any funds that exceed our goal will go toward the care of our remaining foster children and their college funds.

$1,002,755 raised of $25,000 goal
400.2K donors
501.9K shares
200.3K followers

DRAFTS

FROM: "Eden Chase" <e.r.c.2007@springmail.com>
TO: "Kevin Hartwell" <hartwell.kevin@irving.edu>
DATE: July 6
SUBJECT:

I saved one girl's life only to kill another.

I seem to make killing people a habit. I got my mother killed too, after all.

All because I couldn't control my temper.

It was like signing her death warrant.

If I hadn't thrown that tantrum (I can't even remember over what). If my father hadn't told her to *get your daughter under control*. If he hadn't come after me, red faced and shouting when I refused to calm down. If none of that had happened, she wouldn't have put herself between us. He wouldn't have finally hit her.

She wouldn't have finally tried to leave.

We wouldn't have been in the car at three in the morning when that drunk asshole decided to run a red light.

I don't know why I'm telling you this. (I'm not really telling you anything, I guess.) But Oblivienne is dead because I took her out of the wilderness. Because instead of supporting her when her world fell apart, I yelled at her for hurting her sisters. And I don't know how to forgive myself.

30

U̲NCLE J̲IMMY POKES HIS HEAD into the guest room.

"You awake, Rhi-Rhi?" he asks. "Mari Ibanez is on the phone. She was hoping to speak with you. Just checking in."

It is past noon. Oblivienne has been dead for approximately thirty-three hours. Rhi has been in bed for the last sixteen.

Suicide is contagious.

She overheard someone say that yesterday, whispered it, as if speaking it too loudly would make it more likely to catch. She can't remember who it was. It was more than one person, now that she thinks about it. She can't remember any of them.

"Rhi?" Uncle Jimmy asks again from the doorway.

His voice is so gentle, a fresh flood of tears washes over Rhi's cheeks.

Hours later, when she finally gets up to pee for the first time since yesterday, one creaky floorboard on her way out of the bathroom is all it takes before Uncle Jimmy is standing in the hallway. He looks *so relieved* to see Rhi out of bed that she almost starts crying again, but she manages, this time, to hold the tears back.

"You're up," he says. "And I bet you're starving. Let's get some food in you." He takes her by the elbow, guiding her into the living room, to the breakfast counter that separates the living room from the kitchen. Uncle Jimmy sits her on one of the pub chairs and goes to the refrigerator where he starts pulling out an absurd amount of food.

She can't tell him she doesn't deserve any of this kindness. She doesn't deserve good food made with love. She doesn't deserve him worrying about her. She can't tell him this, because he will argue with her, and she does not want anyone to talk her out of this shame.

"Right . . . I suppose most of this is too rich if you haven't eaten in a bit," Uncle Jimmy says, putting nearly everything away. "Soup, though. That's the one. Nothing cures what ails you like a bowl of soup." He opens the lid on the plastic quart container of matzo ball soup and pours it into a saucepan, turning on the gas flame with a few clicks of the ignition.

Purrdita rubs her teeth on Rhi's legs, scratches helplessly at her pajama pants.

Uncle Jimmy grabs a can of orange-flavored sparkling water from the refrigerator and sits next to Rhi. With a determined look, he pops open the can and puts it in her hands. "Hydrate," he instructs.

"I told Epiphanie I'd call her," Rhi suddenly remembers, clumsily dropping the can of sparkling water on the counter, then catching it before it topples. "I told her I'd call and I never called." She is half out of her chair, breathing hard, short, fast.

"Shhhh," Uncle Jimmy says, putting his hands on her shoulders and encouraging her to sit back down. He rubs her back as she tries to catch her breath. "Shhhh."

Disgust crashes over her and bile rises in Rhi's throat. Before she knows what she's doing, she slips off of her chair on the side opposite her uncle and stumbles away, backward, staring at him as if *he* is the one who killed Oblivienne.

Rhi covers her mouth with her hands, eyes wide. "I'm sorry," she whispers.

She shakes her head to rid it of the disgust that doesn't fit here, that shouldn't be a part of this moment.

Uncle Jimmy is alarmed at first. He looks at his hand that was on Rhi's back in confusion, shakes his head the tiniest fraction, then looks back at Rhi as though he's realizing something horrible.

"Rhi—"

"It's nothing," Rhi says. "Nothing. I'm just . . . I'm just . . . I'm just exhausted. Delirious." She pulls her hands through her hair. "I need to shower and change. I . . . I need to go see the girls. They need me right now."

Uncle Jimmy looks deeply concerned as he opens his mouth to say something more, but he shuts it just as fast, thinking better of it.

"You eat some soup before you do anything," he says, standing and walking back to the stove. He sets a bowl on the counter, looking sternly at his niece as he does so. "I'm not letting you walk out that door until your stomach is full."

WHEN RHI FINALLY ARRIVES AT the Quakers—Uncle Jimmy dropped her off because he didn't like the idea of her driving in her condition—it is a blur of shining eyes, faces, hands, arms, bodies. No one asks her any questions. No one blames her for ruining their lives. They simply fold Rhi into the weave of their fabric, let their tears fall in her hair and on her skin, let her tears stain their shirts, until no one knows whose tears are whose, whose shoulder is whose, whose cheek, or arm, or breast racked with sobs.

Rhi's pain is the same pain that moves through Epiphanie, the same pain that moves through Sunder, the same pain that moves through them all. Even when she scolds herself, tries to tell herself she has only known Oblivienne for a few months, these girls are her *sisters*, the pain of the whole coalesces inside of her as if it *belongs* to her.

Which is why she knows they feel her pain, too, in all its peculiarities: the shame. The responsibility. The doubt. But each new wave brings new caresses, new embraces that erode the jagged edges of shame in Rhi's heart until it is smooth, and cool, and dull, like sea glass.

GRIEF HAS A WAY OF breaking time. In the first throes of grieving, you are a boat run aground, unmoving, lodged against the riverbank, the pain too heavy for the voyage. And yet the other boats continue to stream by. For minutes, hours, days, even. Years, maybe, if the grief is more than you can bear. The rest of the world is still rushing by, swept up in a current that will weather your boat down to nothing if you do not return to the water, eventually.

And you will return to the water, eventually. When your grief grows light enough to carry with the rest of your cargo.

Or, perhaps, when you have built a boat large enough to hold it.

THANKS TO DR. IBANEZ AND the Quakers' gentle explanations, the Wild Girls of Happy Valley know about funerals now. They know about caskets, which are also called coffins, and no one in that room really knows the difference. They know about cemeteries, and headstones, and eulogies. They have learned all about this society's way of marking death, but it is not their way.

"We would like for you to grieve Oblivienne in the way that helps *you*," Dr. Ibanez says before she leaves. "But her body will be buried at the Happy Valley Cemetery."

"Can we—" Epiphanie starts, interrupted by her own breathless grief. "Can we have a lock of her hair?"

Dr. Ibanez inclines her head with sympathy. "I'll see what I can do." She makes eye contact with Rhi before leaving, the same offer as always written on her face. *If you need to talk . . .*

Rhi just wipes her eyes and looks away.

Now, sitting on the floor in Sunder's bedroom, the girls look at one another with eyes rimmed red from crying, their keen awareness of Oblivienne's absence broadcast like a silent requiem. They've been asked to contribute to the memorial ceremony, but they have no sense of how to say goodbye to their beloved sister.

Rhi watches Sunder, especially, as the girls ponder. Sunder who believes so fervently in the future Mother promised. What would happen to *her* if she stopped believing? Does she still believe, even now?

Does *Rhi* believe?

She isn't sure. She's never *been* sure—of who she is, or what she believes, or where she belongs. She has never fully given into the desire—and it was a desire, like any other deep and urgent want—to believe in Leutheria and the five princesses, but she doesn't know if that's because she knows it can't possibly be true, or if it's because she's been conditioned to believe only in the facts she can prove—never mind the things she has experienced with her own senses since the girls came into her life.

The grief-dark haze of the last forty-eight hours has not made things any clearer to her; it only begs the question: Did Mother know this would happen, too?

"Rhi," Verity asks softly from her seat on the plush carpet. "What did you do at your mother's funeral?"

Rhi tightens into a ball, her legs drawn up to her chest, arms wrapped around her knees. "I wasn't allowed to go to my mother's funeral. My father said I was too young." She blinks away the memory, looking at the girls again. "But that day, while my father was away and the caterers were setting up for the reception, my babysitter and I did our own ritual. First, we made my mother's chocolate chip cookie recipe together. Then, I took my mother's hair from her hairbrush, and cut a lock of my own hair, and tied the two together with a silver chain I had found on the ground the last time my mother and I went to the park. I tied that to a rose from my mother's garden, and we went to the creek in the woods, and I told the babysitter my favorite memories of her and all the things I would miss about her." Rhi's eyes sting. "Eventually, when I was ready, I placed the hair and the rose in the creek and let the water take them away from me. Then . . . we sat together and ate cookies until the reception started." Rhi smiles weakly.

The girls look thoughtful for a moment, immediately understanding the instinct of the ritual.

But Sunder shakes her head, fresh tears streaking her face. "We have none of Oblivienne's things. They won't even let us have her journal. We have no part of her except for what is inside of us. How do we let her go without cutting ourselves open?"

Epiphanie, fingering one of her long black braids, looks at her sisters with knowing in her eyes. "I have an idea."

31

THE GIRLS ASK RHI TO help them mourn Oblivienne's death the way they want to.

She drives them into town to the thrift store to pick out mourning shawls, which they now wear wrapped around their heads and draped over their shoulders like cowls, fairly swallowing their faces. Sunder's is a sky-blue and gold pashmina; Verity's is dark-green silk the color of late summer leaves; Epiphanie's is eggplant purple with tiny silver feathers embroidered along the edge. Rhi has chosen a plain black shawl, for as much as she feels she is a part of this pack now, she would still rather blend into the background if she can help it.

The casket is at the front of the chapel, a gleaming wooden brick that says nothing of the girl whose body is inside it. There is a wall of flowers on either side of the coffin, traditional white calla lilies, wreaths of white roses, garlands of white hydrangeas. They are too manicured, too homogenous—Rhi would have preferred to see wildflowers, or at least an imitation of something truer to the nature of the young woman they are mourning. The enlarged photo sitting atop the coffin is from the *Jenny Ro Show*, a posed headshot for marketing material; Oblivienne's smile is weak, and forced, and does not belong to her. Her eyes, at least, are real, and wide, and searching.

When the service begins, the funeral director speaks secular words of philosophy and comfort, and a well-practiced reading of "Do Not Stand by My Grave and Weep" by Clare Harner. He then opens the floor up to anyone else who would like to speak.

There is a long, uncomfortable moment of stillness before press cameras begin to click and flash. To Rhi's surprise, Mrs. Lynch is approaching the lectern.

"Hello," she says sweetly. "My name is Muriel Lynch, and I was Oblivienne's foster mother. If you knew Oblivienne, you know it was impossible not to fall in love with her. You know how sweet and gentle and agreeable she always was. She was a blessing. And the other children—they *adored* her. She told them stories about her time in the forest, and they ate up every last bit of it." She pauses here to smile and dab at her eyes with a handkerchief. "But she was still a wild thing, wasn't she? She was still always climbing trees and running around barefoot, forgetting to brush her hair or turn her clothes right side out. And we didn't know she climbed up to the roof at night—we never could have guessed it. We didn't know how to think like a child raised in the wild. But I know—however the accident happened—that Oblivienne was *happy* before she fell. She was *happy* in our home, with her new family." She goes on, for a while, painting a picture of a life that would now never be. Finally, she looks at the casket. "Oblivienne, we are so, so sorry to say goodbye to you . . ." She breaks off into a sob, or at least makes the sounds of grief, pressing the handkerchief to her mouth as more bulbs flash from the back of the room.

Finally, Mr. Lynch escorts her down from the podium. The girls watch her as she goes. They know as well as Rhi does that Mrs. Lynch was not speaking about the real Oblivienne—just some version of Oblivienne she wants the rest of the world to believe was real.

Before Rhi knows what she's doing, she is climbing the stairs to the podium. She is standing before the crowd, angrily leaning into the lectern and saying: "Oblivienne was not just a *happy girl*. Oblivienne was *fierce*. She was curious, and thoughtful, and passionate, and stubborn, and sometimes even violent, if she needed to be. When Oblivienne was protecting the people she loved, she could be downright frightening." Rhi takes a shuddering breath as she leans into the microphone. "And her sisters loved her for that. *I* loved her for that."

Rhi looks around, doesn't know what she means to say or even what she's saying, but the words keep rising in her throat because they're true, and because *someone* has to say them, and she, of all people, owes it to Oblivienne to make sure she is remembered correctly. She sees Uncle Jimmy beside Star, behind the Quakers in the middle of the audience. So many people who did not know Oblivienne.

Uncle Jimmy nods at her.

Rhi's voice shakes when she continues. "Oblivienne was wild. She was born wild, and raised wild, and would have always been wild, no matter how hard the world tried to shape her into something domesticated and . . . and *agreeable*. Not wild as in *feral*, but wild as in *untamable*. No matter how often the world told her who to be or what to believe—Oblivienne would have remained herself. She *did* remain herself. To the very end. A fierce, wild girl, who chose to believe in a world far better than it pretends to be."

Rhi looks at the girls in the front row when she speaks next. "Oblivienne told me once that she and I were alike. She said we both wanted to belong, but we would never be able to lose ourselves long enough to become a part of something else. At first, I'll admit: that hurt. I didn't like the idea of never feeling like I belonged. But I realize now that the most important part of what she said was *we will never lose ourselves*. We're too aware of who we *really* are, the authentic shape of our hearts, which we refuse to let the world shame out of us. And that is a *strength*, not a weakness. A strength that Oblivienne had, that her sisters have, and one that Oblivienne helped me see in myself." Rhi looks at the coffin, eyes blurring with tears. "For that, Oblivienne . . . I will always be grateful."

Rhi walks away from the lectern, blocking her face from the cameras by tugging her shawl farther over her face. She sits down next to Epiphanie, who clasps her other hand tightly and does not let go.

Later, at the cemetery, standing at the open grave, the funeral director says a few last words about the nature of death and returning the body to the earth. The weather is hot and still, with huge white clouds hanging overhead, blotting out the sun. Rhi and the girls stand huddled together despite the heat, sweating under their scarves and shawls. Behind them, Rhi can hear Mrs. Lynch sobbing loudly as the casket is lowered into the deep pit of the grave. She hears other voices too, murmuring prayers, as if Oblivienne cared anything for their gods or saviors.

When the coffin has been lowered, the crowd waits for the wild girls to drop a rose on the coffin, or a handful of dirt. Something symbolic, to say to themselves and the world, *I am letting this person go.*

But the Wild Girls of Happy Valley have no intention of letting their sister go.

Rhi touches Epiphanie's shoulder to let her know it's time.

Epiphanie nods and her sisters straighten. They step forward, one by one, and pull something from the pockets of their dresses. Sunder crouches by Oblivienne's grave and drops a fistful of white-gold hair tied up in a red ribbon. Verity drops a braid of sun-brightened blonde, Epiphanie a braid of black. Together, lying atop the coffin, the hair makes a warm mixture of colors, loose strands slipping down the sleek curve of the casket, into the dirt.

Rhi steps up last and drops a brown braid into the grave before stepping back to stand in a row with the others. Each girl clasps the hand of the girl next to her. They bow their heads as one and imagine a piece of their soul going with Oblivienne, joining her in the after-life, just as surely as they know she has left a piece of her soul with each of them.

As if in response, the wind gusts suddenly and powerfully, swirling around the girls beside the grave. It blows through the trees, shuffling the clouds in the overcast sky until they break over the sun and rays of warm, golden light beam down upon the sepulchral scene. The girls' scarves, no longer held in place by clutching hands, blow back in the wind to reveal the shadowy stubble of four shaved heads.

There are murmurs and gasps from the crowd, but the girls remain where they are, looking down at Oblivienne's casket and the symbols of their time with her, now done forever. They cannot take Oblivienne with them as they did with Mother, but they can leave themselves with her. And they will remember, whenever they run their hands over their shorn hair, what it felt like to snip away each lock, to feel their heads grow lighter, freer, for every fistful of hair that fell to the floor. They will remember the hum of the electric razor mowing down the remaining length, cleansing their minds as the final millimeters were scraped away. They will remember, each time they see their reflections, who and what they have lost.

And as time goes on and their hair grows back, so too will the broken places in their hearts heal. Even if there is now a hole inside each of them, forever.

32

THE ERIKSONS INSIST ON DRIVING Verity to the reception at the Quakers' farm themselves. Mrs. Lynch had claimed that she was too distressed to host, so naturally, the Quakers offered their assistance.

"When did you shave your head?" Blood Mother asks. "How did I not know?"

"She's always wearing that filthy hoodie, that's how," Stepfather says.

"Verity, sweetheart, you can't go doing things like that without my permission," Blood Mother says.

"Mom, it's only hair," Grace says. "It'll grow back."

"Don't you even *think* about shaving your head," Stepfather warns. "It's one thing for her to do it, but you know better. She can't help it. They're all savage little—"

"Baby, it's not normal for a girl to shave her head," Blood Mother says, looking at Verity in the rearview mirror. "And I know when you're young you have all kinds of impulses and desires, but you can't just give in to each and every one."

Verity narrows her eyes. "I must ask permission to remove hair from my head?"

"Yes, sweetheart. What are people going to think? It will take years to grow all that beautiful hair back."

"*God*, Mother. Maybe she doesn't care about what people think!" Grace shouts, exasperated. "She just lost her sister! Let her grieve how she wants to. It's just *hair*."

Verity looks at Grace and inclines her head in appreciation. For an instant, that old spark is there between them, the shared understanding, so elemental that the knowledge of the other is the knowledge of the self.

"Grace," Stepfather says in a low voice. "You do *not* raise your voice like that when you're speaking to your mother. Got it?"

"Why not? Because she pushed us out of her vagina?"

"Grace, watch your language!" Stepfather shouts.

"What language? *Vagina?* Is that a *bad word*?"

Verity's mouth twitches as if to smile, but in the same instant, she senses Stepfather change. He stops the car with enough force that they all jolt forward, then twists around in his seat to grab Grace by the hair.

"Listen you little—*aaahhhh!*"

Verity's arm shoots out, slamming the heel of her palm into Stepfather's elbow, forcing his hand to release from Grace's head. Then, still pinning his elbow, she grabs his wrist with her other hand and pulls his forearm backward, bending it unnaturally away from his body until he cries out.

"Do not touch my sister," Verity says firmly. "I do not care what power you think you have over us, you are not allowed to touch her in anger."

"Verity," Blood Mother whispers, her eyes wide, hand half covering her mouth. "Verity, please, let him go."

"He must give me his word he will never touch her in anger again," Verity says, her voice calm, her expression calm, her body calm. And she is calm. Only her arms are rigid, pinning Stepfather in place. She applies a little more pressure to his wrist, bending his forearm backward, just a bit more.

"Fine," Stepfather says between gritted teeth. "I promise."

Verity releases him and he twists back around to face the steering wheel, still breathing hard.

It is then that Verity notices Grace staring at her—not in awe or fear, but something else. There are tears in her eyes and wonder on her face. Perhaps this is the moment Blood Sister Grace realizes: Verity has only been performing obedience. She has always had the option to be something else.

She reaches out to Verity across the back seat and takes her hand. They both squeeze at the same time.

Without a word, Stepfather puts the car in drive and returns to the road, red-faced, eyes fixed on the dotted yellow line of the country road. They reach the Quakers' farm a few minutes later and as soon as the women exit the car, Stepfather speeds off.

Blood Mother turns pale, but smiles shakily. "He just needs some time to cool off, I'm sure," she says. "Verity . . ."

Verity looks at her. Grace narrows her eyes at her.

"Grace," Blood Mother continues. "Let's find the others, shall we?"

INSIDE THE QUAKERS' HOUSE, Rhi is staring at her phone, at the open email she drafted last night. Not the one about her mother's death, but a new one.

An email she actually intends to send. Maybe.

In the kitchen behind Rhi, Dallas and Giovanna are washing dishes while Dr. Ibanez is telling the foster parents and Mrs. Erikson that the head-shaving was actually a very healthy way to express their grief, even if it's not one our culture has accepted—that cutting your hair is a mourning custom in many cultures.

"I can't believe you did it, too," Grace says, stepping up to the table. She takes a celery stick from a tray of cut fresh vegetables and dips it in hummus, eyeing Rhi as she takes a bite.

Rhi darkens her phone screen, then touches the fuzz on her scalp. "This was how they wanted to grieve her."

"Not gonna lie, it looks pretty sick," Grace says. "You've got a good head shape for it."

Rhi isn't sure how to reply to that. It's the first nice thing Grace has said to her. "Thanks?"

"You're welcome." Grace gestures to Rhi's phone with another celery stick, stepping closer. "So . . . who were you texting just now?"

"I wasn't. I was . . . debating whether or not to send an email to someone."

"Who? A *boy*?" Grace smirks. "A *girl*?"

Rhi's mouth feels heavy, her face suddenly numb. "Someone . . . who has been a big part of my life."

"What's the big deal then?"

The numbness spreads to Rhi's scalp, and she runs her hand over her head again, the soft fuzz of dark regrowth from the last twenty-four hours already enough to draw her nails through. "He's not really *in* my life anymore. I'm debating . . . whether or not it would be worth it to get some kind of closure."

Grace straightens, lifts her chin, makes herself taller than Rhi in more ways than one. "Definitely. Do it. Say what you need to say. Tomorrow isn't guaranteed, you know?"

Rhi wobbles her head from side to side, still considering. Does she want him to know how much he hurt her? Or would she rather he forget she even exists?

Does she want him in her life at all, or does she want him gone for good?

And what would be the consequences, either way?

Rhi tucks her phone into her purse. "Maybe later," she mutters. Her brow furrows. "Why are you suddenly being nice to me?"

Grace shrinks a little. "Well . . . because I also realized recently—or remembered, really—how quickly you can lose someone." Her eyes shift to the back door, through which they can see the flickering light of the bonfire Verity and the others are gathered around, out behind the barn. "And it made me realize the only reasons I didn't like you were A, because I thought I was better than you, and B . . . I was jealous of you."

"*Me?*" Astonished is too weak a word for Rhi's reaction.

"Your relationship with Verity. And how they include you," Grace says. "They think you're their fifth princess. I'm Verity's actual identical twin and they treat me like I'm the goddamn *enemy*."

Rhi looks at Grace and sees, for the first time, no mask of disdain or cruel judgment, but the real and desperate pain of someone who does not know how to make her true self be seen. Rhi has seen that look in the mirror far too many times to mistake it for anything else.

"You're not the enemy," she says. "You were just the evidence that broke their world."

"And I pay for it every day." Grace scoffs. "Do you have any idea what it's like to miss someone for your entire life, only to realize they want nothing to do with you?"

"That's not true. Verity wants to be your sister, she just doesn't know how. None of them know how to *be* in this world. I think *that's* why they've attached themselves to me—not because we share some inner wilderness where we can all understand each other, but because none of us *fit* here. We want to be free in a way we can't quite describe, and can never hope to actually *be*."

"It sounds *exactly* like you share an inner wilderness where you can all understand each other. Isn't that the freedom you want? The one you can't describe?"

Rhi's mouth opens, closes. "Maybe," is all she says. Because maybe that's why Oblivienne left them, because she tried to cut from herself the very wilderness her heart was rooted in to spite the man who raised her. Maybe that's why Rhi has never been able to fit snugly into this world, or her family, or her life—because her heart is rooted in a wilderness that can't be confined to the narrow lot she's been offered.

Grace steps closer, her body charged with intensity, her eyes bright with unshed tears. She whispers sharply, "*I want to go to that wilderness.*" A tear spills free from her left eye, tracing a shimmering path down her cheek.

If Rhi could, she would do what she always does: push her own feelings aside and do what must be done to soothe Grace. But for the life of her, Rhi does not know how to give Grace what she wants. She takes Grace's hand, instead, and squeezes.

For the longest time they just stand there, gripping each other's hand, thinking about what it might mean to be free.

33

THAT EVENING, EPIPHANIE FINDS SUNDER high in the chestnut tree behind the Quakers' barn. Epiphanie has been circling her sisters all day, trying to protect them from the pain biting at their hearts, the raw edges where a piece of them is missing. She knows she cannot keep them from grief, but it is her duty as the eldest to guide them through it. Even if there is no one to guide her.

"Sister," she calls up to the younger girl, and jumps to grab the lowest branch. Epiphanie pulls herself up, branch after branch, as high as she can before she stops trusting the branches to hold her. Somehow Sunder is still several feet above her, but they are at least close enough to talk now.

"You have been hiding," Epiphanie states, concern dusting her words.

"I have been thinking about Mother," Sunder corrects, fiddling with the branches over her head. "I wish he was here."

I am here, Epiphanie wants to say, but she knows this is not about her. She wraps her arm around the trunk of the tree, considering how to address this. "Sister, do you know why Oblivienne died?"

Sunder throws a spiky green chestnut at the ground. "She stopped believing in Mother, and it broke her heart."

Epiphanie frowns. "It is more complicated than that. She was *very sad*. A deep kind of sadness that does not stop. Did you not feel it, when we were together? Is that not why you kept fighting with her?"

Sunder hangs her head. "I did not mean to," she whispers. "But she frightened me."

"She frightened all of us. I have never felt a darkness that deep. And more than just sadness—she was scared, and confused. As we all have been. Oblivienne was struggling to accept that the future Mother promised may never come. That we are, perhaps, not destined to save *anyone*. And . . . I think she desperately wanted someone to save *her*, in the end."

"That is what I said," Sunder says, tears in her voice. "If she had still believed in Mother, none of that would have been an issue. Meeting our destiny would have been enough to get her through the dark times. Even if Mother was wrong about *some* things."

"She wrote about it in her journal," Epiphanie reminds her. "For weeks before the end. Dr. Ibanez showed us—"

"I know."

"Then you know what she was thinking."

If the magic is real, Mother was not lying.

If the magic is real, the magic will save me.

If the magic is not *real, I am ready to die.*

"I know," Sunder whispers, her voice hitching.

"Sunder," Epiphanie says. "We may not ever fully understand why Oblivienne did what she did. But her soul is a part of our souls. We know she would never do anything to hurt us unless her own suffering was unbearable."

"But *this* is unbearable," Sunder sobs, pounding her chest.

"I know," Epiphanie admits, tears falling from her eyes. "*I know it is*, because I feel it too. And yet . . . we *are* bearing it."

Sunder looks down at Epiphanie in the dark, one hand gripping a branch, steadying her. "Oblivienne's pain was worse than this?"

"Worse, maybe. Different. Whatever it was, it made it impossible for her to see how the future could possibly be any better."

"It is not right, though."

"No. And it is not fair." Epiphanie shifts her weight on the branch, balancing on her heels. She scrubs at her face with her hand, breathing through another wave of grief before it can knock her over. "Sister . . . we have seen so much together. We have experienced many things we cannot explain. Perhaps magic *is* real, in its own way, under the right conditions, as Mother taught us. But real or not, it did not save Oblivienne."

"Because she stopped believing in it," Sunder says, resolute.

"But you still believe? Do you believe if you jumped from this tree right now that you could rely on magic to catch you?"

Sunder stands up. It is too dark to make out her expression, but Epiphanie imagines she is glowering, glaring at the world that has taken so much from her, but given so much as well. She stands there for a long time before crouching again.

"The magic started to leave us when Mother died," she says. "But I *do* believe it is still a part of us. And . . ." She looks down at Epiphanie. "Sister, I must confess something. I have determined when the portal to Leutheria will appear."

Epiphanie hesitates, surprised at the old familiar excitement that rises in her. "Are you certain?"

"Yes."

"But . . . when did you figure it out?"

"The night Oblivienne . . ." Her face crumbles. "I told you all that I would figure it out soon. After what happened at the bonfire, I stayed up all night comparing the tables in the almanac. I wanted to surprise Oblivienne. To give her hope. Something to . . . look forward to." She shakes her head and closes her eyes, biting back tears. "I finally figured it out, but I was too late."

"No," Epiphanie says firmly. "Sunder, no. Do not think like that. Tell me. What did you find?"

Sunder sniffles. "Two nights from now there will be a total eclipse of the full moon that will be visible over Happy Valley. It aligns with everything Mother ever told us about how we will get home." She opens her eyes and looks so earnestly at Epiphanie that it hurts. "The portal to Leutheria *will* open in two nights."

"But . . . why would it happen *now*?"

"Mother said it would appear soon after we found our fifth. *Five princesses from five kingdoms.*"

"But there are only four now," Epiphanie says quietly. Painfully. Crushing that old familiar excitement into newly familiar grief.

Sunder's fist twists around the rough bark of the tree branch. After a while, she says in a hoarse voice, "I have been thinking about that all day today."

Epiphanie remains silent.

"We have thought for a while now that Rhi must be the fifth princess. Even when we found out about Grace, I was certain—we *connect* with Rhi. But now that Oblivienne is gone, we are *still* five. Even if I do not feel a connection to Grace, she is clearly connected to Verity in a way that . . . well, a way that *we* are. But we are still five. Five princesses. Five kingdoms. So . . . does that mean it was always meant to be this way? Was Oblivienne always meant to leave us before our destiny was fulfilled?" Her voice shrinks to a whisper. "Did Mother lie to us about that, too?"

"I do not think we will ever know."

"But did he *lie*, Sister?"

Epiphanie treads carefully. She is aware this is the first time Sunder has admitted the possibility that Mother lied, but she does not want to influence her sister's mind one way or another. Epiphanie has lingered in the gray space of unknowing for months now, trying to make sense of what she knows, and make peace with the answers she may never have. But now, with the possibility of the portal to Leutheria so immediately before her, that peace feels impossibly far away.

"I am sorry, Sunder," she says. "But I truly do not know."

Sunder thinks about that for a long while before she replies. "And if the portal appears two nights from now . . . will you go to Leutheria?"

"If the portal truly appears," Epiphanie says, discomfited by the hope that rises in her chest. "Then I will be right there with you when you go through."

34

RHI AND HER UNCLE JIMMY give Verity, Grace, and Blood Mother a ride home because Stepfather never came back to pick them up. Blood Mother lies to Jimmy and Rhi, tells them Stepfather had an emergency at work, but Verity was there. She saw him storm off—*drive* off—in anger, like a child.

She also knows she caused much of that anger, and that makes her smile.

Jimmy is observant, though, like his niece is. When they pull up to the house, he asks for Blood Mother's cell phone and she hands it to him.

"If you're ever stranded somewhere again, I'm around," he says, pecking at the phone. "Happy Valley isn't that big. And if I can't get you, I'm sure I can find someone who can. This CB radio can come in quite handy." He smiles, gesturing with his chin to a mound of electronics on the dashboard.

"Oh, thank you," Blood Mother says jauntily. "I'm sure it won't happen again, but I do appreciate the thought. Thank God for good neighbors!" She smiles too widely and looks at her daughters in the back seat. "Say good night, girls," she instructs as she opens her door and climbs out of the truck.

"Thanks for the ride," Grace says, slipping out the door. "G'night."

Verity moves toward the door, too, but stops, turning to Jimmy. "Stepfather is not a good person. But you are a good person," she says. She nods, and leaves.

UNCLE JIMMY PULLS AWAY FROM the Erikson's driveway and onto the road. It's late and dark, and a Sunday night, so the roads are empty in Happy Valley, even as they near what qualifies as downtown. They pass the café where Star is working tonight and the police station where Rhi has now given two statements, and then the high school where Rhi hopes she will finish her senior year. There is a charged silence in the cab, a tumult of unasked questions, unsaid explanations, and Rhi doesn't know how to diffuse it.

You are a good person.

Verity said those words to Uncle Jimmy, as much of a fact as *the earth orbits the sun.* And Rhi believes it to be true herself.

So why have things not been the same between her and her uncle since that day in the kitchen? Since Uncle Jimmy tried to console her, and Rhi panicked at his touch and pushed him away? She wishes it could go back to how things were, a normal kind of awkward between people who don't know each other very well, but are really, truly trying.

But why *are* they trying so hard?

Because we are the only family we have left. Because we both loved the same person, in very different ways.

But is that enough?

Rhi knows what happened in the kitchen. But she can never imagine explaining it to a man, even if that man is Uncle Jimmy. Even if that man is the kindest, *goodest* person in the world.

Uncle Jimmy clears his throat and Rhi glances at him, notices for the first time that in addition to the charge between them, he looks purposeful. A practiced sturdiness. This is Uncle Jimmy with something serious to address. Normal Uncle Jimmy would lean his elbow out the window and turn on some music while the summer night wind blew through the cab.

"How are you holding up, Rhi-Rhi?" he asks.

A few weeks ago, he might have given her knee a tap to get her attention, to set the tone as playful. But Uncle Jimmy has not touched her, even by accident, for days.

"I'm fine," Rhi says automatically. But in the lingering silence that follows, she wills herself to amend her response, to be more honest with her uncle, who has done *everything* right with her from the second he got the phone call from CPS. "I'm worried about the girls. About them losing each other."

His eyes flick toward her for a moment, then back to the road.

"I'm worried about them losing *themselves*," Rhi admits.

"But what about *you*?" Uncle Jimmy asks. "What about losing *yourself* in these girls?"

She grimaces and runs a hand over her buzzed scalp. "Is this about the hair?"

Uncle Jimmy laughs. "*No*. Actually, I think the hair is pretty cool. Very punk rock, you know? Plus we can rub your head for good luck now." But he does not rub her head. "I'm just checking in. Just trying to do what a good parent would do. I'm still new to this."

Rhi looks at her dark reflection in the windshield, shifting and disappearing with each light they pass. "I'm fine. If anything, the girls have helped me be *more* myself."

Uncle Jimmy nods. "I've noticed. I really have. You know, you've always had such a spark in you, Rhi. I could see it the first time I met you, and in all those videos your mother used to send. But I've watched you smother it over the years—what little I ever saw of you, that is. And when I first came and got you, I was afraid you'd finally done it—finally snuffed out all the bright and fiery parts of yourself. But these past few months you've finally started to let it shine."

Rhi is uncomfortable with his praise, let alone the attention. But she knows it comes from a well-meant place, so she endures the discomfort of being seen long enough to find a bit of joy in the moment.

"Look, Rhi. I know there are certain things you and I don't talk about very often. Like why you're living with me. Or the kind of people you grew up with."

Rhi's whole body has gone rigid. Her shoulders are up, her neck bent, her breathing light and shallow. Her senses are heightened: she smells the coffee and cake on Uncle Jimmy's breath, the last whiff of his only cologne, the scent of freshly cut hay from the Quakers' neighbors still clinging to his hair and his clothes. She notes the way his body has turned to stone, the way a man does when he's made a firm decision and can't let himself be budged.

Her pulse is a butterfly in her throat.

Her mouth is a desert.

Uncle Jimmy bites the inside of his cheek. "So, listen. I got some news the other day. Pretty bad timing but . . . well. I promised I wouldn't keep things from you anymore, and I'm a man of my word. It turns out your father's appeal went better than expected. His lawyer managed to get his sentence reduced to time served, which means he'll . . . he'll be out in two weeks."

"*What?*" Rhi rears back.

Uncle Jimmy moves his hand off the steering wheel, just for a moment, as if he's going to put his hand on her shoulder to ground her, comfort her. But he doesn't. He grips the wheel more tightly instead, and Rhi isn't sure if she is sad or relieved.

"Your stepmother called to let me know. She's going to see some friends in LA first, but she expects to be home by the time he gets out. Your stepbrother is coming back from Germany, too, and Vera wants you both there."

Rhi feels like they've just driven off an overpass, her stomach left somewhere far behind. "No. I was supposed to have time. I was supposed to have time to get out, to finish school, to get away from them—"

"I know, I know," Uncle Jimmy says. "Look, you're going to be okay, you hear me? I'm not going anywhere. I'm going to look out for you, okay?"

"I can't go back there." Rhi blanches, feels the edges of her perception turn wooly and dark. "I can't be around . . . *him*."

"I spoke to your caseworker and I'm filing for visitation rights," Uncle Jimmy says. "It'll take some time, but I'll have a legal right to see you. To make sure you're okay. And hey, you're sixteen—we can file for emancipation at the same time. We can file everything together, I'll help you with everything. And once everything is final you can walk right out those doors and I'll be waiting to *take you home*." He pauses, then adds, "If that's what you want."

"Of course that's what I want," Rhi says, and feels some of the charge between them fly out of the truck. "But that will take *months*." She is trembling.

"Maybe," Uncle Jimmy says, his voice insisting on calm reassurance. "But I'll call you every day. I'll make sure they're treating you right until the day you leave."

"Yeah," Rhi says, but her mind has gone fuzzy. She can't think about going back there anymore—to the life and the girl she locked away, still screaming when she left.

She's thinking about Sunder instead, and her eager belief in a world beyond this one. She's thinking about the possibility of Leutheria. About the magic she has witnessed with her own eyes and felt in her own body.

If all the horrible things Rhi has witnessed are real, why not magic?

Rhi thinks about a world away from here, a world that needs the kind of help and healing only five wild young women can provide, and she wonders what kind of world that must be.

BY THE TIME THEY GET HOME, Rhi has decided.

She lies in bed that night rereading the email she wrote the night before, making sure it's true, making sure he can't accuse her of lying or exaggerating. She makes sure she says everything she needs to say to him, asks him every question she needs answered, because she cannot be sure she will ever get another chance—or if she will ever have the nerve again.

But if there is any version of reality where he is going to be back in Rhi's life, she needs to confront him. For her own sake.

For Eden's sake, she thinks.

For a moment, she wonders if she should forget the email, forget the pain of her past life, and continue on as she has been, ignoring Eden's cries from where Rhi has locked her away.

But she's going to be back in Saratoga Springs in two weeks. Vera and Kevin and Father are going to be back—all of them, in the same house, a family once more. When she tries to picture it, her entire body goes numb.

She cannot go back to living that way.

She cannot go back.

Rhi looks at the screen, at the confrontation she needs to have, the truth she doesn't want to face. But maybe the truth is what will set her free. Maybe his reply will be all the evidence she needs to keep her away from that house for the rest of her life.

Rhi holds her breath and taps SEND.

35

V ERITY IS ON HIGH ALERT when they get home, eager to see how Stepfather has handled their earlier confrontation. They find him in the living room sitting in his armchair. He has drunk too many of the long-necked brown bottles—a bad sign—and is watching greasy, shirtless men wrestle each other on the television. He says nothing when his family walks in through the door, or when Blood Mother greets him with a kiss on the cheek and says kind, fawning things to him.

"It was such a sad affair; I'm glad you didn't have to sit through it," she says, as if she believes her own lie that he was called away for work.

Verity, still standing in the archway to the living room, glances at Grace to see her sister scowling—not at Stepfather, but at Blood Mother. She asks her sister *why*, but only in her mind.

"The Quakers had a nice spread," Blood Mother continues, a birdlike hand on Stepfather's shoulder. "They sent me home with some leftovers for you, of course. I can heat them up if you want. Christopher?"

Grace scoffs, and when Blood Mother shoots a warning look at her daughter, she rolls her eyes and hurries upstairs to her bedroom. Verity watches her sister go, still confused by the direction of her anger.

"Okay, well," Blood Mother says to Stepfather. "I'll put the leftovers in the fridge for now. Would you like another beer? I'm going to head up to bed, so if you'd like anything, let me know now before I turn the lights out. Okay?"

Stepfather does not reply, and it is not because he is so connected to Blood Mother that they do not require words.

Verity remains standing in the archway to the living room, arms behind her back, rubbing the stubble of her scalp against the wooden frame, watching the interaction with dread and fascination—a decent distraction from the grief that has been stalking her all day. Who is this man that he deserves this kind of fawning? Especially after his loss of control in the car earlier. Who is he to treat Blood Mother with such disrespect?

"Verity, why don't you head up to bed?" Blood Mother says sweetly, returning from the kitchen.

Stepfather finally reacts, turning to look at Verity. He looks her up and down with glassy eyes, his mouth tight.

Verity shakes her head. "It is still early. I would like to stay awake a bit longer."

Blood Mother's brow pinches. "You've had a long day though, sweetie. Maybe you'd like to go upstairs and have some time to wind down? I can bring you some tea, and maybe you can take a bath? Have you been using the journal Dr. Ibanez gave you? I'm sure you have a lot of thoughts about the day."

Verity nods. "Many thoughts. Yes." She is still looking at Stepfather.

"Go on upstairs, sweetheart," Stepfather says to Blood Mother. "Verity will go to bed when she's ready."

Blood Mother's face goes slack and pale, because even if her mind is in denial, her body knows the danger of the man she lives with. Verity is beginning to comprehend it as well.

"Oh. Okay. Well then, goodnight you two." She touches Verity's shoulder to warn her she's coming in for a hug—something she began doing when Verity first came home and jumped at every new sound and touch—and embraces her, presses her lips to Verity's cheek, and whispers, "Please don't make him angry again," before pulling away and heading upstairs.

Verity abruptly understands Grace's anger with Blood Mother. Stepfather may be a predator, but Blood Mother willfully ignores that truth and acts as if he is a warrior—worse, she acts as if he is a *king*. As if he can do no wrong. As if all conflict is only a result of their lacking obedience.

Don't make him angry? Don't *make* him angry? As if Verity has explicitly decided to target him, to harass him, the way he has targeted *her* these past six months?

The rage begins to wane as Verity considers how Blood Mother interacts with the world, how she bears responsibility for everyone else's emotions, how she blames herself for the faults and failures of others, for everything she cannot control. Of course Blood Mother would project the same responsibility onto her daughters. Of course she would try to protect them by arming them with the same shields she has used to protect herself. Shields are the only weapons Blood Mother has ever known how to wield.

Verity softens toward Blood Mother's remarks, but remains wary of Stepfather. It is not a quiet wariness, either, but an active alarm, the same kind she experiences when near an unfamiliar wild animal, or when storms are on the wind. This storm started building the moment Verity set foot in this house, and tonight she is nearly certain it is about to break.

At last, after the upstairs noises have ceased and the other members of the household are presumably in bed, Stepfather speaks again.

He looks at her. "Verity."

It begins.

"Did you know your name has a meaning? Not in a distant way, like some names have these abstract meanings derived from ancient Hebrew or Gaelic or whatever. *Verity* isn't even a real name, just a word. It means *truth*. Did you know that?"

"Yes."

"I've been thinking about that a lot tonight. About truth. About you." Stepfather turns back to the television screen. "And the truth is, I haven't been happy since you showed up."

Verity knows she has an option here: to play the obedient, submissive daughter, or not. She thinks of Rhi's words from the funeral, thinks of how much she has had to pretend, and for the second time today, Verity chooses *not*.

"I know that. We all know that."

This is clearly not the reaction Stepfather had hoped for, and that makes Verity smile. Perhaps he wanted her to take it personally, or to feel bad for her role in his unhappiness. But Verity's name does mean truth, and the truth is Verity is not responsible for Stepfather's happiness.

"Your mother was a mess when I met her, did you know that?"

This is the kind of question that is not meant to be answered, Verity has learned.

"She was a *goddamn mess*. Barely making ends meet. Grace was probably more feral than you ever were. Completely out of control, filthy, wild. The police had given up on ever finding *you*, and your mom didn't know how to raise one daughter while she was still mourning the other. She could barely stay sober, let alone raise her child. Then I swooped in and rescued them both. *I* lifted them up out of poverty. *I* let your mom quit her job so she could take care of Grace. I've been their sole support these last five years. I *saved* them. And now you're back . . . and somehow I've become the enemy. How is that fair?"

Verity cocks her head. "Who has called you the enemy?"

"You know what I mean. Suddenly I'm not the head of the household, I'm just the schmuck paying the bills. I practically *raised* Grace, and now you're here, the same damn age as her, and *you* have all the power?"

Verity nearly laughs. She has never felt so powerless in all her life, but she will not offer up her weakness to Stepfather. "What does being part of a family have to do with having *power* over them?"

"You know what I mean. It's not about power. It's about *respect*. They should show me respect for all I've done for them. Before *you* showed up, the girls listened to me. They didn't *talk back*."

Verity bristles. She tries to imagine this dynamic among her sisters: if Epiphanie had demanded respect from the others because she is the eldest, or if Mother had demanded respect from them, or even obedience, because he protected them with his magic. No. She cannot imagine it. She could have never loved or respected a person who demanded it from her. That kind of respect feels like bartering—conditional, even. Not truth at all.

She scowls. "Christopher, do you love my Blood Mother?"

"What is this 'Blood Mother' shit? As opposed to what? That psycho leader of your little cult?"

Verity grits her teeth and considers walking away. But instead, she shifts her weight into the kind of quiet, battle-ready stance that is hard to detect—feet spread a little wider, weight balanced ball to heel, knees unlocked, arms loose at her sides. To any onlooker, she is simply standing, upright, relaxed.

Verity rephrases her question. "*Do you love my mother?* And if you do not, then *why are you here?*" She does not ask if he loves Grace. It does not even occur to her to ask if he loves Grace, the answer is already so obvious.

Stepfather scoffs. "Do you think that's what a marriage is about? *Love?*"

"*Family* is about love."

"What the *hell* do you know about love *or* family? You were a wild animal until a few months ago. You were a *pack*, not a family."

This is not the insult Stepfather probably imagines it to be. Verity has always known she and her sisters are a pack. But while Verity is well aware of the fact that she, like all humans, *is* an animal, she is also aware that many humans see themselves as a superior species—that to be an animal is to be filthy and disgraceful. Sheer ignorance aside, this *is* meant as an insult, but Verity refuses to let shame into her heart. And above all, she refuses to let *this* man shame her.

"If you had ever experienced a true family the way I have, you would see as clearly as I do that no matter how you provide them with material things, you make *everyone* in this house unhappy. Including yourself. I feel sorry for you."

Stepfather scoffs again, but spittle flies from his lips this time. "*Sorry* for me? *You* feel *sorry* for *me*?" As he glares at Verity, the shock gives way to outrage, then the outrage gives way to simple rage. In the flickering light of the television set, a vein bulges and pulses on Stepfather's forehead near his left eye.

He rises from his chair, face scrunched up in anger, eyebrows high and mighty, nose wrinkled, lips pursed, jaw clenched. It fascinates Verity to see how much he resembles the very animals he insults. All that is missing are bared teeth, but he is, after all, at least *attempting* to control himself.

But then, his face smooths over and the rage drains away from his features. He runs a hand through his thinning blonde hair and chuckles humorlessly. "Okay," he says.

Verity shivers and goose bumps rise on her skin, hunching her shoulders forward. Every instinct tells her to leave, to *run*, to get away from this predator before it strikes, but she also knows if she moves now, he *will* chase her.

For the moment, he picks up his empty brown bottle and starts walking toward the archway leading to the kitchen, where Verity is still leaning against the frame. He does not *look* like he is heading toward her; he looks like he is going to the kitchen to get another brown bottle. His eyes are focused on the refrigerator door—too focused for a man with a casual destination.

Verity's whole body is heavy with dread.

Just as Stepfather is about to step into the kitchen, he drops his bottle on the carpeted floor and seems to teeter, as if falling sideways, toward Verity. But he is not falling—he is slamming his forearm into her chest, her newly shorn head knocking against the wall. He grabs her throat with both hands and squeezes—not tight enough to choke her completely, but enough to make her wheeze and struggle to breathe.

"Listen, you little savage," Stepfather growls, jostling her as he does. "I want you out of here by tomorrow morning. Pack your things and get the hell out of my house. Not a goddamn word to Grace or your mother. You did fine in the wilderness before, I'm sure you can do it again. I'm sure it's what you've *wanted* all this time, anyway, you fucking animal. So here." He laughs. "I'm giving you a gift. I'm setting you free."

But while he has been speaking, Verity has laced her fingers together to form a wrecking ball. She punches up between his elbows and strikes Stepfather in the nose, and continues the momentum to bring her arms up between his, forcing his arms apart and his hands off her throat. Quickly, while he is still stinging from the blow, Verity kicks him in the groin. When he doubles over, she knees him in the face, sending him sprawling to the ground, blood gushing from his nose. Stepfather grabs the brown bottle he dropped earlier and throws it at Verity's head, but she easily dodges it. It smashes against the wall instead.

"I'll kill you!" Stepfather roars, pink toothed.

"Christopher! Verity!" Blood Mother screams from the top of the stairs. "What on earth is going on—oh!" She gasps, hands covering her mouth.

Grace is several steps ahead of her, arms clamping around Verity, pulling her away from the crawling, dripping monster on the floor.

"This . . . *animal*!" Stepfather sputters. "She attacked me! Completely unprovoked!"

Verity is rubbing her throat when her eyes widen.

So he is going to *lie* about it? *That* is how he plans to have his way?

Blood Mother is shaking her head, the full whites of her eyes visible around the green of her irises. She is staring between the two of them, unsure who is more dangerous.

"Mom!" Grace shouts at her, a protective arm around Verity's shoulders. "Are you *serious*?"

"Clarissa!" Stepfather snaps. "I swear to God, she just attacked me for no reason! Just like in the car earlier. She's *not* stable. We're not *safe* with her in this house!"

Blood Mother's hand is still clamped tight over her mouth, as if to speak would be the absolute worst thing imaginable. As if the wrong words could somehow destroy everything she has built for herself, everything she stands to lose. But clearly, every cell in her body is telling her to shout.

"Mom, don't just stand there!" Grace warns her, pulling Verity toward the stairs, as if *upstairs* could protect them if they needed to be protected. "Call the fucking cops!"

Finally, the hand falls from her mouth, fisted to her chest. "They'll take her away again!" Blood Mother cries.

"Clarissa, she *needs* to be taken away!"

"You shut your mouth!" Grace shouts. "Mom, *he* attacked her, I saw it with my own eyes!"

"What?" Stepfather scoffs.

Verity knows this is a lie like she knows the heart of it is also the truth, but she supposes Grace feels exactly the same way.

In which case, does it matter?

"Mom!" Grace shouts again. "Listen to me right now. I am your *daughter*. I am watching you hedge your bets instead of protecting your *children*. You will end up losing us *all* if you don't get your head out of your ass and call the police *right now*!"

Verity doesn't understand every word of her sister's powerful roar, but she feels the outrage and defiance in it, and she swells with pride.

"Grace!" Blood Mother gasps.

"Mom!"

Blood Mother steels herself, looks at Stepfather, and rushes into the kitchen.

Stepfather jumps to his feet. "Clarissa, do *not* call the cops. Call the hospital! She needs to be taken to the psych hospital! Clarissa!" He storms toward Blood Mother.

Verity leaps from the stairs, out of Grace's arms and into Stepfather's path. He stops short, just barely, as Verity fixes her eyes on him, teeth bared like the animal she proudly is.

"Get back," she growls through her teeth.

Stepfather rears back and raises a clenched fist as if to strike her— but a shattering sound comes first. A spray of white porcelain rains down around him as his eyes roll back and he slumps to the floor, unconscious.

Grace stands behind him with the remains of a table lamp in her hands, the rice-paper lampshade now bent out of shape. Her eyes are wide with the shock of what she has done.

In the kitchen, Blood Mother is staring open-mouthed at her daughters, holding the kitchen phone in her hands as if she does not know how to use it.

"I believe the phone number you want is nine, one, one," Verity offers.

CLICKMONSTER

BREAKING NEWS:
A Wild Girl "Reverts to Violent Ways" in Savage Domestic Assault—And It's Not Who You Think

Police and emergency services were called to the Eriksons' home late last night after a physical altercation left two people injured. Verity, formerly Mathilda Godefroy, sustained mild injuries, while her stepfather, Christopher Erikson, has been hospitalized with a concussion and other injuries.

"We never would have expected this from Verity," a source who wishes to remain unidentified said at the scene. "She's been a pretty good egg. Not a peep since she came home. If we had to predict which one of them would have gone off like this, it definitely would have been the little one [Sunder]."

But was it Verity who initiated the fight? Late last night, around four a.m., Grace Erikson made a public post on her Instagram, a picture of bruises on a neck presumed to belong to Verity, along with the caption: "HE ATTACKED HER. #LOCKHIMUP" ClickMonster News has been unable to verify whether the picture is real or edited.

"Of course she doesn't want her sister to be blamed," the unidentified source said. "They'll probably want to lock her up again after this. But the reality is, Chris is a decent guy and a respected member of the community. Hard to imagine a world where he'd assault a teenage girl right after her friend's funeral. Seems way more likely the grief made her snap and revert to the old violent ways she used to survive in the wild."

But Emergency Room staff do not seem to agree with the source's observations.

"All I'm saying is," an anonymous paramedic told us, "it's *refreshing* to see a grown man claiming his daughter assaulted him. Half the time a woman needs our help it's because of quote, unquote *fine, upstanding citizens*, usually male, usually folks who look a lot like this guy. Fathers, husbands, boyfriends. The 'usual suspects,' as I like to call them."

The Erikson family was unavailable for comment.

36

RHI FEELS LIKE SHE BARELY slept last night, but the morning after the funeral she awakes to a series of unread text messages—from Grace, of all people. All sent in the middle of the night, but Rhi had left her phone on DO NOT DISTURB.

She rubs the sleep from her eyes and swipes to unlock her phone.

GRACE
🔋🔋🔋 Chris/our stepdad fucking attacked Verity

She's OK mostly, just some bruises

He's in the hospital. He's saying she attacked him unprovoked

DO NOT BELIEVE A WORD OF IT

Shit is messy. I'll update when I have more info

Rhi sits up in bed and types out a reply immediately.

RHI
Jesus
Keep me updated.
Let me know if you guys need anything

Rhi tries to go about her day like normal, but it was never going to be a normal day—the day after Oblivienne's funeral, and the day after she found out her father is getting out of jail in just two weeks.

When she gets out of the shower, she sees Grace has replied.

GRACE
Thanks.
Fucker decided to press charges 😒

RHI
What does that mean for Verity?

GRACE
Not sure yet. Dr. I has been calling mom a lot though

RHI
Do the other girls know what's happened yet?

GRACE
Verity just talked to them.

Verity and I have to go to the police station for questioning. What is this bullshit?!?!

Police want a psych evaluation on V, maybe all of the girls
😳

Now they want one for me!?!

GRACE

I want a god damn lawyer

RHI

What can I do? How can I help?

It is several hours before Grace replies—hours that Rhi occupies by cleaning Uncle Jimmy's house, scooping Purrdita's litter box, scrolling through social media, and fighting the urge to refresh her inbox every five minutes. She'll get a notification if an email arrives. There's no point in checking.

GRACE

Can you pick us up from the police station?

RHI

Yes. Now?

GRACE

Yeah. Can you take us to Sunder's house? And let the other girls know we're coming

RHI

Be there in five

Rhi texts Uncle Jimmy before she leaves the house—Going to the Quakers, be back late—then hops in her truck. On the short drive, she wonders where Mrs. Erikson is, wonders why they want to go to Sunder's house instead of home.

When she pulls up to the police station, there is a huge crowd on the sidewalk out front, crushed against the railings that lead from the street to the front doors. Rhi texts Grace.

RHI

Reporters out front. Meet me in back?

GRACE
Ugh

Rhi circles around and finds a narrow entrance behind the Main Street shopping strip that city waste management uses for dumpster pickups. She pulls up behind what she thinks is the police station—a freshly painted New York State seal on the back wall gives it away: the allegorical figures of Liberty, with her staff, and Justice, with her blindfold and scales.

Within seconds, Grace and Verity emerge from a heavy metal door, a police officer following. He stands by the door with his thumbs hooked in his belt while the girls climb into Rhi's truck, but Rhi can't read his expression from this distance. Grace takes the front seat; Rhi turns to look at Verity in the back seat, and immediately feels her throat tighten.

"Are—are you okay, Verity?" she manages to ask as her hands clench the steering wheel.

Verity nods, but she does not look okay. She looks angry, and disappointed, and sad, and her throat is covered in small, dark bruises that clearly resemble the shape of two hands wrapping around a neck.

Rhi tries not to imagine it, tries to keep her mind in the moment, in her truck, with Grace and Verity, and not in the memory that is clawing its way to the surface: an August morning in New York City. A bus window. Eyes she could not recognize staring back from her own reflection.

Grace curses loudly, pulling Rhi back to the present. She stamps her feet on the floor of the cab and roars in frustration, thrusting her middle fingers up at the state seal.

"Tell me what happened," Rhi says. "Just, start from the beginning."

"Verity?" Grace prompts her sister.

Verity tells Rhi everything in a weary voice while they drive away from the police station and into the rolling farmlands of the valley. By the time they reach the road where the Quakers' farm is situated, both girls have told their sides of the story, and Rhi doesn't understand how the police could have it so backward.

"The police know he attacked you first, right?" Rhi asks, pulling into the long driveway that leads to the farmhouse.

"They're trying to discredit our statements," Grace huffs. "So if the psych evaluation can prove Verity is unstable, then they're going to claim she was a bad influence on me, causing me to not only attack my stepfather but lie about seeing him attack her." She grimaces, puts her head in her hands. "Which I did lie about. Shit."

Rhi slows her truck as they drive up to the Quakers' farmhouse. She is relieved there are no reporters out here, but keeps an eye out nonetheless.

"I *had to* though," Grace goes on. "Mom wasn't listening! She was acting like there was a *choice* to be made." Grace is crying now. Not bawling, but tears are streaming from her eyes and her face is scrunched with the sting of her mother's betrayal. "*No one* fucking listens to teenage girls."

The truth in Grace's words tears something open inside of Rhi, a wound that has been there longer than she knows.

"Dr. Ibanez believes us," Verity says.

"Dr. Ibanez isn't the one doing the evaluations," Grace says.

"Who is?" Rhi asks.

"Some jerk appointed by the state. He said they want someone unbiased, that Dr. Ibanez has formed too much of a bond with the girls to be impartial. But this guy is definitely *partial*." She sneers. "He said it's Verity's job to *soothe the fears and conform to the expectations of the community*."

Rhi bristles, anger flaring momentarily before worry rushes back to drown it out. "So, what happens if his evaluation is negative?"

Grace looks at her sister. "They were throwing the word *institution* around an awful lot."

Before Rhi can reply, there is a gentle knock on the car window that nearly makes her jump out of her skin.

It's Dallas, looking concerned.

"Sorry, didn't mean to startle you," Dallas says when Rhi rolls down the window. "Ma's gone to get Epiphanie, but I guess there was an incident this morning at her foster home. Maggie is freaking out."

"An incident?" Rhi says. "What do you mean?"

Dallas's eyes slide from Rhi, to Grace, then widen when he sees Verity. "I'm not sure. But it sounded . . . not good."

37

WHENEVER A WOMAN IS DECLARED dangerous, there is always a man eager to subdue her. Whether it's because he can't stand the idea of a woman with power, or he can't stand the idea of a woman having more power than *him*, Rhi doesn't know. But she knows the story Epiphanie tells them as if she has lived it.

"It was my foster brother Bradley," Epiphanie says, stroking a darkening bruise on her arm. She's sitting on the Quakers' living room floor, Verity beside her. Everyone else is on the edge of their seats, waiting for Epiphanie to explain—except for Sunder, who is pacing like a caged tigress as she listens.

"He heard about what happened with Verity before the rest of us," Epiphanie says. "He barged into my room in the morning and showed me the headlines on his phone, but did not let me read the articles. He said Verity had been arrested, that they were going to arrest all of us, lock us up in cages and never let us out again." She winces. "He was taunting me. I know that now, but I could not see that, at the time. I was too scared. The idea that this world was turning its back on us— that it would put us in cages—it was too easy to believe. I started to panic—I did not know what to do. Where I could go. All I knew was that I had to find a way to protect you, Sisters, but also that it was impossible to do so. I could not even protect myself." There are tears in her eyes as she remembers, as she presses a hand to her chest.

Verity puts an arm around her sister's shoulders, pulling her close.

Rhi tries to swallow the lump that rises in her throat, easily imagining how frightened Epiphanie must have been. She hates that anyone could be so cruel to her.

"I was so frozen by my own fear, the fear itself became terrifying," Epiphanie continued. "My thoughts were going so fast, and Bradley was still talking—I cannot tell you what I was thinking or what he was saying. And then . . . then he laughed." She looks up at everyone, scowling. "He said, *Oh my god, are you crying?* and then laughed even harder. He said, *It was just a joke, calm down.* And then . . . when I realized it wasn't true, that no one was coming for us—that my *terror* had been for nothing—I did something I am not proud of." She looks at her hands. "I grabbed his wrist. *Hard.*"

"That's all?" Dallas blurts. "He deserves a lot more."

"Perhaps," Epiphanie says. "But I acted in anger, and in that moment, I saw he was afraid of me. He fought back, of course. And I won, because I am a better fighter than he is. I knew I would win, even if he is bigger than me. That is why I should not have done it."

"And did he blame it all on you?" Grace asks, bitterly.

Epiphanie looks up, around, as if coming out of a trance. Her ghost-pale eyes settle on Rhi, searching for something. "Was it not my fault?"

"*No,*" Rhi breathes, all the tension in her body transmuting into ferocious protectiveness. "You were provoked. That was—that was psychological *torture.*" But she hesitates, understanding why this is bad for the girls. "Maybe grabbing him wasn't the *best* idea, but no one can blame you for it. Can they?" She looks at Mrs. Quaker.

"Folks can blame a person for anything they can imagine, these days," she says. "It certainly doesn't look good to Maggie or to Child Protective Services that it ended in a physical fight, but you're not the first foster siblings to scuffle."

"I am ashamed that I acted in anger," Epiphanie says, bowing her head. "But I am more ashamed of how I reacted when I believed what he was saying. I *did nothing*. I froze. If Bradley had been telling the truth, I would have still been frozen when they came to lock me up." She looks at Verity beside her. "I *never* froze in the wild—I never doubted my next move, even when I was face-to-face with a mountain lion."

"Sweetheart," Mrs. Quaker says gently. "There's no need to be ashamed of that. You were scared out of your wits, and understandably so." She looks thoughtfully at all of them. "Has Dr. Ibanez ever discussed the fight or flight response with you girls?"

Epiphanie shakes her heads, her sisters following a moment behind.

"It's like a hormonal reaction to stress, right?" Rhi says. "Your body pumps you full of adrenaline so you can either fight or run away."

"More or less." Mrs. Quaker nods. "It's an animal instinct we all have that's helped our species survive. Epiphanie, if Bradley himself had been threatening to lock you up, my guess is your instinct to fight him would have kicked in right away. And Verity, it sounds like your fight instinct was in fine form last night."

Verity looks up at Grace on the couch, who looks proud when she smiles back.

"But there are two more instincts one doesn't hear about as much, though if you ask me they're much more common nowadays," Mrs. Quaker continues. "The *freeze* and *fawn* response."

Rhi sits up. She's never heard of that.

"They're precisely what they sound like," Mrs. Quaker says. "Freezing and fawning. They show up in more complicated situations than facing a mountain lion—usually when the danger is not exactly life-threatening."

"Like psychological torture?" Rhi asks, still furious at Bradley.

"Very much so," Mrs. Quaker says. "Epiphanie, when you froze, that was your animal instincts trying to protect you. Your body said, in that moment, it was better to be still than to run or fight. And I think you girls know how important it is to trust your instincts."

"Is that why it took our mom so long to call the police last night?" Grace wonders aloud. "She just . . . *stood* there. I thought she was weighing her options but . . . I mean . . ." She looks at Verity and her voice quiets. "It was pretty scary seeing you two like that. Maybe she froze."

Rhi can imagine the scene vividly. Mrs. Erikson is so protective of her daughters, the sight of one in danger—a danger she has placed her in—would have unraveled her. But she knows about frightened mothers and cruel fathers. She knows how hard it is for the mother to know when to fight or flee. Perhaps Mrs. Erikson did freeze. After so many years of fawning, what else did she know?

"Verity," Epiphanie says turning to her, brushing Verity's bruised throat with her fingertips. "Dear Sister. Tell me what *did* happen to you?"

"Stepfather showed me his true nature, that is all," Verity says, arm still wrapped around Epiphanie's shoulders. "I am fine now. My sister protected me." She looks at Grace again.

"No big deal." Grace waves a hand. "I've always wanted an excuse to smash something over his head."

"It's a big deal to the state, unfortunately," Mrs. Quaker says. "Social services will want to do an evaluation on your family. And you too, I'm afraid, Epiphanie."

"Yeah," Grace says, scowling. "The police made it pretty clear they're on Christopher's side."

"So what are we going to do?" Sunder asks, stopping her animal pacing behind the couch to face the room. "They are *looking* for a reason to lock us away. What can we do to make people stop fearing us? What do they *want* from us?"

"They want us to all roll over and be good little girls," Grace says. "They want obedience, silence, all that sugar and spice bullshit. Sorry, Mrs. Quaker."

Mrs. Quaker shakes her head. "No need. But I will say, as much as I understand your cynicism, I think there is something to be said for playing their games. With a strategy, of course."

Rhi tries not to frown. "You want them to pretend to be something they're not?"

"I want them to be *free*," Mrs. Quaker says. "And sometimes that means playing along, at least until their eyes are off you."

"What does that mean, exactly?" Epiphanie asks.

"Let the doctors do their evaluations. Tell them you feel bad for causing harm, but that you acted in fear. They'll respect that more than they'll respect a young woman standing up for herself." Her lip twitches before she continues. "Most importantly, tell them how badly you want to fit into this world, how eager you are to go to school and make new friends."

"In other words," Dallas says. "Tell them what they want to hear."

"Lie to them," Verity clarifies.

"Not exactly," Grace says, almost smirking. "Think of it as *soothing their fears*."

Rhi's mouth twists into a smile as her phone buzzes. She glances at the screen, but there are no new messages. Instead, her notification bar shows a tiny envelope icon.

She has a new email.

"We should not have to play their game," Sunder growls, dropping to sit on the floor with her sisters. She tucks herself into Epiphanie's side, under her arm. Verity, arm still draped over Epiphanie's shoulders, rubs her hand over the soft fuzz of Sunder's head.

"As unfair as it seems, you all have to make a choice," Mrs. Quaker says. "You can either stand your ground and possibly end up back in that mental hospital, or you can pretend, for one afternoon, to be the girls they want you to be. It's up to you."

"It's not right," Dallas mutters. His knee bounces.

"No one claimed it was," Mrs. Quaker says. "But until things change, or someone gets them to change, that's the way it is." She looks around the room at the girls and claps her hands together. "Now then, I assume you're all staying for dinner?"

INBOX

FROM: "Kevin Hartwell" <hartwell.kevin@irving.edu>
REPLY TO: "Eden Chase" <e.r.c.2007@springmail.com>
DATE: July 16
SUBJECT: RE: I need to say something.

Edie,

Wow.

I don't know where any of this is coming from, but I'm really sorry you feel this way.

Can I ask how I went from being your best friend to being this apparent monster that you detailed in your last email? When was the precise moment I switched from protecting you from our parents, to manipulating you into doing things you didn't want to do? What was it that I "forced" you to do? Go shopping with money from my trust fund? Spend days at the waterpark, or the zoo, or the arcade? Or was it just spending time with me that was so terrible?

To be honest, Edie, your whole email was so crazy I almost didn't reply, but I'm worried about you. I know we haven't talked in ages, but I've seen you on the news. (Yes, even in Germany.) I've been following what's been happening with you and those girls you rescued. I was so sorry to hear about Oblivienne, by the way—I can't imagine what it must have been like to find her body.

Are YOU okay? That is an awful lot for one person to deal with, on top of everything going on with your father. And from the looks of your email, it doesn't seem like you're handling it well.

Please write back to me. Or reply to my texts. I miss you, Edie. I worry about you all the time. I've worried about you since I was thirteen years old. You shouldn't have to deal with all of this on your own.

Anyways, even if you don't write back, I guess I'll see you in a couple of weeks. It's going to be one hell of a family reunion.

Please take care of yourself. I need to know someone is looking out for you when I'm not there.

No matter what, you're still my best girl, right, Edie?

Love,

Kev

PS: We can talk about what happened last summer when I see you again. I don't think email is the correct forum for that.

38

R HI IS STANDING ON THE Quakers' front porch with her cell phone in her hand. She is staring at the screen, rereading Kevin's reply over and over again.

Why is it so difficult to comprehend? She knows the words. She understands their meanings. Why are they not sinking in? Why is her mind—her *body*—rejecting them?

Her pulse is thumping and insistent in her throat. She thinks she might vomit. Maybe she has cramps. Maybe she's PMSing. Maybe something from lunch isn't sitting well. Did she eat lunch? She can't remember now.

You're still my best girl, right, Edie?

It was a question he'd asked so many times that Eden's reply had become automatic. Never let him doubt. Never let him down.

You're still my best girl, right, Edie?

Yeah.

Of course.

Or a simple, silent nod if she couldn't make the words come out.

The screen door opens behind her and the needle of Rhi's pulse leaps around the speedometer in her chest, sending too much blood to her nerves and muscles and not enough to her head. She feels dizzy, sick; she's sweating, she's freezing, she wants to be somewhere else, but where? There's nowhere she can *go* to get away from this feeling.

Kevin, we need to talk about what happened when I visited you last summer. But we also need to talk about what happened before that. At home. Ever since I was little.

"There you are," Grace says from the doorway. She steps out onto the porch, over to Rhi. "Whoa, you look like you need to lie down. You okay?" She puts her hand on Rhi's shoulder.

Rhi thinks of Oblivienne.

Sometimes I look at you, and I do not see Rhi. I see . . . Eden.

She turns her eyes to Grace. The girls have made Rhi come alive over the past few months; they have always been able to see the truth of her even when she thought she was doing her utmost to hide herself. But Grace might be the only one who could possibly understand the conflict inside her—the kind that comes with being a girl growing up in America, surrounded by broken, toxic boys and men, and women so full of their own self-hatred that they don't know how to protect their own daughters.

The conflict is too much—too heavy—too hard.

"Rhi?" Grace asks. "What's happening? You're freaking me out."

Rhi's eyes slide away. "I just needed some air," she says, smiling, stepping away, toward the house.

You're still my best girl, right?

Rhi stumbles, throat tightens. She can feel Eden trying to claw her way out of that closet in her mind, but Rhi is stronger than that. She is stronger than the pain—she doesn't have to feel it. This is just a problem to be solved, that's all. No need to get emotional.

You don't have to be so dramatic.

Whose voice was that? Her father's? Kevin's?

Rhi doesn't remember.

"Are you sure—" Grace starts.

"I bet Mrs. Quaker needs help with dinner," Rhi interrupts. She fumbles with the door as she hurries away from Grace's questions, back into the house.

LATER THAT EVENING, when Sunder has started a fire in the pit and the kids have all gathered around it, Grace finds Rhi in the kitchen washing dishes by hand.

"Here," Grace says, opening the dishwasher. "Just put them in. Come join us by the fire."

Rhi tenses, stepping back slightly.

"Or not," Grace says. "Let me dry, then."

They work together in silence: Rhi washing the dishes, Grace drying and putting them away. Rhi's head is spinning as she works, rushing from one thought to the next, circling around a truth she can't fully hold on to.

She has these memories . . . but she's been told they aren't real.

But they are more than fleeting moments—they are life-altering events.

But the person she once loved and trusted most in this world claims she is misremembering them.

So what about New York City? Is she remembering that correctly? And if she isn't, what the hell is wrong with her that she would imagine that?

Rhi's phone chimes in her back pocket.

She drops the plate she was washing and it shatters against the ceramic sink. She swears loudly, puts wet hands on her shorn head.

"It's okay," Grace says, stopping what she's doing to drag over the kitchen garbage can.

Rhi tries to shake it off, reaches to pick up the broken pieces from the sink, and curses again when she cuts herself.

"Okay, just—sit here," Grace says, taking Rhi by the shoulders and shoving her onto one of the dining room chairs. "I'll take care of it."

Rhi holds her injured finger out in front of her like something offensive. She watches as the blood rises from the slice, only half an inch long, from the pad of her fingertip. It coheres, building a fat blackish-red droplet until mass and gravity have their way and the bonds break, letting the blood trickle down to the crease of her finger, drop to the floor.

Grace appears with a paper towel and first aid kit. She starts to clean and wrap the cut.

Rhi watches her work. Grace doesn't need to be here right now. She could be out by the fire with her sister, with Dallas, who Rhi is pretty sure Grace has a crush on with how much they pick on each other. But she's choosing to be here. Maybe that means something about Grace. Maybe it means something about Rhi.

Grace looks up while Rhi is studying her. They make eye contact, and something electric passes between them in that instant, thrusting them both from blurry impressions into high-def. Rhi suddenly and fully comprehends that Grace is not just *Verity's twin sister*, or *the perfect, normal girl*, and she senses that Grace realizes Rhi is not just *the quiet new girl at school* or *the girl who was adopted by a bunch of feral teens*. They are both complex human beings living complex lives, all while trying to navigate the *endless* complexities of being women in the world, and teenagers at that.

And Rhi understands more clearly than ever, there is something wild inside her that has been caged for too long.

In that moment, she is certain there is something wild about Grace, too.

Grace stands and finishes cleaning up the broken plate. She turns and looks at Rhi, crossing her arms over her chest. She reconsiders this and puts her hands on her hips.

"So . . . do you wanna talk about it?" she asks.

Rhi stands, wrapping her arms around herself. She walks up to the sliding glass door and stares out into the blue-green night, burnished by the bonfire. Her whole body says *no*.

"You don't have to," Grace says, following Rhi into the dining room. "But, you know, sometimes it helps to say things out loud. To have someone else hear what you've been through."

Rhi wonders if Grace, as an outsider, can give her the answers she can't seem to find in herself. She can feel, somehow, that Grace wants to help her. But for Grace to help, she would have to understand *everything*. Rhi would have to tell someone about the monster she's kept locked in her closet for years, long before she shoved Eden inside and tried to reinvent herself—and Rhi isn't sure she can do that.

Can she?

"It's complicated," she says finally, a grimace pulling at her mouth. "It's not just one thing . . . it's my whole life."

Grace nods. "Okay. But can I ask you something?"

Rhi shrugs.

"Does this have to do with the person you wanted closure from?"

Rhi's skin buzzes all over as the words come rushing back—her words, his words, a lifetime of words trapped and rattling around in her panic-soaked brain. "Yeah."

"Okay," Grace says gently, as if the wrong words will make Rhi shatter as easily as the plate did. "Can I ask something else? I've seen you get text messages that you delete without even reading. They all seem to be from someone in your contacts named 'NO.' Does *that* have anything to do with what's going on?"

Rhi's brain is now a hurricane of adrenaline, snatches of memories tossing on the waves.

It is five in the morning, and she is in an elevator.

No.

It is six thirty and the pharmacy is finally open.

No.

It is six thirty-four and the pharmacist is looking at her with far too much sympathy for a girl who really, if she's being honest, has only herself to blame.

No.

It is seven in the morning and the bus is pulling out of Penn Station.

No.

It is two minutes past seven and Eden has just deleted the first of many texts she will not reply to.

NO.

> Why'd you rush out so early, Edie?

As if nothing is different. As if nothing happened.

NO.

It did happen, didn't it?

YES.

Rhi turns around, facing the dining room table. She leans heavily against it, palms flat on the dark rustic wood.

"His name is Kevin," she says, trying not to cry.

"What did he do to you?" Grace asks sharply.

But Rhi knows the sharpness is not directed at her—the sharpness is for Kevin. She can sense Grace's words are a knife that she is waving in the direction of an enemy she can't see, has never met, does not know—but knows, already, in her heart, that he is the one to blame.

And that sharpness—that understanding—is enough for Rhi to risk unburdening herself, finally, of this terrible weight.

"He's my stepbrother," Rhi whispers. Her voice is shaking and her mouth doesn't want to work because there is still *so much* fear in her. But there is also anger, simmering beneath. "He's seven years older than me. And I loved him, because he was the only one who was ever kind to me."

Rhi glances at Grace again to see what she thinks of this. She fears her judgment—how pathetic must a person be to say those words?—but there is only furious compassion on Grace's face.

It is enough.

It is enough.

She keeps going.

"My stepmother is awful. And my father is worse. After my mother died, there wasn't anyone in my life who treated me with even a crumb of kindness. Except for Kevin."

Something on Grace's face tells Rhi she knows where this is going, because this is where a story like this always goes. This is why people were so certain Mother was abusing the girls, why even now people insist the girls have only suppressed their abuse: it's more shocking that a man alone in the woods with four young girls *wasn't* a sexual predator than if he had been.

"I was so desperate for affection," Rhi continues, wincing, explaining, justifying. "When he did things that made me uncomfortable, I just . . . assumed I was wrong. I convinced myself that he was just comfortable with me. That sexual things never crossed his mind. I thought *I* was broken, that *I* was disgusting for even *considering* he might have anything but the purest motives." She stops herself, bites her lip, overwhelmed by a slew of memories: the way she would dissolve into some semiconscious state, dissociating from her body, desperate to preserve her image of the one person who treated her with anything even remotely resembling love.

"There were always so many more good times than bad when he was home. I kept telling myself *that's* what mattered." Rhi can see herself now: young Eden in her bedroom, counting down the days until Kevin would be home from boarding school; eagerly awaiting his arrival on the first day of winter break; rushing to meet him in the driveway as soon as he got out of the car, waving a construction paper greeting card she'd made for him at school.

She had loved him *so much*.

The sob that rises in Rhi's chest takes her by surprise. It rattles the cage of her composure, shakes tears loose as a needle of pain stings the backs of her eyes.

"I was a *child*," she gasps. "He was a *teenager* when we met." She trembles, eyes widening as the words come out, painting a picture ten thousand times clearer than the picture she's been carrying in her head, all by herself.

Grace puts a hand on her shoulder but doesn't speak. Maybe she knows if anything interrupts Rhi, she'll never get to the end of the story. Or maybe she is simply speechless.

Rhi wipes her face, tries to catch her breath. "At first, it was so infrequent. And it was just . . . touching."

"It's just touching, Edie. It's not wrong." A weight beside her on the mattress, curling around her small body. Hands roaming over her skin like waves of nausea.

She slumps into a chair and leans her elbows on the table, barely holding her head up. "He really *was* kind besides that," Rhi whispers. "He protected me. He argued with my parents when they were too strict with me, and snuck me food when my stepmother made me go on crash diets, and always wrote me letters when he was at boarding school." She shakes her head, tries to fling the memories out of her skull. "But I *knew*. Part of me *knew* it was . . ." Rhi stares ahead at nothing, into her past, furious with herself—furious with Eden, that stupid, desperate girl.

Why hadn't she stopped him?

Why had she never confronted him until it was too late?

"Rhi," Grace says gently after a long pause, bringing Rhi back to the Quakers' dining room. "You can't blame yourself for what he did."

But Rhi's disgust with herself is still too loud, too clamorous in her mind.

She feels fragile, and exposed, and full of regret.

She shouldn't have told Grace.

She shouldn't have told anyone.

Some part of her must have been okay with everything that happened, otherwise, how could she have let it keep happening?

"Regardless of what you did or didn't understand," Grace says firmly. "You were a *child*. Even if you never tried to stop him—even if you never said no—*he* is the only one who should feel shame here. And I hope he's drowning in it."

Rhi goes cold. She feels the distant burn of an anger so weak it is more like a memory, and pulls her phone from her pocket. She puts it on the table, blank screen up, reflecting her haunted face in the black glass, like a ghost.

No.

No.

NO.

The anger burns a bit brighter.

The weight on Rhi's chest seems to double as a colorless fog rolls into her brain, pulling her backward through time: before Oblivienne's suicide; before finding the Wild Girls of Happy Valley; before her father's arrest; before the fragile threads holding her universe together were forcibly unraveled.

"But I did say *no*," Rhi whispers. "Eventually."

NYC

IT IS AUGUST. KEVIN HAS been accepted into a study abroad program in Germany for his final year of his MBA program. He is leaving in two weeks.

Eden is expected to visit him at his apartment in New York City for the weekend. It is important to him that she be present for his going-away party. *Of course* Eden comes, because she cannot stand the thought of a whole year without Kevin coming home—a whole year without Kevin to protect her from the casual cruelty of their parents. Despite everything she tries not to think about, Eden still sees Kevin as her protector. Her only friend. The only person who has ever loved her for who she is.

So she goes to New York City, on a bus, by herself. She never thinks about who Kevin becomes at night—she only lets herself think of who he is during the day, when he is gentle and generous and endlessly kind.

But that is not the person who greets her at the bus station. From the start, Kevin is cold and distant, inattentive and brusque. He drags Eden around to run errands while hardly speaking to her. He ignores her and talks on his phone to people Eden doesn't know. At his apartment, a small one-bedroom in Harlem, there is no movie watching at night like they used to do back home. Kevin goes to bed early and

Eden sleeps on the foldout couch. She is confused, afraid she has done something to irritate or offend him, but equally afraid to ask him what she may have done.

The next morning, over stale bagels and black coffee, Kevin warns Eden to act mature at his going-away party that night so she doesn't embarrass him in front of his friends.

Eden is determined to oblige him.

Kevin takes her out for more last-minute errands, decides to buy her a gorgeous, pale-green cocktail dress that is several shades lighter than Eden's summer-tanned skin, and makes her look like a woman five years older than she is. It is not a style or a color she likes, but she is used to wearing whatever Vera buys her, so it does not faze her to be just as obedient to Kevin.

The party starts at nine. Out of nowhere, Kevin is nice again. He is kind and solicitous, making sure Eden has eaten before she drinks anything with alcohol in it, making sure she is introduced to each and every one of his friends. He is showing Eden off to his friends, as if he is proud of her.

He drinks, and Eden drinks—and she knows she shouldn't, that she's just barely sixteen despite how her dress makes her look, but she is so happy Kevin is being nice to her again, and she wants to *act mature* for Kevin, wants his friends to see her as the mature young woman he thinks she is.

But Eden has never drunk anything besides a glass of wine at dinner before, and these are cocktails made with strong liquor. Every time she looks at her hand a new brightly colored beverage is staring back at her, half-empty. Soon, Eden is talking to a handsome young man, an undergrad at NYU. He has pale skin and chestnut hair and beautiful blue eyes that follow Eden's lips when she talks. They are in a corner of the apartment somewhere, talking for what seems like ages, and Eden is feeling mature, and experienced, and brave, and strangely alive, so she leans forward during a lull in their conversation and kisses him. His lips are eager as he kisses her back.

Suddenly, the man is gone. There is a cracking sound, and the clatter of items falling to the carpeted floor. Kevin is there, and he is punching the man in the face, knocking over an end table as they tumble together to the floor. Eden covers her mouth to keep from screaming.

There is something terrifying in Kevin's eyes that she has never seen there before.

The crowd swarms forward, swallowing the tangled knot of Kevin and the NYU undergrad, spitting them out as two separate entities. The young man is pushed to the door and leaves, glaring at Kevin as he goes. He does not even glance back at Eden.

The party dissolves within minutes.

Kevin and Eden argue.

Eden is drunk and angry and foolishly fearless. She calls Kevin an asshole. *He's five years older than you, Edie!* Kevin shouts. Eden tries to defend herself, to defend the man, yelling about maturity and making her own choices, pointing out Kevin's behavior was no better than Father's. But Kevin just keeps repeating, *He's five years older than you!* Until finally, Eden shouts back, *Well you're* seven *years older than me and that never stopped you!*

They both freeze.

It is the first time Eden has ever said anything about who Kevin becomes on the nights she wishes she could forget.

Kevin's face turns red. He howls in fury as he picks up a glass and hurls it against the wall, smashing it into a thousand pieces. Then he whirls around and grabs Eden by the throat, pushing her up against the bookshelves, that same terrifying glint in his eyes that she saw earlier. Kevin squeezes just for a moment—cutting off Eden's breath, just for a moment.

But a moment is all it takes for everything between them to change.

Kevin releases her and backs away. He immediately starts to cry, covering his face with both hands, broad shoulders shaking. Eden has only seen him cry once before, when he was seventeen, after Father brutally mocked and demeaned him—for standing up to him in defense of Eden, of course.

Guilt overwhelms her, the fear of Kevin's temper quickly replaced by the fear of losing him. She apologizes profusely, tries to comfort him, to soothe his wild emotions. She calculates what it will take to calm him the same way she has calculated how to calm people all her life. They sit down on the couch. Eden holds him awkwardly as he cries into her lap.

After a little while, Kevin stops crying. He sits up and wipes the salt from his face, looks at Eden with eyes that are glazed and swollen from both tears and alcohol.

"I'm sorry," he says.

"I know," Eden says, throat still tender from his grip.

"You're still my best girl, right, Edie?" he asks, as he always does.

"Of course," she replies, as she always does.

Kevin smiles faintly, then leans in and kisses her on the mouth.

Eden freezes.

Everything else he has ever done she has been able to explain away with intense mental acrobatics, but she cannot explain away a kiss like this. When he jams his tongue into her mouth, she knows there is no way to explain this as anything but sexual. But she can't make herself do anything about it.

She is so ashamed.

And confused.

Her whole life, Eden's stepmother has taught her the greatest value she has as a girl is the value men place on her body—that to be desired sexually is the height of female empowerment—the best she can ever hope for—the ultimate goal of womanhood. And Eden craves affection, more than she can possibly explain.

For an instant, she thinks she should enjoy it. She is getting the attention she desperately needs.

But this is not what she *wants*. It has *never* been what she wanted. And tonight, with whatever drunken courage she has left, she is finally going to say *no*.

Eden pushes Kevin away from her.

"Kevin, *stop*! I don't want to do this."

Kevin looks at her, bemused. Then he laughs.

Eden stares back, baffled, until he pulls her back to him, kissing her again.

She is stunned. She has always assumed, on some level, that if she told him to stop, he would. He might be mad, and maybe he would hate her, and she would be miserable about that, but she always thought *he would stop*.

How incredibly stupid she has been.

Eden has no idea what Kevin is capable of.

There is nothing left for her to do but endure it. She reaches for her usual escape and the alcohol in her blood makes it easier than ever: she detaches from her body, lets her awareness float away from what is happening. Logically, a kiss is no worse than anything he has done before. Eden can survive this. That's all she needs to do: just survive the next ten minutes or so, and things will go back to normal.

She keeps telling herself this is nothing—this is the same as it has been for years—this is familiar, even.

Until he unzips his pants.

Eden slams back into her body. There is something decisive about the sound that makes her realize he doesn't intend for it to be like all the other nights.

Eden pulls herself backward. "*No*," she says, or maybe she shouts it, because the syllable booms in her ears. She pushes against his chest to get him off her and the next thing she knows they are tumbling off the couch, onto the floor.

Before the room stops spinning, Kevin takes her hands in his and pins them over her head. He leans down by her ear and whispers, "It's okay, Edie. Shh. It's okay."

Eden turns her face away from his. She focuses all her attention on the teal wall-to-wall carpeting, rough and faded, speckled with stains. It is filthy from the party and the fight, littered with crumbs from the toppled food and grit from dirty shoes. It smells dusty, like concrete. Sharp pieces of detritus bite into her bare arms, her naked shoulders, her exposed back, infinitesimal injuries too numerous to count. She numbs herself to their sting.

She numbs herself to everything.

She is not here.

This is not happening.

39

"Jesus," Grace breathes.

It is the first time Grace has spoken in ages, and it has broken the spell that Rhi has been under. She emerges from a dark fog, nearly gasping for air, as if telling this story has cost her twice as much oxygen as other words. She feels the table under her hands, the waxy, uneven surface of the wood, the impossibly loud yet noiseless pounding of her pulse in her head. If she could see herself now, she imagines her eyes would be wide, her pupils dilated, her face and lips bloodless.

"Yeah," Rhi says, suddenly aware of the tremulous weakness in her voice as she tries to claw her way through the shame wrapped around her like a cold, wet, moldering blanket. "When it was over . . . I still thought it was my fault."

"It was *not*," Grace says quickly, angrily, climbing to her feet with the urgency of her insistence. "One hundred percent, it was *not* your fault, and it was *never* your fault before that night, either. There is nothing in the world you could have done to *make* it your fault. You never gave consent—you *couldn't* have given any kind of consent that would have *mattered*. You told him to stop, you said *no* . . . and even if you *hadn't* . . ." She swears. "Rhi. It was *never your fault*."

Rhi looks down at her fingernails, newly bloody from her nervous picking, her whole body shivering. "I know that, now. But it doesn't make the shame go away."

With that, some part of her collapses inside, like a sick child who has finally dragged themselves to bed. She has said what she needed to say. She has shared the thing she feared sharing most of all.

And she is still alive.

Rhi feels raw. Her heart is still pounding, as if it were one of the Quakers' deerskin drums instead of a vital organ. She is exhausted.

She hugs herself, not wanting to take up space, not wanting to be perceived anymore, but desperately wanting Grace to repeat herself:

It was never your fault.

It was never your fault.

It was never your fault.

"What did you do . . . after?" Grace asks instead, her voice uncommonly small and cautious.

Rhi lifts her head, tries to hold it high as she returns to the memory of that weekend. These scenes are more familiar to her than the rest. She has let herself replay these memories, over and over again, in search of absolution.

"I snuck out in the morning with my things and went to a pharmacy to get Plan B. The pharmacist made me come in back for a consultation and asked if I'd been assaulted. She was very kind. She really wanted to help, I think. But I was still trying to convince myself it was nothing. Also, I was . . ." Rhi loses her breath for a moment, finds it again in a whisper. "*Ashamed.* For that night, and every night—every time he'd ever touched me . . . I was *so ashamed.*"

Rhi finds herself shaking her head, thinking as she has a hundred times before: *But if it was my fault, then I don't have to blame Kevin.*

If it was my fault, then I don't have to lose him.

If I made it happen, then I never lost control of the situation.

If I was complicit, it wasn't that bad.

It would be better if it was my fault.

Tears prick at Rhi's eyes again, but she doesn't try to stop them. This time, they aren't full of panic and terror. They are just sad—truly, wholly sad—for herself, and for the girl she was eleven months ago, and for the girl she has been, all these years. The girl she no longer wants anything to do with.

"I told the pharmacist I was fine. I just made some bad choices." Rhi hesitates, even now thinking, *Maybe that's all it was, maybe it wasn't as bad as I remember, maybe I just did a fucked-up thing and now I regret it and I'm lying to protect myself because I can't stand to be wrong, just like my father.*

But then she looks at the dark glass of her phone screen and forces herself to remember.

No.

I said no.

I said NO.

"The pharmacist gave me a bunch of info for Planned Parenthood," Rhi continues. "And RAINN and, weirdly, a Starbucks gift card from her own wallet. She said there was like eleven dollars left on it and I should go get myself something high calorie because Plan B can be a bitch on the body. But I knew . . . I knew she didn't believe me. I mean . . ." Rhi touches her throat and whispers, "I didn't realize until later, but I had bruises on my neck. Not as bad as Verity's today, but it was clear something bad had happened." She clears her throat as if she can still feel his hand there. "I still have the gift card, I think. I just took the Plan B and went to a bus station and got a ticket home." She scoffs. "My parents didn't even ask me about the bruises when I came home."

Grace scowls. "And what about Kevin?"

Rhi studies her phone on the table, at the plain black protective case around its edges, bland and unobtrusive and easy to ignore, a case that says nothing about the personality of the person who chose it—or maybe everything, after all.

"He texted me while I was on the bus and asked why I left without saying goodbye. And I got so angry—that he could *ask* me that, that he could act like *nothing* had happened . . . he was acting so normal that I started doubting it had happened at all." Rhi looks Grace in the eye. "But just as I was doubting myself, I caught my reflection in the window. I saw the bruises. I *knew* I wasn't making it up. But I was so angry, and confused, and . . . heartbroken." She shakes her head and looks again at her phone's blank screen. "I didn't respond. But I changed his name in my contacts to 'NO,' because no matter what really happened that night, *I remember saying no.* And I couldn't let myself forget that." Rhi slumps a little in her chair. "I haven't spoken to him since then. Until the email I sent last night. Where I confronted him about . . . everything."

"Oh," Grace says softly. Realizing. "And he replied this afternoon."

Rhi nods, glaring at the phone now, because now that she's said it out loud, now that Grace has heard her and affirmed her innocence, Rhi can see her childhood clearly now. Despite the nagging doubt and shame and horror lingering inside her, she can see Kevin's actions for what they were. And she knows, now, that his reply to her email was nothing more than another attempt to manipulate her.

"He's acting like he doesn't know what I'm talking about," Rhi says weakly.

"That *motherfucker*," Grace hisses.

"I don't know what I expected. Remorse? Some kind of justification? An admission of guilt?" Rhi shakes her head. "Honestly, any of those reactions would have created a new hell for me to navigate. Maybe even led me to forgive him, or make me hate myself more than I already do. Gaslighting me like this—pretending I made it all up— it's probably the only way he could have responded that would actually *break* me. That would force me to finally tell someone, just so I knew I wasn't going insane." Rhi is still not sure whether that is true, but she knows it makes her sound stronger, more certain, than she is.

After a long silence, Grace takes a deep breath. "Rhi. Can I hug you?"

Rhi shrugs, and Grace wraps her arms around her so tightly that it feels like she's trying to meld them into one girl. "I am so sorry," she whispers. "I'm so sorry you had to go through that all alone. I'm so sorry your parents are such awful people that *Kevin* was the one bright spot in your childhood. I'm so fucking sorry you felt responsible for how he hurt you. I'm so sorry you still feel shame about it."

She makes an angry noise in Rhi's ear and drops her voice to a whisper. "You were a *child*. You were just trying to survive. No one can blame you for that."

Rhi breathes deeply, trying to inhale the truth of Grace's words and make them stick to her bones. But how do you make the truth stick when you are so used to avoiding it?

"But Rhi," Grace says, pulling away from her. "You *need* to change your phone number. Or block his number. Something to keep him from contacting you."

Rhi almost laughs, the concept is so absurd to her mind, but instead she begins to cry, very quickly, very suddenly. "I can't. I know it's pathetic, but I'm still afraid of not having him in my life. He was the only person I loved for so long . . . how can I just . . . *lose* him?"

"Because you've *already* lost him," Grace says, her tone kind but her eyes livid. "The first time he touched you like that. The moment he crossed that line, he stopped being someone who deserved your love. You *have* to let the good version of him go. He's been gone for a long, long time—if he ever really existed at all."

Rhi hugs herself again, tears streaming even though no sobs shake her body. It's as if she is simply too exhausted for that. "Either way, it doesn't matter. We'll be living in the same house again in two weeks."

"What?"

"My father won his appeal. Kevin is finished with grad school. My stepmother is already on her way home." Rhi shrugs, even as her mouth bows continuously deeper into a frown. "So long as Kevin denies everything, no one will believe me."

"Maybe not your parents," Grace agrees. "But you need to tell the cops what he did."

"What?" Rhi reels back as if Grace has just slapped her. "I can't do that. My family will literally murder me. There's no evidence, no proof. It'll just make a mess."

"But there's a witness," Grace says, eyes bright. "If you can find that pharmacist, I bet she remembers you."

"No. No way. My parents would ruin my life. They would rather see me dead than see Kevin get into any trouble—and make *them* look bad for letting it happen under their roof. And if they didn't kill me, they'd find a way to make my life absolute *hell*."

"But you're not *alone* anymore," Grace reminds her. "For one, you're kind of a public figure now, so if anything happened to you it would make national headlines, and then *I'd* make a big stink about it. But also, I'm sure Dr. Ibanez will help you. And your uncle. They won't let you go back there once they know—"

"Grace," Rhi stops her, shaking her head, terrified by the prospect of having to tell Eden's story again, having to cut herself open and pour herself out like this for anyone else. "No. I can't."

Grace opens her mouth to speak again, but she is interrupted.

Somewhere outside, a girl is screaming.

40

IT ALL STARTS WHEN GRACE leaves the bonfire to go inside and check on Rhi. Sunder, who does not entirely trust Grace, feels a pang of envy toward the girl as she walks away: envy because she understands their new sister in a way they cannot. Anger, too, because Grace was once bitter toward Rhi—though something in her has changed since Oblivienne's death.

Imagining Grace being the one to comfort Rhi makes Sunder feel powerless. Sunder has never been good at speaking about feelings, even if she knows how to express them. But her feelings are like clouds, visible and obvious, always in motion. Rhi's feelings seem to be like hidden wells and springs churning underground: invisible, but eroding nonetheless, until a seismic shift cracks the earth.

How long can a person carry such an ecosystem inside them before they collapse or erupt?

Perhaps once Rhi is in Leutheria, she will be able to leave that burden behind. Perhaps meeting her destiny will cure all her ills.

"Sisters," Sunder whispers, even though they are not alone around the campfire. She knows Dallas and Giovanna may overhear, but there is no time to waste. "We should speak about the portal. Tomorrow night—"

"Not now," Verity says, snapping a piece of kindling in two. "We are worried about Rhi."

"She feels like Oblivienne felt," Epiphanie whispers. "Before the end."

"Similar . . . but different," Verity agrees.

Sunder does not like to admit that she has felt the same thing. But this time, she will not be too late. She will give her newest sister hope, even if she cannot give her relief.

"That is why we need to talk about the portal," she whispers to Verity again, too low for Dallas and Giovanna to understand, but Verity only gazes into the fire as if she has not heard her either.

"Do you guys have any idea what's going on with Rhi?" Dallas asks, glancing back at the house. "She seemed distracted during the funeral yesterday. Really focused on her phone. It was so unlike her."

"That thing has always made her brittle," Sunder says agitated. "It beeps or vibrates, and she turns into an eggshell."

"An eggshell?" Dallas wonders.

"Delicate," Epiphanie says. "Sharp when broken."

He frowns.

Giovanna tosses a half piece of kindling into the fire, watches it catch and curl in the heat. "I wonder if it has to do with her family," she muses.

"I wish she'd let us know how we could help," Dallas says. "It's not like Gia and I don't understand shitty families."

"She does not speak of her grief," Verity says.

"But she has always carried it, since we met her," Epiphanie adds.

"It is an old grief. Always becoming new again."

"How can you tell?" Dallas asks.

"Because we are connected to her," Sunder says, tossing a handful of dry grass into the fire. It flares and fizzles in seconds. "Just as we are connected to each other." She gives Verity a meaningful look again, but she does not return it. When she turns to Epiphanie, her face is grave as she watches the fire.

"But you all grew up together," Dallas says. "You've had years to form a bond like that."

"It is not *time* that forms a bond like ours," Sunder says. "It is more than that."

"Is it?" Verity wonders.

Sunder is taken aback. "We have always been connected to Rhi," she says. "Just as we have always been connected to one another. And as you have been connected to Grace. Our destiny is what binds us."

"Destiny?" Giovanna asks.

A heavy silence falls over the girls. Sunder stubbornly tries to wait it out, hoping one of her sisters will acknowledge the fate awaiting them tomorrow night.

"Have you both completely given up on everything Mother taught us?" Sunder asks after a moment, her voice shaking.

But she already knows in her heart that her sisters' faith in Mother's prophecy has faltered, just as she knows in her heart that the portal *is* going to appear tomorrow night.

"Sunder . . ." Epiphanie tries.

"I was not lying when I told you last night," Sunder says, shouting now. "The portal will open tomorrow, and we must be ready."

"*There is no portal*," Verity says firmly. "And Mother was *not* a good man."

Sunder stares at her sister, heart dropping into her stomach.

"He *stole our childhoods*," Verity insists. "And he tried to take away our *future*, too. He assigned us a destiny so early on, none of us ever had a chance to imagine an alternative. None of us ever imagined a future at all—we only pictured what Mother described." She shakes her head. "It is no wonder Oblivienne felt so helpless. She could not believe in the future Mother promised us, but she could not imagine a different future, either. She could not see anything but more of the same—disappointment, and manipulation, and lies—"

"Mother *did not lie!*" Sunder shrieks, launching herself at Verity. Verity catches her as if Sunder is coming in for an embrace, but immediately falls into a somersault, the two of them rolling on the ground, thrashing at each other like wolves.

Giovanna cries out for them to stop, but the sound barely penetrates Sunder's awareness. She is full of rage and betrayal and fierce loyalty. Striking Verity does nothing to let the pressure out. It only makes Sunder feel more savage, more terrible, replacing rage with a pain she cannot quite describe: deep and broad and changing, like the moment the castle fell, rather than the moment her leg was bitten by that metal jaw.

When Verity strikes back, catching Sunder's cheek with her nails, the depth of the pain turns to burning sadness, turns to shame. She thinks of the bruises on Verity's throat, the bruises on Epiphanie's arm, all of it invisible in the dark.

Violence, violence, violence. Is this what this world would have her become? It is not the first time she has fought with one of her sisters, but she does not want to be like the men who did those things.

She lets herself go limp and Verity rolls her off her, pins her to the hard, dry ground, looks her in the eye with such furious hurt and concern, Sunder almost wants to forgive her for her betrayal.

"What the hell is going on?" Grace's voice breaks through the hum in Sunder's head.

41

WHEN THEY REACH THE BONFIRE, Rhi is surprised to see Giovanna clinging to Dallas, her face buried in his shoulder. More surprising is Verity, kneeling on Sunder's stomach, pinning her to the ground, her teeth bared like a wolf.

Grace jogs over and pulls Verity off Sunder. Epiphanie helps Sunder sit up. Her cheek is bleeding.

"Dallas," Rhi says, her voice low and calm. "You should probably take Giovanna inside."

Dallas wants to protest, she can tell, but after a moment, he nods. "Come on, Gia," he says. "It's late. We're all tired and cranky. Let's get to bed." He climbs to his feet, pulling a sobbing Giovanna with him, and leads her back to the house.

Rhi studies the remaining Wild Girls of Happy Valley. She is not shocked by their violence, only saddened by what it means: their pack is dividing. Their indelible bond, once so powerful and certain, has been worn away by their time in this world.

"What is this about?" Rhi asks. She has shoved aside all vestiges of panic from her conversation with Grace—a skill she developed thanks to her family, she realizes—because the girls need her. They need one another more, but maybe she can help them.

"Tomorrow night," Sunder says, her tone sullen. "The eclipse. The portal. We should be preparing, making a plan."

"The portal," Rhi repeats, and something in her surges with hope at the thought.

"You can make all the plans you want," Verity says, coolly. "There will be no portal. And then you will see what a monster Mother truly was."

"Verity," Epiphanie warns.

But Sunder does not snap. She turns away, closing her eyes. In the firelight, Rhi can see tears leaking from the corners of her eyes, and something about that is far worse than her temper.

"Then I will go alone," she says in a tone just as regal as the first time Rhi ever heard her speak.

"Sunder . . ." Epiphanie tries, and then starts again. "Sisters, I believe in Leutheria." She clutches her fists to her stomach, desperate for her sisters to understand. "I have been trying to find a way to say this so you might understand. I do believe in Mother and Leutheria. But differently than before. I wonder if, maybe, his stories were not what we thought they were? Maybe it is like the fairy tales we have read. Not a lie, and not completely true. A symbol. For something real."

"A fairy tale, exactly," Verity huffs. "Just another lie."

"No, that is not . . ." Epiphanie makes a noise of frustration, not quite able to find the words. And more than that, Rhi can see—she is unable to make her sisters understand, the way she used to, before words became so important.

Rhi can see their divide as clear as day: Grace and Verity stand together on one side of the fire, Sunder and Epiphanie separated on the other. When she first found the girls, they were huddled so closely together she could hardly differentiate their limbs; their minds were so connected they hadn't needed to speak a single word to understand one another, or even to call down a rainstorm. Looking at the girls, Rhi suddenly feels a grief so huge it cannot possibly belong to one person. It swirls around her, inside her, just like the magic did that day in the hospital when the girls asked her to help them heal Sunder's leg—only this time it is heavy, and cold, and suffocating, like being tossed on the dark waves of a brutal sea.

Is it coming from them, she wonders? Has the world Rhi brought them into finally torn them apart? Is this what happens when such a powerful bond is broken?

"Rhi?" Sunder asks. Her eyes are open now, the usual contrast between them lost to the dance of flames reflected there. The set of her features has never been more stoic, more quietly determined. "Will you come with me to the portal tomorrow?"

For a moment, Rhi can almost taste the hope leaking out of Sunder, a citrusy ray of sunshine breaking through the clouds. She grabs onto it like a life preserver, hauling herself out of that ocean of grief, and starts to imagine a life where her past is not hanging around her neck like a noose. A life where she doesn't flinch when her phone rings or when someone touches her. A life where she doesn't mistrust every kindness, every moment of happiness. She wants that life so desperately, her whole body aches at the thought.

And she wonders for the second time: If every nightmare she's experienced has been real, why can't magic be real, too?

Rhi walks over to Sunder, making her choice.

"You can't be serious," Grace says. "Rhi—"

"I don't know if Mother was a liar or not," Rhi says sharply, interrupting her. "But if tomorrow night a portal to another dimension appears somewhere in Happy Valley, I want to be there. I want to walk through it. I would happily fight monsters in Leutheria instead of staying here. At least in Leutheria, the monsters might have hearts that can be stopped."

"And if there is no portal," Verity asks, "will you both concede? Will you finally admit that *this* is the only world we are ever going to have a chance to save? Or will you look to every full moon and every eclipse for another way to run away from the truth?"

Sunder looks at Rhi, then at Verity and Grace. "Yes. If there is no portal . . . we will accept it. And if there *is* a portal, will *you* accept that Mother did not lie to us?"

Verity shakes her head, frustrated, her voice unexpectedly shaking. "No. I am sorry, Sunder. Even if there is a portal, I cannot go through it. And I cannot watch *you* go through it." She frowns, the sheen of tears turning her eyes to glossy embers as she takes Grace's hand and grips tightly. "We will not be coming."

"What?" Sunder breathes, bewildered by this betrayal. "Not even to see if the portal is *real*?"

"I do not want to live my life for Mother anymore!" Verity shouts. "I am sorry you cannot see it, but Mother was *not our savior*. I do not want a *destiny*. I do not want anything to do with portals, or other worlds—or Mother!" She grimaces as tears begin to roll down her cheeks. She puts a hand over her heart. "It hurts me too, Sister—to lose Mother a second time. But this . . . this is the truth of how I feel."

It takes several moments, but Sunder nods—once—to her sister. Rhi can see she is grief-stricken, but unwilling to beg, unwilling to yield.

"Epiphanie?" Sunder asks. "Will you come?" And then, softer: "Say you will come. You said you would."

Epiphanie suddenly looks exhausted. "You know how I feel, Sunder. You know what I think. And it hurts me too much to keep pretending I still believe in something I do not. We *all* need to make peace with this world. To start living *fully* in this world." Her mouth bends down into a frown as she speaks. "I am sorry, my sisters, but I cannot come with you either."

Sunder hisses, as if she's been struck. She grips Rhi's hand tightly.

"Then you have made your choices," she says, the pitch of her voice rising. "Rhi and I will go alone. We will try to save Leutheria, just the two of us." Her face crumples, furious tears streaking from her eyes. "And when the people of Leutheria ask about the other princesses, I will tell them you chose to stay in a world that does not even *want* you!"

Sunder whips around and stalks back to the Quakers' farmhouse, her small form swallowed by the shadows beyond the bonfire's light.

After a moment, Rhi exhales a long, slow breath, and follows.

"Rhi!" Grace shouts after her. "Look, I know things suck right now, but you can't just run away from your problems. That's not—"

"Thank you, Grace," Rhi interrupts her, heart pounding low and steady in her chest. "For listening to me earlier. But there are some things you will never understand . . . and I hope you never have to."

The Wilderness

Excerpted from *Savage Castle:*
A Memoir of the Wild Girls of Happy Valley

SUNDER'S LEG WAS HOT WITH pain. The wolf-kin kept the wound clean, kept her blood from leaving a trail as we carried her through the wilderness toward an unknown future. All the bickering and irritability of the previous weeks had fled from our pack. We were a unit, once more, moving as one in symbiosis, praying for Sunder's relief, for a destination that would welcome us.

The shock of our loss was still heavy on our minds, obscuring our grief, our fear. We only knew we had to keep moving, that our destiny lay beyond the wilderness we had called home for so long. There was no other option but forward.

On the third night, though the moon was full and the forest well lit, Sunder could move no more. She alternated between hot and freezing, fever threatening to consume her as infection set in. We huddled with her beneath the thickly layered shelter of a hemlock's low branches, wolf-kin pressed tight to our flanks as we called on our power to heal our sister. Each of us laid our hands on Sunder's clammy skin and suffused her with all the healing magic we could summon from within the deep wells of our hearts. Eventually, Sunder's temperature dropped. She slept fitfully, her head on Epiphanie's lap, as night blanketed the mountain.

"How much longer can we keep going like this?" Oblivienne whispered in the dark, and even though it was merely a whisper, her words were thick with fear.

"We will keep going until we can go no farther," Epiphanie replied, brushing mud-streaked hair away from Sunder's scrunched-up face. Epiphanie turned to look at Oblivienne and saw her real question, written in the shadows on her face.

Are we sure this is what Mother intended for us?

Wordlessly, Epiphanie replied: *Whatever path we walk is the path Mother has set us upon.*

Are you certain?

Neither Mother nor I would ever lead you astray.

Oblivienne relaxed, finding peace in her sister's reassurance as she leaned against the wolf-kin at her side and joined her sisters in sleep. Come morning, the raw flush of day turned the sky a hazy pink, summoning a dense fog as pale as bone. Something stirred in the forest ahead of us, rousing us from shallow sleep to greet the morning with wild eyes.

Something is coming, we realized.

Our wolf-kin's ears twitched as they climbed to their feet, sinking their heads low to peer through the wall of fog. We huddled even closer, surrounding Sunder with our bodies, moving her as carefully as possible to hide behind our wolf-kin. The fog beyond us was impenetrable, even with our keen eyesight. We could have been sitting out in the open for all we knew. It could have been an angry bear out there, hunting our scent, tracking Sunder's fevered blood.

But this was the path Mother set us on. This was the only way forward. Whoever's feet or paws were loudly crunching over sticks and squelching through mud was a part of that path. A part of our destiny.

Another twig snapped.

The wolf-kin stepped forward, their tails flicking low to the ground.

The footsteps stopped abruptly.

Disturbed by the wolves' movement, the fog began to dissipate, revealing the outline of a girl. A young woman.

It is her.

We do not know who thought it first, but the thought moved between us like the fog, intoxicating us with hope. Still, we had to be wary. Mother warned us the people from this world were often not to be trusted.

But as the fog cleared and the girl came into focus, the truth became obvious. The naked hunger in her eyes. The way she carried herself with the weight of an object out of place. The way she never wavered when she saw us, despite the fear running off her like heat waves.

We knew it in our bones before we accepted it in our heads: this was our fifth sister.

We were finally on our way home.

42

WHETHER OR NOT THE PORTAL is real, Rhi has no idea what to pack for a trip to a parallel world. She tries to imagine the future she glimpsed last night as she stuffs clean pairs of balled-up socks and underwear into her backpack: a world where she is not only free from her miserable family, but free to be as wild and powerful as the girls once were, before this world tried to break them down. That thought makes her sad though—imagining Epiphanie and Verity left behind, and Oblivienne gone forever. But Epiphanie and Verity's minds are made up, and Rhi knows better than most that she cannot force them to do or believe anything they do not want to.

Her mind turns back to Leutheria instead. Mother had told them it was their destiny to defeat a great darkness that had fallen over the realm. If Rhi is truly the fifth princess, the *daughter of wolves* Mother spoke of, is there some kind of power she might uncover once she is through the portal? What kind of strength does she have that the other girls do not, that required her to be raised apart from them?

Dr. Ibanez might say it's her ability to stay calm under terrible circumstances—her ability to turn off all the painful things that weigh her down and never look at them again. Dr. Ibanez would probably not approve of that last part, but Rhi hasn't found a better solution yet. Besides, what good would it do to dwell on the past now? If the portal is real, then Rhi is about to be free of everything she's ever tried to run away from. Everything she blacked out when she couldn't run away. Everything she ignored in order to survive.

If the portal appears tonight, then Rhi will never have to face her family, or any of the pain that goes with them, ever again.

She sees her mother's Syracuse University hoodie hanging over the back of her desk chair, and feels a squeeze of love so sudden it knocks the breath out of her. She sits on the floor in the middle of the guest room, grabbing the hoodie on her way down. Holding the dark-blue fabric and faded orange print in her hands, Rhi struggles to find her breath. As she drags air into her lungs, it feels like she is pulling something up from the bottom of a deep, dark well, covered in sludge and debris and an infinite number of lost things.

In many ways, Rhi has actually been free for a very long time. She may have been trapped in a haunted house full of monsters, but she has never belonged to anyone—not since her mother died. She has never been constrained by the unspoken commitments that come with love—and even the perverse obligation she had felt toward her stepbrother had been dashed to pieces the moment she said *no*.

Her obligation, now, is only to herself—to Eden or Rhi, she is not yet certain. She will not let weak, defenseless Eden be locked in that haunted house again. She will not let the dream of Rhi and this life she has created in Happy Valley die the silent, unmourned death of a powerless, terrified teenage girl. She would rather both girls die fighting.

But she does have one other obligation: to the girls. Or what's left of them.

"Knock knock," Uncle Jimmy says softly, rapping gently on the half-open door with his knuckles. The door swings open as Purrdita pushes between his feet, running to rub her face on Rhi's knees the moment she catches sight of her. "Everything kosher in here?"

Rhi folds the sweatshirt in her lap and nods, putting a hand out so Purrdita can rub her face on Rhi's fingertips. "Yeah, just . . . putting some stuff away."

Uncle Jimmy raises his eyebrows. For seven months, Rhi has left her clothing in neat piles around the guest room, on top of the dresser, in the bottom of the closet—as if to settle in would mean she belonged here—that she deserved a home here.

"Dinner will be ready soon," he says. The look on his face changes slowly from suspicion to concern. "You sure you're okay? You look a little . . . I don't know. Scared?"

Rhi forces a laugh. "I'm fine. It's the shaved head—makes me look more like a giant baby bird than a punk."

"Hmm." Uncle Jimmy watches her for a few moments, clearly not convinced. "Is that old thing your mother's?" He points with his chin to the hoodie in her lap.

"Oh," Rhi says. "Yeah. From Syracuse."

"You know, I think I still have some of her things if you ever want to look through them. After your grandmother passed away, everything in that old house went to me. In fact—" He smacks his forehead with his hand. "I can't believe I didn't think of this before, but I have her old letterman jacket from high school. You should really have that."

Rhi smiles, her heart aching a bit at the thought of leaving Uncle Jimmy behind. "Yeah, I'd like that."

"I'll see if I can dig it up. Anyways . . . dinner in ten," he says, and is about to walk away when Rhi speaks again.

"I'm going to the Quakers again tonight. After dinner. For a sleepover."

"I thought Dr. Ibanez wanted the girls to take it easy after what happened with Mr. Erikson? The news has not been treating those girls too kindly these days. It might be safer for everyone to just stay home tonight."

"They don't want to be alone after . . . everything. We're just going to have a bonfire and some, uh, girl time." The lie feels like mud on her tongue.

Uncle Jimmy cocks an eyebrow. "Makeovers and pillow fights?"

Another forced laugh. "Are you kidding? I'm sure they'd be lethal even with pillows."

"Hmm," Uncle Jimmy grunts again, thoughtful. "Hey. How about tomorrow you and I go on a little road trip to Syracuse? We can check out the campus if you want, or we can go to the mall, or the museum . . . whatever you want. Just you and me."

Rhi takes too long to reply, so Uncle Jimmy starts to offer answers to questions she hasn't asked.

"I just think, you know, it's great you want to be there for your friends. Really. But what you're going through, that's hard too. I just don't want you feeling responsible for all those girls when the only one you *are* responsible for is yourself. And . . . maybe it's selfish, but I'd like to spend some time with you. Before . . ."

"I have to go back," Rhi whispers.

Uncle Jimmy is careful to keep his expression blank. "Yeah."

Purrdita sinks her teeth gently into Rhi's finger, purring loudly as she rubs her face aggressively against her hand. Rhi does not hesitate this time. She smiles up at Uncle Jimmy from the floor and says "Okay" before the lie can choke her.

LATER, AFTER SHE HELPS CLEAN up from dinner, while Uncle Jimmy is digging through boxes in one of the closets, Rhi gives Purrdita a few last pets and scritches under the chin. She looks around at the small cabin she's come to love, the cat-fur-covered back of the sofa, the counter where she ate meals with her uncle, who never looked twice at what she put on her plate except to see if it was enough. She thinks Uncle Jimmy will understand if she never comes back. He won't take it personally. He knows some of what she's up against. That soothes her guilt a little.

"Uncle Jimmy!" she calls as she slings her backpack over her shoulder. "I'm heading out!"

"Hold up! I found it!" he calls. There's a soft clatter as what sounds like the lids of several plastic storage tubs fall to the floor. Uncle Jimmy jogs out from his bedroom holding a roomy gold-and-black jacket with a big gold *W* on the front right side, right under the name *Abrams* embroidered in gold. "Your mom was on the varsity track and field team in high school. Got herself a scholarship for college and everything—I think that might have been how she met your father, at a track meet—anyway. Check this out." He turns the jacket around with a flourish so she can see the back. "What do you think?" Uncle Jimmy grins.

Rhi stops breathing.

"What . . . is that?" Rhi asks, forcing a smile, even as her heart jams in her throat. It takes everything she has not to let her emotions play across her face.

"Technically it should be a she-wolf because it was the girls track team, but they just called themselves the Happy Valley Wolves, so . . . it's a *wolf*, I guess. But what do you think? Badass? Corny?" He jostles the jacket while waiting for her reply. "Maybe it's *ironically* cool?"

"It's incredible." Rhi brushes her fingers over the thick embroidery of the massive gray wolf's head, the yolk-yellow eyes, the sharp white fangs of its open jaws.

"Well, go on then." Uncle Jimmy hands it to her. "It's yours now."

Rhi takes her mother's jacket in both hands, gripping it to her chest. "Thank you, Uncle Jimmy." She says it too quietly, so she tries again. "Thank you so much." And before she knows what she's doing, she's hugging him, half to hide the tears that want to burst from her eyes, and half to hide the wild excitement she's sure must be beaming from her face.

A daughter of wolves, Rhi thinks.

Holy shit. It is me.

MR. AND MRS. QUAKER ARE upstairs in their bedroom, sitting around like they do every night, reading their books and writing in journals. This is their evening ritual, after everything has been cleaned up from dinner and they've watched some television and made sure Giovanna is ready for bed: they climb the stairs to their room and change into their sleeping clothes and stay in their room for anywhere from fifteen minutes to an hour before one of them comes downstairs again, says goodnight to whoever is still awake, locks up the house, and then both go to bed.

This is how Sunder knows she has at least fifteen minutes to sneak out of the house before the Quakers might catch her and try to stop her. She doesn't believe they could stop her, but it's an altercation she would rather avoid if she can.

She is standing at the sliding glass doors in the kitchen, her backpack slung over both shoulders. Giovanna is reading another book of fairy tales in bed. Sunder has kissed her on her forehead and wished her sweet dreams, and felt the pain of leaving her sharper than expected. Dallas is in the barn working on his motorbike. Sunder has not found a way to say goodbye to him yet—she is too afraid he will try to stop her. She wrote him a letter and left it on his pillow instead.

Sunder knows she will miss Giovanna and Dallas when she is in Leutheria. She has grown accustomed to Giovanna's gentle and eager nature, how she loves so openly and without reservation. She has become fond of Dallas and his obsession with motorcycles and engines, his fearless ability to mount mechanical beasts and soar across the pavement. And she has become absolutely soft for the Quakers and their nurturing kindness. They remind her of Mother, in many ways: seemingly endless wells of wisdom, patience, and comfort.

Mother loved her and her sisters—no matter what other doubts have entered her mind, she has always been certain of that. But Mother is gone, and the Quakers and Dallas and Giovanna are here, and she knows they love her, too. Sunder thinks she loves them back—and is that not amazing, how the idea of family can grow and change? Is it not incredible how love can appear where there was none before?

Sunder realizes she will miss them much more than she expected when she is in Leutheria. And she worries. This world is so full of monsters that they have come to look like human beings. What will happen to Giovanna and Dallas as they grow older in this world?

But Sunder has a promise to keep to the land she came from and the people she is meant to protect. She cannot abandon them, just like she cannot abandon Mother's teachings.

When the heavens meet the Earth and your fifth sister has arrived, the way home will be revealed. You will return to Leutheria and save your kingdoms.

Sunder is resolved. She will find the portal. She will walk through it, and she will face her destiny.

Even if she has to do it alone.

Sunder looks out through the glass door at the darkening sky. She can already see the moon overhead, full and glorious in all her radiant splendor. The barest feather of a shadow is creeping at the moon's edge as the eclipse begins. Waiting to reveal the doorway to Leutheria. The portal home.

She shifts her weight and thinks about that word, *home*.

The digital clock on the microwave blinks to 8:15.

Sunder opens the back door and slips outside.

"So, you're actually going," Dallas's voice comes from the gray-dark.

Sunder's eyes take a moment to adjust to the twilight, but she sees him there, sitting on a bench at one of the picnic tables on the back deck. His elbows are on his knees, hands clasped. He looks like he's been waiting for her.

Sunder steels herself against the squeeze of remorse.

"I have a destiny to fulfill," she says plainly.

"Mom and Dad are going to be heartbroken, you know," he says. "And Gia."

"They are strong. My absence will not undo them."

"*I'll* miss you."

Sunder frowns. "I know. Because I will miss you, too."

"So . . . stay."

She shakes her head, but for the briefest moment, she cannot remember why it is so important that she leave.

And then Mother fills her mind: Mother carrying her through the woods on his hip when she was small and too tired to walk back from the creek; Mother laying a fur over her shoulders as he told the story of how he rescued her from the monsters in Leutheria who stole babies and sold them for piles of gold coins; Mother teaching her how to use magic to lull bees to sleep so she could taste their honey; Mother

MADELINE CLAIRE FRANKLIN / 321

holding her while she sobbed after a fight with her sisters; Mother telling them, again and again, of their destinies in another world—of a fifth princess who would join them—of a portal that would open, when the time was right.

Mother's body, vacated, lying helpless on the ground.

Oblivienne's body, all alone in her coffin, six feet deep in the earth.

"I have to go," she says, swallowing her grief. "Leutheria needs me."

Dallas nods. "Okay. But . . . what if this world needs you, too?"

Sunder curls her toes against the still-sun-warm wood of the deck. "Then it should have been more welcoming."

IN THE WOODS THAT RUN alongside the Quakers' farm, Sunder feels like herself again: wild, free, and clean. The grass underfoot and the trees around her are once more connected to her through the invisible filaments that keep her heart pumping, just as sure as they keep the sun rising and the stars in the sky. She feels pure, like cold spring water, and as lithe and powerful as a mother wolf—except when she remembers. She has imagined this fated night a thousand different times, in a thousand different ways. But she never imagined walking this path alone.

It is not long before she hears the snap of twigs and branches behind her. She knows it must be Rhi—her other sisters would never make so much noise. Sure enough, Rhi appears beside her, ashen faced but bright eyed, with a backpack slung over her shoulders.

"You came," Sunder says, not smiling, but feeling it in her chest. She takes Rhi's hand in hers.

"I wasn't sure if I'd be able to find you," Rhi says, panting a little.

"Of course you would find me, Sister," Sunder says, squeezing Rhi's hand tightly. "This is our destiny."

"Yes," Rhi says, reaching into her pack. "And Sunder, I have to show you something. This belonged to my mother—*look*." She holds up a piece of clothing—a coat or a jacket of some kind—with a picture of a wolf's head stitched into the back almost as real as a photograph.

"It belonged to my mother. She was on a team when she was younger, the Happy Valley Wolves—"

"You *are* a daughter of wolves," Sunder realizes. Of course, she had known Rhi was one of them, had always believed that from the moment Rhi pulled the jaws from Sunder's leg. But this was *proof* that Mother's prophecy was not a lie. Mother *had* told them the truth. Mother *was good*.

"Come, dear Sister," Sunder says, grinning, taking Rhi by the elbow. "It will not be long now."

THE TWO OF THEM JOG into the forest, Sunder taking the lead, guiding them into the thicket where no one has blazed any trails for them to follow. She seems to know where she's going, though Rhi is not sure how. Maybe some remnant of the magic Mother instilled in them is guiding her—or perhaps Leutheria itself is calling her home.

All day today, Rhi had been softened by a persistent, enveloping calm. At times, she had felt downright peaceful, relieved by the possibility that she would be leaving this world behind. Discovering her mother's jacket had blown up that inner peace, replacing it with an intoxicating excitement Rhi had not felt since—well, ever. She had nothing to compare it to, the heady high of knowing, and purpose, and being in motion. Had the girls felt like this all their lives, before they came to this world and were forced to question their own reality? If so, she ached for them more than ever, knowing that *this* was the feeling they had lost.

Now, her excitement has been transmuted into riveted focus, her insides shivering with the pounding of her feet and the hum of her blood. She is reaching out all around her with her senses, trying to feel something, *anything*, pushing or pulling her in any direction. She listens for a call from another world, a hum or a whistle or a whine, anything that would further signal that she is the right person, on the right path. But maybe she doesn't need to hear or feel its call—she has Sunder, after all. Maybe she just needs to keep trusting. Keep having faith.

In the distance, she hears the dull *whooop* of a police siren turning on and cutting off. It's very far away, but distinct in her ears, that aural signal flare of impending trouble. Is the siren for them, or is it merely coincidence?

Sunder seems to hear Rhi's thoughts, because they pick up their pace. The run stretches on over tree roots, up an almost imperceptible incline, but it doesn't faze Rhi. She has had years of jogging experience to prepare her for a run like this, thanks to Vera's treadmill addiction. She wonders if *that* is a sign she is meant to be here.

"Sisters!" A voice calls from behind, but they don't slow down, don't stop.

Suddenly Epiphanie is there, falling in on Sunder's right-hand side, jogging alongside her. "I may not believe as you do," she says, looking at her sister, then at Rhi. "But I will not let either of you face this alone."

Sunder finally looks at Epiphanie, her eyes wide with tenderness. She grins, turning back to face the invisible path ahead.

"However, the police have sent dogs after us," Epiphanie says, voice shaking with each pounding step. "I snuck out of Maggie's house—but I think Bradley saw me leave."

Sunder nods, her eyes shining. "We will get there long before they can find us. We are almost there."

Yes, Rhi thinks to herself, her spirit lifted by Epiphanie's appearance. *The bond between these sisters is too strong to be broken. The truth of Mother's prophecy is holding them—us—together.*

The three of them continue through the forest, breaths coming in measured huffs as the running begins to take its toll. Through the trees, Rhi catches glimpses of fireflies rising like a mist over the forest floor, electric and flickering. As the full moon darkens, she spots a flash of silver on her right, then her left—*wolves*, she thinks, but they are glowing and moon bright in the dark. Ahead of them, the trees seem to part for the girls as they run, slipping roots underground so they won't trip, leaning slim trunks aside for them to pass. The whole forest is guiding them, urging them forward, to a destination that has been waiting for them their entire lives.

Finally they break through the edge of the forest and find themselves atop a hill overlooking the Little Salmon River just a few hundred feet below.

To Rhi's surprise (but also no surprise at all), Verity and Grace are already there, standing atop the hill in the now full dark of night, Grace panting and pressing a hand to her ribs, a cloud of fireflies forming a star-bright shroud around them. The girls keep running until they are almost on top of them.

Rhi doesn't need to wonder how Sunder knew to take them to *this* spot, how it is that Verity and Grace also knew where to meet them. Because the answer is so clear, so obvious.

Our destiny is real. And it is calling to all of us.

43

THE SHIFTING LIGHT OF THE fireflies casts an eerie glow over them, but the love on Verity's face is unmistakable. She puts her long arms around as many of her sisters as she can, pulls them to her chest and says, "We are a pack," as if that's all they need to know.

Grace nods her agreement, though her doubt is clearly written on her face.

But she is here. They are *all* here—*five princesses from five kingdoms*, and the sliver of moon hanging in the sky overhead, gently dimming by the second as Earth slides into position between the sun and the moon.

"It is nearly eclipsed," Epiphanie says.

Somewhere in the forest, the police dogs bark, padding closer by the second.

"Let's go," Sunder says, urging them forward.

Everyone follows as she rushes eagerly down the hill, toward the smooth surface of the river where the moon's reflection is wavering on the water, diminishing rapidly. The hill is steep, though, full of too many divots and rocks, and the girls must slow themselves despite the danger pursuing them in the forest.

And Sunder's bad leg, though it did heal faster than any doctor expected, has never been quite the same.

So when she steps just wrong enough into a divot, her heel landing too soon and the ball of her foot not landing soon enough, it strains the scarred muscle over her shin. Pain jolts through her leg, and Sunder loses her footing.

"Sunder!" Verity shouts, reaching for her—but not soon enough.

Sunder tumbles head over heels down the rest of the hill, landing with a groan on the grassy bank of the river. The girls hurry as fast as they can to the bottom of the hill to help her.

"Are you hurt?" Rhi asks as she skids to a halt and kneels before her, examining her leg.

The answer is obvious: Sunder's ankle is already ballooning.

"Jesus," Grace says. "That's not good."

"You will be okay," Epiphanie says as Sunder's eyes turn wild. "Sunder, you will be okay. It is just a sprain. You have seen much worse—"

"That is not what is wrong!" Sunder shouts, tears streaming. She points to the water as the light from the full moon completely disappears overhead. "I will never make it! I cannot get to the portal like this!"

Silently, all five girls look at the water.

Rhi holds her breath.

Hovering in the air above the undulating surface of the water, just a few feet from the riverbank, is the earthbound form of the lunar eclipse—a red circle of light pulsating around a murky, shadowy center.

The portal. It is here.

It is real.

Everything Rhi has not dared to fully let herself believe—every hope she's had since her father was arrested—a future free from the monsters and ghosts that have haunted her heart—it is all there, *right there*, inside that red corona: her chance to leave all this pain behind and become something bigger than a scared little girl, afraid of the dark.

But at her side, Sunder is sobbing.

"I cannot make it," Sunder weeps. "I cannot make it! Leutheria—"

"Sunder," Verity pleads, resting her hands on Sunder's arms, eyes ricocheting between her little sister and the glowing red circle hanging over the water. "If we are meant to go through that portal, why are you unable to go? Why would you be hurt?" She grimaces and takes Sunder's hand in hers. "Something is not *right* . . ."

"What if that is not even a portal?" Epiphanie says, almost in a whisper. Her brows pinch together. "What if it is only an illusion? A trick of the light?"

"It is real!" Sunder cries. "It is *right there*! Can you not see it?"

"Sister," Verity says, leaning her forehead against Sunder's. "We have all seen *so much*. Just because we see it does not mean it is good. It does not mean we need to embrace it."

Sunder's grimace stretches into an anguished bow of parted teeth, half snarl, half silent howl. "But Mother *told us* . . ."

"Mother told us we would *know*," Verity says. "Mother told us the way would be *clear*. This is *not* what Mother said it would be like."

Epiphanie strokes the fine short hair on Sunder's head. "Sunder," she says with such wretched tenderness it makes Rhi's heart twist. "It is okay for Mother to have been mistaken. It does not mean he loved us any less."

Tears stream down Sunder's cheeks, veins of quicksilver in the dim starlight. She leans back into her sisters' arms, recreating the tableau from the day Rhi first found them in the woods. Only this time, Grace is here instead of Oblivienne.

Oblivienne, who was driven to despair by the disparity between what she believed to be true, and what she could not accept.

Oblivienne, who was ready to die rather than live in a world where the person she trusted most of all turned out to be a villain.

Oblivienne, who understood that some kinds of pain simply cannot be endured.

Rhi turns to the portal, a keen desperation sensitizing her mind. She can feel it, now: the pull she had been searching for earlier, the tug from the threads of her own destiny, drawing her toward Leutheria.

She can also feel the weight of the past around her neck, the weight of a future she cannot bear to imagine like a leaden rope trailing down back through the woods, through Happy Valley, all the way back to the girl she locked in a closet in Saratoga Springs.

It is a very easy choice, to slip that noose from around her neck, to leave it on the grassy bank of the river to be washed away with the next storm. Really, it is the only choice that makes any sense at all.

"What if they are waiting for us?" Sunder cries to her sisters, voice shaking now with the fury of her own impotence. "What if they need us, and we never come? *What if we fail them?*"

"But Sunder," Epiphanie pleads. "What if they need us *here?*"

"No," Rhi says, because she understands now. She understands why, if she is the fifth princess, she had to be raised apart from the others. They were never meant to join her in Leutheria. They were only meant to guide her here. Tonight.

Because Rhi is the only one of them with a life worth walking away from.

"Sunder," she says. "You haven't failed them. You brought me here. And I won't let Leutheria down."

She climbs to her feet and rushes toward the river. It is effortless, like a horizontal free-fall, as if some other force is yanking her forward. The portal hums and wavers, gaping at her, a deep, fathomless maw waiting for her, *calling* to her—

("Rhi!" someone shouts, but she does not know who.)

Yes, *finally*, Rhi can hear it calling to her. She can see what waits for her on the other side so clearly in her mind's eye—the waving fields of silver grain, the cobblestone streets waiting to welcome her home. The darkness will still have to be defeated, and the kingdoms will have to be rebuilt, but Leutheria has magic, and now that Rhi is certain she is the fifth princess she knows she will be able to wield that magic and fulfill her destiny. It is her destiny calling to her, reaching for her, pulling at her, promising her a future: a place where she is powerful, and wanted, and knows where she belongs. It is promising her a life—promising to lead her *home*.

Maybe *this* is why Rhi has always felt rootless and displaced, like an alien in her own world: because she has always belonged to someplace else. Not to her mother or her father, definitely not to her stepmother or Kevin.

She has never belonged to any of them.

Maybe Rhi has never really been a part of this world at all.

Maybe she has always belonged to Leutheria.

("Rhi, no!" Grace shouts somewhere behind her.)

And now she will return to Leutheria. She will use all the strength she has gained from her suffering to help her people defeat the great darkness that has consumed their kingdoms.

Yes.

It all makes sense now.

("Rhi, stop!" Epiphanie cries after her.)

All the long years of isolation and confusion and pain . . . they were preparing her for this. And now, they'll soon be over.

The portal is a few feet out from the bank, but Rhi can make it through, easily. Eden Chase set the school record for the girls' long jump when she was fourteen—Rhi has got this, no problem.

She runs, and as she runs, she feels the weight around her neck dissolve, no longer able to hold her down when the promise of a future—a *true home*—is right in front of her.

At the river's edge, Rhi leaps from a jutting rock, into the air, and wonders who she will be when she lands. For a long moment, she is flying, buoyed by the mystical energy that surrounds her, that has possibly always surrounded her. She is defying gravity, defying physics, defying everything she ever thought she knew was true.

Rhiannon Chase is sailing into the warm black maw of the portal to Leutheria, leaving this life behind.

44

S HE IS FLOATING.

Or maybe time has stopped.

Or maybe she is dead.

No.

White noise fills her head, the rush of blood and water. The impenetrable dark dissolves like dust blown away from a photograph, revealing a vast plane of wild grasses whispering in the breeze; the crumbling ruins of a kingdom scattered along the horizon; a solitary figure moving toward her from the field; all of it cast in the color of bruises, silvered by moonlight.

The white noise fades to silence as the figure comes closer, replaced with a piercing, high-pitched whine instead. The figure is small. She can make out wild dark hair, hollow dark eyes. For a moment, she thinks it is Oblivienne—for another moment, she thinks it is Eden, some younger version, before she was broken beyond repair. Either way, she understands: this is a haunting.

The figure stops, still too far away for her to make out their face. They thrust an arm out, pointing: *back*. She does not need to turn to see what the figure wants her to see: Epiphanie and Grace scrambling toward the river, screaming a name that does not belong to her; Verity and Sunder watching in horror as she disappears without them. And somewhere else, Uncle Jimmy is sitting on his couch with Purrdita, texting Star for recommendations for cool shops to take his niece to in Syracuse.

But somewhere else, her stepmother is hiring staff for their house in Saratoga Springs. Her father is serving the final weeks of his sentence. Her stepbrother is packing up his apartment in Germany, preparing to come home. To face her. To tell her that her memories are not true.

A cry in the dark pulls her vision back to Sunder, but it is a memory now: Sunder, anemic, mud streaked and grim, lying in her sister's lap, the spring trap still biting into her calf. Oblivienne is holding her head, looking up with coal-black eyes, pleading—no, demanding—that she save her sister. That she not abandon them. That she not make the same mistake Oblivienne did.

She turns her vision back to Leutheria, but the figure is gone. She is alone in the dark, in the space between two worlds. The only sound in her ears is the susurration of the field of silver grain. An imitation of an ocean she has never seen. White noise. The rush of blood and water.

She has one more choice to make.

45

"RHI!" SOMEONE SCREAMS.

There are hands on her wrists—now arms under her arms—pulling her backward, up, out of the river. Away from the portal.

She is coughing, shivering, soaking wet. Earthy water is spewing from her mouth, her nose. She doesn't remember being in the river.

"Rhi," Epiphanie says firmly when they stop, holding Rhi's back to her chest. "You cannot do this. *You cannot leave us.*" Her voice is shaking. "*We cannot lose another sister.*"

A lump rises in her throat, but she keeps staring at the portal, shimmering and beckoning, promising her a *home*, a place where she can exist without fear, without pain, without shame—promising her the only true freedom she will ever know.

But she knows now, even if Leutheria is real, it is a false promise.

How could she possibly defeat the monsters of another world if she cannot face her demons here?

"There's no way out," she says, hot tears streaking down her cold cheeks.

Grace tightens her grip on Rhi's arm and leans down to whisper in her ear: "Listen to me. You don't need to leave this world in order to be safe. You don't need to leave this *life* in order to be free."

Rhi sinks back against the other girls, shaking with cold and a grief so huge it might as well be the river she has just been dragged from. Before their eyes, the vision of the portal dissolves into nothing but night sky and fireflies.

The portal to Leutheria is gone.

Rhi is still here.

They are *all* still here, in the shadow of the eclipse: Rhi, crying. Grace and Epiphanie, holding on to Rhi as if she might run at any moment. Verity and Sunder sink to the ground on Rhi's right side, arms still around each other for support. Verity's free hand takes one of Rhi's, squeezing it like she's trying to verify the truth of her existence. Sunder grabs the back of Rhi's head. She looks her straight in the eyes for an interminable moment before pressing their foreheads together. Sunder says nothing, but Rhi understands everything.

Sobbing, Rhi clutches the arm around her chest—she does not know who it belongs to, but it does not matter. She is suddenly desperate to hold on to the world she was willing to throw away mere moments ago.

Somewhere behind them, above them, dogs are barking. Men are shouting.

"We have to hide," Grace hisses somewhere near Rhi.

"Wait—look," Verity says in a hushed voice.

They all turn to look up. At the very top of the hill, Rhi can just make out two huge pale dogs, watching the girls on the riverbank below.

No, not dogs.

Wolves.

They turn away as the sound of barking dogs creeps closer in the night, their tails flicking low to the ground.

And then they bolt.

The girls below can't see what happens, but they know the dogs and the police never come. The barking and voices fade as they twist off in another direction, following some unseen trail and the sound of wolves howling at the shadow moon.

While the wolves lead the police astray, the girls crowd together in a pile on the riverbank. Verity finds clothing in one of their backpacks, uses strips of torn cloth to wrap Sunder's ankle. Epiphanie holds on to both Sunder and Rhi, crying silent, furious tears. Grace, with her arms still wrapped around Rhi, whispers to her all the little acts of chaos and rebellion they can do to keep Rhi safe and free, all the ways she can escape the cage of her life to live fully in this world.

"We're going to tell Dr. Ibanez everything," she says. "And we're going to find that pharmacist in Harlem. And we're going to make sure your parents and your dipshit stepbrother never see you again. And you're going to use this whole goddamn experience on your college application essays someday—if you want to go to college. And if not, well, we'll figure that out. But you're going to stay alive, Rhi. You're going to live to *spite* those motherfuckers. You're going to live wild and free and never be caged again, unless you get arrested at like a protest for women's rights or something. Because this world *needs* you, Rhi. *We* need you. Alive, and kicking, and screaming. Got it?"

"Yes," Epiphanie says, though she can't possibly understand all of what Grace has said. "*We need you*, Rhi. And we will not abandon you in your time of need."

Rhi says nothing, tears streaming down her face as she imagines this life Grace has described. She can't really imagine it at all, not for herself. She can imagine it for Grace, easily. She can imagine it, even, for the wild girls around her who have been actively caged and tamed these last four months.

But Rhi? Wild and free? Impossible.

She would have to rid herself of all the roiling pain in her bones before she could ever be free. And who is she, then, if she isn't living in constant fear of making more wrong choices? Who is she, if she isn't a girl reduced to nothing but survival instincts: freezing and fawning and fleeing?

Is such a life possible?

Rhi cannot imagine it—not in this world.

But Grace can. And Epiphanie can.

So maybe—just maybe—it *is* a possibility, existing somewhere out there among all the possibilities her life may unfold into.

And if that possibility does not exist, then maybe—just maybe—she can build it.

But she realizes, as she looks at the river, at the place where she nearly disappeared forever: she will never be able to build a future if she is using all her strength to run away from the past.

"Eden," Rhi chokes out, and feels a childish desire to wail building in her chest.

"Huh?" Grace asks.

Epiphanie puts her hand over Rhi's heart, her ghost-pale eyes like an afterimage in the dark. She holds Rhi's gaze as she speaks, *willing* her own strength into Rhi.

"My real name. It's Eden."

But that's not quite right, either.

The Long Way Home

Excerpted from *Savage Castle:*
A Memoir of the Wild Girls of Happy Valley

IN THE SHADOW OF THE eclipse, on the bank of the Little Salmon River, in a kingdom known as Happy Valley, we tended to our wounds, visible and not. All hands were our hands as we wrapped gashes in torn fabric, as we wiped tears from our eyes. Each heart was *our* heart, whether lifting or breaking, or something in between. A great weight had been taken from our shoulders: the salvation of a world we had never laid eyes on; the stewardship of kingdoms we had no memory of. But that weight left a deep impression where it once lay. For many of us, it would even leave a scar.

We supported Sunder between us as we returned to the forest, to the unmarked path that would lead us, once more, away from the wilderness. Our wolf-kin howled in the distance, leading the hounds astray, but also mourning with us for all that we had lost—or perhaps celebrating the release of all that we were finally letting go. The scythe of the moon followed us in the sky, a lidded eye opening—so slowly—as the promise of Leutheria settled in our hearts, no longer a looming question or an impossible answer. Now, it was only a memory of a dream.

We ached with the memory, and we would ache for quite some time. But there was relief, too. And groundedness. And the comfort of our sisters, who we knew would be here for us, in this world, no matter what the future held.

We did not know it then, but we were beginning to grasp what Epiphanie had realized long before us—what she had tried to explain to us the night we nearly fractured, but did not have the words for.

One truth does not always negate another. We may never have all the answers to our questions, but there is room for uncertainty in this world—in fact, it is built upon it. There is room for the unknown, the undefined. There is room for magic, and wildness. There is room for so much more than any of us had ever dared to imagine.

And how beautiful this world must be, to contain so many possibilities.

46

IT COULD HAVE BEEN HOURS or days before they reached the Quakers' farm, emerging from the woods cold and damp and weary. Dallas meets them there with the Quakers' golf cart; had he been waiting there all night? Had he seen them stumble out of the woods and come running? Rhi/Eden can't tell. Swathes of time are slipping from her grasp: one minute Rhi is dragging her feet through the tall grass of the pasture, the next minute Eden is in the barn, kneeling on straw, safely squeezed between Verity and Grace, who are whispering to each other about something she cannot follow.

Rhi/Eden is not even sure who she is, right now. She is not sure she can face that, yet.

They are all hiding now. The Quakers are talking to the police, denying they know anything, insisting their own foster child is asleep in bed and will not be awoken for this without a warrant. The girls are huddled in the barn while Epiphanie wraps Sunder's ankle in a proper bandage and Dallas silently forces water and ibuprofen down her throat.

Then they are moving again, and Rhi/Eden is soaking wet and freezing one minute, then naked and stepping into a hot shower the next. She is leaning her forehead against an unfamiliar white tile wall as steaming water pummels her neck, her shoulders, her back. Somewhere on her leg there is a scrape she doesn't remember getting, stinging as the water washes the crusted blood away. She closes her eyes and focuses on the pain until it dissolves, numb and vacant, like every other part of her body.

But Eden has been trying to tell her: *that's not how things work.*

Soon she is out of the shower, standing wrapped in a plush purple towel as she stares at a pile of clothing that does not belong to her. But it is dry and smells like the pale bars of lavender soap Eden's mother used to keep in her dresser drawers. Rhi/Eden has the curious notion that if she puts on these clothes she can become another person—again. That somehow, when she was inside the portal—or when she was immersed in the Little Salmon River, maybe—she shed her skin, her body, her very identity, and became . . . not *new*, but liminal. In-between. No longer Rhi, but not quite Eden, either.

Or maybe she had never truly been either.

And if she puts these clothes on, now—the unfamiliar fit of another person's well-worn jeans; another person's plain, black T-shirt; another person's clean white underwear—she has the feeling she can become a whole new person: not Rhi, who abandoned Eden, and not Eden, who made all the wrong choices to begin with—

No. That feeling—that thought. It breaks her heart.

Rhi/Eden looks into the mirror over the bathroom sink. Vera would lose her mind if she saw her now: two dress sizes bigger and completely shorn of her "mother's Jewish hair." She is almost unrecognizable.

But even as that thought brings her a flicker of pleasure, a wail swells inside her chest—a child's wail, deep and unconstrained as only a child's wail can be. But she doesn't let it out—not yet. She listens to that child wailing inside her, the one who *knows* she deserved to be loved without conditions; the one who *knows* her trust was broken, over and over and over again, not just by her parents or her stepbrother, but by *herself.*

Rhi was never Eden's chance at rebirth.

Rhi abandoned Eden the night she came to Happy Valley.

She abandoned *herself*.

"I am so sorry," Rhi says to Eden's reflection, as tears well in their eyes. "I'm so, so sorry I tried to leave you behind. Just because we were hurting. Just because our pain was too much. I'm sorry."

Her words pierce her heart—Eden's heart. Suddenly she is a child again, crying for her mother. Crying for her loneliness. Crying for the injustice of her existence. She puts her hands on the sink as her knees buckle, as she folds in three, her body wracked with breathless sobbing. For a long time, that is all she is: the deep throb of old pain, the bitter agony of unexpressed sorrow, and the tectonic shift she has caused by acknowledging their existence.

When she has exhausted herself, she pulls herself to her feet, leans heavily on the vanity counter, and looks up, once more, into the mirror. Through the blur of her tears, she thinks she can see her true self for the very first time, both the little girl she was, and the young woman she has become: full of fear and anger and longing, and so many huge, wild emotions, it makes her want to run away again.

But she wants more than a life of running and numbing. She wants contentedness and calm, curiosity and clarity. She wants affection, and safety, and freedom, and simple, easy joy.

Rhi/Eden knows the only way to get to that place is through feeling everything she's locked away for so long, and releasing the part of herself she tried to abandon. She knows it will be hard—devastating, even. She can feel her child-self's wail still waiting inside her chest, scouring the edges of her soul like steel bristles over bare skin, portending what awaits her.

But *feeling* that—processing every savage thing she's hidden beneath her quiet, placating exterior—that has to be better than living with it buried inside her, festering and metastasizing, constantly threatening to consume her. It has to be better. *It has to be.*

Because she can no longer live that way. Not in this world, or any other.

RHI/EDEN FEELS SELF-CONSCIOUS WHEN SHE comes downstairs to the dining room, borrowed clothing hanging loose from her frame. It is not because of the clothes that she feels self-conscious, but because of the transformation she's gone through—a transformation she's not sure she can explain.

The girls, minus Sunder, are seated in silence at the dining room table along with Mr. and Mrs. Quaker and Dallas. There's a kettle still steaming on the stove and several mugs of tea on the table, the cream and sugar service at the center.

"Is Sunder okay?" Rhi/Eden asks.

"She'll be fine," Mr. Quaker assures her, his tone as soft as the well-worn clothing his wife has loaned Rhi/Eden. "Just a sprain. Nothing ice, rest, and time won't heal."

Epiphanie makes a face. Rhi/Eden catches her eye, understanding. It's more than just the ankle they're worried about. But she knows in her heart, as grieved as Sunder is to have lost her chance at Leutheria, she is comforted by the fact that, in the end, her sisters showed up for her. They remained a pack, until the very end.

It was only Rhi who tried to stray.

"Are *you* okay?" Dallas asks, sliding a mug of tea in front of her.

Rhi/Eden shrugs and sits on a stool between Verity and Dallas, putting both hands around the warm mug.

"Girls," Mrs. Quaker says after a moment. "I don't pretend to know what happened out there—and I suspect whatever it was that happened *had* to happen in order for some of you move on from your past. But I have to say: it can't happen again." She frowns. "Lying to the police . . . to fellow foster parents . . . I don't intend to do these things again."

Epiphanie's eyes are sharp as they focus on Mrs. Quaker. "You will not have to," she says. "My sisters and I know how close we came to losing each other tonight. Whether to Leutheria, or to the police, or to institutionalization . . ." She shakes her head, looks decisively at the older woman. "We have agreed: We will do what we must to fit into this world. To not scare people. To be safe."

Rhi/Eden frowns.

Sensing her disapproval, Verity looks at her. "We will still be true to ourselves—only now, we have a chance to discover who we really are, without a prophecy shaping us." She turns to Grace. "We cannot go back to the wilderness knowing what we know now. And we cannot escape into any other world."

"The only way is forward, and the only way forward is through," Epiphanie says. "Which means finding a way to connect with this world and the people who live in it." She smiles faintly at the people around the table. "And we have connected with all of you, so it cannot be that bad."

The only way forward is through, Rhi/Eden repeats to herself, and swallows the lump in her throat.

"It is hard," Verity says, leaning wearily back in her chair. "To balance who you really are with what the world expects you to be. Sometimes the world is correct, sometimes it is not. It seems like a person could spend their whole life learning to tell the difference."

"And when the world is incorrect," Epiphanie muses, "perhaps it is up to you to change the world. One expectation at a time."

Rhi/Eden startles as the clock over the Quakers' mantle strikes an ungodly hour. "We should get you home, Epiphanie—come up with an excuse on the way."

"Are you okay to drive?" Grace asks.

"Yeah," Rhi/Eden says. "Let's go home."

Outside the Quakers' farmhouse, the four of them climb into the truck Uncle Jimmy bought for Rhi, hidden between Mrs. Quaker's minivan and a small tractor. They squeeze together in the cab, Epiphanie in the middle, Grace in Verity's lap. For a moment, Rhi/Eden looks at the keys in her hands, the thick plastic head of the key to her truck, the slender gold key to Uncle Jimmy's house, the green-and-black boondoggle keychain Sunder made for her while the girls were all still in the psychiatric hospital.

Quietly, Grace asks: "So what should we call you now? Rhi, or Eden?"

Rhi/Eden buckles her seat belt and sticks her key into the ignition. She doesn't turn it though. Instead, she leans heavily into the scuffed and torn leather of the driver's seat and looks out the windshield, up at the sky where the moon hangs like a silver thumbprint on the night, misshapen by the tail end of the eclipse. "That depends. Is changing your name just running away from your past, or is it creating a better *now*?"

Epiphanie begins to speak, but hesitates until Rhi/Eden glances at her.

"Mother told us once," she says. "That he hid our old names so that we would always be free of masters and kings."

Rhi smirks. "I like that idea."

"He also said, when a name is *true* it holds great power," Verity adds. "When I found my blood family, they told me my real name was Mathilda. That name means nothing to me. It has no power over me, but it has a great deal of power over them." She looks at Grace, thoughtfully. "For them, Mathilda was *their* truth. But the power it has over them is not a kind power. *Mathilda* reminds Blood Mother of the daughter she *lost*, not the daughter who came back to her. So she honors my new name—the name that is *my* truth. I think it has helped her accept how things are, not what they could have been. And both of those things bring us closer together, bit by bit."

"I think what she's saying," Grace says, leaning forward to look at Rhi/Eden, "is that it's okay to spare yourself unnecessary pain. It's not running away. It's like . . . moving out of a house made of broken glass and into a cozy log cabin."

"But, Verity—Epiphanie," Rhi/Eden says. "When we first met, you all said *Rhi* wasn't my real name. That *Eden* was."

"Because it was—then," Epiphanie says. "You wore the name *Rhi* like a piece of armor, not as a part of yourself. The name *Eden* was woven into you."

"And now?"

"Now . . ." Epiphanie looks thoughtful. "Now it is up to you. The life you lived as Eden will always be a part of you, no matter what name you choose."

"Just as Mother and the wilderness will always be a part of us," Verity says softly, reaching for Epiphanie's hand.

"But does the name *Rhi* even belong to me? Or is it still just . . . armor?"

Epiphanie puts her hand on the back of Rhi/Eden's head and leans close, as if she is about to tell her a secret. "You are asking these questions as if there is only one answer—as if our answer is more important than your desire. But there is no right answer, Sister. There is only a choice that *you* must make: Do you *want* to be Rhi? Or do you simply *not* want to be Eden?"

47

"Thank you, Rhi," Dr. Ibanez says. "For trusting me with this." Her tone is so soft, so delicate—as if the slightest hint of unkindness could make the girl before her crumble like ash in the wind.

Rhi is sitting in the now familiar chair across from Dr. Ibanez, wringing her hands because her fingers are already stinging from where she's picked too much at her cuticles. She hangs her head, desperate to hide the shame burning her cheeks—shame she knows she should not carry, and yet lives in her all the same.

"I want to be clear," the doctor continues. "Before I say anything else. *You are not to blame for any of what has happened to you.*" She holds Rhi's gaze for a beat, and then another, until Rhi can't see her through the blur of tears that suddenly threaten to spill down her face. "Especially what your stepbrother did to you. I need you to know, not a single moment of his abuse was your fault." She leans forward slightly, resting her forearms on her desk. "You have *nothing* to be ashamed of, Rhi."

"You say that. And Grace says that. But why do I still feel so . . . disgusting?" she asks, her whole body hot with loathing.

Dr. Ibanez takes a deep breath. "The answer to that is pretty complicated. But feelings aren't facts. We must let ourselves feel them, but we can question them, too. Feelings of shame are often rooted in *beliefs*. What do you believe about this situation that makes you feel shame?"

Rhi doesn't need to dig deep. Her beliefs run through her head on a loop, no matter how often she tries to contradict them, but they all come down to the same thing. "I should have done more to stop him."

Dr. Ibanez nods. "Is that true? Or is it only true based on what you know *now*?"

Rhi looks at the doctor's manicured hands, thinking. "I don't know," she says finally.

Dr. Ibanez thinks for a moment. "This is just the beginning of our conversations, but I want to explain some things to you now, so you can better understand what happened to you. The need to be loved and feel like you belong is a *biological imperative*. That's why so many people stay in abusive situations for so long: they convince themselves it's not as bad as it is because the alternative—being alone—feels like a threat as real as death. For a child, that threat feels especially true. But your parents never tried to meet your emotional needs. And Kevin took advantage of that, whether he knew it or not." Dr. Ibanez offers Rhi the box of tissues on her desk.

Rhi takes one and swabs her face.

"Do you still feel panic when you think about him not being in your life?"

She nods, shamefaced.

"That's perfectly normal. And it will fade over time. You'll probably experience a whole range of overwhelming emotions, from grief, to rage, to happiness."

"Happiness?" Rhi wonders, confused.

Dr. Ibanez softens her expression again. "Of course. Happiness is as unavoidable as grief. And some days you'll feel guilty about being happy. And some days you'll feel good about it. It's all a process. But you'll get through it—as long as *you believe* you are worthy of happiness and healing. And you are. We all are."

"Even my parents? Even Kevin?"

Dr. Ibanez cocks her head. "Well, that question is more in the realm of moral philosophy than psychology . . . but it's also not something you need to concern yourself with. Their happiness has *never* been your responsibility. Right now, you need to focus on *yourself*. On pleasing yourself, and *being* yourself, and figuring out who you are when your parents and stepbrother aren't telling you who to be. Maybe the girls can help you with that."

Rhi wipes her face again and smiles a little. "Yeah. I think maybe they already have."

"I'll talk to your caseworker at CPS this evening and make sure you stay with your uncle when your father is released, at least until they can finish their investigation. There's no guarantee of the outcome, of course—if your father fights for custody, it could get messy. When are you going to the police?"

Rhi bites her lip. "In a few days. Grace and I are driving down to Harlem tomorrow to see if we can find the pharmacist. If we can't, or if she doesn't remember me . . . it's probably not worth reporting it."

Dr. Ibanez nods. "Well, your uncle and I will support you no matter how you decide to proceed." She grabs a business card from her desk drawer and writes something on it. "Come to my house on Wednesdays, seven p.m. I have a private office." She hands the card to Rhi and clasps her hand as she does so.

"It may be a long road ahead, but we'll get you through this, Rhi. I promise. You're not alone now." She smiles. "And you're going to be okay."

THE PHARMACIST REMEMBERS Rhi very well, it turns out. She has thought about Rhi almost every day since she gave her that Starbucks gift card, wondering if she was safe. She is more than happy to give a witness statement, too, that when she had seen Rhi in the pharmacy that August morning it was clear there had been an assault—from the bruises on Rhi's throat to the vacant look in her eyes, which she has unfortunately seen on many young women seeking medication after an assault they can't bring themselves to report.

The state prosecutor's office has told her it is not enough evidence for a conviction on its own, but it is enough for Rhi to obtain a temporary restraining order in the meantime.

And Rhi was correct; her father and stepmother do not believe her accusations. But in a fortunate twist, they told her caseworker they no longer wanted to have anything to do with her (though the caseworker stressed that they would still have to pay her uncle child support until she is twenty-one). And though the finality of their abandonment had stung like swallowing a fistful of glass, Rhi told her caseworker that was just fine.

Once, Rhi had been terrified of abandonment. She had been absolutely paralyzed with fear when she thought about being cast out by the only family she had ever known. But she's finally realized her family abandoned her ages ago.

"Are you sure about this color, Rhi-Rhi?" Uncle Jimmy asks, paint roller in hand, cocking an eyebrow at the streak of turquoise on the wall before him.

They're in Rhi's bedroom—formerly her uncle's guest room—all her worldly possessions at the center of the room, under a drop cloth.

"For that wall, yeah," Rhi smiles, dipping her brush into a tray of rich, royal purple. "Turquoise over there, purple over here, orange over there."

"What about the wall with the door?"

"I got chalkboard paint for that one."

"Well, aren't you fancy?" Uncle Jimmy chuckles.

"Wait till you see the spray paint I got for that desk we thrifted."

"If it doesn't have the word 'glitter' in it, I'm not interested."

Rhi grins. She crouches and drags the flat end of her paintbrush along the wall just above the baseboard, making sure to get all the edges before they start rolling the rest, just as she did with the turquoise wall.

"So, are you ready to go back to school next week?" Uncle Jimmy asks, rolling paint up and down his wall.

"I think so," Rhi says, even as anxiety creeps into her chest at the thought. But she takes a breath and reminds herself: she doesn't *have* to fear it if she doesn't want to. It doesn't make the physical sensations of anxiety go away, but it helps keep her mind from racing. "I've decided to do something a little crazy this year."

"Oh?"

There's a note of concern in Uncle Jimmy's voice, concealed under a layer of humor, but Rhi can hear it even in a single syllable.

"Yeah," Rhi says. "I think I might actually try to *join* some stuff."

"Oh." The relief is apparent. "What are you thinking about? Stage crew? Drama club? You know, I used to be *quite* the theater kid myself, if you can believe it."

"Oh, I can believe it." Rhi finds herself smiling as she glides her paintbrush up along the corner of the wall. "But I'm not really sure yet. The girls' track and field coach wanted me to join up last semester. I could be a *she*-wolf like my mother." She smirks, knowing Uncle Jimmy will appreciate her zoological accuracy.

"Very cool. What about the internship with Mari you two were discussing last spring?"

"Um, that's off the table for now. Too much of a conflict of interest."

Even with their backs to each other, the silence that follows feels heavy.

Uncle Jimmy knows, of course, what Rhi has told Dr. Ibanez, and the police, and the paralegal who works for the prosecution for the state. Not all the details, but the gist of it. He went through his own phases of grief when he found out—denial that something so terrible could happen to his niece (which he thankfully did not direct toward Rhi), anger that it happened, guilt that he couldn't have prevented it, depression that Rhi had been living with this for so long, all by herself. He even finally displayed some of the toxic masculinity that it turns out he's not entirely immune to—he disappeared one day, and when he returned that night, he explained that he'd started driving to Saratoga Springs to find Kevin and "beat the shit out of him," only he realized when he got there that beating up Kevin would only make him look like a victim. Not to mention, if Uncle Jimmy earned himself a police record it would be that much harder for him to remain Rhi's legal guardian.

Rhi was touched, on both accounts: that he was furious on her behalf, and that he decided his feelings were not as important as her safety.

But she doesn't want him to feel uncomfortable now, so she tries to ease his mind (even though she's been working with Dr. Ibanez on understanding that it's not her job to make people comfortable with her experiences. But figuring out how to be okay with other people's discomfort is not something one learns overnight).

"But it's a good thing," Rhi says. "Just means I have time to work part time at the ranger station again. If you guys still need the help."

"Maybe, maybe," Uncle Jimmy says. "But I also happen to know Star is planning on opening up their own café soon. Probably pays better, *and* you'd get tips. Plus, you know . . . less likelihood of finding wolves or feral children on the job."

"Oh, I don't mind the wolves and feral children."

"Hmm. I've noticed. Speaking of which, are you sure you want the girls to help with this paint job?"

Rhi smiles. "Absolutely," she says, drawing the paintbrush up along the corner where it meets the other wall.

The girls and Grace will be arriving soon to help with the hand-painted final touches Rhi has envisioned for her bedroom: a riot of flowering vines breaking through at the seams, and a starry night sky for her to sleep under. Rhi feels a rush of warmth when she imagines her friends filling the small bedroom with excited conversation, the wild girls' unchecked curiosity and wonder helping Rhi to see everything through new eyes. She imagines the joyful mess they'll make, together, Grace rolling her eyes at all of them but smiling just the same.

They would have all been there sooner, but they are with Verity, who has court today; she's filling countercharges against her stepfather (and Rhi has spent more than enough time in court this summer herself). Despite the police department's psychologist's poor attitude during his evaluation, he confirmed Dr. Ibanez's conclusion that Verity is of sound mind, exhibiting no extraordinary tendency toward violence, and is extremely capable of reasonable self-regulation. Dr. Ibanez's testimony, Grace's testimony, and Mrs. Erikson's testimony—*against* her husband, in the end—along with photographs and forensic evidence of the injuries Mr. Erikson inflicted on Verity, would be enough, their attorney assured them, to clear Verity's name. What the family will do after their court case is resolved, Rhi is not sure. But she knows things will be hard for Grace and Verity, whether or not Mr. and Mrs. Erikson are really split up for good. Rhi is determined to be there for them, no matter what happens.

She grabs the ladder from beside the door and sets it near the soon-to-be-purple wall, ready to start edging at the ceiling. She puts the bucket of paint on the tray shelf and starts climbing, brush in hand.

"Rhi?" Uncle Jimmy says after a while.

Something in his voice makes Rhi pause and turn to look at him.

Uncle Jimmy is smiling a small, wistful smile that makes Rhi see her mother's face in his for the very first time. It is a little sad, but mostly happy.

"I just want you to know: I think your mother would be so proud of you."

Rhi's throat almost closes, the clench of tears is so sudden. "For what?" she whispers.

"For everything. Standing up for yourself. Surviving everything you've been through. Rescuing those girls and helping them through all they've been through. Heck, even shaving your head." He looks thoughtful for a moment before turning back to the wall to paint. "You know, you're a lot like her when she was a teenager."

Rhi smiles. "Really?"

"Absolutely. Your mother was the best big sister anyone could ask for. And part of that was because of her huge heart, obviously. I know—cliché, right? But let me tell you something you probably don't know: she was also one hell of a troublemaker . . ."

Rhi paints and listens as her uncle regales her with tales of her mother as a teenager, as seen through the eyes of the little boy Jimmy Abrams once was, before Angie Abrams grew up, got married, and became Angela Chase. She aches for them both: for the little boy who lost his big sister; for the woman who lost herself, and then her life. Mostly, she aches for her own losses: the mother she never got to know; the childhood she never had.

But instead of talking herself out of the pain as she has done her whole life, Rhi lets herself feel the deep ache winding through her, an artery of grief and loss too significant to cut off or ignore. She is supported, inside and out, by the traces of magic the wild girls have instilled in her; by the words of validation and reassurance that have been offered to her, for the first time in her life; by the people in her life now, who she knows are not perfect, but she knows she can trust.

Even now, as tears form in her eyes, Rhi realizes the ache of her grief is not as devastating as she had once feared it would be.

In fact, it almost feels like love.

The Long Way Home

(. . . continued)

Excerpted from *Savage Castle:*
A Memoir of the Wild Girls of Happy Valley

IN THE END, THE DESTINY that united us was almost the thing that tore us apart.

We had *wanted* to believe in Mother. We had wanted to know for certain that he had not lied to us. But more than anything, we were terrified that everything at the core of who we were was nothing but the result of one man's psychosis. We could not stomach seeing ourselves as mere victims of his long, intricate delusion, a delusion passed on to us in the form of a wild childhood trapped within the rigid confines of destiny. The thought was too much—too heartbreaking to entertain. It still is, some days.

The truth is, we can never know if Mother was a madman or a prophet. Perhaps he was right about everything, and we simply misunderstood his meaning. Perhaps we passed through the portal to Leutheria long ago, that foggy spring morning our wolf-kin led us to our fifth sister. Perhaps *this* world has always been our home.

But regardless of whether Mother's prophecies were real, both these things remain unequivocally true: we are, undoubtedly, from this world of walls and pavement and laws and contradictions; and yet, we are not.

Sometimes, the five of us return to the riverbank where the portal hung those brief moments in the air over the water. We return to think about the choices we made, and the choices we could not make, that night. We wonder about what we might have found on the other side of the portal. Perhaps Mother would have been there, and Oblivienne, born again into some new form. Perhaps our blood families would have been waiting for us. Perhaps there would have been five kingdoms, a star-shaped land besieged by darkness, waiting for our return.

Or maybe we would have only found ourselves splashing into the river, five girl-shaped salmon, desperately swimming upstream.

In the end, we did not choose one world over another. We chose each other. Whether that meant going through the portal to Leutheria or staying in this world, we knew there was only one option: to live this life as we always had, or in some cases, had always dreamed we could: not just as individuals, but as a pack.

And what is a pack, after all?

A pack is more than a family. A pack cares for one another in times of hardship. A pack shares its abundance, inspires joy in each other, challenges each other. A pack holds space for one another's pain, protects each other, lifts each other up. A pack is *belonging*.

A pack is *home*.

And though life may take us to different places and push us in different directions, our pack—all five remaining Wild Girls of Happy Valley—will always find our way home.

ACKNOWLEDGMENTS

When I was about ten years old, I became known as "the writer." Not just to my family, but to my friends, my classmates, and my teachers, too. This was mainly thanks to my fifth-grade language arts teacher, Mrs. Gauger. Though she is no longer with us, I have known since I was that child of ten, writing my very first manuscript on my mother's clunky word processor, that she would have to be among the first people I thanked in my acknowledgments. So thank you, Mrs. Gauger. I hope I am doing justice to your legacy as a teacher.

Of course, how much more of a struggle would it have been had I not had the complete support of my family? Mom and Dad, I cannot thank you enough for encouraging me and believing in me as I pursued my dreams, no matter how long it took (or how painful the journey could be at times). Brothers, thank you for taking your little sister's writing seriously. It pains me to admit that your opinions matter to me, but there it is. To all of you: thank you for being some of my first readers, my most insightful critics, and my loudest cheerleaders. I am so, so grateful for you.

Thank you to Pete and Katie who founded the original Buffalo Writers Group (Higher Grounds, we miss you!), and to all the members who made that group so special. We had a lot of fun together doing writing exercises, critiquing each other's work, and occasionally becoming performance/installation artists or filmmakers when the need arose, but more than that, our weekly gatherings were the fuel I needed to keep telling stories all through undergrad and beyond. Thank you also to everyone who read my "too weird to publish" web serial *The Poppet & The Lune*, especially those of you who kept reading when I tried my hand at self-publishing, and *especially* those of you who are still here, reading this book. You gave me faith that someone other than myself wanted my strange stories in the world, and that they could find a home somewhere. I suppose the world is ready for my weird now.

To my various mentors and peers: thank you so much to Nova, the first person to read the very first pages of the very first draft of this novel and to encourage me to keep going. Thank you to VCFA for accepting me into your incredible MFA program, to the whole VCFA WCYA community, especially my classmates, The Writers of the Lost Arc. Thank you especially to Ann for starting me on that path, and being a guiding light and inspiration all the way to this moment. Of course all of my advisors and workshop leaders left their marks on me, but Martha, our work together on my critical thesis profoundly changed how I approach storytelling and made it possible for me to write this book; and Amanda, all the work we did together was vital in expanding my ability as a writer, but the purple Post-it note you gave me the morning after my chapters were workshopped was absolutely *the thing* that gave me the courage I needed to keep going (it's still hanging on my fridge).

A HUGE thank you to my Ocean City ladies! Six years of supporting each other, checking in, and encouraging each other to keep going (I am writing these acknowledgments in OC while some of you are in the other room, actually). And thank you especially to Lenore who volunteered to read the first complete draft of this book and reassured me that it did, in fact, make sense, and was not, actually, a steaming pile of nonsense. I hope we continue our tradition for many years to come, no matter what life throws at us.

I probably wouldn't be living this moment today if not for the care of two very important doctors: Dr. Patel, who brought me back to life after years of an increasingly incapacitating mysterious chronic illness; and Dr. Conant, who did the same thing but for my emotional and mental health, and helped me process a lot of junk that needed to be processed in order to write this specific story. Both of you knew the main metric of success for my healing was: *Is she writing again?* And thanks to you, I am.

But I would be absolutely nowhere without my agent, Danielle Burby of Mad Woman Literary Agency, who took a chance on me and this wild book. I knew from the moment I saw your agency name that it was meant to be! You helped me not only get this manuscript into shape, but you got it into the hands of all the right people—people who would recognize the heart of it and fight to be able to bring it into the world. You blew my expectations around selling my first book completely out of the water. Thank you for loving my wild girls as much as I do. Here's to the next adventure!

That brings me to my editor, Tiff, and her editorial assistant, TJ: thank you both so very, very much. Your guidance has helped me make this story the very best version it could possibly be and allowed me to grow and improve as a writer and storyteller in the process. I often picture a novel as a giant, unwieldy IKEA bag filled with stuff; alone an author can only do so much to keep it all organized and stop it from spilling onto the floor. With your help I was able to contain the whole bag, trade out some of the items with upgraded versions, and just hold the whole thing together until each piece was exactly what it needed to be. An author only really gets to debut once in their life, and I'm so grateful my debut experience was with you and the excellent people at Zando.

Of course I must thank our cover artist, Tim O'Brien, and our art direction team, Jessica Handelman and Sarah Schneider, for the stunning work of art that has become the face of this novel. I never had a vision in my head for a cover, but you managed to pull something out of the ether that is just as eerie and captivating as I hope the book inside to be.

Navigating the process of all that comes after your first book deal really does take a village. I want to thank my incredible fellow 2024 debuts who created such a warm, generous, caring community on our private Slack, where no question was too silly, and no fear too absurd, and no win too small to celebrate. No matter what happens next, we'll always be the 2024 debut cohort, and I'm proud to be a part of that.

Finally, to the family I've created, and the ones who supported me emotionally through the grueling drafting of this novel: Rusty, Nadja, Luke, Leto, Mort, and Lando (may his memory be a blessing), you can't read this because you are animals, but you have seen me through the brightest and the darkest times of my life. Thank you for existing and reminding me to take a walk, or play, or bask in the sun when things get tough (or in Mort's case, thank you for teaching me it's okay to be an emotionally unstable jerk sometimes). But most importantly, to my partner, my love, my best friend, my favorite person: thank you for being you. Thank you for listening to me talk about this book for half a decade, for talking through its problems with me, all the changes big and small that I struggled with. Thank you for seeing how important this story is even when I could not. Thank you for reminding me to be kind and true to myself, no matter what. Thank you for being my one-man PR team without my ever asking. You are the best man I know, and there is no one else I would rather be on this journey with. You and the fur babies are my pack. I love you all more than you will ever know.

And finally, Reader: thank you, thank you, thank you for reading.